# JOHN O'E

# TIPPING POINT:
# THE FIFTH TUNNEL

## BOOK VI OF TIPPING POINT

# Ares Virus

Ares Virus: Arctic Storm

Ares Virus: White Horse

Ares Virus: Phoenix Rising

# Red Team

Red Team: Strigoi

Red Team: Lycan

Red Team: Cartel Part One

Red Team: Cartel Part Two

# A Shrouded World

A Shrouded World: Whistlers

A Shrouded World: Atlantis

A Shrouded World: Convergence

A Shrouded World: Valhalla

A Shrouded World: Asabron

A Shrouded World: Bitfrost

A Shrouded World: Hvergelmir

A Shrouded World: Asgard

# Lifting the Veil

Lifting the Veil: Fallen

Lifting the Veil: Winter

Lifting the Veil: Emergence

Lifting the Veil: Risen

# Tipping Point

Tipping Point: Opening Shots

Tipping Point: Escalation

Tipping Point: OPLAN 5015

Tipping Point: Penghu

Tipping Point: Korea

Tipping Point: The Fifth Tunnel

# Author's Note

Well, we're here on the fifth book and the goalpost keeps
Well, here we are again. At this point, I feel like I may owe some
an apology for not moving the story along very far. Yes, you
heard correctly. As much as I'm aching to move to a different
part of the storyline, I wasn't able to progress very far. Like my
other series, the story gets told how it wants to be expressed. I
feel as if I'm merely the conduit for putting the tale out there for
you to enjoy…or not, I suppose.

I do like writing this story. Often while I'm progressing
on what I believe is the path the books are taking, I am often
surprised by some of what comes up. Or I'll sit bolt upright in
the middle of the night as an idea takes hold. It holds me in its
grasp until the early hours of the morning and then I'm at the
laptop trying to capture the essence of what flooded my mind
during the wee hours.

So, I'll just come out with this semi-spoiler; there will be
at least one more book following this one. There's just too much
story to be told to contain it. It would be doing you an injustice
to rush the tale to its conclusion. To be honest, I'm not exactly
sure how it's going to end. I have some ideas, but the story will
often prove me wrong and head in a completely different
direction. There is still so much to tell that it's overwhelming at
times. Sometimes I feel like my head is going to explode from
all the information crammed inside. I tell ya, it's not easy
keeping all of the moving parts together. Or perhaps I'm not
keeping them whole and that's just an illusion.

Now I'm babbling. Aside from the editing and looking
forward to getting this book out, I'm also planning out a dozen
different hikes that I've yet to go on this Summer. It won't be
long until the sun starts to fade and I'll find myself back at the
keyboard, staring at the raindrops falling outside of the window
and longing for Spring and Summer.

One of the difficult things about writing about this
alternate history is that world events seem to often crop up that
tries to turn this fictional story into reality. I'll write some detail

or head down a path only to find that it's being partially revealed in the real world. I feel like I'm in a race at times to get this story told before it becomes reality. There are times when the mimicry gets a little too real and I feel like I should walk away from telling the rest of the story.

Well, I'm going to keep this short as the sun is beckoning and the wildflowers in the Alpine meadows are blooming. So, without further ado, I'll leave you to read on while I throw my pack in the Jeep and head out. I hope you enjoy this next edition of the ongoing story.

Take care and thank you so much for all your support. You are truly the best!

John

# Cast of Characters
## US Personnel

### Presidential Cabinet

Jake Chamberlain, *Secretary of the Navy*

Tom Collier, *CIA Director*

Elizabeth Hague, *Ambassador to the United Nations*

Imraham Patel, *CDC Director*

Aaron MacCulloch, *Secretary of Defense*

Bill Reiser, *NSA Director*

Joan Richardson, *Homeland Security Director*

Fred Stevenson, *Secretary of State*

Frank Winslow, *President of the United States*

### Joint Chiefs of Staff

Phil Dawson, *General, USAF—Joint Chiefs of Staff Chairman*

Kevin Loughlin, *General, US Army—Joint Chiefs of Staff Vice Chairman*

Tony Anderson, *General, US Army—Army Chief of Staff*

Duke Calloway, *General, US Marines—Commandant of the Marines*

Brian Durant, *Admiral, USN—Chief of Naval Operations*

Mike Williams, *General, USAF—Air Force Chief of Staff*

### US Naval Personnel

Jerry Ackland, *Commander, USN—Captain of the USS Texas*

David Avelar, *Commander, USN—Captain of the USS* Topeka

Peter Baird, *Commander, USN—Captain of the USS* Cheyenne

Charlie Blackwell, *Vice Admiral, USN—Third Fleet Commander*

Kyle Blaine, *Lieutenant, USN—F-35C Pilot*

Shawn Brickline, *Admiral, USN—Pacific Theatre Commander (USPACCOM)*

Jeff Brown, *Commander, USN—Captain of the USS* Connecticut

Alex Buchanan, *Captain, USN—Indo-Pacific Watch Commander*

Ralph Burrows, *Captain, USN—Captain of the USS* Abraham Lincoln

Chip Calhoun, *Rear Admiral, USN—Carrier Strike Group 5/Task force 70 Commander*

Alan Cook, *Commander, USN—Captain of the USS* Springfield

Bryce Crawford, *Admiral, USN—Commander of the Pacific Fleet (COMPACFLT)*

Jeff Dunmar, *Commander, USN—Captain of the USS* Seawolf

Sam Enquist, *Lieutenant (j.g.), USN—F/A-18F Electronic Warfare Officer (EWO)*

Ed Fablis, *Rear Admiral, USN—Carrier Strike Group 9 Commander*

Scott Gambino, *Commander, USN—Captain of the USS* Ohio

John Garner, *Captain, USN—Captain of the USS Theodore Roosevelt*

Steve Gettins, *Rear Admiral, USN—Carrier Strike Group 1 Commander*

Matt Goldman, *Lieutenant, USN—F/A-18F Pilot*

Myles Ingram, *Commander, USN—Captain of the USS Howard*

Tom Jenson, *Lt. Commander, USN—Executive Officer of the USS Howard*

Zach Keene, *Lieutenant (j.g.), USN—F/A18-F Electronic Warfare Officer (EWO)*

Tyson Kelley, *Captain, USN—Captain of the USS Ronald Reagan*

Carlos Lopez, *Lieutenant, USN—P-8 Pilot*

Ryan Malone, *Lt. Commander, USN—Executive Officer of the USS Springfield*

Brent Martin, *Commander, USN—P-8 Combat Information Officer*

Ben Meyer, *Commander, USN—Captain of the USS Illinois*

James Munford, *Lt. Commander, USN—Executive Officer of the USS Texas*

Michael Prescott, *Rear Admiral, USN—Carrier Strike Group 11 Commander*

Carl Sandburg, *Rear Admiral, USN—Carrier Strike Group 3 Commander*

Kurt Schwarz, *Captain, USN—Captain of the USS Nimitz*

Nathan Simmons, *Commander, USN—Captain of the USS Preble*

Patrick Sims, *Commander, USN—Captain of the USS* Columbus

Mike Stone, *Commander, USN—VFA-137 Squadron Commander*

Chris Thompson, *Lieutenant, USN—F/A-18F Pilot*

Warren Tillson, *Vice Admiral, USN—Seventh Fleet Commander*

Chris Walkins, *Captain, USN—Captain of the USS* Carl Vinson

Tony Wallins, *Lt. Commander, USN—Executive Officer of the USS* Preble

Charles Wilcutt, *Lt. Commander, USN—Executive Officer of the USS* Cheyenne

Joe Wright, *Commander, USN—Captain of the USS* Mississippi

### US Air Force Personnel

Wayne Blythe, *Major, USAF—B-52 Pilot*

James Blackwood, *Captain, USAF—B-2 Pilot*

Edward Brewer, *Lieutenant, USAF—F-16 Pilot*

Jeff Hoffman, *Captain, USAF—C-130 Pilot*

John Faden, *Captain, USAF—A-10 Pilot*

Mark Foley, *Captain, USAF—F-15E WSO*

William Gerber, *Lt. Colonel, USAF—F-15C Pilot*

Phil Hamilton, *Captain, USAF—F-16 Pilot*

Dave Lowry, *Captain, USAF—F-16 Pilot*

David Miller, *Captain, USAF—F-15E Pilot*

Jerry Munford, *Captain, USAF—F-22 Pilot*

Alan Johnson, *Captain, USAF—F-16 Pilot*

Vince Rawlings, *General, USAF—Air Force Pacific Commander (COMPACAF)*

Keith Restucci, *Captain, USAF—A-10 Pilot*

Chris Tweedale, *Major, USAF—B-1B Pilot*

Steve Victors, *Captain, USAF—F-22 Pilot*

Tom Watkins, *Colonel, USAF—Schriever AFB Watch Commander*

Jake Weatherly, *Lieutenant, USAF—F-16 Pilot*

Amy Weber, *Colonel, USAF—NORAD Watch Commander*

### US Army Personnel

Vincent Cardillo, *Lieutenant, US Army—AH-64E Gunner/Co-pilot*

Brent Carson, *Sergeant, US Army—M-1 Tank commander*

Walter Carswell, *General, US Army—ROK/US Forces Commander*

John Coley, *1st Lieutenant, US Army— AH-64E Gunner/Co-pilot*

Dwight England, *Captain, US Army—AH-64E Pilot*

Sara Hayward, *Colonel, US Army—USAMRIID Commander*

Karl Neilsen, *Sergeant, US Army—Stryker Crew Member*

Sam Marshall, *Lieutenant, US Army—11th Engineer Battalion*

Carl Rowe, *Captain, US Army—AH-64E Pilot*

Charles Warner, *General, US Army—Special Operations Command (SOCOM) Commander*

**CIA Personnel**

Tony Caputo—*CIA Operator*

Andreas Cruz—*CIA Operator*

Felipe Mendoza—*CIA Operator*

John Parks—*CIA Operator*

**NSA Personnel**

Allison Townsend—*NSA Analyst*

\* \* \* \* \* \*

## Philippine Personnel

President Renaldo Aquino—*Philippine President (as of 17 May, 2021)*

General Ernesto Gonzalez—*Philippine Rebel General*

President Andres Ramos—*Philippine President*

\* \* \* \* \* \*

## Chinese Personnel

Wei Chang, *Minister of State Security*

Sun Chen, *Admiral, PLAN—Captain of the aircraft carrier,* Shandong

Hao Chenxu, *President of People's Republic of China (PRC), Paramount Leader of China*

Tan Chun, *Commander, PLAN—Captain of the* ChangZhen 17

Lei Han, *Minister of Finance*

Hou Jianzhi, *Sergeant, PLA—Special Forces sergeant*

Cao Jinglong, *Captain, PLAN—Captain of* ChangZhen

16

Jian Kang, Sergeant, *PLA—Special Forces sergeant*

Li Na, Colonel, *PLA—Penghu invasion force commander*

Tien Pengfei, Captain, PLA—WZ-10 Pilot

General Quan, *General, PLAN—Fiery Cross Commander (as of 30 May, 2021)*

General Tao, *Fiery Cross Commander (prior to 30 May, 2021)*

Hu Tengyang, *Captain, PLAN—Captain of* ChangZhen 14

Huang Tengyi, *Captain, PLAN—Captain of* Kilo 12

Liu Xiang, *Minister of Foreign Affairs*

Zhou Yang, *Minister of National Defense*

Xie Yingjun, *Captain, PLAN—Captain of* ChangZhen 15

Zheng Yunru, *Major, PLAN—H6M Pilot*

Hu Yuran, *Captain, PLAN—Captain of* Kilo 6

Lin Zhang, *Admiral, PLAN—Southern Fleet Commander*

Xhao Zhen, *Captain, PLA— WZ-10 Pilot*

\* \* \* \* \* \*

## Taiwanese Personnel

Cheng-han, *Captain, ROCAF—F-35 Pilot*

Chia-ming, *Commander, ROCN—Captain of the ROCS* Hai Lu

Chia-wei, *Captain, ROCAF—F-CK-1 Pilot*

Chih-hao, *Sergeant, ROCA—Penghu Defense Command*

Chin-lung, *Major, ROCAF—F-16 Pilot*

Chun-cheih, *Vice Admiral, ROCN—Flotilla Commander*

Hsin-hung, Chief of General Staff

Kuan-yu, *Captain, ROCAF—F-35 Pilot*

Kuan-lin, *Sergeant, ROCA—Penghu Defense Command*

Pai-han, *Commander, ROCN—Captain of the ROCS Hai Lung*

Shu-ching, *President of Taiwan*

Tsung-han, *ROCAF Commander*

Wei-ting, *ROCA Commander*

Wen-hsiung, *Penghu Defense Commander*

Yan-ting, *Minister of Defense*

Yu-hsuan, *ROCN Commander*

\* \* \* \* \* \*


## Iranian Personnel

Omar Hasani, *Iranian Supreme Leader*
Ahmad Nazari, *Iranian President*
Mohsen Fakhrizadeh, *Chief of Iran's Nuclear Program*

\* \* \* \* \* \*


## Israeli Personnel

David Cohen, *Mossad Agent*

\* \* \* \* \* \*


## North Korean Personnel

Yun Baek, *Commander, Korean People's Navy – Submarine captain*

Choi Ju-won, *Sergeant, Korean People's Army —*
*Sapper*

Kang Yun, *Captain, Korean People's Army — Tank*
*company commander*

\* \* \* \* \* \*

## Russian Federation Personnel

Grigori Aleksander, *Major, Russian Federation Air*
*Force — Mig-29 Pilot*

\* \* \* \* \* \*

## South Korean Personnel

Park Chan-woo, *Captain, Republic of Korea Air*
*Force — F-35 Pilot*

Cho Dae-hyun, *Commander, Republic of Korea*
*Navy — Captain of the ROKS* Sejong the Great

Kwon Dae-jung, *Captain, Republic of Korea Air*
*Force — F-15K Pilot*

Choi Ji-hu, *Lieutenant, Republic of Korea Army —*
*Recon Leader*

# What Went On Before

China pushed to become the global economic power, engaging in a trade war with the United States. At the same time, they sought to expand their empire into the South China Sea by creating manmade islands and building military bases. The territorial waters China claimed was challenged in the World Court and ruled that they had no basis for making the claims. China ignored the ruling and continued to claim the waters surrounding the Spratly Islands. It was a claim that was continually challenged by warships of the United States, who conducted FONOPs (Freedom of Navigation Operations).

Along with their attempts to push into a world economy, China sought to establish the Yuan as world currency. Nations balked at using the Yuan as a trading currency, thus keeping China relegated as the world's second largest economy. Although many of the nations in Southeast Asia were swinging in China's direction, the Chinese government sought a quicker remedy to their sluggish economic gains. The devised a virus which would run rampant throughout the world and disrupt the various economies. China's goal was to emerge from the crisis as the number one economy. Markets fell as the highly contagious virus spread throughout the world. However, other events soon overtook China's attempts.

One general was fed up with the constant intrusion of the United States into what China viewed as territorial waters. One warship was targeted, but in a procedural lapse, the defensive systems were left in automatic mode and missiles launched. The USS *Preble* and the USS *Pinckney* fought valiantly but just didn't have enough time to fend off the sudden swarm of missiles. Hit several times, the USS *Preble* sank rapidly. Only twelve survived.

China rescued the twelve survivors and kept them hostage, claiming them as prisoners. The United States sortied their submarine fleet in case matters turned south. Fed up with China's refusal to release the twelve sailors, United States SEALs conducted a rescue. This rescue was coordinated with a follow-on attack which levelled the island of Fiery Cross, the Chinese military installation from which the USS *Preble* was fired upon. In response, China devised a response along many fronts and sortied their own submarine fleet.

\* \* \* \* \* \*

As part of their response to the American attack on the Chinese base on Fiery Cross Island, China fire submarine-launched cruise missiles at Anderson Air Force Base situated on Guam. Undersea battles ensued between LA-class fast-attack subs and the Chinse vessels who fired the cruise missiles and their accompanying escorts. Backed into corners and not wanting to show signs of weaknesses, both nations reinforced their presences in the South China Sea.

After much deliberation, the United States launched attacks against the remaining Chinese military installations located in the contested Spratley Island Chain. The destruction of those two bases prompted China to strike out against the two American aircraft carriers operating in the South China Sea, resulting in the sinking of one carrier and a cruiser. This ignited a regional war between the two superpowers, expanding into the East China and Philippine Seas. Most of the preliminary battles were conducted undersea between fast-attack submarines.

In the ensuing battles, the United States sank one of China's aircraft carriers while damaging a second. China damaged a second American carrier as it was departing San Diego, thus limiting the firepower that the United States could bring to the Far East.

Nudged by China, North Korea mobilized its forces and began a march toward the demilitarized zone separating North and South Korea. There were also signs that China was gathering an invasion fleet pointed toward Taiwan. Although the United States destroyed much of China's submarine fleet, they now found themselves facing attacks on many fronts. They urgently needed to eliminate a second surge of Chinese submarines so they could bring their carriers within striking distance.

* * * * * *

The undersea war continued unabated as China prepares for its invasion of Taiwan. The threat from North Korea built as men and equipment were sent south to staging areas near the DMZ. Meanwhile, the United States was slowly building its forces with Guam, Japan, and Okinawa receiving a massive influx of reinforcing aircraft.

As tensions built in the region, Taiwan sortied its naval fleet in anticipation of China sending invasion fleets. An encounter with a Chinese nuclear fast attack submarine and Taiwan anti-submarine assets led to a rapid escalation of events. In a night filled with hostilities, fighters from both sides took to the skies. Before long, the strait separating the two nations became a warzone as cruise missiles crossed the narrow waterway.

Dawn arrived with Taiwan's navy no more than pieces of twisted metal lying at the bottom of the East China Sea, and their air force decimated. However, the island's forces were able to damage China's ability to wage war. Cruise missiles flying out from Taiwan destroyed a number of China's mobile launch platforms. In a mad dash north, under constant fire from China's land-based anti-ship batteries, Taiwan's navy managed to send volleys of missiles into the ships China was planning on using for their invasion. When morning arrived, funeral pyres dotted the countryside of both countries.

The next evening, China ramped up their invasion plans by initiating cruise missile attacks against Taiwan's defenses and communications. The island was pummeled by hundreds of low-flying missiles. Having been forced back to the defensive, Taiwan waited for the invasion ships from China to arrive.

With North Korea ignoring warnings, the United States initiated one of their contingency plans against the secretive state. OPLAN 5015 called for a preemptive strike against the north if war seemed imminent. The resulting attacks focused on North Korea's command and control structure, their artillery and anti-aircraft platforms, along with their ability to use weapons of mass destruction.

\* \* \* \* \* \*

The USS *Nimitz* sustained damage from China's hypersonic missile attack, forcing the United States to enlarge the Rules of Engagement. In order to preserve the carrier groups waiting in the western Pacific, the ROE scope allowed for the intercept and destruction of Chinese ballistic missiles above the nebulous sixty-thousand-foot vertical boundary.

The subsequent destruction of Chinese missiles pushed China into action. Amid doubts of pursuing his conquest of Taiwan, President Hao ordered the invasion to proceed. Previously undetected by western intelligence agencies, a small flotilla of ships set sail for a grouping if islands off Taiwan's western coast. Airborne battalions boarded an armada of helicopters which stormed across the Taiwan Strait, landing at the Penghu Islands main airport. Facing the thousands of Chinese soldiers was the Penghu Defense Command, consisting of two Taiwanese battalions with attached units.

The main island of Penghu was quickly overrun. However, demolitions by Taiwan set back China's timeline. The main port and airport were quickly put out of action, forcing China to alter their plans. Ensuing battles, ambushes set by the Taiwanese forces, slowed China's takeover of the island chain.

China's firepower eventually wore down the Taiwanese defenses, forcing the remains of the Penghu Defense Command into a headlong retreat. Being chased by a Chinese push to envelop the second largest island, and pinched between opposing forces, the Taiwanese commander opted to force a breakthrough. Threatened by the loss of his entire command, Colonel Wen-hsiung had no choice but to cross the long expanse of the Penghu Great Bridge. As the Chinese forces were closing in, Mother Nature intervened, closing the door to China's push to eliminate the last of Taiwan's defense.

\* \* \* \* \* \*

As events were transpiring on Penghu Island, The Korean peninsula began heating up. OPLAN 5015, the Republic of Korea and the United States operational plan called for preemptive strikes in the event North Korea showed imminent signs of an attack south.

American aircraft swept over the North, effectively decimating their Air Force. Cruise missiles and long-range bombers attacked the strategic infrastructure, disrupting communications and the air defense network. Also targeted were the launch and known storage facilities for North Korean weapons of mass destruction.

With their forces massed and poised for an attack south to reunite the two countries, North Korea waited for China to make their move against Taiwan. The hope was that China's invasion would draw off American forces, making the drive south easier. However, the preemptive strikes by the United States set the Democratic People's Republic of Korean forces in action.

Armored and mechanized columns began their march south along the few roadways leading south. General Carswell, the 8th Army Commander, opted to continue attacks against the miles long columns. In particular, the attacks focused on major river crossings where bottlenecks occurred.

Leading the attacks, F-16s punched holes in the air defense networks near the DMZ. Follow-on attack fighters surged across the DMZ, at first firing standoff weapons and then closing in. Streaming out of narrow valleys, A-10s swooped down onto the armored columns. Defensive fire, in the form of MANPADS and mobile radar guns, ate into the attacking Warthogs.

North Korea opted to send their remaining fighters aloft. The antiquated fighters, not well suited for night combat, were essentially eliminated by the F-15s flying cover. South Korean F-16s and F-35s joined in on the fray, achieving air supremacy over the battlefields by the time the sun again rose. Allied long-range artillery and loitering munitions in the form of drones also aided in the attacks, relieving some of the pressure against the American attack fighters.

When the American and South Korean attacks started winding down, North Korean artillery emerged from their hardened artillery sites. Punishing fire was delivered toward designated targets south of the DMZ. Of note was the chemical attacks against Seoul, Camp Humphreys, and Osan Air Base. This opened the door for escalatory measures, but the United States and South Korea opted for constraint, waiting to see if the North would continue their NBC attacks. When dawn rose, North Korean forces poured from hardened bunkers all along the DMZ.

# Chapter One

*Camp Humphreys, South Korea*
*2 August, 2021*

North Korean mechanized divisions and regiments were on the march, both on the road networks and along railways. Thousands of artillery pieces had emerged from within their hardened bunkers like dragons raging from their lairs, delivering devastating bombardments across the DMZ. Concealed within that madness, the 8th Army Intelligence Division knew were hidden the specific platforms that were responsible for firing weapons of mass destruction (WMDs).

North Korea had launched chemical attacks against the South, and General Carswell had ordered the 8th to locate the long-range enemy MLRS platforms. The intel shop was a hive of activity. Aside from having to sift through a myriad of information coming in from multiple sources in order to ascertain enemy movements and intentions, analysts had to dissect every scrap of intel to locate specific vehicles amid the masses.

A team of analysts were pulled aside and given Priority One orders: Pinpoint the North's KN-09 MLRS vehicles.

The group of seven intelligence officers knew that merely searching through photographs wouldn't be enough. For one, the firing range of the KN-09 was about 200km, so the few systems that North Korea possessed could be anywhere within a hundred miles of the DMZ. And even if they managed to spot the vehicles, the intel would be old and the targets could easily have moved. Searching the photographic evidence was a starting point, but then the MLRS platforms had to be found tangibly to allow for artillery or aerial units to conduct a strike that would have a chance of eliminating the vehicles.

The mission to locate the long-range systems was urgent. The North had already shown their propensity to use WMDs in the course of their advance, and there was no reason to suppose they wouldn't do so again. The initial observations were that

North Korean leadership wanted to sow chaos and disrupt the allied ability to respond to their attack. At least those were the assumptions that intel shops submitted. It was the best they could do without having direct proof from intercepted comms or actually being inside the North's planning rooms.

With North Korea demonstrating that they wouldn't flinch from launching such escalatory weapon types, the 8th Army intel assessments also concluded that the North was likely to continue to use such measures to facilitate a breakthrough in the defensive lines. The forces of South Korea and the United States were equipped and prepared to function in such pressured environments, but the North's rapidly escalating tactics hampered operational efficiency. While the use of chemical weapons may not have sown the chaos the North was hoping for, the allied forces couldn't afford to conduct operations at anything other than peak efficiency. Timely resupply and reinforcements, the ability to freely maneuver, and real-time intel were the keys to the success of the allied defenses.

There were worries of more aggressive tactics, including persistent chemical or biological agents that could be fired against major command posts, supply routes, or the front lines. The team tasked with locating the long-range vehicles knew they were operating against the clock; the North could conduct these horrific attacks at any time. General Carswell was right to be worried. His anxiety was reflected in the orders he issued to locate the systems immediately, before a more devastating attack could be launched.

The fact that North Korea only had approximately ten of the KN-09 systems was both a blessing and a hindrance. Any additional long-range chemical or biological attacks would be limited by the number of rockets and vehicles the North possessed, however, finding those ten vehicles, camouflaged like Mamushi snakes within the mass of enemy equipment on the move, or secreted anywhere among the rough terrain north of the DMZ, was a tall order. They could even be hidden in some warehouse or scattered across any number of buildings in one of the North's cities, protected from the allied forces by the surrounding civilian population.

The task of identifying the KN-09s was daunting, seemingly almost insurmountable. And if the assignment had come during World War II or the first Korean War, then it truly might have been an impossible task. But the team of analysts had a wide assortment of technological resources at their disposal. Along with intelligence assets, they had an immense stockpile of data that they could employ in their search.

While a handful did indeed spend their time poring over stacks of photographs or reviewing video files in case something was missed, a team of two took another approach. They accessed the radar tapes of previous counterbattery reports. By analyzing the information, they were able to determine the locations from where the long-range rockets carrying the chemical weaponry had been launched.

After pinpointing the various firing locations of the KN-09 rockets, the two then brought up the historical data of vehicle movements. The information was derived from the airborne JSTARS aircraft, which was subsequently stored in data banks. By running the vehicular movements alongside the counterbattery reports, they were able to follow the movements of the specific KN-09s they were ordered to find.

Before venturing further, the two analyzed satellite photos taken at the time of the launches. As they had a specific location, they were able to discern the heat signatures and positively identify that they were tracking North Korean KN-09s. Once they were confident they were on the right path, the two then ran the JSTARS data backward to locate the vehicles' starting points. There they identified a hidden hardened bunker.

They next ran the tapes forward, individually tracking each of the ten identified MLRS vehicles as they departed. Each of the paths led back to the specific HART site from where the KN-09s originated. Then came the lengthy part of their investigation. They had to sift through every minute of every hour of the tapes that came from the aerial command post, to include the present date. This was to make sure the vehicles hadn't moved in the interim.

They ran through the videos twice and then had another analyst verify their findings. In the end, they were reasonably certain that they had discovered the present locations of the North Korean KN-09s. Based on the final assessment that came out of the 8th Army's intel shop, the site was kept under constant watch via drones, the command post aircraft as they rotated through their shifts, and satellite coverage, when feasible.

Now it was time to determine what to do with the information. The hardened artillery sites constructed by the North were all but impervious to anything the United States or South Korea could throw at them, short of using nuclear weapons. And even that wouldn't have guaranteed success.

Although it wasn't a comfortable decision, General Carswell didn't see any other option than to wait until the vehicles again emerged from within their shelters. And when they did, he couldn't rely on attack fighters, even if they were placed on alert status. It would just take too long to fly north, having to weave through the North's anti-air defenses, to attack.

"Jim, we're going to have to take a battery of M270s offline and allocate them to this task. I want them loaded with ATACMS and held on standby. If the JSTARS sees any movement from that HART, I want them hit, and I want them hit hard. Those long-range MLRS systems are a priority target. We need those platforms gone," Carswell stated.

The ops officer paused in his reply. He knew they needed everything they currently had to fire on the North Korean artillery in counterbattery support. The enemy bombardments were unrelenting, and the frontline units needed all the relief they could get. Plus, there were the identified enemy supply routes and depots that needed attention. Even taking six of the M270s out of action would be a blow. And who knew for how long they'd be redeployed?

"Jim, I see those gears cranking in that head of yours. I know we need those systems online, but we can't allow those bastards to shoot chemicals at us whenever they feel like it. Who knows what they'll send our way next?" the general added.

"I know, sir. I was scrambling to come up with another way. We're going to need everything when the North crosses the DMZ and hits our boys up front. But you're right, sir. We'll have to manage somehow. I'll see to it," the ops officer responded.

General Carswell understood his ops officer's concern. The divisions and brigades at the front had to absorb the initial hits without buckling. Every rocket, every shell, hell, every bullet that they could fire into the advancing forces would be needed to minimize the impact. But when he envisioned the front being peppered with chemical or biological agents, his decision to keep a battery offline and focused solely on these specific targets made sense. The WMDs could have a devastating impact. It was something that couldn't be ignored, and could likely mean the difference between holding the line or having a breach sliced into the defenses.

The dilemma was one of where to best use the scant resources given to the 8$^{th}$ Army. If he kept the battery in place and used it to provide fire support to the troops on the front line, he was essentially giving the North Koreans a free pass to use chemical weapons. Although the front line was the most immediate threat, in his mind, the long-range chemical attacks presented the greater danger. No, taking the battery offline to deal with the North's WMDs was the correct decision.

Every time he thought of the chemical attack or any subsequent mention of WMDs, a shiver went up his spine. It wasn't that he was worried so much about the North Korean KN-09s. Yes, they had to go, but the idea of chemical or biological weapons being used on the troops scared the piss out of him. He couldn't treat it as a marginal problem, it was deadly serious. But it wouldn't be those long-range rockets that would deliver nuclear warheads.

When the chemical warheads had fallen on Osan, Camp Humphreys, and Seoul, he'd nearly shriveled. The North didn't care how they achieved their victory; they went against the boundaries of warfare that even the most feared leaders didn't dare cross, whether because of moral sensibility or international reprisal. But the nation on the other side of the DMZ had no such reluctance. They were ready to use anywhere in the neighborhood of forty nuclear warheads.

As far as he could tell, North Korea hadn't managed to construct tactical nukes. That was a double-edged sword. On one hand, Carswell was thankful they hadn't because he had no doubt that the Northern leadership would use them if they had them. Especially considering their use of chemicals at the outset of hostilities.

The other side of the blade was that the nukes the North did possess were blockbusters. Their deployment would devastate whatever place they struck. And that's what scared the shit out of the general. If the North escalated in that manner, no one on the southern peninsula would be spared. It would result in a hellish scenario, as the United States wouldn't have any choice but to respond in kind. It could mark the end. At the very least, it would mark the end of the life he knew.

But even though it affected his thinking, the identification of those systems was in the hands of others. He had done his part in finding the platforms responsible for sending chemical agents deep behind the lines, and had ordered measures which would hopefully neutralize them before they could do much more harm. However, even with that, he knew the enemy vehicles could conceivably launch another volley before being hit themselves.

"Jim, when we eliminate those North Korean MLRS systems, remind me to reward the intel shop. They did a mighty fine job," the general commented.

*　*　*　*　*　*

*Joint Base Pearl Harbor-Hickam, Hawaii*
*2 August, 2021*

While the intel apparatus associated with the 8th Army

was searching for the long-range delivery vehicles capable of deploying chemical and biological agents, there were others who were focusing on the third leg of the NBC (Nuclear, Biological, and Chemical) triad of WMDs. With the major launch facilities heavily damaged during the preemptive attacks, and without finding any indication of underground silos, that only left mobile launching systems with which North Korea could send aloft their short-range, intermediate-range, and intercontinental ballistic missiles.

Years before, South Korean intelligence had identified three distinct belts of North Korean missiles. The first of these was located thirty to sixty miles north of the DMZ and contained some five-to-six hundred short-range Scud ballistic missiles. However, most of the missiles were in storage, but this first belt contained approximately forty active transport erector launchers. These shorter-ranged weapons were only capable of delivering chemical warheads, as intelligence had indicated that North Korea hadn't yet managed to miniaturize nuclear warheads enough to load onto these systems. Other agency analysts would assist the 8$^{th}$ Army intelligence operations to locate the TELs in this first belt, but for the most part, that would be an 8$^{th}$ Army operation.

The second belt identified by South Korea was in a region sixty to seventy-five miles north of the DMZ. Here, the North had placed around three hundred intermediate ballistic missiles, all capable of carrying nuclear warheads. Again, many were in storage with perhaps thirty active mobile launch vehicles. The third region contained a mix of medium-range and intercontinental ballistic missiles, again, with thirty TELs operating in the area. It was in these second and third belts that the Indo-Pacific and CIA analysts would focus their efforts. Their prime directive was to locate mobile launchers capable of delivering nuclear weapons to Japan, Guam, and possibly beyond.

Not much was known about the secretive nation, but it was believed within the intelligence community that North Korea would follow Chinese protocol with regards to nuclear-tipped missiles. The majority of the nuclear warheads was likely to be stored separately from the missiles and mounted only when orders came directly down from the North Korean president. In accordance with perceived doctrine, that indicated that North Korea could likely have three of their intermediate missiles fitted with nuclear warheads.

At this time, with war not only looming, but about to commence, it wasn't known whether that order had already been issued. Or if it might come soon. For that reason, it was imperative that the mobile launchers capable of carrying North Korea's arsenal of intermediate and intercontinental missiles be located.

The North's chemical weapons and their delivery systems would be handled by the 8th Army intelligence operations. Little was known about the North's biological weapons, but they were believed to be limited, as the North had demonstrated a reluctance to stockpile such weaponry, considering them too dangerous to handle.

There was another aspect that had defense and intelligence agencies worried. There were whispers floating around that North Korea had managed to construct a rail-launched system for their KN-23 short-range ballistic missiles. It was common knowledge that the North had been interested in this type of launch system for years, but it was increasingly rumored that it was about to be tested and possibly made operational.

The problem lay in the fact that, while the North had a limited roadway system as compared to South Korea, they far exceeded them in relation to railway lines. North Korea had over twice the rail mileage, spread across the entire country. Many of the rails north of the DMZ went through tunnels, some of which were over a mile long. Much like they had with their hardened artillery sites, these could provide the North with cover for their short-range delivery systems. They could hide their rail-based launchers securely and with little chance of discovery until the missiles were already in the air.

The task for the analysts nestled within the confines of

Pearl and within the bowels of the CIA was far more difficult than that facing the 8th Army. They didn't have past radar tracks with which to backtrack to the vehicles. They had to rely on slower means of discovery. Using JSTARS data, both live and historical, teams pored over tapes.

The thought process was that the transporter erector launchers would be kept separate from the mechanized columns in order not to draw attention, even if they were hidden away underground as well as in the open. The analysts filtered out the amassed traffic and searched individual tracks to their terminus. They then pulled up recent satellite pictures and zoomed in, searching intently for any sign of the vehicles.

A great majority of the time, the hunts ended without locating anything of significance. With most of North Korea's missile arsenal believed to be in storage, finding thirty vehicles spread across each of the defined missile belts was an immense undertaking. As North Korea could very well be poised to launch a potentially devastating attack on Japan, Okinawa, or Guam, the task had to be completed post-haste.

"There you are, you bastard," one analyst at Pearl stated.

She'd been searching numerous possibilities, eliminating each one through several painstaking hours. Sitting up after leaning over a large table for hours on end, she arched backwards, knuckling her lower back in an attempt to straighten it. She'd been at it for so long, she was convinced she'd be permanently hunched over for the rest of her life. Rubbing her tired eyes, she leaned back over the satellite footage. Suddenly, there it was. The magnifier showed the bed of a North Korean WS51200 vehicle. Riding on the back of the monstrous sixteen-wheeled TEL was the long, foreboding shape of an intercontinental missile.

The analyst immediately circled the vehicle and sent the picture and coordinates up the chain. With the chance of the mobile platforms moving, and thus again becoming lost, any sightings of the North's mobile launchers were quickly moved through and transmitted overseas. Within minutes, the data arrived in Japan or South Korea, depending upon the target's location. Those found within the first missile belt, the one closest to the DMZ, were to be targeted by the wings stationed in South Korea. Those located within the second and third belts were to be targeted by the F-15E Strike Eagles sitting on alert in Japan for this very reason. As this was one of the North's ICBMs, it was positioned in the third belt, almost on top of the North Korean nuclear testing site at Punggye-ri.

\* \* \* \* \* \*

*Joint Base Pearl Harbor-Hickam, Hawaii*
*2 August, 2021*

Admiral Brickline leaned back in his chair, the remains of a catered lunch sitting on the table before him. If he'd been alone, or at least in the comforts of his home, he might have belched loudly to relieve some of the pressure against his belt. As it was, he held a linen napkin to his face, politely covering the expulsion of gas.

The Indo-Pacific Commander noted the others around the table finishing off their meals and dabbing their lips. Brickline, the overall commander of the Pacific Forces, hoped he hadn't been as obvious as the others. It made him chuckle inside to think that these important commanders, those whom the citizens of the United States depended upon to defend their western shores, thought themselves impervious to bodily functions. It wasn't as if they thought they were above natural human frailty, but they pretended to others that they were, himself included.

He almost mentioned the thought aloud, nearly remarking that they should invoke a new law within the code of military justice outlawing burping, farting, sneezing, or hiccupping. In fact, he should throw in loud breathing as well. Placing his napkin on his plate, he then considered the opposite, of how these strategy meetings would be so different if it was commonplace to burp or pass gas at will, and he wondered if that's how the Chinese conducted their meetings. No, he'd take what courtesies they recognized over the images that came to mind of the men in the room, older as they all were, farting their way through a meeting that had important relevance on the lives of millions.

He imagined Admiral Crawford leaning to the side and farting as he was delivering a report on the conflict being waged in the Far East. As amusing as Admiral Brickline thought it would be, he could very easily imagine the gruff admiral doing just that, and not even excusing himself. As a matter of fact, he was a little surprised that he wasn't observing the Commander of the Pacific Fleet performing that little feat right now. Instead, the admiral sitting across from him made an odd expression and adjusted himself in his chair. He held a napkin to cover his lower face then wadded up the cloth and tossed it on a plate to his front as if he was giving a table scrap to the family dog.

To his right, General Rawlings seemed more proper than his naval compatriots. Brickline smirked. It was a fairly typical stereotype that Air Force officers thought themselves more refined than the other services. To date, the admiral hadn't seen anything to disprove that analysis, although the refined airs they put on certainly didn't mean incompetence in the field.

The Indo-Pac Commander thought about the differences in Navy and Air Force pilots. Naval aviators came flying down through turbulent storms, groping their way down to find their ships embroiled in wave-tossed seas. And upon vaguely spotting the carrier through clouds sweeping past, they had seconds to orient themselves toward a deck that rose and fell thirty or more feet at a time, before slamming down on an almost impossibly short landing strip in a manner that resembled a crash more than a landing. Air Force pilots, on the other hand, eased their aircraft onto an unmoving surface that stretched two miles, gently landing five hundred feet down the runway and slowly rolling to a stop. But whatever their differences, they each dropped bombs on target with a precision few other countries could imagine.

The last person in the room, the Commander of the Submarine Forces in the Pacific, seemed more subdued than usual. The admiral guessed that the reason behind the tension coming in waves from Admiral Ramsey was because of their previous meeting. Ramsey had wanted to engage Chinese submarines that had been located inside China's territorial waters. Brickline had cautioned him not to pursue that particular course of action. Although the Indo-Pac commander wasn't wanting to risk an escalation with China, the real reason was because he knew with some certainty that the wrecks would be discovered, and all fingers would point back to the Pacific submarine commander. The outstanding service of the man would be tarnished, or ruined, for disobeying the rules of engagement. With the restraint emanating from Admiral Ramsey, Brickline became suspicious that some of the reports that had crossed his desk regarding enemy losses had been altered. Though that would be a serious accusation, he'd be willing to bet that the coordinates of some sinkings had been adjusted.

Admiral Brickline eyed the submariner, thinking for a moment that he should look into the orders issued from the man's office more clearly. But then again, what was done was done, and he wasn't going to be the one that brought it to anyone's attention. He felt it was best that no one looked at those particular ones too closely, as long as the allied forces came out on top. He caught Ramsey's eye, giving him a look that he hoped said that all was okay, at least with him. The man nodded, folding his napkin and placing it tidily on the near empty plate to his front, seeming to relax just a bit.

Admiral Brickline knew that his thoughts in the fleeting moments at the end of the meal were merely delays on his part for the discussion that was to come. He nodded toward the men and women hanging on the edges of the room. They came forward, collecting the plates, silverware, and other scraps from the table. In short order, clean glasses and fresh decanters of water, beading with condensation, were brought. With a word of thanks, Brickline cleared the room.

On a monitor near the head of the table, General Carswell came onscreen.

"How are you holding up, Walter?" Admiral Brickline

inquired.

"Well, sir, we're taking a beating from their artillery, but we're managing to hold our own. I hate to think what it might've been like had we not conducted the preemptive strikes," Carswell answered.

Brickline nodded. "And how's Virginia doing?"

"You know, sir, feisty as ever. She puts up a brave face, but she's dealing with a lot right now," Carswell replied.

"If there's anything we can do for her, or you, from this end, you have but to mention it," Brickline stated.

"Thank you, sir."

"I mean it, Walter, anything."

"I'll let you know if we need anything, sir."

The admiral nodded. "All right, let's get down to the meat of this get-together. As that grimy little bastard has shown, the North Koreans aren't afraid of using WMDs. And right or wrong, our administration has elected not to respond in kind — for the moment. So, gentlemen, it's up to us to figure out how to counter the threat. After all, we can't sit back and let them fire against us at will. That could very well unhinge our defensive efforts. Now, we haven't seen any additional attacks of this nature. Is that correct, Walter?"

"Nothing has been reported, sir," Carswell answered.

"Right. Although unlikely, it could be that the North Koreans were testing the waters to see if and how we'd respond. If we do nothing, then they could view it as permission to continue. It looks to me like we have no choice but to respond to any overture. So, the question becomes, what do we do about what's already gone down?" Brickline queried.

"Well, sir, we've identified the location of the long-range rocket systems responsible for the attacks. Unfortunately, they're back in their underground site. We're monitoring the hardened shelters, but I don't really see that we have much of a choice but to wait for them to reappear. Considering our response time, there is the likelihood that we'll have to absorb another attack. We managed well enough here at Camp Humphreys and Osan, but Seoul was hit pretty hard. Another chemical attack could end up a lot worse, depending upon where they strike," Carswell responded.

"That only answers a very small part of what the North Koreans might bring to bear. Those three hundred-some scud missiles in the first belt alone would be devastating. That's not to mention the mobile launchers in the secondary and tertiary lines," Brickline said.

"The guys and gals in intel have identified a few of the mobile platforms housing their intermediate and intercontinental missiles. We've initiated strikes against those targets, some of which should already be in the air," General Rawlings chimed in.

"We need to keep looking for these, twenty-four seven. I consider them to be priority targets. If the enemy conducts a massive launch using their vast chemical stockpiles, then we could be in real trouble, gentlemen. And God forbid they actually use any of their nukes. This thing has the potential to quickly spiral out of control," Brickline stated. "It's imperative that we find these launchers. And I mean they need to be found yesterday!"

"Sir, while I agree, I also feel it necessary to voice a concern around this. If we individually target these mobile platforms, the North has to realize that we're systematically eliminating them. That could become problematic. If they panic, they just might decide to fire the missiles rather than wait for them to be destroyed. What I'm saying is that our attempt to subdue their capabilities could very well trigger the exact response we're trying to avoid, especially if we take them out piecemeal," Rawlings responded.

The room quieted for a moment as the Air Force general's statement was digested.

"What do you suggest we do about it?" Brickline asked, finally breaking the silence.

"Well, one possibility is that we identify the mobile launchers and keep track of them. Then we send in a massive attack and attempt to take them all out at once, or at least as many as we can locate," Rawlings replied.

Brickline shook his head and whistled lowly. "That's a dangerous line to walk, General. I hear what you're saying, but if we wait to attack, that'll leave a whole hell of a lot of missiles laying around, ready to fire. You mentioned that was one possibility; what others do you see?"

"Well, sir, I should have said the *only* other possibility. I don't see any other way at the moment."

"We hit their missile storage sites in our initial attacks, didn't we?" Admiral Crawford inquired.

General Rawlings nodded. "The ones we were able to identify, yes, sir."

"So, our main concern is over the hundred or so mobile launchers staged throughout the country, am I correct?" Crawford asked.

"What are you getting at, Bryce?" Brickline said.

"Well, I'm kind of with General Rawlings on this one, sir. We pinpoint the launchers and then hit them in one massive strike. In the interim, we place a line of available destroyers with ballistic missile defense systems along the west coast of Japan. Guam and South Korea have the Terminal High Altitude Area Defense systems in place. North Korea is ringed by ballistic defense measures, so we simply blast anything the bastards send aloft," Crawford commented.

"As you're aware, we don't have a whole bunch of destroyers available to establish a picket line," Brickline replied.

"Have the Japanese Navy send some of their ships. They have, what? Eight destroyers with the SM-3 terminal-phase interceptor missiles?" Crawford stated.

"That's possible, but they could only fire on missiles deemed to be targeting Japan. And we can't run joint patrols. We can't run the risk of introducing Japan into the conflict—we cannot in any way make it look like they are involved in this fight with North Korea, or the one with China," Brickline said.

"Hell, sir, they *are* involved," Crawford responded.

"Only as far as serving as launching points for *our* aircraft and ships, not in the actual shooting. We just can't risk Japan being seen as becoming more committed and have North

Korea start targeting our bases in Japan, or have China start doing so for that matter. We're operating on a razor's edge as it is," Brickline replied.

"Very well. Japan can patrol their western seaboard and act in defense. They only have terminal defensive measures anyway. I'm sure they'll be more than agreeable to defending their shores from North Korean missiles. So, we have three destroyers assisting Guam with ballistic missile defenses, and the high-altitude defenses for Guam and South Korea. That leaves Okinawa. We place three destroyers equipped with SM-2, SM-3, and SM-6 missiles around the island. That will take care of ballistic threats to our bases there. Then we hunt down those mobile bastards and take them out in one fell swoop," Admiral Crawford said.

"If it were only that easy, Bryce. But I'll admit that the plan seems sound," Brickline responded.

"What about the aircraft that are already in the air?" General Rawlings asked.

"How many targets are we looking at, Vince?" Brickline inquired.

"As far as I know, four."

"I don't see an issue having the aircraft continue," Brickline replied. "Anyone else see a problem?"

The three others around the table and General Carswell on the monitor all shook their heads negatively.

"I do have a question, though," Admiral Ramsey said. "Are we going to be under the same constraints as with China? By that I mean, apart from certain missile types, we have currently imposed a limit of five Chinese missiles that must be fired before we are allowed to engage over their homeland. Will we be applying the same constraints in this instance?"

"I say we hit any goddamned thing that lifts off higher than ten feet from that pigsty of a country," Crawford chimed in.

Admiral Brickline stared at the Pacific Naval commander, a look that ordered him to calm down.

"Good point, Nick," Brickline turned. "For now, we

won't place any limitation. As our esteemed fleet commander so eloquently advised, we hit any ballistic target that rises from North Korean control. I'll clear it with Washington, but for now, we'll operate in that manner."

"I wish we had more of those laser weapon system demonstrators," Crawford mumbled.

"Yes, well, we have what we have, and there's no use musing over what could have been," Brickline cautioned. "Okay, I think we've about covered it. Walter, how are we holding up in the south?"

"Sir, as I mentioned, we're taking a beating but doing okay so far. The lead North Korean mechanized units will cross the DMZ within the next twenty-four hours. We'll know more then. As we've seen, a lot can happen in a day. Our ammunition expenditures are exceeding our forecasts. We'll need an increase in our resupply amounts, especially with regards to artillery ordnance. Barring anything unfortunate, we can hold— provided we're well supplied."

"We'll see what can be done on our end to up the numbers being delivered. Admiral Crawford?" Brickline responded.

"Rawlings and I will confer immediately after this meeting to address the situation. You'll get your ammo, Carswell," Crawford said. "You have my word on it."

"Very well," Brickline said. "On to our next order of business. China. Bryce, do you want to take it from here?"

"All right. First, I want to say a kudos to Nick here. His subs have done a number on those Chinese boats. Our estimates show that the Chinese have lost well in advance of, what, eighty percent of their underwater fleet?" Crawford began.

"Ninety-one," Admiral Ramsey chimed in.

"What was that?" Crawford asked.

"Ninety-one percent."

"Fantastic. Thanks to those efforts, we'll soon be able to move to the next phase of operations…luring the Chinese bombers out. First, however, we have to do what we can about those fleets that are about to cross the Taiwanese Strait. Our estimates show that the Chinese will hit Taiwan's shores on the morning of the 3rd. We believe they'll cross in the night and be in position when the sun rises," Crawford said. "At the moment, there is little we can do to affect the situation. We have four carriers that are out of range and will have to remain so until we take care of the bombers. Until that happens, I'm afraid to say that our surface vessels will mostly remain out of action. Nick?"

"Um, well, yes. Right now, we have the *Michigan* and *Louisiana* in the East China Sea, each with a hundred and fifty-four Tomahawks. They'll target the escorts protecting China's northern fleet. The *Ohio* assisted in the preemptive strikes over North Korea and is on its way to rendezvous with the USS *Frank Cable* to resupply. They'll be out of action for the next few days.

"It's a different story in the south. Most of our boats were off chasing after China's Kilos and are therefore playing catchup. The *Greenville* and *Missouri* are in place to intercept and attack the southern fleet, with the *Seawolf* and *Jimmy Carter* shadowing." Admiral Ramsey cleared his throat. "The danger lies in China's airborne ASW assets. While they don't have many remaining, so there's not much we can do to chase them out of the South China Sea area of operations like we've been able to in the East China Sea. We'll only get one chance to launch, as the boats there will likely be beset upon shortly afterward. Until our other boats catch up, that's about all we have to hit the Chinese invasion fleets with."

"Vince, is there anything we can do to assist the boats to the south?" Brickline asked.

The Pacific Air Force commander shook his head. "I'm afraid not. As you know, sir, the talks with the Philippine government are ongoing and as yet, we haven't reached the point where we've established bases. If we were to launch fighters, say from Okinawa or Guam, and have them ride with tanker support, then maybe. But they'd be picked up a long ways out and intercepted.

"However, as per our plans, we do have bombers stationed in Guam. They're loaded up and are only waiting for the Chinese ships to poke their heads out. Once they leave the twelve-mile limit, we'll pounce on them with a variety of anti-ship weaponry."

Admiral Brickline nodded. "Sorry, Nick. Those boats in the south will have to endure what comes at them. We need the weapons they have onboard."

"Understood, sir. They'll do what's needed."

"Okay. The Marines on Taiwan have NMESIS anti-ship missiles, along with what Taiwan has remaining. It's too bad we couldn't convince the Taiwanese leadership to go after the escorts, but I can understand their reluctance. And that's about it concerning Taiwan.

"We'll come at them with our underwater boats and bombers. When they leave their territorial boundaries, we'll start driving one or more of our carriers toward Taiwan, using them as bait to hopefully lure China's bombers out. Once we eliminate that threat, we'll move our carriers in and aid Taiwan. In the meantime, Walter, we're gonna need you to hold out."

"We'll hold, sir," Carswell responded.

"Very well. Bryce, which carrier is to be our bait?"

"I was thinking the *Nimitz*, seeing it's already damaged," Crawford answered.

"All right, gentlemen. We have some planning to do. The next twenty-four hours are going to be interesting."

# Chapter Two

*Sea of Japan*
*2 August, 2021*

With a misting spray of jet fuel, which quickly evaporated in the cold, thin air, the F-16CJ eased aft of the tanker. Banking sharply to clear the KC-135, the Wild Weasel fighter tore out from view of the tanker's boom operator, sliding over to rejoin the other three flight members, who appeared to hang motionless in the clear blue.

The four F-16s had been modified for the particular role of suppressing enemy air defenses. They were to lead a flight of Strike Eagles who were being sent after identified North Korean mobile launchers. Ever since the North had dropped chemical weapons on several South Korean locations, the efforts to locate and destroy North Korea's ability to deliver that type of weapon had ramped up dramatically. Even though the northern nation utilized a bevy of archaic weaponry, they still had the capability to cause tremendous harm.

With intel estimates of North Korea possessing anywhere from thirty to forty nuclear warheads, it was quite conceivable that Japan, Okinawa, and Guam could be annihilated, or at the least, rendered unusable. The deeper levels of intel were attempting to find out whether China had put the northern nation up to it, or whether North Korea had acted alone.

More importantly, they were trying to fathom how far North Korea would go with their use of WMDs. Was their plan to use them only to break through the South's defenses, or would they use chemical agents or nuclear-tipped missiles to destroy the busy ports that were feeding the Southern armies? Would they dare to send their ballistic missiles after the harbors of Sasebo or Yokosuka? The airfields and ports of Guam or Okinawa? If that happened, then the United States would surely lose its position of power in the Far East. Taiwan would fall, as would South Korea. Aside from the tremendous loss of life, it could quite possibly send the outer American defenses in the

Pacific back to the shores of Hawaii, and by extension, change the global balance of power.

And who knows where the escalation would end? There was no doubt the United States would react. How could they not?! The only question would lie in to what extent? Would the United States threaten the use of nukes against Chinese invasion forces? Would that then invite China to respond in kind? It could easily invoke the kind of escalation path the world had dreaded for nearly a century. That reasoning was why it was imperative that North Korea's mobile missile launchers be found and destroyed — before it was too late.

The future ramifications might have been in the back of the pilots' minds as they flew high over the blue waves that comprised the Sea of Japan. However, their immediate attention was on their SEAD mission. They were to create a gap from which the following F-15Es could punch through the North's air defense networks. Each of the modified Falcons carried four AGM-88F HARM missiles, along with three AIM-120 AMRAAM long-range air-to-air missiles, and a single AIM-9X Sidewinder, for shorter engagements.

The air-to-air missiles were carried in the event North Korea opted to send what was left of their shattered air force up to intercept the flight of F-16s. The only other threat to the flight streaking high above the white-capped waves would come from North Korea's long-range KN-06 surface-to-air missiles. As the flight would be engaging any hostile radars at the edge of the AGM-88F's envelope, the threat stemming from the North's long-range missiles was minimized. However, air defenses, both radar-guided and heat-seeking, would be a constant threat for the Strike Eagles ingressing to their targets.

To the north, circling out of sight from the flight of F-16CJs, flew an E-3C. The airborne command post controlled the allied aircraft either patrolling over the Sea of Japan, or conducting strike missions against North Korea from the east. The E-3C also served as a clearing house of data, which was then handed down to the aircraft under its control, filtering only the information needed by each.

The radar screens of the F-16s remained as clear of the enemy as the sky was of clouds, but the squadron of four pilots knew that would change as they approached North Korea's coastline. The first warning came when the flight was about a hundred and fifty miles from the nearest enemy shores. The signal strength, frequency, and range denoted it as a "Flap Lid" phased-array radar system. It was most likely part of a North Korean KN-06 battery guarding the eastern reaches. The signal grew stronger as the four jets few west at near Mach speeds.

At a hundred miles, additional radars began pinging the aircraft. There was no doubt in the minds of those responsible for the North's eastern air defenses: four hostile aircraft were over the Sea of Japan and aiming straight for the heart of North Korea.

*   *   *   *   *   *

The North Korean officer alerted when the first warning came in. At the outer edges of the radar's range, four unidentified blips appeared onscreen. He watched as the specifics of the bogeys came in. They were flying high and fast, their course changing neither left nor right. They were aimed straight at the radar station.

The operators at the consoles conducted tests to determine if the station was being jammed. The initial analysis concluded that the four blips on the screen were legitimate returns. The officer had witnessed several American patrol aircraft flying over the Sea of Japan, all of them originating from the island that gave the expanse of water its name. Those flights had flown just outside of the KN-06's range, orbiting or flying along a north-south line.

He wasn't part of the eastern defenses when the Americans had struck, so he hadn't seen the multitude of targets that swarmed over North Korea's shores. Still, he was embarrassed by the poor showing of the Northern air defenses, and promised himself that he wouldn't let that kind of shame come to him or his family. He would make sure his country was defended.

Based on the profile flown by the aircraft, the computer system classified the incoming blips as hostile. The officer concurred with the analysis, watching the scope for additional tracks. He was sure that there had to be other American aircraft out there, perhaps loitering just out of radar range. The officer had been taught about American doctrine, which stated that there also had to be one of their airborne radar planes somewhere over the body of water separating them from Japan. The Americans loved their spy planes, so it would also be likely that one of those were snooping somewhere along the fringes.

As the officer watched the blips draw closer, he became slightly perplexed as to why there weren't others showing on the scope. Surely the Americans wouldn't be attacking with just four planes. From what he had heard from those who had been privy to the initial American attacks, their forays had come en masse, and from low altitude. Subsequent strikes had followed that pattern. The high-riding nature of the aircraft coming almost right at him didn't match the attack profiles he had heard about.

As his team readied the batteries of long-range surface-to-air missiles, the computerized system selecting the missiles to be used based on their positions to the bandits, the North Korean officer wondered what the four aircraft were up to. Worried that he was missing something, he had the technicians again check for jamming. The offset check didn't reveal anything of that nature, and the four aircraft still advanced at speeds nearing six hundred knots.

A myriad of thoughts cycled through the leader's mind. Were the Americans testing the eastern defenses, measuring what radars were active along the shores? Perhaps they were testing reaction times? Or were the four bandits a cover for something coming in low-level? With each mile the four aircraft narrowed the distance, the officer became more concerned that he was overlooking something vital.

Preliminary data was sent to the individual launchers arrayed across the countryside, some of which were situated just behind waves that rolled peacefully onto beaches, or those that crashed against rocks that were resisting the eons old battle between sea and shore. The missiles stood ready, the three tubes of each TEL already raised into their upright position. The tracked data was relayed to the selected batteries, a steady update of information for when the projectiles would be freed from within their confines, waiting only for the order from their human captors.

The officer watched as the targets neared the outer range of the KN-06s. He thought perhaps the Americans had become overly arrogant, thinking themselves impervious to North Korean defenses; something that would not surprise him. They had to note the radar emissions, but still they came on, straight as an arrow. They weren't practicing any subterfuge that the officer could determine. Well, he'd prove to them that their confidence was misplaced. The advanced missiles streaking along at over Mach 4 would show them that North Korea wasn't a country to be trifled with.

In the confines of the control vehicle, the officer waited. He'd do so until the Americans closed to well within the range of the KN-06s. That way, they couldn't escape, as had many he'd heard about on the southern border.

\* \* \* \* \* \*

The threat warning system aboard the F-16CJs had been long-silenced when the aircraft flew within a hundred miles of the radar emitting off their nose. With a signal from the lead pilot, the planes spread out into a semblance of a tactical formation. The second element was a mile out with the wingmen extended several hundred yards in a line abreast configuration.

Everyone kept an eye on the surrounding blue expanse, periodically glancing downward in case the North Koreans tried to sneak in underneath. They all knew that even though they had a tremendous lead on technology, it was wise not to rely on that advantage alone. If North Korean pilots scooted along at wavetop level and locked on at the last moment, they might get warning, but it could easily prove to be too late, even given the North's old equipment.

The closer they drew to the northern shores, the more radars came online. Or rather came within range. Several of the emissions were out to sea. With the data being handed down from the E-3C and the positioning of those radars, it was apparent that there were several North Korean patrol boats operating in the Sea of Japan.

Again, like much of the North's military equipment, the vessels were decades older than the US armament. Few of the North Korean warships were known to possess any anti-aircraft capabilities, let alone have long-range abilities. If they had any anti-air weaponry, it came in the form of short-range IR Igla surface-to-air systems. Most of the ships in the PKN were for coastal protection, configured chiefly for the anti-ship and ASW warfare roles. However, the radars could theoretically be joined in with the main enemy air defense network and provide information to the waiting surface-to-air missiles. If they couldn't necessarily participate in the acquisition of targets, they could certainly relay positions to those that could. And that could be a problem, with the F-15Es streaking in. There wasn't any choice to but engage the outer radar pickets, which meant that the few HARM missiles tucked under their wings, couldn't be used for the more lethal inland radars.

Chosen by operators buried inside the E-3C Sentry, targets were selected for the AGM-88Fs. With the clearance to fire, missiles were dropped from their hardpoints and began streaking away from the flight of F-16s. Glowing dots of fire slowly faded from sight. Streaking ahead of a thin, white trail of exhaust, the projectiles gradually arced down through the freezing atmosphere. As they descended toward their targets, the anti-radiation missiles flew through a cold layer of air, each leaving a short contrail that formed and hung against the blue of the sky, leaving behind a band of white ribbons vaguely resembling the teeth of a comb.

*   *   *   *   *   *

Crammed into the small compartment of the Flap Lid radar control room, the North Korean officer in charge of the KN-06 battery eyed the screen. The four bandits were steadily approaching, their course unchanging. They were all well within the firing parameters of several missile launchers, but the officer withheld the order to engage. He wanted the targets closer so they couldn't merely turn around and slip back out of range.

Everything changed when additional radar returns suddenly appeared. It was as if each of the four hostiles had divided into four additional tracks and sped up. The information coming from the radar's software showed the new targets had accelerated to over Mach 2 and were all following different courses. One of the new radar tracks appeared to be heading directly for the center of the monitor, which meant it was coming straight at him.

At first, the officer thought they were perhaps being jammed, the enemy conducting electronic misinformation warfare. His initial analysis was that the original four were attempting to show false locations. However, the new courses were too linear to be subterfuge, at least in his opinion. With the four original blips now making turns away from the eastern shores, a lightbulb popped on inside the officer's head.

"Engage!" the officer shouted.

His demeanor suddenly turned frantic as he concluded that the American aircraft had fired their anti-radiation missiles, which meant that the Flap Lid radar he was in charge of was in peril. His gut tightened when he realized that he needed to keep the radar operational for a moment longer so the selected missiles would receive the latest data and fire. That was time wasted. He had to shut down and get the vehicle moving if he was to have even a chance of escaping the American attack.

Along major and secondary roads lining the eastern shores of North Korea, launch vehicles received their orders. One at a time, the silo caps flew off as missiles were ejected from their individual tubes. After being thrown several feet into the air, sudden sharp pops echoed across fields and beaches as the solid propellant of rocket motors ignited. Trailing long strings of fire, the anti-aircraft missiles tore into the skies. With rumbling roars, sounding much like gigantic sheets of heavy paper being ripped, they tore across sandy beaches sleepy with the gentle caresses of low, rolling waves and sped into the cloudless heavens.

Inside the radar control, the operators and officer verified that the missiles were functioning and underway, flying after the four original targets. The officer knew there wasn't any time to dawdle or to allow the long-range radar to send updates to the KN-06s.

"Shut it down! Shut it down!" he ordered.

The room became a mix of control and chaos as the operators turned off the emissions and prepared to move the imminently threatened vehicle. The surface-to-air missiles stopped receiving mid-flight updates and switched to their internal tracking software. They were now on their own.

External communication antennae were lowered as the systems were powered down. The crew knew they only had minutes, if that. Stepping outside, the officer noted one of his men yanking at a grounding stake, attempting to pull it clear of the clay-like soil.

"Never mind that, you idiot!" the officer yelled. "Get the vehicle started! We need to leave!"

The operators raced for the cab, the slam of metal doors ringing across the open expanse of ground. The diesel engine coughed to life, belching a cloud of dirty smoke. With some of the white trails of the departed missiles still visible as they drifted on the light breeze, the vehicle lurched forward as it was put into gear. The eight wheels started rotating, picking up speed as the control vehicle accelerated. Pulling up the grounding stake as it drove away, the vehicle trailed a long wire which bounced erratically, threatening to wrap itself around one of the large tires.

The secondary road was barely wide enough to

accommodate the big vehicle. The narrowness of the road, in truth more of a track than anything else, made the driver hesitant to go any faster, even though the officer was spewing orders to do so. The crew jostled as they rode over the bumpy path, each looking toward the skies outside their windows, nervously watching for any sign of the descending threat.

\* \* \* \* \* \*

A North Korean officer in charge of a separate KN-06 battery chose another form of action. He too had recognized the American attack for what it was. However, instead of fleeing the location, he opted for a different measure. His radar was situated on a hilltop, and the road winding its way down was a tricky one to navigate. Plus, he didn't want to abandon his ideal location and possibly leave a gap in radar coverage for any incoming American strike.

Normally, the individual batteries were under control of their higher commands, but the communications network was still compromised from the devastating American attacks days prior. That left some of the individual batteries seemingly on their own, with orders regarding engagements either delayed or not arriving at all.

The officer of the hilltop battery, considering the rough terrain and the significance of his post, made the decision to remain in place. After firing a volley of long-range anti-air missiles, the crew shut down the radar transmitter. Under the officer's direction, the unit then began jamming the incoming missiles.

\* \* \* \* \* \*

The AGM-88F targeting the fleeing radar control vehicle lost the radar emissions it was passively homing in on. The guidance software noted the last known coordinates of the target and self-guided toward that location. As it descended and entered its terminal phase, the system activated the onboard infrared seeker and searched the area for a heat signature comparable to its target. It located one moving away from the coordinates and adjusted its course.

Activating its millimeter wave radar, the HARM also scanned the area, emitting an electronic signal for the first time. The secondary sensor also saw the vehicle traveling away from the original coordinates. The software determined the moving object, located through both scanning sensors, to be the target it had originally been tracking.

It again made a slight course alteration, the onboard computer constantly analyzing the movement of the target and missile. With a final calculation of an intercept, the AGM-88F dove toward the large vehicle bouncing over the uneven surface. Arriving over the top of the target, proximity sensors activated and the warhead detonated.

\* \* \* \* \* \*

The North Korean crew were bounced and jostled, their efforts to keep an eye on the sky disrupted at times. The officer in the front passenger seat was still shouting for the driver to speed up, the sound of his voice as disruptive as the bumping of the truck. Amid trying to keep his forehead from slamming into the window, one of the crew saw something in the sky. A long line of white was growing bigger and was definitely curving toward the vehicle. The operator, rather than issuing a warning, thinking there wasn't time to do so, opened the door and jumped.

The officer, in the middle of turning around when he heard the sound of a door opening, was interrupted by a deafening, intrusive noise. He barely caught a glimpse of a roiling ball of fire before the vehicle seemed to compress downward. The officer was launched forward when the truck lurched to a stop, the engine torn apart from the AGM-88Fs fragmentation warhead. At the same time, he felt like his breath had been forcibly expelled from his body. He tried in vain to catch his breath as the light inside the cab dimmed significantly. Everything seemed to slow down to the point that seconds stretched indeterminately long. In this odd period of distorted time, the North Korean officer noticed a fascinating mix of oranges and yellows on the other side of the window glass, the patterns constantly changing.

When he hit the dash, time appeared to resume its normal pace all at once. The roar that had filled his ears vanished, as had all sound. The pattern of colors shot ahead of the truck, wrapping around the windshield as if engulfing it in a blanket. Then, the mysterious ball of lava vanished, and the cab again became filled with the light of day.

Confused, the officer looked toward the driver, wondering what in the hell the man had done and why they weren't still fleeing. Why had he suddenly stomped on the brakes? Then he saw the man hunched over the steering wheel, his head turned toward the officer as if responding to the unasked question. The man's eyes stared through the officer. A long string of red hung from the driver's open mouth, reaching for the floorboards.

The officer's awareness returned in increments until he finally realized that they had been attacked. Picking himself up, he looked into the back only to see another of the crew slumped over and not responding. He shouted but wasn't able to hear his own words. He was sure he had said something...he came to the realization that an explosion had deafened him.

With the sensation of increasing heat and smoke penetrating the cabin, the officer reached for the door and saw that the glass window had shattered. Pushing against the reluctant door, and with panic rising, thinking he was trapped inside a burning vehicle, he slammed his shoulder even harder.

The door opened and the officer tumbled the few feet to the ground, hitting hard on the solid surface. He rose to see the rear compartment of the radar vehicle in flames. Stumbling upward, he staggered down the rutted pathway, going to his knees when he was distant enough that he felt he wouldn't be involved in the burning conflagration.

Looking back, he saw the vehicle nearly covered in a sheet of flame, a dark column of smoke billowing upward, the pillar bending in the light breeze. On hands and knees, the officer suddenly worried he would be court-martialed for losing a valuable asset and not successfully defending his country. Would they go after his family?

Another thought overrode his current predicament. He realized that he had seen his driver and another of his crew dead inside the now burning truck. Where was the fourth? The opening door he'd heard; did the man jump out? And if so, where was he?

The officer rose in the dirt road, standing unsteadily. He gazed toward the truck, searching for any sign of the missing crewmember. Unable to locate him in his initial search, the officer turned in a circle, looking farther across the surrounding countryside. There wasn't another indication of life anywhere in sight. He was in the middle of nowhere. What in the hell was he supposed to do? Where was he supposed to go? Nowhere in any of his training did they cover what to do in an event like this.

He gave the flaming wreck a wide circle and hobbled back down the road, searching for his lost crewmate. He finally found the man, lying beside the road. A dark pool of blood, spreading in a wide circle around him, had soaked into the ground. The soldier had his hands wrapped around his thigh, tightly gripping his leg. The pantleg of his uniform had been cut wide open and the officer saw that something had sliced into the inner thigh.

Dropping to his knees, the officer quickly unfastened his belt and wrapped it around the injured man's leg. He cinched it tightly until the bleeding from the deep wound slowed to a trickle. He then offered the man a drink, which the soldier eagerly accepted, coughing as he tried to choke down too much at once. Holding the belt tight, the officer again wondered, *What now?*

*   *   *   *   *   *

One of the HARM missiles going after the radar site

located atop the hill also lost the emissions it was tracking when the facility went offline. The internal guidance software then recognized a jamming signal coming from the same location. Because it was passively homing in on an electronic source, the jamming coming from the North Korean station was ineffective.

Due to the likelihood of a jamming source and a radar being co-located, the missile's programming changed its mission and started passively tracking the jamming signal. Streaking out of the daytime skies, the projectile exploded over the top of the radar station. The truck erupted in a secondary explosion as shrapnel from the AGM-88F warhead punctured fuel tanks and ignited servo fluids. Like the fleeing radar vehicle, the radar site serving a series of long-range anti-air missiles was put permanently out of action.

* * * * * *

The Nampo-class corvette rode over the rolling seas, its narrow bow knifing into each swell as if it were a descending axe. The strong breezes that had swept through the morning had moved eastward, but the seas had yet to be restored to their usual calm. The latest additions and most modernized of North Korea's larger vessels, the ship was patrolling a section of the eastern coastline. It was on the lookout for attempts to land special forces via small craft or submarine. Although not anticipating any direct confrontation with South Korean or American surface ships, it was equipped with four Kh-35 anti-ship and land attack missiles. It also carried a variety of anti-submarine weapons with which to deter any approach to the coast. Its wide band search radar kept a watch on the skies, ready to warn the land-based defenses of approaching enemy aircraft.

The ship rode over a crest, the bow then plunging down. A hard shudder went through the vessel as water arced outward, the droplets hitting the sea with an angry hiss. Inside the bridge, North Korean sailors recovered from the collision of man and nature, bracing themselves for a repeat as the bow cleared the crest and began another downward arc.

The captain of the corvette kept an eye on the radar scope, fully aware of the four American airplanes heading toward his country's eastern shores. He had radioed a warning, but that was about all he could do. Armed only with Igla short-range anti-air missiles, the enemy warplanes were far outside his effective range. The heat-seeking missiles were purely for close-in defensive measures.

The abrupt appearance of additional blips sent a wave of tension through the combat center. All knew that the new tracks were missiles fired from the four enemy aircraft. The software monitored the incoming radar tracks, noting the trajectories, and determined that one was on an intercept course. It could possibly be tracking the ship's radar emissions.

When the four aircraft initially appeared, the captain ordered the crew to battle stations. With one of the American weapons targeting the vessel, the crew manning the Igla IR missiles and those crewing the 14.5mm Gatling guns searched the blue skies for the first sign of the incoming threat. The two 30mm radar-guided close-in weapon system (CIWS) swiveled on their mounts, waiting for the inbound missile to come into range.

Traveling at over Mach 2, it didn't take long for the enemy projectile to enter the envelope of the Igla missiles. With the sun in the east, it was difficult for the crew to find a good heat signature with which to lock onto. Sweat trickled down their helmeted faces as they attempted to get valid tones.

A *whoosh* shot up from the aft deck when one of the operators thought they had a valid tone. The rocket, trailing smoke, rose into the blue sky. Unable to track the incoming missile due to the offset angle, it locked onto the sun and raced eastward. Those crewing the manual guns swiveled barrels as they squinted through the sunlight, searching for the first visual dot that would then grow larger by the second.

With a whine from the rear decks, the radar-guided AK-230 twin 30mm revolver cannons began spitting out rounds, the *chunk-chunk-chunk* of each gun punching through the noise of the ship plowing through the seas. The hiss of the spray, coupled with the sound of the guns firing, created a symphony filled with staccato basses accompanied by the clash of symbols.

Tracer rounds sped across the rolling wavetops, reaching out toward an unseen object, the separate streams seeming to converge at a distant point. With the constant movement of the ship riding over the waves, the tracers seemed to conduct a mid-air dance. The up and down movements also made it more difficult for the close-in weapon systems to accurately track the incoming missile.

"Full port rudder, increase to flank speed," the captain ordered.

He was hoping that putting the stern of the ship toward the threat, and thus the presentation of a narrower view, would give the enemy missile a harder target to hit. He wasn't aware that the enemy weapon was homing in on the corvette's radar emissions, the very thing that was guiding the vessel's only reliable form of defense.

The Nampo-class warship heeled over as it conducted a high-speed turn, the waves assisting as they slammed into the sides of the turning ship. On the aft decks, the two 30mm systems swiveled on their mounts as they strove to stay aligned with the target painted by the radar. On the raised mid-deck, another missile went flying. It rose, and then the trajectory immediately flattened as it tore after the heat source it registered.

The guidance software aboard the heat-seeker and the kinetic weapons plotted intercept points and made minute adjustments. Those manning the crew-served 12.7mm weapons opened up when the missile came into view, the projectile coming toward the vessel at impossible speeds. Waves slammed into the side of the ship, rolling the vessel and making it even harder for the gunners to maintain their balance and aim.

Just behind the stern, a tremendous explosion rocked the ship as one of the guns of the CIWS found its mark. The fireball grew, the fire-encrusted ball of smoke expanding. Shrapnel pinged across the decking, slamming into the metal structures with pings that went unheard above the thunderous roar of the explosion. The rolling ship, now speeding at close to forty knots, distanced itself from the dissipating cloud of smoke.

In the aftermath, empty shell casings rolled back and forth with the ship's motion. The crew searched the skies, afraid that there might be more, but the clear air remained empty. One sailor manning the 12.7mm weapons leaned over and vomited, the anxiety and subsequent relief becoming too much.

"Right standard rudder, come starboard to zero one zero, slow to twenty knots," the captain ordered.

He let a breath out and wiped his brow. His ship and crew had performed well, but it had been such a close call, too close. He wasn't sure they'd be so lucky the next time.

\* \* \* \* \* \*

Not far away, a North Korean Najin-class frigate was patrolling a similar stretch of water off the eastern coast. One of the AGM-88Fs was homing in on the beam of the air search radar, closing at over Mach 2. Having been somewhat modernized in recent years, the vessel sported a close-in support weapon system similar to the Nampo-class corvettes. However, the radar guided automated 30mm turrets didn't have the same capability as the newer North Korean warships.

The air search radar identified the American aircraft and subsequent missile launches. Turning to the west and accelerating to twenty-five knots, the older ship didn't fare well in the swells hitting broadside while at speed. The ship rolled, bucking and heaving like a bull in a rodeo. The 30mm cannons tried keeping up with the speeding threat, but they weren't able to adjust fire as readily as had the Nampo-class vessel.

The missile sped over the stern and detonated just over the top of the bridge. The explosion seemed to compress the ship, appearing to halt the forward momentum for a split second. A fireball rolled around the bridge, momentarily blinding the crew to what was occurring outside.

As if set free of its bonds, the ship surged ahead, the ball of smoke fading aft. When the vessel cleared the blast, the tall mast and other components that were housed above the bridge were nothing more than a tangled mass of twisted metal. Whatever elegant lines the ship may have boasted in the past were no longer present. A dark smudge encircled the forward structure.

The search and fire control radar systems were offline, reducing the warship's capability to that of an anti-submarine vessel without the capability to defend itself from threats beyond visual range. And even then, any fight on the surface would be an iffy proposition, considering the ship would have to manually target their enemy.

Other HARM missiles targeted radar emissions positioned off the eastern coast, likely coming from other corvettes or missile boats of the North Korea's East Sea Fleet. In one instance, one of the anti-radiation missiles homed in on a Komar-class guided missile patrol boat. The weapon's explosion tore the small patrol craft apart, leaving it to flounder in the swells.

Although the United States SEAD mission took out several active radars, it didn't create a wide gap, as had the squadrons along the DMZ. But it did give the follow-on attack aircraft a much better chance at penetrating the eastern section of North Korea.

\* \* \* \* \* \*

Several minutes after the F-16CJs departed the tanker, an F-15E Strike Eagle came alongside the aft end of the KC-135. The light turbulence caused the larger plane to oscillate, the smaller attack fighter following suit. Riding the same currents, the two separate aircraft engaged in a synchronized dance. Matching the tanker's airspeed, the twin-seat fighter then slid directly behind. Bumping the throttles slightly, the F-15E eased closer.

"Forty feet," the boom operator radioed.

As the jet neared, the operator continued, "Thirty

feet…twenty feet…ten feet."

Flying the boom, the operator began extending the refueling probe. With the three flying through the little bumps prevalent in the air, the tanker, the fighter, and the boom constantly required small adjustments. The end of the probe slid down the F-15E's refueling slot and connected with the receptacle.

"Contact," the operator stated, her voice calm.

Captain David Miller acknowledged and eased the throttles back to again match the tanker's airspeed. From here, it was a matter of flying close formation while the fuel transfer took place.

"Ease closer and smile for the camera."

The F-15E flew closer to the KC-135, the big plane's shadow blocking the sun, making it easier for Captain Mark Foley, in the back seat, to monitor the connection and process.

"Down five," the operator instructed.

David eased the stick forward, the Strike Eagle responding by descending. "Do you guys provide room service?" he asked.

"It depends on what you want," the operator responded.

"A Dr. Pepper and a roast beef sandwich would hit the spot," David said. "Maybe throw in a Butterfinger."

The operator, flying the boom with one hand, reached to one side with her other hand and grasped a can of soda, turning it around so the Dr. Pepper lettering could be seen.

"You mean like this one?" she said, taking a sip.

"That's just cruel," Captain Foley remarked.

"Wait until you see this," the operator said.

Returning the soda can to its holder, she then reached into the leg pocket of her flight suit and withdrew a candy bar, holding it up to the window.

Looking at the boom operator window mere feet away, he saw a Butterfinger with the smiling face of the operator behind.

"You know that I'm a Yelper, right? I'm afraid I'm going to have to file a bad review about the service here. One star."

The operator chuckled, "It wouldn't be my first, sir."

Fuel began streaming out from the vent ports on the trailing edge of the wings.

"I guess that about does it," David radioed.

"Copy that," the operator said, disconnecting the boom. "Good disconnect."

"Copy that. Enjoy the rest of your day—and don't choke on that Butterfinger."

"Good luck to you, too, sir! I'll see what I can do about that drink and candy bar," the boom operator replied as the boom retracted back into its stowed position.

Popping a single flare as a way of saying thank you and goodbye, David eased the aircraft off to the right of the tanker, banking harder as he cleared the aft end.

"Disconnected F-15E is down to the right," the operator stated over the tanker's intercom.

David switched back over to the radio channel of the E-3C directing the air operations for the mission. "Yukla four-three, Sugar three-three is back on freq," he radioed.

"Sugar three-three, Yukla four-three, copy. You are cleared for route Charlie five," the operator aboard the Sentry replied.

"Copy Charlie five."

David eased the throttles back and began a descent toward the blue waters below. The mission profile was to be a high-low-high one, meaning that he would conduct the first part of the mission at high altitude, dropping down low for the ingress, target run, and egress, then pop back up once clear of North Korea's radar and long-range anti-air systems.

The target, one of the North's mobile missile launchers, was on the edge of the Strike Eagle's combat radius. The reason for the top-off from the tanker was to ensure that they remained well within margins for the mission. Somewhere across the expanse of blue, other F-15Es were enroute toward other transport erector launchers that had been identified.

The mission planning had been hectic at best. Alert to takeoff had occurred within minutes of the launchers being located. And with the TELs being mobile, it was imperative to hit fast and without warning, lest they scatter and had to be found again. Long-range cruise missiles could have been utilized instead, but with the launchers being a high priority asset for the North Koreans, it was a good bet that they'd be on the move at the first indication of a missile attack. But F-15Es could readjust and bomb the targets directly, even if they were on the move. This would ensure the priority targets were destroyed with the initial attack, instead of having to relaunch the missiles, or worse, lose the targets entirely.

As the F-15E descended toward the Sea of Japan, David allowed the aircraft to accelerate to Mach speeds so they could catch up to the F-16CJs. The plan was for the F-15Es to pass ahead of the Falcons on their SEAD mission. Being at low level, they would remain hidden from North Korea's search radars for longer and reach the edges of enemy radars just after the AGM-88Fs were due to hit. This would hopefully allow for the F-15Es to scoot past any primary screening radars before any secondary ones activated.

Leveling off at three hundred feet, David ran the throttles up. The deep blue swells rolled underneath the attack fighter's nose at nearly unbelievable speeds. In the back seat, Captain Foley ran through the weapons check, ensuring that the eight GBU-53/B StormBreaker small diameter bombs hanging off their specialized racks were ready to go.

The glide bombs could be deployed up to sixty-nine miles away, however, with this mission and the planned profile, that kind of distance capability likely wouldn't be utilized. The SDBs could also strike a moving target at up to forty-five miles, which could prove to be useful in this scenario. And that did give the pilots the flexibility of using that distance capability, should they need to, such as if they ran into heavily defended areas.

If that became the case, the StormBreakers would have the GPS coordinates input into the system, the Stike Eagle climbing to lob the bombs gliding toward their designated location. Once near, StormBreakers would activate their millimeter wave radar and find the target. Of course, that would put the pilots at greater risk, having to climb to a release point. There they would be more vulnerable to longer-range surface-to-air defenses.

"Sugar three-three, Yukla four-three. Primary target is on the move, heading northwest from Alpha one."

David clicked the mic button twice, acknowledging the call with minimal electronic emissions.

"I'm on it," Foley said over the intercom.

The WSO pulled up a map of the area and located the primary target, denoted as Alpha one. The mobile launcher, one of North Korea's largest TELs, had been near a railway station at Punggye-ri. The position was, incidentally, just down a valley from where North Korea had conducted their nuclear tests underneath Mount Mantap.

"Okay, I think I have it," Foley stated. "If they're heading to the northwest, then they'll be travelling up a narrow valley toward, if you can believe it, a beach volleyball training center."

David chuckled and started slapping the side of his helmet.

"What the fuck are you doing up there?" Foley asked.

"I don't think my helmet is working. I swear I heard you say a beach volleyball training center...in North Korea," David answered.

"You heard me right," Foley responded.

"I never, in my wildest thoughts, would have imagined North Korea having a beach volleyball team. You think they wear Speedos? I wonder what in the hell that place is like."

"Well, let's see...I imagine it's comprised of, I don't know, lots of sand, balls, and nets? Maybe some courts?" Foley remarked.

"Fuck you."

"Well, whatever they have there, it's about to get a whole lot more interesting for the team," Foley remarked.

"You got that right."

David glanced toward the heavens, trying to see if he could make out the tiny dots of the F-16s they were now flying under, at least according to the data replicated from the circling E-3C. According to the mission profile, those aircraft should be firing their HARM missiles anytime. It was getting time to buckle down and get serious. This far out, David had only seen a couple of larger fishing boats riding the swells, but that would change as they drew closer to the North's eastern coast.

Minutes passed as the Strike Eagle raced over the seas, seemingly alone in the vast expanse of blue water and skies. David could easily imagine him and his backseater being the only ones in the world, alone in the sky, or perhaps part of a space expeditionary force on some remote water planet. For some reason, he liked that fantasy and would often incorporate it into some of his favorite daydreams.

"Well, would you look at that," Foley commented.

"What?" David inquired.

"Look up."

Taking a quick peek, lest he plow the racing jet into the sea, David saw several short contrails curving their way across the blue sky. He knew what they were from, and the sight of them made him sit a little more upright. The ball had been kicked and the game was on.

"I sure hope the guys up there know what they're doing," David mentioned.

"Or what? Are you going to write a review on Yelp?" Foley asked.

David chuckled and felt a little heat rise in his cheeks. "Hey, it was all I could think of."

"You're going to have to work on your witty comebacks, man. Maybe keep a list handy."

"Yeah, I admit it wasn't my best," David said.

"Your best? Damn, man. That was close to the dumbest thing I've ever heard you say. And I've been flying with you for a while, so I have quite the list to compare it to."

David jerked the stick suddenly.

"Dammit!" he heard Foley exclaim as the backseater readjusted maps and target data sheets.

"Sorry, bud. Turbulence. Now, what were you saying?"

"I was saying that I'm filing a restraining order against you as soon as we get back. You made me fucking drop my favorite grease pencil. Fucker's under the seat now."

As the F-15E drew closer to the shore, and thus nearer to North Korean defenses, David edged the laden aircraft lower until he was streaking a mere hundred feet over the wave tops. The data coming from the E-3C showed that the attack by the F-16CJs had been effective. There were no active radars showing near the planned entry point.

However, an object became visible off the nose of the fighter, rising on the swells and almost vanishing from sight as it sank into the troughs. Thinking it was a fishing boat, David nudged the aircraft onto a different heading. It could just as easily be one of North Korea's many small patrol vessels, but the object didn't look like it resembled much of anything. Even though there weren't any radar emissions coming from ahead, if it was a patrol boat, it could still have weaponry, including portable air defense systems.

Zooming past the object, David could see that the vessel was damaged, the remains of a patrol boat, more than likely hit by one of the AGM-88Fs and turned into a floating wreck. The sheen of a fuel slick surrounded the floundering vessel. A little distance away was a life raft, the heads of several people poking above the rim.

"I'll bet they've had better days," Foley commented as the raft faded behind.

"Yeah, I reckon so. Nothing a little volleyball wouldn't cure."

The tone of a radar pinged and just as quickly vanished. It then returned, coming and going with more frequent intervals.

"Looks like the boys overhead missed one," David said.

The enemy search radar appeared on the screen. The airborne command post had also picked up the transmissions.

"It looks like it's coming from Yang-do Island. Either that or it's a stationary boat," Foley suggested.

"Well, there goes the easy way in," David commented.

The planned route would have taken them straight to the long valley in which the large North Korean mobile launcher was situated. With a new search radar coming online directly in their path, the two would now have to navigate a more circuitous route.

"Guess it's on to Plan B. Come right to zero one zero. Let's hope that they're a little more inviting farther north," Foley directed.

David yanked the aircraft into a steep bank to the right, the wingtip seeming as if it would scrape the wave tops. Behind the aircraft, water rose as the wingtip vortices left in the wake encountered the seas. Rolling out on the new heading, David searched the waters ahead for any sign of an enemy vessel. The air defenses that were suppressed by the F-16s were mainly intended to clear the primary route. Now that the crew of Sugar three-three had to head inland at another point, the chances of running into active air defenses increased.

In the back, Foley brought up the secondary route to the target, replacing it as the primary course and setting the entry point.

"Okay, everything should be good to go."

David noted the new navpoint and set a heading to take them directly there. It wouldn't be so much of a deviation that fuel would be an issue, but his concern was that his target might now be on the move, possibly heading toward the tunnels that were still at the testing site. Although why anyone would want to go there was beyond his comprehension. From what he'd heard, the North Koreans weren't too particular about safety regarding their underground nuclear blasts. As a matter of fact, he'd read somewhere that no one involved in those tests was allowed in Pyongyang because of the contamination. Whether that was true or not, he still wouldn't want to drive a hunk of iron into a zone that was said to be radioactive.

The target tracking performed by the E-3C still showed the vehicle moving up the valley, but that it was still some distance from the testing site. Provided they didn't run into any more complications, they should be able to intercept the mobile launcher well before it reached the tunnels. That was assuming there weren't other, closer bunkers carved into the rough terrain that rose above the narrow valley.

Reaching the start of the secondary route, David rolled the aircraft back to a westerly heading. Ahead, a dark smudge on the horizon marked the beginning of the North's coastline.

"All right, let's try this again," David stated.

The smudge grew more defined, almost by the second. The route remained clear of radar emissions, at least according to the replicated information. As the shores grew larger in his vision, David wanted to switch on his own radar, just to reassure himself that the last miles were indeed clear of patrol vessels. The passive sensors didn't detect any radar beams, but that didn't mean that there weren't other threats out there.

Through the windscreen, streaking just feet over the tops of the rolling waves, David started making out stands of trees. Then he could see the individual trees and the line of white just below them where waves crashed into the rugged coast. And then they went feet dry as they crossed the boundary between water and land.

"*Warning, missile launch. Warning, missile launch.*"

Those words in David's helmet unleashed a burst of adrenaline. While keeping the aircraft from merging with the forest below, the captain started searching for the tell-tale sign of a missile streaking for them.

"Missile trail, eight o'clock and coming fast!" Foley shouted.

The countermeasure system, set to automatic, began dispensing volleys of flares and chaff out to the side. The flares burned intensely hot as they arced toward the ground.

"*Warning, missile launch. Warning, missile launch.*"

"There's another one!" Foley stated, the adrenaline coursing through his body, recognizable by his frantic tone.

David yanked the aircraft right, bracing for the impact of the missiles. He visualized reaching for the handles and ejecting, knowing that he'd only have a split-second to react. Turning away from the missiles would present the engine exhaust to the incoming threats, but he hoped the extra second would allow another set of countermeasures to deploy. That could make all the difference; also, it was really his only option.

"Fuck! I lost sight of 'em!" Foley exclaimed.

Pulling hard, David reversed his roll and felt the aircraft shudder. Thinking he'd been hit, he glanced quickly inside and noted the engine instruments still read normal. The Master Caution light wasn't illuminated, and there weren't any audible alerts.

Out of the corner of his eye, amid the glare from the descending flares, he caught a brighter flash of light, which dissipated almost immediately. Reversing his turn again and focusing on keeping the jet out of the trees, David pulled into another high-G turn.

Although they were banking hard left and right, the F-15E continued roughly inland, leaving the coast gradually behind. Feeling that they should have already been hit, David rolled out and checked the instruments. They behaved as if nothing out of the ordinary had occurred, the G meter showing they had pulled just over 8 Gs. The stick in his gloved hand felt normal. He did feel a little movement and could see his WSO in back turning this way and that, searching for any more threats.

"Shit, man, I'm definitely going to contact my union rep. This kind of treatment is bullshit," Foley remarked.

"Going to file a grievance, are ya?" David asked with a chuckle, the adrenaline starting to subside.

"Damn straight! I need a raise, man. Okay, let's see where your drunk driving took us."

"Drunk driving?! That's the thanks I get for saving our asses?"

"Ha! Man, you were swerving all over the place! Next time set me down on the beach first. Okay, we need to be in the valley to our left," Foley said, his voice calming.

The coastal mountains along the eastern section of North Korea weren't as divided as some of the more central highlands. There weren't any long, definable valleys or ridge lines, but more a jumble of dips and rises. David thought it looked more like the surface of a brain than anything else. In order to remain on the plotted course, he had to weave through the terrain. It felt as if he were constantly turning one way or the other, sliding magically between two higher points of land where none seemed to exist moments before.

All the while, he was keeping watch on the surroundings, especially where the trees gave way to openings. When they'd crossed over the coast, the missiles came out of nowhere, and he was feeling a little gun shy.

Racing along a short, narrow valley, David saw the hills closing in ahead. Between two hilltops, a gap led out of the valley they were in. Beyond, another ridge seemed to block the path. The two pimple-like rises in land were quickly past the wingtips and he brought the F-15E into a hard bank to the right, the G-suit inflating with a rapid onset of pressure. Standing the aircraft on its wing, with the ground and hillside racing past in a green blur, the Strike Eagle knifed into another small valley.

In the middle of the valley was a clearing. Still pulling hard and tensing with the Gs, David's breath nearly exploded out of his lungs as he thought he saw the outlines of a truck with missiles pointed skyward. He was about to click his countermeasures button and started to reverse his roll when he realized that he was going to fly directly over the threat and that turning wouldn't do any good. As he raced over the vehicle, the captain saw that what he had taken to be a KN-06 launcher was in fact only another small stand of trees. The shadows were arrayed in such a manner that they resembled the outline of a large truck, weapons upright, until looked at more closely.

"The fuck was that about?" Foley asked.

"Uhhh, nothing. I was just checking if you were still awake back there," David answered.

"Uh huh. I'm more worried that you're falling asleep at the wheel."

"How the fuck could I with this ridiculous route you planned."

"Ridiculous, huh!? I slave away back here, and this is the thanks I get," Foley jested. "I swear. I get no credit for all that I do. No respect, man."

As much as he could through the constant application of Gs, David chuckled.

They were streaking through a line of ridges that connected the coastal range with the interior mountains. It was another route that navigated through mostly unpopulated areas, but they were coming to an end of the higher ridge lines and about to cross over one of the major roads running along the eastern part of North Korea.

"Okay, here's where it's gonna get interesting," Foley commented.

"Oh...*this* is where it's going to get interesting, eh? Guess I better buckle up then!" David replied.

Coming out of the rougher terrain of the coastal mountains, the landscape became rolling hills covered with thick belts of trees and bushes, with cleared fields along the edges. Keeping an eye on the radar altimeter, David kept the F-15E rolling with the undulations. Hedgerows flashed underneath with a myriad of small streams running in chaotic patterns across the land.

David's focus however, was directed dead ahead. There, the next big threat ran straight across his route. Flying low, the major highway didn't come directly into view; instead, David's first glimpse of the thoroughfare came in the form of a long line of vehicles traveling bumper to bumper as the convoy proceeded south. No sooner had the captain glimpsed the dark line of mechanized armor and personnel carriers than he was screaming directly over, laying a string of flares along his path.

The column was there and then gone just as quickly as the land's folds again swallowed them from sight. The threat warnings remained silent, the enemy unable to bring their weapons to bear fast enough. The Strike Eagle had been visible for mere seconds, the sound of the jet fading almost before any of the North Koreans even registered its passage.

"Probably shit their pants down there," Foley joked. "But that's a lot of fucking vehicles." He shook his head, wishing they had racked a few more of the StormBreakers.

"Perhaps we'll pay them a return visit, if we have anything left after our primary and secondary targets," David mentioned.

"Wishful thinking," Foley added.

They both knew the chances of conducting their own strike against the convoy was near zero. Gone were the days where attack fighters roamed the countryside, looking for targets of opportunity. In today's world, there was scant fuel for lengthy loiter times. The proliferation of hand-carried anti-air defenses had also created greater risks. It was still nice to think about, especially with the vehicles packed together and lined up so perfectly.

Ahead, the terrain began rising, ridgelines making up the central mountains climbing sharply from the flatter farmlands. Nudging the jet over a touch, David lined up the aircraft with one of the valleys flowing at the bottom of steep, forested slopes. These ravines provided for straighter courses, but the corners they did make had to be navigated at speed more precisely.

At one such bend, David yanked the F-15E into a hard turn, sinking deep into his seat as he pulled the aircraft around. The hillsides were so steep and the valley so narrow that the wrinkled landscape flashed by seemingly feet from the top of the cockpit, while the green blur of the opposite side hurled under the belly. A narrow stream, which had flowed for over a millennium, looked as if it was being carved out by the aircraft's wing.

Rolling out, the valley knifed its way between two sharp ridges, the end blocked by another steep crest.

"Our valley is just over that ridge," Foley said from the backseat. "According to the Sentry, the target is moving northwest, three miles from where we'll come out. Hop over that ridge, turn right, and then parallel the valley."

"Roger that," David responded.

His eye was on the last ridgeline, mentally going over the maneuvers he would need to make to align himself with the valley and target. He double-checked the countermeasures, ensuring they were set to automatic and the sequencing set accordingly. Although briefed on various surface-to-air threats, there was no certainty of what he might actually face once he crested the ridge ahead, one that was quickly drawing closer. The fact that the target was on the move decreased the possibility that it was protected by dedicated air defenses, theoretically. If it had remained parked in its original location, it was likely that it had some anti-air defenses stationed nearby.

"Okay, here we go!" David said.

He pulled back on the stick, the Strike Eagle shooting up the slope in response. A flock of birds flew up from the trees and scattered, some passing underneath, others flashing over the tops of the wings and canopy. There wasn't a damn thing David could do about them other than hope he didn't hit any of them or suck one down an intake. They were everywhere; it felt like he was riding under the curl of a wave, or like the nose of a sub creating a swell of water while motoring on the surface. Almost magically, the rising flock parted like water around the speeding fighter.

At the top of the crest, David rolled the plane onto its wing, pushing on the bottom rudder to bring the nose down. He then pulled hard to bring the attack fighter around parallel to the wider valley. A central stream and its smaller tributaries meandered over a bed of sand and rocks, with a narrow dirt road running alongside the waterway.

As he grunted through the Gs, David looked up through the canopy, spotting a drifting line of dust to the northwest.

"I see 'em," Foley stated as the aircraft rolled back to level.

David could see a giant vehicle motoring along the dirt roadway. The WS51200 rolled along, the 16-wheeled monster appearing far too big to be traveling on such a narrow path. As it crossed over the creek, it looked like it might topple into a pool near the ford.

Foley centered the laser over the launcher, a large missile draped across its back.

"Okay, he's painted."

David searched the hillsides and floor of the valley for any sign of a missile launch or tracers streaking upward. All he saw were walled compounds that made up the beach volleyball training facility Foley had joked about earlier.

*Looks more like a prison*, he thought.

The aircraft jostled as two GBU-53/Bs were ejected from their racks, the aircraft becoming lighter by almost five hundred pounds. Winglets on the glide bomb immediately swung into position. The sensors acquired the scattered light of the laser and began homing, making minute adjustments as the moving target's speed and direction changed.

Being so close, the StormBreakers calculated that they were already in a terminal phase and activated their millimeter wave radar. Both bombs saw the launch vehicle and determined it was within the parameters for the programmed target. The guidance software switched over and used the radar to home in.

As soon as the bombs were away, David pushed the stick over hard to the left and pulled. The Gs hit quickly as the laden attack fighter was brought into a tight turn, flares and chaff ejecting as it sought to escape the valley.

Grabbing the handrail and straining through the high-G maneuver, Foley kept his eye on the screen. The erector launcher, one of the largest in the North Korean inventory, was centered, with the target reticle positioned directly on the missile it carried. Coming in from the bottom of the screen, something dark flashed into view.

The first glide bomb soared down, still adjusting as it sailed over the top of the ballistic missile carrier. The hundred-pound warhead went off just above the huge rocket strapped to the back. A ball of fire and smoke rose upward, the explosion echoing off the canyon walls, rolling up and down the valley. A second bomb came gliding in and a second detonation reverberated through the valley.

Foley was watching the hits, seeing pieces of launcher blown outward and skip across the dirt, when his screen went almost completely dark. As the two bombs sent fragments through the thin skin of the ballistic missile, the hot shards pierced the fuel tanks and contacted the liquid propellant.

The resulting flash of light was blinding, even in the bright sunlight washing down on the valley. The stream, over which the launcher was crossing, vaporized when the white-hot explosion rolled over it. Trees along the stream's course were sheared by the force, toppling to lay outward in a concentric circle around the blast. Smaller ones were thrown some distance, tumbling over the ground like toothpicks caught in a typhoon. Most of the launcher's sixteen tires were blown from their axles and sent tumbling and rolling away from the stream crossing.

Pieces of the missile and launcher were flung to the sides, thick shards cutting deep into and through trees on the boundary of the explosions. In the training compound, one athlete had just bumped a volleyball into a high set. The air, compressed by the huge explosion, rolled over the training area and caught the ball, driving it far beyond the compound's walls.

The white intensity roiled into the sky, yellowing as the heat from the abrupt combustion cooled. As the fireball expanded, downed tree crowns burst alight. Like a miniature nuclear blast, the angry coil of heat and fire rose into the sky, mushrooming as it climbed.

"Whoa! Whaaat...In...The...Fuck!" Foley exclaimed.

"Yeah. I'm betting practice just got a little more interesting," David commented.

Trainees in the facility, seeing the burgeoning boil of heat rise above the walls, stood stunned by the intensity of the explosion's thunder. It rolled over the compound as players watched in awe as the storm exploded a short distance away. The surrounding trees, bent from the ripping wind, swayed hard as they returned upright. When the blast cleared, water rushed in to fill a deep crater, nullifying the ford. Little remained of the transporter erector launcher. It lay devastated in the bottom of the pool; a spiderweb of bent, torn, and flattened metal.

"Yeah, no shit!" Foley responded. "Note to self...Do NOT fly directly over one of those motherfuckers when bombing them."

The aftermath left both the pilots mostly speechless as they banked left and set a course to the southeast. The two captains had seen plenty of explosions, but they had never before seen a secondary eruption the likes of what they had just witnessed. It was enough to rattle anyone, and it truly set into stone the magnitude of what they were out here doing.

On the flight out, weaving down the valley, it was again all business as they struck a power sub-station at Kilju, the name alone sounding ominous to the crew. They also hit a major railyard in the same town. There wasn't a thought given to returning to strike the armored column they had seen on the way in, even though they had two GBU-53/Bs remaining. It was time to go home.

Once they were out over the Sea of Japan, and had climbed back up to altitude, David announced, "FOD check."

He then rolled the aircraft inverted and pushed the stick slightly. Both men became light in their seats as they floated in zero to negative-G. One object in the back seat came floating to the top of the canopy.

"Oh, hey! Look at that. My grease pencil returns," Foley remarked. "Thank you."

"My pleasure."

"I take back every nasty thing I said about you...and, well, thought about you."

A couple of days after the two landed, they walked into their flight room to find two cans of Dr. Pepper and two Butterfingers with their names on them. Attached was a note:

"Courtesy of the 909th ARS. We aim to please. Don't forget to mention that in your Yelp review."

# Chapter Three

*Beijing, China*
*2 August, 2021*

On this day, the mural of the farmer on the wall seemed to taunt the Paramount Leader, the peace and serenity it used to portray all but lost. The longer the fight with the Americans went on, the farther down this path his country ventured, the more Hao felt like he was pulled along with events rather than being the one directing their course.

First were the reports coming from Minister Zhou and the National Defense Minister's office. The losses China had sustained during the course of the battles in the South China and Philippine Seas had been dressed up, the numbers falsified. Wei Chang, the Minister for State Security, had shown him the true losses. Although he felt that the intelligence minister was backing him, Hao wasn't entirely sure, and would probably never know. Minister Wei had stated that he worked for China's security, but the old man never said outright that it meant that he was in Hao's corner. The mysterious minister played his own game, cementing the security of his position in the process.

The other high-level ministers around the table conducted their own games as well. A definite rift lay under the surface of their discourse, with subtle power plays in action, and some not so subtle. Minister Zhou, the head of the National Defense, was walking a dangerous line. Hao could have him discarded over the falsified reports, but was biding his time. It wouldn't do to have that kind of strife made public while the invasion of Taiwan was just hours away. He would have to act soon, though. If the invasion was a success, then Zhou could ride the wave of a national hero, becoming almost invulnerable. The lies would be swept away and forgotten, were he instrumental in bringing Taiwan under China's control. Hao's timing would have to be perfect.

As for the Foreign Affairs Minister, Hao wasn't exactly sure where the man stood. At times, Minister Liu appeared to support him. At others, the president was sure that he and Zhou had been in consultation. If Minister Wei knew that, he wasn't sharing the information. Minister Lei could also be behind Zhou. With the current state of inflation and the decreased exports, the finance minister didn't wield quite the power he had when China's financial growth was soaring. Perhaps he was looking to reclaim that prestige.

The power plays had always been there, and would likely continue in one fashion or another, that was the nature of politics. However, that wasn't why the old farmer in the painting seemed to mock him. It was the news spreading across the globe that North Korea had used chemical weapons against the American and South Korean forces. China's backing of North Korea put China in a precarious situation. If they continued to support the North Korean regime, then they ran the danger of encountering global sanctions. That would further increase China's economic woes, likely erasing years, or perhaps decades, of work. Nations that were becoming friendly might begin to shy away from trade and military agreements.

Already, the war with the United States was causing many Southeast Asian nations to turn away from China, thus strengthening the surrounding blockade of hostile nations. With the inroads they had made into Africa, and the European nations coming around, China had stood poised on the brink of an economic explosion. However, the pandemic and subsequent war for control of the South China Sea had put China's burgeoning economy in jeopardy, to the point of a recession they might not recover from for years.

And now that they were all in on bringing Taiwan under control, failure in any arena wasn't an option. Even now, with their ships only hours away from Taiwan's shores, Hao was having doubts. It was as if the news coming out of Korea put more weight on his shoulders than all else combined. But there was nothing he could do at this stage. Once set into motion, there were some things that he simply couldn't do anything about. He had to let their situations play out.

"I think our best course of action is to do nothing," the

defense minister stated. "We take the stance that we do not have proof that the incident took place. After all, we personally have no concrete evidence that what the Americans are stating is true."

The other ministers around the table thought over the statement. As was his usual, Hao refrained from commenting or making any gesture that he agreed or disagreed. They had been discussing this situation for the past hour.

"We add a declaration that we are solidly against the use of weapons of mass destruction, unless as a means to defend China, of course," the foreign minister offered. "The Americans are going to want to bring this to the UN security council. The question is, do we use our veto when the inevitable vote is taken?"

"Of course we do!" Minister Zhou emphasized. "We cannot afford not to."

Paramount Leader Hao allowed his neutral mien to slip, showing displeasure at the defense minister's outburst. He quickly reigned it back in. He couldn't allow his personal dislike of the man to show. It was one thing to have power moves play out behind the scenes, and another altogether to bring them into the open. China stood on the brink of greatness, which could be destroyed in a blink. Reshuffling of power would have to take place at a later time, and at a point when Hao was assured of his backing.

"The defense minister is correct, as is Minister Liu. We state that China does not have definitive proof that our North Korean neighbors used chemical weapons. We continue with our party message that the North is merely responding to the aggression of the United States and South Korea. Have the United Nation's ambassador remind everyone that the Americans were the first to send their warplanes across the globally recognized demilitarized zone.

"When any initiatives are brought to the security council, we will abstain, then use our veto only if it appears that the United States will garner the required nine votes for passage. Make sure we are communicating with our friends to ensure their votes."

"Perhaps this might work to our advantage," Minister Wei chimed in.

"Explain this," Hao responded.

The Minster for State Security cleared his throat and stood. With both hands clasped behind his back, he began walking back and forth, portraying the image of an elder statesman delivering wisdom.

"Does anyone here remember Blue Crane?" Wei asked, his gaze directed around the ornate room.

"Blue Crane? That sounds vaguely familiar," Minister Zhou said, his face quizzical as if trying to remember something in the deep past.

"It should. It was one of many contingency plans created after the Korean ceasefire. It was written by those who thought we had made the wrong decision in allowing the Americans to drive all the way to the Yalu."

Minister Wei paused in his pacing and turned back toward the table.

"Let me clarify that the contingency plan wasn't for us to attack the Americans at an earlier stage of the previous war, but to invade and conquer North Korea before the Americans could drive north. It was felt that the Americans would then have halted in place."

Wei continued his leisurely pacing and staring off into space.

"Subsequent negotiations would have delivered North Korea into Chinese hands, thus creating a buffer zone. There were those who believed that relying on other leaders to rule these buffer states was too risky," the minister stated, turning back toward the others, "just as we are now seeing today."

"Are you implying that we send troops into North Korea...to fight North Koreans?" the foreign minister exclaimed.

"I am implying nothing. I am merely suggesting that perhaps this is the right time to dust off Blue Crane and see if it might perhaps suit our current situation," Wei responded.

"After all, if I remember the stories correctly, the architects of the plan envisioned that a future scenario might develop when the plan could again be of value."

Minister Wei again took his seat, the noise of his chair sliding back the only sound in the room. It was apparent that his words had spurred a great deal of internal thought. The leaders of China worked over possibilities, running several scenarios through to their conclusions. Each had a different perspective on the matter. How might such a plan affect economic concerns? What would allies think of China just overrunning one of its supposed friends? Would that turn more of the world against China? Cause more of an exodus of global corporations?

Hao saw the potential but wondered if it was worth the risk of global condemnation. It was already a tough world to navigate, with the impending invasion of Taiwan. It would further reinforce the American global push to view China as an imperialistic expansionist.

"Having North Korea *would* give us direct access into the Sea of Japan," Minister Zhou stated, almost as if he were talking to himself.

"And allow more extensive control of the Yellow Sea," Minister Liu followed.

And that was the central theme of most of the scenarios envisioned by the council. If they could take Taiwan *and* North Korea, they would have de facto control over a lion's share of the shipping lanes. As they thought farther, other possibilities also began to emerge.

"If North Korea's forces managed to weaken the United States and South Korea enough, we could even push the entire length of the peninsula," Minister Zhou breathed, his face flushed with the greedy thought. "I mean, think of it. Korea *and* Taiwan. We would be on the doorstep of Japan. The Americans would be on their heels and the Pacific open to us."

"Let us not get ahead of ourselves," Hao reminded the table. "North Korea would be one thing, but we would have to directly confront the American soldiers if we pushed farther south. This would no longer be a war at sea, or between us and Taiwan. This would open the war, possibly escalating it beyond our capacity to manage."

"But think of it, Hao. Think of what we stand to gain," Minister Zhou insisted.

"Do not forget whom you are addressing, Zhou," Hao replied, his tone cold and menacing.

"Forgive me, Chairman. I allowed my enthusiasm to get the better of me," Zhou responded, nodding his head in respect.

"This plan, however, has merit, if we only control our ambition to what we are certain we can achieve. Let us look at this together and update it as necessary. Once I have reviewed this contingency, I am not against the idea of placing troops along the border, with the possible aim of driving south to fold North Korea under the wing of China," Hao further stated.

"The Americans will see troop buildup and think it part of a plan like the last war. They will not fathom our true mission until it is too late," Minister Zhou said.

"If we do this and succeed, the Americans will have no choice but to accept the results or risk expanding the war. That is nothing either of us wants," the foreign minister added.

"I want to make this clear. I am authorizing updating the contingency plan and placing troops along the border. That is all for now. Am I clear?" Hao stated, his gaze locking momentarily on each of the ministers.

They each nodded as his scrutiny rested on them.

"To recap. We are to stand by our commitment that the use of nuclear, biological, and chemical weapons is to be used strictly in the defense of our homeland. If pressed, we remain vague as to what defines our 'homeland.'

"We muddy the waters, claiming that we do not have proof of North Korea's usage of said weapons. If the Americans demonstrate proof, which they will, we allude to the fact that any results could be falsified. We can demonstrate that the Americans accused us of faking proof that we did not release SARCoV-19. Anything that may cast doubt on the accusation.

"In the United Nations, we work to stall any initiatives in

the security council. If enough votes emerge to cause passage of something detrimental to our cause, we will use our veto. And finally, we will reopen Blue Crane, positioning troops along the Yalu. But hear me again, they are not to venture south unless I directly order it," Hao said.

Once the ministers had departed, with Hao the last to leave, the farmer seemed to again bestow a measure of peace to his heart. Although he still felt that events were pulling him along, he also believed he had regained initiative, taking back a measure of control over his country's destiny.

*   *   *   *   *   *

North Korean mechanized columns poured from their underground lairs like Saruman's orcs. The artillery barrages undulated in intensity throughout the 2nd of August, delivering fire on known and suspected American and South Korean force concentrations.

The two sides traded artillery fire. North Korea sought to diminish the defensive capability of the Southern forces, while the South conducted counter-battery fire, attempting to minimize the amount of fire the North could bring to bear.

North Korean and allied remotes crisscrossed the DMZ. Most were surveillance drones spotting for artillery or conducting intel on opposing force dispositions. Counter UAS systems were kept busy. Radar systems deployed along the front lines detected incoming North Korean drones. Coyote UAS drones were dispatched to deal with the enemy unmanned aerial remotes that came across the DMZ in waves. It was one of the many levels that played out during the first hours of the second Korean War.

Seoul received more than its share of attention as heavy artillery rounds and rockets smashed into the city. High-rise offices and apartment buildings hit by explosives sent chunks of concrete crashing to the streets below, the tumbling glass of shattered windows flashing when caught in the sunlight. Sirens rang through the mostly empty boulevards, their screams adding shrill notes to the dull booming of explosions. Mixed in with the cacophony of sound, car alarms, triggered by the multiple explosions, sent their own shrieking notes echoing down avenues. Dozens of dark smoke pillars rose from the once vibrant city.

Many who had chosen to remain, going against the evacuation orders, wished they had followed the path of those who'd fled. Several civilian cars swerved madly through the city streets, driving around hazardous debris. A few buildings had tumbled over completely, blocking some of the exit routes. Drivers turned corners with tires squealing, their need to clear the metropolis frantic once the decision had been made, only to find their pathways blocked by smoking piles of rubble.

In the madness, military vehicles held in cover near the Han River. Engineers constantly monitored the mined bridges, ensuring that the incoming artillery didn't sever connections to the wired explosives. Other soldiers stood ready. They knew it wouldn't be long before the forces of the North Korean army appeared on the opposite shores.

But before that happened, the South Korean Seventh Corps would have to cross over the bridges. They had been positioned to cover the northern routes to the city, there to fight delay tactics meant to slow the enemy marching south. Once the last had crossed, then the bridges would be blown and the defense of the Han in the Seoul area would fall to the South Korean "I" Corps.

Soldiers, tucked into cover, winced when a 155mm shell slammed into the side of a high school adjacent to the river. A ball of fire and smoke shot out from the nine-story building, tossing blocks of concrete onto the nearby roads. Chairs, their plastic melted and scarred, their metal legs twisted, bounced across once busy thoroughfares. Flaming sheets of paper rode the drafts, their charred remains breaking apart to float downstream in the waterway.

Subjected to pressures greater than it was built to withstand, the building shuddered amid the tinkling sound of glass hitting the ground first as dense smoke rolled out of the structural void the blast created. Like an avalanche gaining momentum, the front of the building gave way with a crash. Sliding into the parking lot, rubble fanned out, finally coming to rest in a haphazard mosaic of books, desks, computers, and other furniture mixed in with rebar-studded concrete.

Thanks to the relatively ancient military equipment used throughout the North Korean ground forces, the city was spared the devastating bombardments that some of the more northern cities experienced. Most of the North's artillery was limited in their range. But the built-up areas along the National Routes within fifteen miles of the DMZ were hammered relentlessly. Especially those along the three major routes leading to Seoul. It was there that the South Korean Seventh Corps, the United States First Cavalry Division, and the United States Second Infantry Division endured the onslaught, holding their ground, poised to meet the first columns of North Korea's mechanized forces.

\*   \*   \*   \*   \*   \*

The night of the 2nd was like an apocalyptic storm. Red and yellow flashes lit up the night sky, the horizon strobing as blazing bolts rained down from a distant, hellish tempest. Acting in concert, fiery streaks shot upward with sharp, reverberating cracks that split the night. In the background, deep rumbles roared over the landscape, accentuated by sharp, punctuating crashes. The ground shook and trembled as if the earth itself were fracturing and coming apart at the seams.

Artillery on both sides fought duels throughout the evening while North Korea's mechanized columns, some of them battered and bruised, rolled southward. The newer brigades, entering the picture after emerging from their hardened shelters, and as yet untouched by the American and South Korean air and artillery strikes, stood ready to punch through any weaknesses found, or made, in defensive lines.

The leading North Korean forces approached the DMZ, the commanders cautious but ready to hurl themselves into whatever fight they came across. Previous rolling barrages across the demilitarized zone had hopefully cleared pathways through the minefields. The Southern forts that ran across the boundary, which they expected to have to fight through, had been hammered by both sides.

With the distant thunder of artillery in the background, the first main battle tanks, grouped with armored personnel carriers and infantry fighting vehicles, rolled past North Korean outposts. The earth trembled at their passage, the armored mechanized units rolling down from the last friendly outposts. They hit the churned soil that stretched between opposing sides. No longer would the two sides merely eye each other through high-powered lenses. The lead North Korean units crossed the line.

Though the initial efforts of the sappers were thorough, explosions still rolled through the separating valleys; not all of the mines had been taken care of. Explosions would rock vehicles, the armor coming to a halt as they ran to the end of their broken tracks, often with smoke pouring from within. Follow-on vehicles would come upon stalled units and swerve around, some then running into additional mines. Gaps started appearing in the once elegant formations as they powered up the far side, anxious crew members waiting for the first crack of anti-armor weapons firing.

In the very early hours of the morning of the 3rd, with exploding artillery shells marking their progress, North Korea entered South Korea.

# Chapter Four

*Near the DMZ, Korea*
*3 August, 2021*

The eastern skies had just started to lighten, portending a dawn that was just around the corner. Hidden at the edge of a clearing, diesel smoke belched from rusting exhausts. The bluish smoke drifted among the thin trunks, dissipating in the light breeze. Underneath the forest canopy, uniformed crews clambered over an older transport vehicle, removing camouflaged netting draped over the short-range ballistic missile attached to its back.

With the covering removed, the sound of the heavy diesel motor revving echoed throughout the wooded area and across a small meadow. As if it were a predator that had been crouching in the shadows, waiting for a meal to come within striking range, the big launcher emerged from the tree line. Traveling just far enough so the entire vehicle was clear of the forest, the North Korean TEL came to a halt with a hiss of brakes.

A whine of hydraulics accompanied the sound of the idling diesel. In the semi-darkness, the silhouette of a missile took shape as it was raised from its bed. The Hwasong-9 Scud missile locked into its firing position with a loud clank, the harness mechanism lowering back to the launcher. Afterward, there came an almost awkward pause, like a speaker waiting for applause that never arrived.

The awkwardness was replaced by anticipation when vapor began leaking from the large projectile, the thin cloud streaming toward the ground. A small flame then appeared near the nozzle. Suddenly, a loud hissing sound was followed by a sharp crack as the liquid fuel ignited.

A roar reverberated throughout the clearing, startled birds taking wing in the dim light. Flame shot from underneath, and the giant missile tore off into the heavens. Gaining altitude quickly, the projectile angled toward the south, the flame extending out from the engine, then fading as the rocket accelerated to Mach 5.

*   *   *   *   *   *

In a similar event with a far different outcome, a Scud missile rose from its pad and lifted into the air riding a seat of orange flame. Clearing the launcher, the surrounding area illuminated in a flickering yellow glow, when suddenly, a blinding white flash deprived the world of all color. The liquid fuel tanks erupted in an explosion that obliterated everything within a hundred yards.

Momentum carried flaming debris upward before arcing back to earth as gravity again became the dominant force. The compressed air spread outward in a concentric ring, hammering stands of smaller trees, and leaving behind splintered trunks in its wake. The crew standing off to the side were knocked off their feet, their eardrums bursting from the intense explosion.

One North Korean soldier was decapitated by a spinning piece of metal. The edges, sharpened by the extreme forces, easily tore through gristle and bone. Instantly dead, she was considered lucky. The pain felt by the other crewmembers when their eardrums burst was nothing compared to the agony they experienced when the remaining liquid fuel fell burning among them. It stuck to their clothing and naked skin like napalm, the heat instantly catching everything it touched on fire. Like human kindling, they writhed on the ground in the worst pain imaginable. It might be considered a blessing that their individual screams were unheard by the others.

Mercifully, their torture didn't last, their minds shutting down long before the flames reached their full intensity, incinerating them to smoldering piles of ash.

Another Hwasong-6 missile never even made it that far, erupting in a mighty explosion before making it a foot into the air. Most of the crew, standing in a loose group only a slight distance in front of the transport erector launcher, were taken out when the heavy vehicle was shoved away from the massive explosion. The TEL hit them like a semi speeding down a Texas highway, the large stains of splattered blood barely visible on the matte olive drab paint.

One of the crew was launched into the air, flying across open ground. He hit hard against a tree trunk before landing in a crumpled mess on the forest floor. There he lay unmoving for several hours, more bones broken than whole, every part of his body in pain before eventually succumbing to his injuries.

These weren't the only occasions where the antiquity of North Korea's equipment self-destructed catastrophically. Some of the older artillery pieces were put out of action when the barrels split, or when older ammunition prematurely exploded. The northern artillery crews found out the hard way that age and explosives don't mix.

\* \* \* \* \* \*

The crash of artillery fire from north of the DMZ ebbed and flowed throughout the night, increasing as the dawn neared. Adding to the intense bombardments, some seventy short and intermediate range ballistic missiles were launched from the first two identified North Korean missile belts. Accidents attrited the number that made it past their launches and into their boost phase to fifty-one.

\* \* \* \* \* \*

The advent of North Korean ballistic missile launches brought additional Southern air defenses into play. The first of these systems were the Terminal High Altitude Area Defense (THAAD) units thinly spread across South Korea. Due to the limited number of available systems, and in some part to regional politics, only a few batteries had yet been deployed to South Korea. The inclusion of additional batteries was due to North Korea's increasing number of missile tests and their capability of putting nuclear warheads atop their ballistic missiles.

The second systems were the Patriot batteries spread

throughout the northern half of South Korea. More specifically, it was those that housed the PAC-3 version of the missile. The smaller and more agile variant was better suited for ballistic missile intercepts, whereas the PAC-2 was geared more for defending against aircraft, cruise missiles, and unmanned aerial systems. With North Korea's large inventory of short, medium, and intermediate range ballistic missiles, most Patriot batteries, and launchers, carried a mix of both variants.

Referred to by some as the "Catcher's Mitt" when discussing terminal phase intercepts, both the THAAD and Patriot systems, having smaller missiles, were designed to intercept enemy ballistic missiles in their terminal phase. This phase usually lasted less than a minute, therefore, reactions had to be perfectly timed. Using the terminal phase interceptors often felt like a last second effort to avoid destruction, an act of desperation.

Only the Aegis system's SM-3 missiles, carried by Arleigh Burke destroyers and Ticonderoga class cruisers, and the larger missiles of the Ground Missile Defense systems, could intercept ballistic missiles in their mid-course phase of flight. However, due to the quick flights North Korea's short and medium-ranged ballistic missiles made to their targets, and the subsequent brief time the warheads were in their mid-courses, the ships of the United States patrolling Japanese harbors and out in the Pacific on escort duties were unable to assist with the intercepts.

With the pre-dawn blue lightening the eastern skies, missiles left their launch tubes, streaking into the heavens. As the fifty-one missiles fired from North Korea began their descents toward targets scattered along the South Korean peninsula, the THAAD systems stationed at Seongju and another at Osan reacted, blasting skyward to catch them.

As the THAAD weapons were capable of exoatmospheric intercepts, they were the first to begin targeting the inbound threats. With the North Korean launches, nerves within the airborne and ground command posts stretched to the breaking point. Their responses were split-second; a miss here could mean devastation. The questions on everyone's mind were twofold. The first, the Northern leadership had already demonstrated a willingness to use chemical weapons and had threatened nukes, so what was on the fifty-one inbound warheads now heading toward different parts of the South? And secondly, would the defensive weapons be accurate enough to stop them at the last possible moment?

\*　\*　\*　\*　\*　\*

The battle was going to be waged far above the earth, opening when a flare of light suddenly lit up the area, illuminating a tan eight-wheeled vehicle. On its back, eight tubes were angled upward, poised to meet their opponents. Whitish-blue smoke engulfed the tubes and vehicle as a projectile tore away from its launcher. Shortly after leaving, the missile corkscrewed in the air, conducting an energy steering maneuver meant to burn excess propellant before streaking upward again. A long tongue of flame accelerated away, quickly fading to a fiery glow as the THAAD missile sped away at Mach 8.2. It only had seconds in which to intercept a descending enemy weapon that could contain anything from conventional explosives to a nuclear warhead.

On the heels of the first interceptor, another missile raced away from the launcher. In the space of seconds, eight interceptors were speeding toward the dimming stars, each seeking an enemy, becoming dots that blended with the faraway galaxies. The lead missile made a series of minute adjustments as its targeted North Korean warhead slowed from increasing friction as it entered the outer fringes of earth's atmosphere.

Using its specialized imaging infrared seeker, the missile homed in on its opponent. The violent intercept happened at astonishing speed; the kinetic interceptor traveling at over six thousand miles per hour slamming into a warhead traveling nearly three times that velocity. Their collision was like a miniature nova, at least on the infrared spectrum. The speed and generated heat obliterated the descending threat, sending the remains of the warhead tumbling.

The second interceptor's seeker, a cleanup missile aimed at the same target, located the largest remaining section and crashed into it, generating a second, smaller nova of heat. The remains of the North Korean warhead, aimless and deprived of its heat resistance, burned up as the pieces entered the atmosphere.

A series of smaller flashes dotted the outer atmosphere as successful intercepts were performed, but there were misses as well, due to guidance systems issues or the timely deployment of countermeasures by the North Korean missiles. But there were failures with the North's deployments as well, resulting in a greater number of intercept successes.

\* \* \* \* \* \*

On the ground, the space battle was orchestrated by a tactical control team of humans. The AN/MPQ-65A Active Electronically Scanned Array radar first identified the multitude of targets. The software reviewed the speed, altitude, radar cross-section, and profile of the tracks, matching them against data parameters in the system. Determining them to be ballistic missile targets, it presented them on the LCD screens of manstations 1 and 3 within the Engagement Control Station.

With only seconds for a decision, the tactical control officer, seated between the two stations, concurred with the computer's appraisal and authorized the system's launchers to be brought out of standby mode. With the system now fully operational, the Patriot battery's computer, while interfacing with the THAAD system, automatically selected the launchers containing PAC-3 missiles which would have the highest probability of a kill.

Because of the threat of chemical warheads, part of the parameters in the system contained a "keep-out altitude parameter." The inbound targets had to be destroyed above a certain altitude to prevent contamination.

Having determined the specific launchers for the upcoming engagement, the system automatically fired the PAC-3 missiles. Selecting two missiles for each descending target, it ripple-fired the projectiles with a 4.2 second separation. The AESA radar continued to provide guidance to the interceptors, which were now traveling at over Mach 4. A series of small attitude control motors steered the weapons, keeping them on course toward their targets.

Before the sweep had ticked down thirty seconds, the first two missiles determined they had reached the terminal phase of their intercept and activated their onboard radars. The seeker identified the targets and the control motors, near the front of the missiles, fired in a series of tiny course adjustments.

As with the THAAD interceptors, the PAC-3 Patriot missiles were kinetic kill vehicles. However, they also had lethality enhancers, small explosive warheads that shot out twenty-four tungsten fragments. As with the THAAD system, the first missile would slam into the target, the second would then find and go after the largest remaining section.

One by one, targeted tracks were eliminated from the screens. With each successful intercept, the tension among command post officers relaxed by degrees. Between strikes, the room was silent. With the speed of the ballistic missile terminal phase, there wouldn't be time for a second round of intercepts. The first ones had to be spot on.

When the THAAD and Patriot missiles had concluded their intercepts, the successes and misses were tallied. The radars still showed five ballistic warheads untouched by the missile defense systems. Although already warned, Osan Air Base, Kunsan Air Base, Camp Humphreys, and the Gyeryongdae military complex were placed on heightened alerts.

Suddenly, localized Patriot and other radars picked up additional incoming tracks from the southeast at high speed. The systems determined that the new objects didn't fit within established parameters and thus held back firing air defense missiles. However, the operators aboard the E-8C were aware of the inbound objects, and had been ever since they were fired, but a failure in communication didn't propagate the information to ground air defense units. Nor to headquarter command posts.

After travelling for nearly two hundred miles, Aegis SM-2 Block IV missiles, fired from South Korean KDX-III destroyers patrolling the straits and supply routes near Busan, began to arrive. Proximity fuses aboard the interceptors triggered 137-pound blast fragmentation warheads. The intense pressures from their blasts and shrapnel finished off the remaining North Korean ballistic missiles before they detonated.

With the five having reached lower altitudes, there were some anxious moments establishing whether there was still a danger from chemical agents. Great efforts were made to locate and set up perimeters around any fallen segments of the destroyed warheads, including those that were hit at high altitudes. Subsequent investigations attempted to prove that North Korea had again launched weapons of mass destruction, but no evidence of that was ever recovered.

When the last of the enemy warheads were eliminated, many in the command posts released breaths they never realized they'd been holding. One stage of the initial North Korean invasion had been thwarted. But there were a vast number of other ballistic missiles still in the North's possession. And their leading forces were about to collide with the Southern defenses.

*   *   *   *   *   *

Aside from the communications failure coming from the E-8C, the operators located the mobile launch platforms responsible for the ballistic launches. Rather than target them with artillery units already engaged with the approaching North Koreans, their supply depots, and suspected command posts, they only kept note of the launcher positions. Once the missiles had departed, the TELs weren't a threat—until they were reloaded.

When any of them began moving, they were tracked. For those that remained stationary, their positions were marked and subsequent operators coming on station were instructed to watch for vehicular movement nearby. Although North Korea had many missiles, they only had about a hundred launchers of all sizes. They would have to be reloaded before missiles would again take flight. That would be accomplished either through vehicles bringing missiles to them (a highly unlikely scenario as the process was a complicated one) or by traveling to where the weapons were stored. The location of those storage facilities was information the South Korea/United States combined forces command badly wanted.

*   *   *   *   *   *

*35,000 feet, west of Cheongju*
*3 August, 2021*

"Sir, I have movement from priority target, Alpha 364," an operator stated over the intercom. "Five vehicles have departed...wait, sir, make that six."

Alpha 364 was where the North Korean KN-09 MLRS launchers had come from and retired to after firing their long-range rockets filled with chemical agents. Drones deployed to the area had determined that the position was a hardened bunker which had thus far defied all attempts to fully destroy it. General Carswell had given it two days of observation before seeing if B-2s carrying GBU-57 bunker busters could target the location.

When the last of the vehicles exited the bunker, ten long-range rocket launchers were on the move. After verifying the report and the data, along with all of the other gathered intelligence, was transferred to a ground station module via the airborne commander's tactical terminal then disseminated to other ground stations. It was quickly determined that the KN-09 mobile launchers weren't within range of an M109-A6 Paladin battery that had Excalibur shells available. Because of the munition's ability to quickly hit moving targets at moderate ranges, it had been one of the resources allocated for the destruction of the North's vehicles. The distance was also beyond the range of the Phoenix Ghost and Switchblade 600 drones.

The commanders therefore opted to go with their original plans. This was the less desirable solution, as it might allow the North Korean long-range MLRS vehicles a chance to fire their ordnance prior to being hit. This meant that any allied forces in the northern half of the South Korean Peninsula were under the threat of another possible chemical attack.

Preparation orders were sent to an M270 ATACMS unit stationed far to the rear. In addition, a flight of South Korean F-15Ks, that were also on alert for this very mission, were scrambled. With a thin bank of blue hanging on the horizon, four of the Strike Eagles tore down the runway, their afterburners roaring. Lifting into a sky whose stars were beginning to fade, the laden attack aircraft turned northeast, hoping to vanish in the rugged terrain of the central mountains.

The data coming from the E-8C was a constant stream. The mission commander responsible for the elimination of the North Korean KN-09 systems monitored the launchers' movements as they emerged from their hardened shelter. The F-15Ks were carrying GBU-53/B StormBreakers, glide bombs designed to hit targets up to seventy miles away, but only effective against moving targets out to a distance of forty-five miles. Provided the enemy mobile launchers remained on the move, the attack fighters would hit them when they came within range, thus preventing the KN-09s from firing.

However, if the data showed that the vehicles had stopped, that meant they were getting ready to fire. In that case, the coordinates would be handed down to the ATACMS unit and the fire mission approved. The problem with that scenario was that the North Korean weapons could theoretically launch within the time it took to initiate the response. It would be a race to see which system prevailed. Could the ATACMS missiles arrive before the North Koreans were able to prep their vehicles and attack?

The presumption was that the vehicles wouldn't travel very far from their bunker, so they could return quickly once they had fired their ordnance. The uncertainty meant directing a lot of resources toward a mere ten mobile platforms, but those long-range systems could hit half of South Korea from their present positions and deliver a wide scope of warheads. It was vital to the defensive endeavors that these damaging systems be taken out as early as possible.

The worry in everyone's mind was whether North Korea had managed to miniaturize nuclear warheads. There was no doubt that they had the capability to put nuclear payloads on their larger ballistic missiles, but the answer no one knew for certain was whether they could field tactical nukes. If they successfully fired even a very few, then the defense of the southern peninsula would be over. That was the fear that picked at the back of General Carswell's thoughts. It was a nightmare scenario that suddenly became real when the first of the chemical warheads detonated over South Korea.

*   *   *   *   *   *

Weaving through the creases that formed deep valleys between steep-sided hills, it didn't take too long for the ROK F-15Ks to work far enough north to be within range of North Korea's long-range MLRS vehicles. Data from the E-8C operating in the west still showed the ten KN-09 launchers were moving, working their way slowly along narrow secondary roads.

Ensuring that their ECM pods were active, four South Korean Strike Eagles pushed their throttles up and pointed their noses at the sky. The selected GBU-53s tucked in their specialized racks accepted their programming. Leaving the confines of the ravines, all four aircraft began dispensing chaff countermeasures. Almost immediately, alerts within the cockpits came alive as enemy search radars panned across the flight of four F-15Ks.

The North Korean air defenses near the DMZ were still

attempting to reorganize themselves into a cohesive network. With the previous attacks against communication centers and radar facilities, it was a patchwork effort at best. The search and fire acquisition radars that were still viable were only active for seconds at a time. The SEAD missions of the United States and South Korea had instilled a caution in the operators, the commanders knowing that keeping radars on for any length of time invited swift responses.

The result of this caution was that air defense gaps were created along the North Korean frontier. And with the communications still degraded, there wasn't any broader coordinated network of air defense systems. Most of the longer-range search systems came online, allowing for a full sweep before shutting back down. If they found enemy aircraft withing range of their attached missile launchers, then the fire control radars would target them, staying active only long enough to fire.

A further problem for the North Korean air defenses was that the number of their more advanced KN-06 surface-to-air missiles had been significantly reduced. Or rather, many of their associated radars had been put out of action. Until additional radars were brought forward and the system restored, the Northern defenses were down to their aging SA-2 and S-200 guided missiles. The inherent difficulty was that these anti-aircraft systems were only semi-active radar-guided missiles, meaning that the projectiles themselves weren't smart enough to continuously home in on their target; land-based radars had to remain locked on for the weapons to achieve an intercept. And that meant the radar station had to keep operating throughout the engagement, leaving it vulnerable to anti-radiation missiles.

With the Strike Eagles powering into the pre-dawn skies, the hint of the sun just beyond the horizon became more pronounced as the altimeters wound rapidly upward. The release points for the GBU-53s were set to automatic, the onboard computer determining the optimal release points. Almost in unison, the first four StormBreakers broke free of their perches, each one lofting before settling into a glide as they separated from the F-15Ks.

In a ripple effect, more of the weapons were ejected from their racks. With the forward and tail wings deployed, the bombs grew distant as they headed after their targets. At the same time, the alerts within the cockpits continued. Several of the older North Korean S-200 missiles had been fired, the battery commanders opting to risk letting their radars remain active.

With the last of their bombs sent toward their targets, and still ejecting chaff dispensers, the South Korean Strike Eagles rolled inverted and pulled, their noses crossing the horizon line as they sought lower altitudes. Descending at steep angles, the flight of four attempted to evade the pursuing Mach 8 threats closing in on their positions.

In another area, a flight of four F-16s loitered miles behind the DMZ. These Falcons deviated from their standard combat loads, carrying four AGM-88F HARM missiles along with an AIM-120, an AIM-9X, and two external fuel tanks. The four were on suppression of enemy air defense missions, searching for North Korean radars to remain active long enough to target. The S-200 surface-to-air launches were exactly what the four were waiting for.

Under guidance from the E-3C, the four Falcons turned north, pushing their throttles up. They had been orbiting just out of range of suspected North Korean KN-06 sites. In moments, they were at the edge of the missiles' parameters. With "Magnum" radio calls over the air advertising the launches, anti-radiation missiles sped away from the streaking F-16s, pushing north. Long, fine white lines marked weapon paths.

Some of the North Korean radar sites heard the American radio calls coming from the aircraft far to the south. They knew what "Magnum" meant, that anti-radiation missiles had been fired. The North Korean battery commanders faced two choices. They could play it safe, shutting down the radars and attempting to move the mobile sites before the missiles arrived, or they could continue the engagements and hope they weren't one of the targeted sites.

For the commanders who chose the first option, the radar sites became hives of activity as they shut down their equipment and made haste to drive away. For the others, the atmosphere within the cramped radar command centers became permeated with nervous tension.

The four South Korean F-15Ks that were streaking earthward heard the radio calls of the F-16s on their SEAD missions. Thinking it couldn't hurt, the flight leader copied the radio calls, giving his call sign and announcing "Magnum."

More Northern radar sites went offline as the commanders' nerves wavered. The S-200s that had been receiving guidance from the radars lost their tracking information. As per their limited programming, they "safed" themselves and began falling from the skies, defeated by a bluff.

The Strike Eagle flight's radios became alive with sightings of North Korean missiles.

"Blaze-three, missile, seven o'clock low."

"Blaze-two, missile five o'clock, break right."

"Blaze four status?"

"Blaze four is still with you."

Several of the older radar systems had locked onto the fine chaff threads floating on the winds in dense groupings. The missiles, flying at nearly five thousand miles per hour, ran through the countermeasures and exploded when their proximity fuses issued the commands. Other S-200s were locked onto the aircraft as they engaged in high-G maneuvers. When the pilots saw the missiles angling for their jets, they waited and then pulled hard into the incoming threats. This was to give the missiles' tracking sensors more difficult angles to intercept. The large, antiquated projectiles weren't very maneuverable and couldn't turn as hard as the more agile attack fighters.

The pilots and WSOs gave momentary sighs of relief when thick white trails went powering past their aircraft. Some of the missiles that missed made wide arcing turns as they attempted to come back around, but most kept flying ahead. In several instances, the ECM pods carried by the South Korean jets fooled the missiles into thinking the attack fighters were in different places, the North Korean weapons detonating in empty space.

During the minutes of intense maneuvering, the ROK Strike Eagles managed to evade the North Korean anti-air missiles, thus preserving the Eagles' perfect combat record. Regrouping after eating up miles of sky maneuvering, the flight of four F-15Ks again entered the low-level environment and were directed back toward their base.

The North Korean air defense network became further degraded as most of the sixteen HARM missiles found their targets. Some of the North Korea commanders had tried jamming the incoming threats, but that only prompted the anti-radiation missile guidance systems to activate their home-on-jam capabilities.

As for the commanders who had opted to turn off their systems, they met with marginally better success. With the loss of a radar signal to passively home in on, the AGM-88Fs scanned the area with their millimeter wave radar. Some found targets on the move and made to intercept. Several of the fleeing mobile radar sites managed to get under overhead cover and lost themselves from the missiles seeking them out.

While these actions were playing out in the air, the glide bombs continued their descents in their semi-autonomous modes. Their three sensors, millimeter wave radar, infrared homing, and semi-active laser homing, fused the input coming from the ground. The guidance computer analyzed the data and determined that the class of vehicle they were homing in on matched the type of target it had been programmed to attack.

Dropping silently out of the sky, the GBU-53s came at the moving KN-09 MLRS vehicles from different angles. Some snuck up on the slow-moving vehicles from behind, gliding toward the large trucks as if being towed. Others came out of the dark from the sides, the soldiers inside perhaps hearing something strange in the night before fireballs erupted overhead.

The shaped charges of the glide bombs created both blast

and fragmentation effects. Gouts of flame engulfed most of the vehicles as fast-moving shards of metal punched into the thinner skins of the mobile launchers. Secondary explosions rocked the areas as the solid propellants of the rockets carried by the trucks were set off. More dangerous were the chemical agents that were released, and the droplets that survived the intense fires were carried on the explosive air currents, and even by breezes. Any soldiers that survived being hit by the two-hundred-pound warheads succumbed to painful and lingering deaths as they absorbed lethal agents. Most didn't understand the effects as they had no idea what they carried onboard.

Two of the KN-09 launchers were untouched. One of the bombs missed due to a guidance system malfunction. Another was unable to hit because its sensors lost track of the target when it passed through a narrow defile, a hill on the southern side interfering with the bomb's ability to "see" the truck.

\* \* \* \* \* \*

The E-8C and those in the ground command center at Camp Humphreys closely monitored the attack against the North Korean KN-09s. The data coming back from the glide bombs showed that they had hit eight of the ten targets. Orders were about to be sent to the E-3C and the F-15Ks to re-engage when the sensors on the JSTARS indicated that the two remaining vehicles had come to a stop.

The news sent alarms throughout the command. That meant that the North Koreans were preparing for launches with unknown types of warheads. Initial indications from passing satellites were that the destroyed vehicles might have been carrying chemical agents, but that information had yet to be fully verified.

Firing orders were immediately sent to the M270 unit that had been placed on alert. Coordinates were handed down from the E-8C to the ground station and subsequently to the battery. In short order, ATACMS rockets blasted away from mobile launchers, the long-range weapons arcing over Seoul and the DMZ.

While the American M270 battery was faster at getting their weapons in the air, partly because they were already set up and were only waiting for coordinates, the North Korean soldiers crewing the KN-09 batteries were agile in getting their systems online. In short order, sixteen 300mm rockets were fired from the two Northern vehicles that had survived the initial aerial attack, although the soldiers of those two systems were as yet unaware they were being tracked.

Shortly after watching their fiery streaks vanish into a pre-dawn sky, the North Korean soldiers that manned the KN-09 launchers were obliterated when the American rockets came hurtling down. Smoke-encrusted fireballs lifting into the air signaled the demise of North Korea's long-range artillery capabilities. However, their last statements were already spoken and enroute.

*   *   *   *   *   *

The sixteen 300mm rockets fired by the North Korean KN-09s struck in front of a South Korean company of 7th Corps soldiers situated to the northwest of Paju, South Korea. They were part of a regiment tasked to guard the Unification Bridge and the Imjingang Railway Bridge crossing over the Imjin River, and to destroy North Korean leading units as they drew near.

The large caliber rockets arrived in a mixed bunch. Eight of them were carrying conventional explosives. Those detonated amidst other artillery rounds of various calibers landing in the area in attempts to prevent South Korean forces from destroying the crossings. The only difference, noted by a very few, was that the blasts seemed larger than the others.

What went almost entirely unnoticed were the eight that detonated in the pre-dawn skies, with barely anything to indicate their arrival. The rockets went off with soft pops, their cargo unseen in the early morning light.

The nature of the deadly warheads was revealed when several of the company, who weren't wearing their full MOPP gear, collapsed to the ground. Their convulsions signaled the second chemical attack by the North. Again, the word went out and was quickly disseminated to all ROK and United States units. The order to adhere to chemical warfare operations was emphatically reinforced.

The attack was intended to happen on a much grander scale. It was meant to disrupt the South Korean and American front lines at a time when the mechanized columns were due to hit the Southern defenses. This was achieved only in a small, localized area, but it did manage to spread a fear among the soldiers manning the forward defenses.

\* \* \* \* \* \*

When the leading North Korean units crossed the DMZ and scaled the southern slopes leading up to and around the enemy forts, the supposed first line of defense, it didn't take long to realize that the frontier had been abandoned. Mines and booby traps took some toll on the advance screens, but for the most part, the border was breached without much effort.

When it became clear that the ROK and Americans had abandoned the area, North Korean commanders grew cautious. Many suspected a trap, which slowed their progress, resulting in a timetable that was thrown off almost before the invasion began.

The initial strategy had been for North Korea to steamroll over Southern defenders and keep driving, slamming into the main line of resistance just as the sun was peeking over the horizon. Some regimental and brigade commanders kept to the plan, moving briskly forward, but others proceeded with caution. The spotty communication, partially stemming from the ongoing electronic warfare conducted by the South, led to poor cohesion between units along the line. It even caused a lack of coordination between those supporting the offensive, namely the artillery, seeing as most of the attack fighters had been destroyed.

This meant that the massed artillery slamming down in

South Korea, intensifying with the coming dawn, didn't benefit the mechanized columns as much as it was intended. The leading North Korean stormtroopers were still miles away from their first contact and weren't moving as a cohesive front.

*   *   *   *   *   *

While the aerial and artillery attacks conducted by the Southern forces made it appear as though South Korean and the United States was winning handily, the fact remained that they were barely holding their own. The overwhelming numbers of northern artillery raining down was seriously hurting some units. This resulted in some of the reserves being held to the south having to be shifted north much sooner than planned.

Equipment and men had to be replaced so leading defensive lines could be held at strength for when the brunt of the swollen North Korean forces finally struck. The only relief came from an unexpected enemy strategy. The Southern commanders were thankful and felt fortunate that the Northern leadership had opted to split their artillery fire. It seemed that half of the seven thousand artillery pieces were hitting civilian infrastructure rather than focusing entirely on military targets.

Frontier towns, devoid of citizenry, were taking a beating. Thick pillars of dark smoke rose from dozens of smaller settlements and larger cities alike. The ground rumbled from continuous barrages. And that only increased as the eastern sky began glowing orange. The surge warned frontline Southern commanders to expect the North Koreans at any moment, but the major thoroughfares remained empty. The drones that were constantly being flown to the north showed that the leading enemy forces were still miles away.

At the moment, the artillery duels being waged were the only active ground engagement, but the distance was closing. It was like watching a giant wave approaching stone bluffs; those watching anxiously anticipating the booming crash that the two colliding forces would produce.

# Chapter Five

*South Korea*
*August 3, 2021*

After a long night, the pre-dawn blue finally turned to a thin line of red. As if the slow approach of the sky's lightening was startled into catching up to real time, the red turned to orange and spread quickly, widening, and then rising upward. The stars gave a last twinkle before disappearing until they could again shine in all their glory in half a day's time.

As if the building tension of a thriller had reached its nail-biting climax, the tip of the sun rose above the horizon. Shadows scampered as light stretched across the war-torn landscape. The normally clean light of the dawn cast a brownish tint, reaching dimly through a gritty haze. Columns of smoke spiraled up, bending as they reached altitudes where they caught stiffer breezes. On the South Korean peninsula, the advent of dawn went mostly unheralded as the sounds of war rolled across the lands in its northern reaches.

The thunder of artillery was a constant, the distant barrages a background rumble with the sharper cracks of nearby explosions. The larger city of Seoul and its surrounding urban areas were mired under the heavy odor of burning, while the lands to the north smelled sharply of gunpowder. Every soldier, from General Carswell on down, braced for the clash that the new day would bring.

\* \* \* \* \* \*

K151 and other light armored vehicles belonging to units of the South Korean 7th Corps raced along the Unification Bridge. Below ran the slow-moving muddy waters of the Imjin River, the lazy flow of the waterway at odds with the frantic racing of the scout vehicles returning from the far side.

Light poles overhanging the roadway on both sides, the morning's first glow stretching their long shadows across the pavement, whisked past as the drivers gave their vehicles almost all they had. The worried faces of the scout leaders were betrayed as they glanced repeatedly in their sideview mirrors, looking for signs of the enemy they knew was coming, perhaps just around the nearest bend in the highway.

Ahead, amid the rising pillars of smoke, explosions rocked the fields on the southern shores. Gouts of earth shot upward as enemy artillery shells landed, their thunder arriving moments later. The fields were pockmarked with craters from previous artillery strikes, looking like some disease had infected the land. Even though it appeared as if the greater danger lay ahead, it was still in rearview mirrors that the soldiers in the front seats watched.

The relief they felt upon reaching the raised roadway on the far side as it stretched across the scarred lowlands, wasn't reflected in the tension that lined their tired eyes. Nor could it be seen when they pulled into the still-manned checkpoint.

The lieutenant in charge of the recon unit waved the lightly armored vehicles behind to continue, pointing to the low hills rising to the east of the highway and south of Majeong-ro.

"Are there any more coming, sir?" a sergeant at the checkpoint asked.

"No, we are the last," Lieutenant Choi Ji-hu answered.

"How far behind are *they*?"

"Minutes," the lieutenant replied, knowing full well that the man knew this. His radio calls had alerted everyone.

The recon officer kept glancing back along the road, recalling his close call with the North Korean advance units. While his small patrol could wield some firepower against smaller infantry forces, they were mere flies to the armored personnel carriers, infantry fighting vehicles, and main battle tanks the enemy had in their vanguard.

\*   \*   \*   \*   \*   \*

Lieutenant Ji-hu hovered next to the drone operator, looking at the tablet in the man's hands. The screen depicted a line of North Korean vehicles in reverse infrared, the dark shapes of armored vehicles stark against the white of the surroundings. Some of the mechanized units were pulled off to the side of a four-laned highway. Dark figures milled about the vehicles.

One of the groups seemed to be mimicking the actions of the lieutenant and his patrol, gathered around a central figure holding on to something. It appeared as though the two sides were attempting to gather information regarding positions in the same manner. Seeing the small group caused Ji-hu to gaze up to the morning sky, looking and listening for a drone he suspected was there, or soon would be.

* * * * * *

Ji-hu's scout platoon of nearly thirty men, three APCs, and two light armored vehicles had been sent to the northern side of the Imjin River in order to fix the position of the lead North Koreans. They had several drones with which to assist. Their secondary mission was to mine the roadway. For this, he had selected a location near a couple of installations where the road was lined with trees on both sides.

Looking from the clear skies toward where several engineers were working, the lieutenant knew he didn't have a lot of time before he had to go. The engineers were planting mines near a fresh crater created by an earlier artillery strike. Vehicles were likely to take the easier way around the crater and thus hit the mines, perhaps effectively blocking the road for a little bit. If the patrol were to get into trouble, it might even buy them enough time to escape.

Ji-hu wanted to hurry the engineers, willing them to move faster. But he knew that handling explosives and working hastily weren't mutually supporting endeavors. But that didn't ease the tension sitting on the officer's shoulders. The three APCs, with their 30mm cannons, and the anti-tank K153C light armored vehicle may look impressive from a soldier's standpoint, but they wouldn't be much of anything if confronted by the North's tanks, which were rolling past the drone's screen.

The plan was for Ji-hu's scout patrol to locate the enemy, plant the mines, and call in artillery fire when the North Korean vanguard blundered into the trap. However, locating the enemy was proving to be difficult as their lead units had been successful in destroying the drones that he had sent ahead.

The lieutenant's eyes roved around his position, looking for ways to strengthen it and still ensure they could get away quickly. At the forefront, he had the K153C, with its twin AT-1K anti-tank missile launcher, positioned inside a partially collapsed building. Also covering the highway were two of the APCs. The third was off to the side, keeping watch over the engineers as they went about their tasks. That vehicle also carried the mines, so placing it nearby was essential. The platoon of soldiers with him were arrayed on both sides of the highway, watching the flanks and distant tree lines for any sign of enemy recon units.

He looked back to the drone's screen and was about to ask the operator to pan the camera so he could see where the lead enemy vehicles were, when several North Korean soldiers pointed directly at the drone. Carbines were raised and a heavy caliber machine gun atop one of the small tactical vehicles swiveled toward the camera. Gunfire winked on the screen, which oscillated, and the video feed went fuzzy. The monitor then went dark.

"Well, there goes our last one," the operator stated.

Ji-hu spat, disgusted that the last of his "eyes" had been blinded. At the same time, a hint of movement caught his attention. Shielding his eyes against the glare of the sun, he saw a small object darting in the sky to the east. Just as his people had done, the Northern operators were using the low sun to shield their drones from being observed.

The lieutenant caught the attention of his driver, who was manning the machine gun atop his own tactical vehicle, and pointed to the enemy drone. The driver pivoted the heavy machine gun and took aim. The chattering of the weapon startled the others in the patrol, thinking they were about to come under fire. Hurried glances told the real story. The barrel of the weapon was angled upward. The soldiers then knew that an enemy drone had been spotted. Tracers fled the barrel in bursts, the streaks of the rounds zipping past the drone, which was now weaving back and forth, attempting to dodge the gunfire.

A few bursts and the driver had the range. One of the heavy caliber rounds slammed into the lightweight aerial drone, shattering its body and ripping off one of the rotor arms. The shattered remains of the drone spun out of the air, falling a short distance away.

"Okay, we need to set up the jammer," Ji-hu said.

The plus side of their last drone being downed was that an active wi-fi jammer wouldn't interfere with their own UAS. It would be preferable if the enemy wasn't able to gather any more intel than they already had. But this was only a consolation prize. The real problem was that Ji-hu wouldn't know exactly where the enemy vanguard lay, and when they'd round the corner just up the road. He wanted to give the engineers all the time he could, but without sacrificing his troops in the process.

As the drone operator was unfolding an antenna for the jammer, Ji-hu walked over to where the engineers were setting up anti-tank mines along the only path around the crater.

"How much longer?" he asked the engineering sergeant.

"We could be here a week and still have more to do. How much time do we have, sir?" the sergeant asked, his gaze going up the road.

"Not much," he shook his head. "Maybe fifteen minutes, at best."

"Well, I guess we had best be wrapping it up then," the sergeant stated.

"That is my thinking. We lost our eyes, and to be honest, they could be approaching our position at any moment."

As if to emphasize the statement, a *whoosh* sounded from up the roadway. A fast-moving streak sped away from the rubble of the ruined building where the South Korean anti-armor vehicle was located. Trailing a fine line, almost completely opaque, the missile raced between the tree lines bordering the road. With a loud *clang*, it struck the front of an armored vehicle.

The tandem warhead went off with a flash, the first explosive detonating the reactive armor bolted onto the main battle tank. Obscured by smoke from the explosion, small, dark objects flew up and outward. Yellow flashed from within a thick smoke cloud that was boiling upward.

A second missile fired from the building, paralleling the previous one's track. Another loud metallic clang sounded, the explosion out of Ji-hu's line of sight. A second pillar of ebony smoke rose above the tree line.

"Get everyone on board and head south! Immediately!" Ji-hu yelled at the engineering sergeant.

He heard the sergeant yelling as Ji-hu began running toward his vehicle. The sharp staccato sound of 30mm cannons followed. As the scout lieutenant ran, he was shouting into his mic, telling the soldiers positioned off to the sides to get aboard the APCs. He didn't really have to tell any one of the teams to get going as they were already on the move. The engineers bolted for the open rear of their nearby APC, while other soldiers sprinted across paddocks for vehicles farther up the road, which were already firing at the enemy.

Enemy tracers appeared, streaking past where the trees hugged the road and zipping into the community structures, many of which were heavily scarred from recent North Korean artillery rounds. A third anti-tank missile sped away from the K153C, racing up the road. Ji-hu didn't hear the sound of a hit as the noise of the battle had grown into a cacophony.

He saw his armored car, his driver behind the upper armor plates as he delivered bursts of fire. Enemy tracers streaked across the fields, chasing after his scattered group of soldiers as they clambered over, under, and through the fence lines adjacent the road. One man lay over the strands, only moving with the sway of the wire as others crossed.

Ji-hu wanted to run and grab the stricken man. Alive or

dead, he wanted to return with everyone. He was about to race over when two other soldiers reached the figure and pulled, the man flopping over as one grabbed his beltline and yanked.

A sharp, loud crack penetrated the din of multiple calibers firing. Ji-hu had heard that distinct sound only a couple of times. There was only one thing that sounded like the long barrel of a tank firing, and that was another tank.

With the sound of his 7.62mm K12 firing nearby, Ji-hu looked up the road. He was just in time to see the building where he'd parked the K153C blossom as an explosion sent debris scattering into the road. A ball of smoke rose above the structure, followed by a thicker column that was propelled upward by an intense heat source. The remaining walls of the structure fell, the building fully collapsing to send a fan of brick and mortar outward.

His anti-tank vehicle was out of action. Ji-hu continued watching the location, waiting for any of the crew to come stumbling away. No one appeared, but one soldier ran up to the building, peered in for a second, and then ran away. That was enough to let the lieutenant know that no one had survived the hit. Under the intense fire coming from the enemy, it would be nearly impossible to retrieve the bodies. In frustration, Ji-hu knew he had to let them go.

The volume of incoming fire was growing steadily. The APCs up the road and still in action were taking hits from smaller caliber rounds. The engineers had loaded up and the rear hatches were closing when the vehicle appeared to take in a deep breath, the hull seeming to expand. It then acted as if it was holding that inhalation—before the vehicle erupted in a gout of flame. The top hatches blew off, tumbling high into the air before allowing gravity to take charge once again.

An intense roar was added to the cacophony as towering flames shot through the openings. Even being a distance away, Ji-hu could feel the heat coming from the destroyed vehicle. It was past time to be gone.

"Back to the bridge," Ji-hu shouted over the radio.

The nearby machine gun that was firing stopped as the

driver made ready to get the fuck out of Dodge. Ji-hu opened the passenger door and waited, looking up the road to see his two remaining APCs reversing toward him, their smoke generators emitting dense clouds. Their 30mm cannons continued to send a steady stream of rounds toward the enemy, the tracers vanishing into a thick fog of smoke. From out of the same smoke cloud, enemy tracers suddenly appeared. The North Koreans were lost from Ji-hu's sight, but he knew the thermal optics of both sides wouldn't be so blind.

The two APCs reached Ji-hu's position and turned around, racing south. The lieutenant jumped inside, slamming the door.

"Let us get the hell out of here," Ji-hu ordered the driver.

"You do not have to tell me twice," the driver returned, flooring it.

The K151 turned tightly, the wheels sending gravel shooting away. Ji-hu looked back in the sideview mirror. Smoke was covering the road. He was about to look away when a long barrel poked ominously through the screen. Smoke shot out of the barrel. The lieutenant almost felt the heavy passage of the shell as it raced close down his side. The enemy round smashed into a tall brick tower ahead and exploded.

Bricks slammed against the windshield and front of the tactical vehicle, along with a downpour of smaller chips. It sounded like he was driving through a hailstorm, the vehicle mercilessly beaten with golf ball-sized debris. Looking up, fear struck Ji-hu as he saw the tall stack begin to topple.

The driver yelled, "Oh shit!" his foot flooring the accelerator.

Ji-hu saw that it was going to be a close-run thing. The top of the tower was falling faster as it gained momentum. It was no longer a solid structure; its shape was now made up of individual bricks all falling at close to the same speed. As the lieutenant watched, it turned into an almost fluid object. The tank was momentarily forgotten as both soldiers' attention was focused on the falling silo.

Individual bricks began landing in the road, bouncing

down the highway toward the armored car. The solid thuds against the front seemed to slow the speeding vehicle. A shadow crossed, the windscreen filled with the sight of literal tons of bricks growing larger by the second. Ji-hu threw a hand up over his head, as if that might protect him from the massive structure breaking apart and falling on him. And then the interior was suddenly flooded with light.

Both men screamed, thinking the sudden brightness was the tower striking the vehicle. The armored car shook and the world was filled with a roar as thousands of bricks hit the highway all at once. Realizing that they had escaped the crumbling silo, Ji-hu swore he had heard a scraping sound as the tower grazed the top of the K151.

Turning to look behind, he saw dust and fine debris floating above a huge pile of bricks strewn across the highway. Beyond, he saw the now fully emerged shape of a North Korean main battle tank, its barrel pointed straight at him. He may have escaped the pot, but he was about to end up in the fire. Ji-hu knew that he was looking his own death straight in the face.

The tank shook. For a brief second, Ji-hu thought it had fired and time had slowed. It would be only a matter of microseconds until the shell arrived. Then he saw a cough of brownish smoke roll up the side of the tank. It had gone around the crater and hit one of the mines laid out by the now dead engineers. They had landed a parting shot before exiting the earth for good.

Thinking the gun could still fire, and with his breath held, Ji-hu stared at the steel behemoth. A secondary explosion shook the monster, thick smoke rising from somewhere inside. With the barrel still aimed at the fleeing armored car, the tank grew smaller until it was lost from sight as Ji-hu and his driver turned another corner.

\*   \*   \*   \*   \*   \*

"If you are going to blow it, now is the time," Lieutenant Ji-hu stated.

With enemy artillery rounds landing to the south of them, the sergeant turned toward the others in the shrapnel-scarred booth and motioned. A helmeted head in the window of the building nodded and darted away. Two seconds later, a series of eruptions thundered to the east. Multiple pillars of smoke blasted into the air and amid the explosions, debris was hurled outward.

To the untrained eye, it looked like any of the other artillery rounds detonating across the countryside. But the rippled blasts could only belong to a planned detonation. In this case, it was the destruction of the Imjingang Railway Bridge. When the rolling blasts subsided, girders of the superstructure lay twisted in the current, along with great slabs of concrete from fallen spans. One of the main routes across this section of the river had been blocked.

The sergeant watched the explosions, the smoke still skyrocketing upward. Most of the debris had already landed heavily in the river and atop adjoining land. He then looked toward the Unification Bridge, his expression one of worry and confusion.

The door of the guard building slammed open, and a South Korean soldier came running out. Panting, he stopped at the side of the armored car. He gave a brisk salute to the lieutenant, and then quickly took his hand away. He'd forgotten that they were now at war, and salutes on the frontline could easily lead to a sniper bullet taking out a commander. With the North Koreans only a short distance away, and with no allied forces now north of the river, it was entirely conceivable that the enemy could have scout snipers already positioned in cover along the opposite banks.

Turning back to the sergeant, the soldier reported.

"There is a problem with the line to the Unification Bridge. It showed green until a few moments ago."

"Do you know where the break is?" the sergeant inquired.

The soldier shook his head. "It could be anywhere along the line."

The sergeant turned toward Ji-hu, the question plainly written on his face but hesitant to outright ask.

"Sir, we do not have enough — " the sergeant started.

"Can you fix the break if we find it?" Ji-hu asked both the sergeant and the soldier.

"Yes, sir," the young engineer eagerly replied, perhaps ashamed that the system, *his system*, wasn't working and was maybe allowing the North Korean vanguard to easily cross as they stood there. The soldier thought that he might conceivably be responsible for single-handedly losing the war.

"Jump in," Ji-hu stated.

"But sir, we were ordered to report in. We are supposed to be heading there with the others," the driver stated, pointing toward the low line of hills.

"That report will have to wait," Ji-hu replied, grabbing for the radio mic.

The armored car jostled as the rear door opened and the engineer climbed in. Ji-hu called for one of the larger K808 armored APCs to turn around. The armored personnel carrier held ten soldiers. It wasn't anywhere near enough to hold off the North Korean vanguard, but it might be enough to bide some time for the young soldier to fix whatever was wrong with the explosives mounted under the spans.

"Thank you, sir," the sergeant said. "*Jalwayo*, sir."

"If luck means that the enemy stays away for a little while longer, I will take it."

It didn't take long for the APC to return, the 30mm cannon and 7.62mm machine gun protruding from the two-man turret. Turning around, the armored car started back down the highway toward the bridge.

"Oh, sir, wait a second," the engineer called from the back seat.

The vehicle lurched as the driver stepped on the brakes a little harder than intended, the soldier's call startling him, or perhaps annoyed that they were once again heading back toward the frontline. When the K151stopped, the engineer sprinted from the car, leaving the door swinging as he ran into the building. He came out a few moments later, carrying something about the size of a smaller car battery. He clambered back in, again seemingly out of breath.

"Just in case," the engineer said, holding up a portable battery coupled with a detonator.

The sight didn't give Ji-hu a comfortable feeling. Obviously, the engineer understood that time was of the essence and that they may not have enough of it to return to relative safety before the North Koreans showed up. As they started out again, the driver developed a nervous tic in his eye caused by heading back, especially considering what they had already gone through.

Ji-hu had the same reservations. He wasn't too keen to face the enemy mechanized advanced forces again and hoped the problem with the line could be discovered and remedied soon. He wanted to get the fuck away from the river that would hopefully stall the enemy advance, and maybe even prove to be an impenetrable barrier. He knew the major units comprising the 7th Corps weren't far away and would be tasked with stopping the North Korean forces, or at least delaying them long enough for the main line of resistance to be strengthened.

A second K808 appeared, joining the small convoy heading toward the Unification Bridge.

"Thought you could get all the glory," the radio blared.

Ji-hu recognized his sergeant's voice, a smile pursing his lips. The man could be the biggest pain in his ass, but was also his greatest asset. "I see you have finally learned how to follow orders," Ji-hu responded sarcastically, only to be met with a laugh.

Together, the two APCs and lone armored car slowly rolled up the vacant highway. As the nearby village to the north had been destroyed, the enemy would surely be rolling up to their location soon. The engineer in back was constantly peering outside, but he was focused on the roadway's edge. He was searching for any obvious sign that the line had been broken. Unfortunately for him, the road began its raised portion soon after departing the checkpoint and the engineer had to get out to walk in order to view the cables, thus slowing the small convoy even more.

The twenty soldiers that had been riding inside the APCs also disembarked and walked along with the rolling vehicles. Nervous glances darted whenever a crescendo of artillery shells escalated, hoping to hell that the North didn't shorten their fires. It was bad enough having to return after having narrowly escaped, but doing so in the midst of an artillery attack wasn't a good plan for longevity. This was especially true on this raised section as there was nowhere to go for cover. There were several who contemplated their chances of survival if they were to jump in case the enemy artillery fires shifted.

"That might be a clue as to why it did not work," the driver stated sarcastically, pointing ahead to a damaged section of the roadway.

Part of the highway had crumbled and was blackened, the crater on the ground underneath indicating that an artillery shell had exploded. Ji-hu didn't remember seeing that on the frantic drive across, and the smoke still drifting from the hole in the ground was a hint that it had occurred recently.

"Hey, maybe there," Ji-hu shouted to the engineer, pointing to where the driver had.

The engineer nodded. "Yes, sir. I was thinking it was the problem, but wanted to check the whole line anyway."

"Time is not our friend," Ji-hu replied.

The soldier seemed to get the gist and hurriedly glanced to the far side of the bridge.

"I will, uh, just get on that, sir."

"If it is not too much trouble," Ji-hu said, smiling as the younger man turned sharply.

The engineer ran ahead, uncoiling rope he had draped around him.

"We might be too late, sir," the driver said, pointing ahead.

Ji-hu looked up from watching the engineer only to see two enemy armored vehicles appear from around a bend in the highway across the bridge. They looked very similar to the

K808s that were in a line across the span, the recognizable sloped front jutting like a beak. Judging by the smaller chassis, the lieutenant thought they might be the six-wheeled versions of the M2010, a replica of the Russian BTR-80.

The two South Korean K808s were quicker on the draw, their 30mm cannons spitting out rounds. Tracers shot down the length of the span. Sparks erupted from the two North Korean armored personnel carriers, or at least Ji-hu believed that was the type of transport he was looking at. The distances made it difficult for a positive identification. Soon, smoke started rising from the two enemy vehicles. Tiny figures darted from the rear of the APCs, disappearing from sight along the road's edges.

The one-sided exchange of fire rapidly changed as tracers came back down the bridge. Loud clangs and sparks erupted from the front of the K808s as heavy caliber rounds started striking.

"Get behind them," Ji-hu shouted to his driver.

He hated to take the K12 7.62mm gun on top out of the action, but there was no way the armored car would last long in this firefight with the heavier caliber weapons.

The windshield cracked as a bullet careened off the glass face. A second chip appeared when another round struck. The K151 screeched as the driver jammed the vehicle in reverse and drove back between the two friendly APCs, swerving as he passed to place the armored car directly behind the one on the right as though hiding behind its big brother.

*   *   *   *   *   *

The engineer stopped adjusting his harness when the firing started. He saw the two North Korean vehicles at a distance and witnessed the hits against them. He wasn't sure if he should continue or run. His decision was made when he realized that the two armored vehicles near his were sticking it out, exchanging fire from those across the river. They were buying him time. The sights and sounds of the K808s being hit spurred him into action.

He worked the rope through the harness as he eyed the structure. The previously empty bridge was now ablaze with tracers, those speeding away and those coming seemingly right at him. There were larger, slower tracers that grew faster as they approached. And then there were the ones that zipped past almost faster than could be recognized. It was a laser light show; enough to become mesmerized and petrified, standing, staring, doing nothing.

Miraculously, at least to him, his fingers were still working, even if his brain was threatening to shut down. Tying off on a nearby lamp post and testing the sturdiness, the engineer sat on an edge of the ramp that had been blasted away, the one closest to the river. With a deep inhale and a final glimpse down the span, he slipped over the edge.

The change was dramatic. Whereas he had been ingulfed in the volume of the firefight, the chugging of the 30mm cannons, the thinner sound of carbines, the whoosh of portable rocket launchers firing, the rolling booms of artillery landing, and the bee-like zips of rounds passing far too close, he was now immersed in a muted world. It was almost like being underwater.

Letting out enough line, he began swinging and was able to grab a handhold near the conduit bundling the electronic cables that would signal the explosives under the bridge to detonate. Managing to wrap his legs and steady himself in a semi-seated position, the South Korean engineer looked at the conduit. It was shattered by whatever had landed underneath. A spiral of whitish smoke rose from the crater and went right into his face, just like the smoke from a campfire that would ceaselessly chase one person. He coughed, nearly dropping the detonator he was still carrying.

He set the device on a ledge just within reach, hoping that the tremors running through the span wouldn't cause it to tumble from its perch. Analyzing the mess of cables hanging from the ruined conduit, he forgot about the firefight occurring just over his head. He gathered the wires and wrapped them together with a Velcro strip. Grabbing a pair of cutters, he evened them and then exposed each individual wire.

Wiping sweat from his brow, the soldier then started splicing the lot of them together one wire at a time. A large tremor shook the bridge, the sound of an explosion reaching him on his perch underneath. The wire cutters turned in his grip and fumbled from hand to hand as he attempted to catch them. A last desperate grab ensnared them. Remembering the trigger device, he reached up just as it was about to tumble off the precarious ledge.

With things back under a semblance of control, he wiped another stream of sweat trickling from his temple. He then set back to work, splicing all the exposed wires to a pair of leads. Holding the detonator in the crook of his arm, he wrapped one of the wires around a post. He was about to do the same to the second one when another loud explosion rocked the bridge.

He managed to stay in place, momentarily wondering how the team accompanying him was faring. He knew the lieutenant had been right that there wasn't time to fuck around and that he had to hurry. Quickly attaching the second wire to the detonator, he suddenly wondered if he was doing the right thing. Should he detonate? He had the previous order, but did it still hold in his current predicament?

A deep rumble penetrated his senses and internal conversation. The bridge was trembling as one might when a large truck passed over it. The sensation grew. With a feeling that it was growing too late, he flicked a rocker switch and was rewarded by the glow of a green light. He then depressed the red button, sending an electrical current down the wires.

A series of blasts shook the span. From underneath, the engineer saw great billows of dark smoke roil from where it crossed the river. The smoke boiled and curled like a brewing storm, the ball growing larger as it rolled toward his position. It then swept past, engulfing him. The feeling was a suffocating one as the world beyond dimmed and grew dark. And then it was past, leaving his lungs spasming.

The bridge shook and bucked like a bronco, the soldier clinging to his perch with all his might. Then, the blast ebbed, leaving the engineer shaken and not entirely sure he was still alive. He then started climbing back to the top, which now seemed particularly quiet.

\* \* \* \* \* \*

Thick, dark smoke twisted up from the far bank as two North Korean APCs burned. The sound of the firefight up top was deafening. The outgoing 30mm and 7.62 mm fire from the nearby K808 APCs could be felt as well as heard. The whine of incoming rounds and the clangs of hits, coupled with the small arms fire coming from the twenty South Korean soldiers arrayed across the highway added to the cacophony.

Even though they had taken out the lead enemy vehicles, Ji-hu knew from experience that this fight could only end one of two ways. Either they would have to conduct a hasty retreat under fire, or the heavier armor he knew was coming would destroy them. It was difficult to see through the smoke on the far side, so he had no idea exactly what he was immediately facing.

From the tracers streaking from the opposite bank, it appeared that he was fighting a force similar to his own. Small arms fire and thicker tracers from 12.5mm caliber fire were passing the outgoing tracers from his own unit. Ricochets off the APC's frontal armor whined off into the distance, some tracers streaking into the morning sky. Sparks flew everywhere from impacting rounds. It seemed as if the very pavement was alive.

With the flat surface of the roadway, cover was almost non-existent. A couple of the soldiers were being assisted behind the K808s, their wounds hastily bandaged. Ji-hu, peering around one of the APCs and adding his own rounds to the fight, glanced toward the crumbled section of the bridge where the engineer had vanished. He wondered how the young soldier was faring and how much longer he'd be.

He'd hold off the Northern forces for as long as he could, but the time was quickly arriving when he'd have to disengage and pull back. The front of the armored vehicles looked like the fireworks on the beach at night during the Boryeong Mud Festival. The lieutenant thought the time for pulling back might have already come and gone. He glanced once more at the hole, urging the engineer to hurry up. Ji-hu knew the importance of destroying the bridge, but that didn't stop him from wishing the soldier would appear and signal that the bridge was ready to blow.

A sharp crack rose above the furious sounds of the ongoing battle. It was followed a second later by a loud *clang*. The ringing was like being up against a giant gong when it was struck. A blinding flash preceded a concussive explosion that rolled over the lieutenant. Knocked to the ground, Ji-hu looked up to see flames leaping from one of his APCs and thick, black smoke towering into the air. The outgoing fire from his side was drastically reduced.

With his ears ringing, the lieutenant rose and stumbled back to the cover of the remaining APC. Peering back down the bridge and bringing his carbine up, he witnessed a missile powering away. He watched as the AT-1K Raybolt arced upward and immediately began a steep descent. A flash from the far bank indicated that the weapon had found a target. He saw a sheet of flame wavering through the haze of battle, another pillar of smoke pouring into a sky that was turning a brownish-orange hue.

More wounded soldiers were being dragged behind the remaining APC, giving a wide berth around the fiery inferno that had been the other KN808. The incoming fire seemed to double while his own outgoing fire was diminishing. This fight was about over, and he was on the losing side. It wouldn't be too much longer before he was overwhelmed and the enemy forces would start crossing.

Heavy crumps started along the shoreline across from him. Help in the way of friendly artillery, the strikes showing through the haze with great gouts of flame and smoke. The small arms fire being directed at him seemed to diminish, although it was hard to believe with the volume of fire still coming from the enemy on the far shore.

Large caliber incoming rounds kicked up chunks of pavement, sending minute pieces in all directions. Ji-hu felt the stings as tiny bits of roadway sliced his cheeks and forehead. The roar of the blazing APC drowned out much of the other battle sounds. Directing fire down the bridge, attempting to aim at the dozens of tiny sparkles emanating from the opposite side, he saw another friendly Raybolt missile soar aloft and descend.

This time, the course of the missile shot off to the side instead of racing down the bridge. Running to the opposite corner of the APC, Ji-hu saw that a couple of North Korean tanks, looking much like the Russian T-72s, had come to the river's embankment. One of them flashed white as the anti-tank missile struck. A secondary explosion rocked the tank, the cupola sliding off the top to land canted next to the flaming wreck.

The lieutenant saw a puff of smoke from the barrel of the second one. Turning, he began to dive away from the APC he was in cover behind. The explosion propelled him faster and farther than intended, the force of it twisting him in mid-air. He fell next to his armored car and slid across the pavement. Rolling the last couple of feet, Ji-hu lay on the surface in agony. He heard only a dim roaring and it felt like his body was on fire in a dozen places.

Pushing himself up, it seemed as if his bones had turned to jelly. At the same time, they felt like they were brittle and would snap under the slightest pressure. Managing to get to his feet, he stumbled toward the driver's side of his armored car. Leaning against the side and using it for support, he lurched forward.

The sparks coming from the pavement barely registered. His mind seemed to be wrapped in cotton and his ears ringing loudly enough to block out any other sounds. The far-off smoke pillars were like some backdrop of a play, portraying a scene that wasn't really a part of his reality. The nearby towering flames also seemed unreal, although the heat coming from them felt real enough.

Suddenly, the world came swooping back in. The crackle of flames, the zipping whine of ricochets, the distant crump of artillery shells landing, all broke through his muted senses at once. Soldiers, his soldiers, lay scattered on the ground. The part of the bridge where the engineer had vanished was blocked by the burning APC. There was no more he could do here. It was time to go, engineer or not.

At the driver's side door, Ji-hu saw an image of himself in the rear view. He didn't recognize the person staring back, the smoke-smudged face with a myriad of cuts was a stranger. It was the eyes that startled him the most, the gaze like that of someone much older, someone who had witnessed a lifetime of events.

He reached for the handle of the armored car and swung the door open. The body of his driver fell out, almost rolling as if he didn't have any bones. Landing face up, Ji-hu saw that a piece of metal had nearly sliced the man's head in half, a deep gouge running completely through from the bridge of his nose.

Pings knocked against the open door as rounds struck. The window glass spiderwebbed from impacts. Ji-hu looked up to see the monstrous form of a tank on the bridge, rolling across the span. Fire winked from a turret and the lieutenant felt something hard slam into his leg. He fell to the pavement, agony running up his thigh, the pain from his other injuries forgotten.

At the sight of the North Korean tank, Ji-hu knew that he had failed. He had killed his platoon, and for what? The enemy had been able to cross. He had waited too long and still lost the bridge. The vibration of the heavy main battle tank on the bridge rolled under him. Laying on the hard pavement, with waves of pain moving through him, he waited for the end.

At first, the sight of the towering explosions seemed unreal, even as they engulfed the tank that had been heading toward him. The bridge erupted in a series of blasts that sent smoke rocketing upward. Even in as much pain as he was in, Ji-hu understood that the young engineer had accomplished his task. Pieces of the bridge crashed nearby, the shorn-off top of a lamppost landing close with a metallic clang. With a smile that must have looked like a grimace, the lieutenant lay back on the roadway, gazing at the brownish-hued sky above.

*   *   *   *   *   *

As his head crested the lip of the bridge, the engineer was shocked at the difference from when he had slipped below. Both of the armored vehicles that had accompanied him were burning. Bodies of soldiers lay everywhere, none of them moving. Even the sounds had changed. When he had gone underneath, the entire bridge had been filled with the noise of a fierce battle. Now there was only the roar of fires and the distant rumbles of artillery landing on the far shore.

Tracers, which had filled the area over the long span, were now mostly gone. A few still raced down the roadway, but it was nothing like before. The soldier pulled himself the rest of the way up, keeping as close to the pavement as possible to avoid being shot. It was a shock to see the lifeless bodies, some with surrounding pools of blood, their fatigues tattered from enemy bullets. Their weapons lay strewn and empty cartridges winked in the weak sunlight.

The engineer looked up the highway, pleased to see that the spans had been dropped and the crossing closed. Glancing again at the bodies, he wondered about the cost of doing so. It came to him that these men had died for him...had sacrificed themselves for his personal mission...so that he could close off the passage to the enemy. Would they soon be forgotten, lost in the turmoil of war? Or would they be remembered as the heroes they were?

As the soldier moved past the fallen, he wondered if they even cared about being remembered as such. As he stumbled past the burning vehicles, with tears blurring his vision, he vowed to make sure that they would be remembered for as long as he lived. He would find out their names and visit their families, would make sure to honor their lives.

At the rear of the burning vehicles, the engineer came

across the body of the lieutenant who had guided them in, lying next to another fallen soldier. The grimace on the man's face and the long stream of drying blood running from his leg told of the pain he suffered. The soldier thought about the officer, and even though he'd only known the man for a short time, he seemed like someone who cared. He too would be remembered.

Amid the background of artillery dropping on the opposite shore, the engineer made his way back to the checkpoint. The crossing had been held, and he would remember those who had fallen until his dying day.

\* \* \* \* \* \*

Resounding booms echoed up and down the Imjin River as the bridges separating north and south, or in some cases, west from east, were blown. One of the problems of defending this first of several rivers flowing across South Korea was that the waterway was shallow in many places. In some locations, it could be easily forded. And in one particular spot, sandbars stretched almost all the way across. It was almost possible to walk from one shore to the other, especially in the summer.

But the spans across were all wrecks of concrete, rebar, girders, and pavement resting on the bottom of the river. The North Korean momentum, their forward movement to force their way through the defensive lines, was halted for the time being, at least in the South Korean 7th Corps area of responsibility.

# Chapter Six

*South Korea*
*August 3, 2021*

Eight AH-64E Apache Guardian attack helicopters stormed up the valley, their wheels clearing small buildings, fence rows, and the occasional tree by mere feet. The hard thrumming of their rotors scattered birds searching the brown fields for meals. Spread across a narrow valley in a staggered formation, Bravo Company of the 1st Battalion/227th Aviation Regiment raced north.

Strung out along the stub wings and attached to hardpoints, each of the attack choppers was configured for an anti-armor role, carrying a complement of sixteen AGM-114 Hellfire Longbow missiles. Behind the "Reapers" came the "Vampires," another company in the same battalion. With the sun rising in the east, the valleys north and northeast of Seoul filled with the beating sound of attack choppers racing toward the front lines. Although smaller skirmishes had taken place between recon units, major ground units of the North and South were about to collide head-on.

\* \* \* \* \* \*

Brown fields raced past, the almost bare dirt screaming by just a few feet below. Captain Dwight England twitched the stick back, the Apache Guardian lifting slightly in response. Applying gentle pressure to the control stick, the chopper lifted over power lines that he swears he could have flown under. Glancing to the side, he saw another of his company undulate smoothly over the lines, popping back down to almost ground level on the other side.

The company approached the front line at extreme low levels to avoid radar that might be prevalent in the mix of North Korea's advance forces. The data being handed down from the E-8C miles overhead didn't necessarily show an abundance of electronic emissions, but the plans called for low approaches, in any case.

Rolled and stacked bales came into view and flashed past. In one field, a lone piece of farm machinery sat, looking forlorn and abandoned. Behind it was a line of stubble, while taller stalks marched ahead of the bailer.

Dwight heard a chuckle over the intercom. "It looks like that farmer decided right there and then to skedaddle."

The captain didn't respond to his gunner sitting in front, just watched as his helmet swiveled back and forth. Dwight often flew with the lieutenant, although the pairing had led to the two being called England Dan and John Ford Coley. Lieutenant John Coley, the gunner and co-pilot, would often just shake his head after hearing for them to sing after entering the O-Club. It had maybe been amusing the first hundred times or so, but it did seem to drain the soul when it kept playing out. Dwight sympathized, sometimes thinking he might forgo the usual Friday night drinks just so he wouldn't hear the calls that would inevitably surface.

Shaking his head to rid his mind of those tiresome thoughts, Dwight focused on maintaining those few feet between him and the ground. After all, the ground always wins in any contest with aircraft. Farther ahead, it wasn't difficult to determine where the front lines were. The rising palls of dark smoke were an easily distinguishable feature.

Glancing at one of the screens, Dwight saw that things on the battlefield ahead were progressing slowly. A drone loitering in the vicinity was sending live video of the location for the first meeting of allied and enemy armored units. Miles beyond a ridgeline that sat in the middle of a valley, magnified views of North Korean tanks, APCs, and IFVs showed enemy armored columns covering the valley floor. They were spread out and deployed in combat formations, dust clouds drifting into the morning skies behind them.

Although it was feasible for any of the choppers in formation to take over the drone, or control any weaponry it might have, today's plan didn't call for it. Perhaps they might have if they'd been scouting to locate enemy forces, and/or perhaps engage them from a longer distance. But as was depicted on the screen, the enemy had already been detected, and had been for some time. Other drones monitored the flanks of the engagement area, and other companies and regiments were responsible for the other valleys that the North Koreans were marching through.

Dwight rolled his shoulders, attempting to ease the tension. He envisioned that the upcoming fight would be intense. Not only that, but it was going to be a long day. The regiment was to be on the front line for most of the day, moving to the battlefield in company formations and returning to reload before heading back. A second attack regiment of the 1st Air Cav Brigade would take over the battle duties supporting the 1st Cavalry Division's front in due time, but Dwight anticipated the next few months to be filled with nothing more than sleeping and flying, and with the latter winning out hands down.

"Hotel six, Crazy Horse three-one, ten miles out," Dwight radioed.

He didn't bother adding that they were eight Apache Guardians or their ordnance as the controller directing battlefield operations already had that information. If any of the attack helicopters had to break away for some reason, they would then use their individual call signs for future calls until they either rejoined the formation or landed.

"Copy that, Crazy Horse three-one. Anchor three hundred yards off the eastern edge of the Alpha three-five-one ridge."

Dwight was on the far right of the company and would serve as the targeting chopper. That meant that he and his gunner would hover behind the ridgeline so that only the sensors mounted on top of the rotor were visible to anyone beyond. This would allow for them to identify North Korean targets in the valley beyond without exposing themselves to enemy fire.

The other seven choppers would hover in line below the crest and use the replicated data from Dwight's helicopter. The entire company would target the enemy armor beyond using the information from Dwight's Guardian. Once targets were selected, the individual attack choppers would quickly rise above the ridgeline and fire, descending immediately, limiting their exposure to enemy anti-air systems. It would look like some convoluted game of whack-a-mole to the North Koreans, with choppers rising for only moments before again vanishing and repositioning.

As the hellfire missiles being carried had dual sensors, one being a millimeter wave radar, they were launch-and-leave weapons which could home in on enemy armor on their own. In front, Lieutenant Coley was in the process of verifying that the other "Reapers" were receiving the data being sent.

"We're all good to go," Coley stated.

"All right, let's do this," Dwight responded.

Inwardly, he was thankful that his gunner didn't have a song ready. As much as he complained about their nicknames, the lieutenant was all too ready to blast into one of the famous duos' songs if it fit the moment.

Dwight angled toward the eastern end of the ridge that was coming into view. The top was being plastered by a series of explosions from North Korean supporting artillery. The captain knew that elements of the 1st Brigade Combat Team were positioned on this side of the ridge, using the rear slope of the hills to protect them from the incoming enemy rounds.

Seeing the blasts as they continually detonated along the top, Dwight was glad he wasn't a ground-pounder. He in no way wanted to be close to what was transpiring and couldn't imagine what it must be like for the tankers and infantry supposedly arrayed along the ridge. He pulled within the specified distance and brought the chopper into a hover, slowly rising until the camera and other sensors on top could see the valley beyond.

He could almost feel and hear the explosions that were lifting clumps of earth and scattering them. Craters formed on top of other craters in some places, but through the smoke, Dwight could see where firing positions for the tanks had been dug. And on the back side of the hill sat the squat shapes of the brigade's tanks, along with other armored support vehicles. Dwight assumed they were waiting for the artillery landing on positions atop the ridge to stop, or at least become less intense.

On the interior screen, he could see the live video from recon drones showing friendly artillery dropping in among the encroaching North Korean formations. Glancing to the side, Dwight saw the others of his company hovering in line with his chopper, waiting for the order to fire.

"Hotel six, Crazy Horse three-one in position."

"Copy. Crazy Horse three-one, standby."

Dwight knew he wouldn't be cleared to fire immediately, as the enemy was still beyond the six-mile engagement distance of the Hellfire. Until the enemy armor drew within that range, the fight would belong to the artillery systems and the air forces of South Korea and the United States.

*   *   *   *   *   *

The sun cresting over the horizon glinted off the canopy as the F-15E Strike Eagle sliced through the thin morning air. Three other gray-painted attack fighters were spread out to the sides, the sunrise hitting the high-altitude aircraft while the waters below were still shrouded in the pre-dawn darkness.

Tucked under the wings and fuselage were an assortment of sleek, sharp-nosed missiles. The longer AIM-120 air-to-air missiles were there to deal with any of their few interceptors that North Korea might decide to throw at the flight. The shorter AIM-9X were nestled adjacent in case the fight became a closer quarters brawl. But the much larger white shapes loaded on pylons under the air-to-air missiles were the main show, and the reason why the flight of four Strike Eagles were currently out over the Sea of Japan.

Each aircraft carried two of the long-range weapons, although recent tests showed that the F-15E could be equipped with up to five of the air-launched cruise missiles. The AGM-158B Joint Air-to-Surface Standoff Missile-Extended Range (JASSM-ER) was a stealth missile that was deadly in its own right, but these carried specialized gear that was intended to do damage the enemy, but not in the conventional sense of explosive warheads.

The missiles were a result of the Counter-electronics High Power Microwave Advanced Missile Project (CHAMP). They were directed energy weapons which projected high power microwaves at targets, effectively destroying electronic gear. This type of weapon could be employed against unmanned aerial vehicle swarms, although they would have to be deployed ahead of friendly lines to avoid interfering with or incapacitating friendly equipment.

Enemy command posts were another priority target for which they were well suited and designed. The normal jamming of enemy electronic emissions and receivers stood the chance of only being partially successful, and was only good for as long as the electronic warfare equipment was deployed. There were also inherent risks that EW aircraft faced, including passive homing attacks and a wide array of anti-aircraft defenses. The JASSM-ER cruise missile was chosen as the optimal delivery vehicle as it eliminated a variety of problems facing the electronic warfare operators.

With the cruise missiles' range of nearly six hundred miles, the flight of Strike Eagles didn't need to venture very far from Japan's western shores. The only caveat to the mission parameters, and for those originating from air bases on the island, was that any launches take place outside of Japan's territorial boundaries. It was a small, but important technical detail that was supposed to keep the island nation out of the nearby conflicts. Theoretically, as long as Japan was not directly involved in the conflict, American ports and bases there were protected from long-range fire from either North Korea or China. This arrangement permitted sanctuaries from which U.S. planes and ships could be refueled and rearmed, while allowing them to conduct strikes away from Japan's territorial boundaries. One important responsibility for these bases was the staging of equipment and ordnance to resupply the forces in South Korea.

The Strike Eagles jostled as the two-thousand-pound cruise missiles dropped from their hardpoints. Gleaming an orangish hue in the rays of the newly risen sun, the rear tail and mid wings of the ALCMs snapped into place. The turbojets ignited and the missiles began to pull away from the jets, slowly descending from their lofty perch. A second set of missiles then fell away and chased after the leaders.

With a casualness that belied their mission, the four F-15Es started gradual turns back to the east. They then nosed over and began descents that would take them to their runways only a few miles away.

The eight AGM-158B missiles continued their journeys to the northwest, descending as they approached the outer limits of North Korea's long-range radars. Hugging the wavetops, the missiles began to fly divergent courses as they sought out the first of their many targets.

Flying nearly seven miles above the earth, and orbiting some distance from the inbound cruise missiles, two airborne command posts and a surveillance drone continued to collect data. From radio emissions, the operators aboard the aircraft had determined the locations of numerous North Korean divisional and regimental command posts. Electronic warfare aircraft operating south of the DMZ had also been able to sniff out possible battalion command posts, adding them to a growing list of targets.

From the E-8C's and other aircraft data, the E-3C directing the cruise missile strikes was able to provide accurate mid-course guidance to the subsonic AGM-158Bs. That limited the electronic emissions from the CHAMP-equipped missiles, keeping them from being tracked by North Korean EW units.

Approximately forty-five minutes after being fired, and with sunlight gracing the shores, the cruise missiles slipped into North Korea. Some crossed over beaches with gently rolling waves hissing across sandy shores. Others rose above rocky cliffs with the thunder of waves crashing against them. Heading inland, the stealth missiles flew up valleys that rose to fertile, higher grounds.

Here the missiles started deviating, some flying circuitous routes in order to bide time. Those hitting closer targets in the east wove back and forth, while those striking targets in the west and northwest flew more direct routes. The idea was for the first targets housed in their guidance systems to be hit at nearly identical times, so that the North Korean military leadership would be at a loss in determining what was happening and perhaps take steps to minimize the damage.

One missile crested a rise and descended the reverse slope. Using its GPS-aided INS, the guidance software determined that the weapon was now entering its terminal phase and activated its internal sensors. The infrared homing sensors identified the first of its targets, a group of vehicles and structures in an open field. Narrowing down the numerous targets, the software matched what the sensors saw with what was stored in its database.

Making a minute adjustment to its course, the projectile aimed directly for a grouping of command tents and an antennae farm clumped nearby. Flying at just under six hundred miles per hour, the internal system aimed the microwave emitters, and at the optimal distance, it fired the high-powered microwave transmitter.

Sparks erupted from radios and other electronic gear as they were hit by a miniature EMP blast. Idling trucks in a small compound shut down. One armored tactical vehicle that was tearing into the command post bucked like a bronco coming out of the chute when the motor just ceased to function, its driver thrown hard against the steering wheel. Blood spattered on the windshield when a passenger collided headfirst into it.

Cell phones carried in hands and pockets warmed and then burst into flame when their lithium batteries caught fire. Monitors, which had held drone footage went dark, some dying in a shower of sparks which momentarily illuminated them as if they had been decorated with blue and silver light tubes. Radio operators frantically grabbed at headsets as loud squeals replaced conversations. In a single moment, a divisional general and his staff were cut off from the lead brigades and battalions that were just now heading into their first confrontations with Southern forces.

Overhead, unheard except by a very few in the ensuing chaos, the AGM-158B turned over the encampment and headed toward its next target. The internal software again shutdown electronic emissions as operators miles to the rear resumed giving the cruise missile course guidance. It would remain silent until it determined that it had again entered its next terminal phase.

Another cruise missile went through similar actions as it approached its target. However, instead of the internal software seeing a sprawling encampment, the infrared sensors observed heat sources emanating from within a fenced area. Thick wires ran through the electric sub-station, crossing insulators and conductors. Sparks suddenly erupted from the outdoor facility as transformers blew with resounding blasts that echoed throughout the countryside.

Power downline from the station was disrupted. Upstream stations noted the interruption of power and stopped it from flowing to the destroyed sub-station. However, many other sub-stations were hit, and the central grids weren't able to compensate for the differing electrical currents. It didn't take too many hits from the JASSM-ERs before the entire electrical grid serving North Korea, which was minimal to begin with, was shut down.

In North Korea's military installations, backup generators kicked on and some of the larger bases had their own electrical grids. When the North Korean main grid went down, they hardly experienced a blip as the supply transitioned to the backups. That was until the directed energy pulses hit the facilities. Some of the more protected facilities managed to locate and shoot down the low-flying stealth missiles before they could complete their missions, but with their capabilities diminished by American strikes, that was a rare occurrence.

Each of the CHAMP-equipped cruise missiles was capable of delivering their high-power microwave energy technology to a hundred targets. All across North Korea, divisional, brigade, and battalion command posts lost the ability to communicate with their units. As the North had a centralized command system (because of their inherent lack of training and trust), this had a particularly drastic effect on the forces conducting attacks against the southern defense lines.

Units who found themselves dealing with the unfamiliar were at a total loss, unable to get orders from above. Not used to acting independently and afraid to issue orders themselves, lower-level officers found themselves stymied and unable to function effectively. Coordination between units and supporting artillery fell apart, resulting in some artillery fires never reaching the front or worse, friendly fire accidents occurring when the coordinates weren't shifted in time.

Even in North Korean units where officers did take charge and try to effectively execute combined arms attacks, they were unable to communicate to rear support units. Artillery fire couldn't be shifted or directed. Higher level command posts conducting drone surveillance or spotting for artillery lost control of their drones when their equipment was destroyed.

It may have only been eight cruise missiles, but the success of their attacks made it seem like eight hundred. All coordination between North Korean units, between their long-range air defense networks, between high command and subordinate units, simply failed at a time when they were needed the most.

*  *  *  *  *  *

England Dan and John Ford Coley weren't the only ones who expected long days and nights ahead. The F-16 and A-10 pilots lifting off from their air bases at Osan and Kusan, in addition to the South Korean F-16, F-15K, and F-35A pilots, knew they were in for weeks and months of little rest. Anticipating that the North Korean forces would eventually battle their way south, and the friendly units only conducting delaying actions, activities in both Camp Humphreys and Osan

Air Base were controlled but hurried.

All of the ordnance and maintenance equipment at the air base was being prepared to move south. If North Korea broke through, Osan Air Base, being only thirty-five miles behind the planned main line of resistance at the Han River, would be largely vacated. With the aircraft becoming vulnerable to long-range rockets, the F-16s would be moved to Kunsan Air Base, which would become quite crowded.

The A-10s were to be distributed to emergency airfields, utilizing some of the larger national routes. That would be inconvenient, but it had been planned for in the operational contingencies. Already, tent cities were being erected at the selected sites with supply convoys constantly moving back and forth.

The move from Camp Humphreys was proving to be a greater task. Although the plan was for personnel, especially the command staff, to remain, General Carswell had ordered the secondary site to be set up to the south. With the camp more than forty miles from the closest point on the Han, they were beyond the range of most of the North's artillery. However, although intel pointed to the total destruction of North Korea's long-range rocket launchers, it couldn't be absolutely assured that they didn't possess more. Only time would tell.

There was also the fact that the enemy had numerous weapons in their rocket forces, which could reach any point on the South Korean peninsula, so those weapon systems were no real factor in the decision to move. The allied forces would have to rely on their ground-based interceptor capabilities, which would be concentrated around the major bases and the southern supply ports.

The A-10s taking off from their airstrips didn't have far to fly before they were within range of their AGM-65 Maverick missiles. As volley after volley was unleashed, the tank busters dove back down into their low-level environment, snaking through the mountain valleys as they threaded their way north.

Following on their heels, flights of F-16s roared down runways. Laden with additional Maverick missiles, the attack fighters took even less time than the A-10s to climb and reach their launch positions. Series after series of missiles raced north, their seekers singling out individual North Korean targets as they maneuvered through South Korea's once populated valleys.

*   *   *   *   *   *

Captain Dwight England continued to observe the video coming from the surveillance drone scouting the leading North Korean armor. The fields and roads were swarming with tanks, armored personal carriers, and infantry fighting vehicles. It looked like a heavily supplied army of ants was on the move, ready to devour everything in their path.

Interspersed among them were short-range anti-air vehicles. A variety of armored chassis sprouted multiple barrels, some with small radars attached. About half of the kinetic anti-air vehicles could be automated with radar guidance, the others having to be manually aimed. The bristling barrels were intended to keep the battlefield clear of enemy helicopters and low-flying attack aircraft, at least in previous decades. Although the initial close-in attacks from the A-10s proved that the older weapon systems were still lethal, in the right environment.

Dwight wasn't too worried about those anti-air weapons as he would be fighting at longer ranges than those defense systems were capable of reaching...or at least he hoped that was the case. He had been around long enough to know that nothing went perfectly as planned. If he had to venture closer, then hopefully the ECM countermeasures would be able to deal with the older enemy radars.

The weapons that made Dwight nervous were the numerous MANPADs he saw attached to some of the North Korean armor. He knew from briefings that the North put a lot of dual anti-air mounts on their tanks, APCs, and IFVs. In particular, the squat shape of the tracked 9K35 launcher, which mounted eight 9K38 Igla infrared missiles, made him worry. The range of those portable IR devices was around three miles. While the Hellfire he carried could be launched from six miles, it was entirely possible that the fight could close to within the range of the North Korean MANPADS. Considering that tank ranges were somewhere between a mile and a half and two and a half miles, it was likely that the AH-64Es providing support could come under fire from the portable devices.

Dwight looked at the hill to his front, hoping that the intervening obstacle and the short time the choppers were above its crest would be sufficient to protect his company and those following from the dangers the IR missiles presented. Glancing back at the screen, he saw that the artillery falling among the North Korean elements had stopped. He knew that the next phase of the engagement was about to begin.

As the last of the smoke clouds rose above the advancing enemy, other explosions started dotting the battlefield. Whereas the artillery was constant but scattered as to where the rounds hit, these new blasts were fewer but more precise. Flashes of fire and smoke hid individual armored vehicles. Even masked by smoke, Dwight was able to observe several secondary explosions flare brightly as vehicles were torn apart by their own ammunition stores. In one instance, he saw a turret cartwheel away from the obscuring smoke cloud, coming to rest inverted a short distance away.

In another, a smaller turret, probably belonging to an infantry fighting vehicle, was catapulted straight up, turning slowly in the air, and then falling straight back down into a rising cloud of smoke. In some instances, armored vehicles rolled through the obscuring smoke clouds which engulfed them, only to stop a few feet later as they ran clear of their treads, their steel wheels becoming hopelessly bogged into the ground. One after another, armored vehicles were hit, coming to a standstill and either smoking or becoming engulfed in towering flames.

The explosions arrived in a series, eight to ten happening seemingly all at once. There would be a short pause before others would come out of nowhere. Dwight knew that the Maverick missiles fired from aircraft miles to the rear had started arriving, each singling out a piece of armor to home in on. It wasn't all perfection. Some missiles struck against already smoking or burning tanks. As destruction rained down, the

North Korean vanguard continued their steady approach toward where M-1s and other vehicles idled on the reverse slope of the long ridge line.

Watching the destruction, it almost seemed unfair. The North Korean forces were taking a beating without being able to fire a shot. The northern armor continued, leaving behind smoking wrecks and blazing husks. Then missiles stopped arriving. There came a pause in which there wasn't any fire hitting the Northern forces.

Watching the drone footage closely while also maintaining a watch outside to make sure the auto-hover was functioning correctly, Dwight saw tracers and smoke trails rising from the midst of the vehicles. Enemy missiles began launching toward the east.

Black smudges started appearing in the clear skies. The North Korean fire was hitting something, but Dwight couldn't see exactly what it was. Then, explosions smaller than the Mavericks began hitting some of the armor. At first, the captain wondered what in the hell could be happening, but figured it out when his gunner chimed in.

"Looks like they launched a bunch of suicide drones," Coley commented. "I don't remember that from the briefing. I thought the sequence was supposed to be artillery, attack fighters, A-10s, then us."

"Yeah, I don't remember hearing anyone mention drones," Dwight responded. "It makes sense, though."

He wasn't entirely surprised. It wasn't a perfect world, and he had been privy to his share of fucked-up briefings that forgot to mention shit. He remembered one such briefing where the briefer had neglected to mention that artillery was going to use the same range they were, at the same time. Oops. A misread notice had nearly spelled the end. He recalled flying in and calling that he was inbound with rockets when large explosions started erupting directly in front of him. He had all kinds of words for command once he'd extricated himself from the midst of that shitstorm, some of which he was sure he'd invented on the spot.

As he watched, it seemed that the drone attack, at least those making it past the North Korean air defenses, were zeroing in on the anti-air vehicles. The skies over the enemy vanguard were filled with new and dissipating trails of smoke, with curving tracers following the inbound threats. Dwight hoped that the North Koreans were blowing through their entire contingent of missiles, which would make his job a whole lot easier down the road.

With more smoking vehicles left behind, the enemy armor kept rolling. Instead of slowing, the intensity of outgoing fire increased. The skies already looked like the aftermath of a fireworks show above a stadium prior to a Super Bowl kick off. White smoke streamers drifted on the morning breeze, growing larger as they dissipated. Still, more tracers and missiles kept coming.

The scene was soon filled with arcing flares as they shot out of their dispensers. A-10s came screaming out of adjacent hills, attacking the armor from the flanks as they had before. Smoke streamed from Warthog noses as their 30mm guns engaged the North Koreans. Sparks flew from tanks as depleted uranium shells slammed into their surfaces. As the A-10s soared over the top, they left behind smoking ruins.

They weren't the only ones inflicting damage. Dwight watched as IR missiles fired by the enemy ground forces hit. Tailing smoke, several A-10s limped from the battlefield. The Apache pilot saw one Warthog get hit and roll, nosing down and crashing in a fireball. Over the top of the combat zone, amid the chaos of flares, missile streaks, and tracers, a parachute flared open.

Like a pendulum, an object below swung twice before landing. Dwight winced as the pilot landed among the enemy forces, wondering if he would be crushed by the advancing tanks or shot outright. He couldn't imagine the pilot lasting long, especially as it was doubtful that allied troops would show up for a long time coming. With so many of the enemy forces in the valley, there was no chance of a rescue attempt. From what he could see, that would be a fatal endeavor for anyone attempting it. The only chance the pilot had was to escape in the mayhem, perhaps hiding out in a nearby ruin until nightfall.

"Poor bastard," Coley lamented.

"Yeah. I hope he somehow makes it."

There wasn't much else to say as both men knew the pilot was likely doomed. And they also knew it wouldn't be the last time they witnessed certain death. But the idea that they just saw one of their own meet their demise, and in such a quietly useless way, made them angry, and that anger grew. A swell filled them with rage, that the piddling little country had caused this war for no reason. And that rage was directed toward one man, the North Korean leader responsible for this mess. The thing was, they couldn't do anything about a madman secured in some bunker, completely safe, and that made it worse.

The Warthog attacks continued, with planes attacking from the sides, coming in from multiple angles like a choreographed dance. A stream of flares announced each new attack, with the tracers and missile trails changing directions as new threats appeared. The long train of the North Korean attack was being hit up and down its length. More pillars of smoke marred the clear morning skies, with new ones rising every minute.

And then the airborne attacks stopped. One second, there were newly added countermeasure flares spanning the width of the valley, with North Korean anti-air missiles and tracers shooting toward the flanking hills, and then there was nothing but the aftermath. Another operational pause ensued. The range to the lead North Korean armor was approaching six miles.

"All right, folks, cinch it up. I believe we're on deck, coming up to bat," Dwight radioed over the company frequency.

Up in the front seats of the AH-64Es spread across the rear of the ridgeline, gunners began selecting targets based off the data being transmitted from the lead chopper. The information was handed down to selected Hellfire missiles, which returned data that they received the target information.

Lieutenant Coley was busy up front tracking some two hundred and fifty-six targets, making sure there were plenty for the company to select. The entire company of eight Apache Guardians, each carrying sixteen Hellfires, could effectively target only half that number. Away from the battlefield, the data from Dwight's attack chopper was being included in the overall data available for every level of command.

On the screen, the lead North Korean armored vehicles drew closer. An RQ-7 Shadow drone that was keeping tabs on the armored force was slowly moving south to keep watch on the lead enemy armor. Other drones were keeping track of the entire line, including follow on enemy units. Some of the UAVs had to be relaunched, their coverage temporarily lost, when they were discovered by North Korean forces. It was a game both sides played, with advance operational units attempting to keep the airspace clear of enemy recon drones. Coyote counter-UAS drones flew out to meet incoming targets when the small radar systems found them.

"Crazy Horse three-one, Ronin two-one. You are cleared to engage," the radio crackled.

"Ronin two-one, copy. Cleared to fire," Dwight responded.

Switching to the company's internal frequency, Dwight broadcast, "Okay, Reapers, let's let 'em have it. Three-two, start us off."

"Copy. Three-two is up."

The pilot of the adjacent chopper held it in a hover for a moment longer.

"You good to go up there?" he asked his gunner.

"As good as I'm gonna get," the answer came over the intercom.

Increasing the throttle and lifting the collective, the Guardian shot straight upward. When the pylon-mounted weapons cleared the crest, the gunner fire the first Hellfire. The missile leapt from the rail and streaked over the top of the ridge, clearing it by several feet. Almost immediately after firing, the pilot descended, the chopper dropping like it had fallen through a trap door.

Tearing through the smoke-encrusted hilltop and emerging out the other side, the Hellfire Longbow missile ripped into the valley at nearly a thousand miles per hour. Its millimeter wave radar identified many targets traveling on the valley floor, but stayed true to the one that had been selected.

After speeding for over three miles, the weapon arced downward. The Hellfire struck the top of a North Korean tank. A tandem warhead set off reactive armor that covered the surfaces of the main battle tank. A second shaped charge then punched through the thick armor. A fireball engulfed the tank, a second one rocking the armored vehicle as hatches blew off. Thick black smoke belched from the stricken vehicle with small flames licking from the hatch openings. The tank lurched to a stop, its pillar adding to the many still spiraling upward from the rear of the formation.

When the first chopper sank back below the crest, the pilot of the next in line made ready.

"Three-three is up."

The chopper soared upward, unleashing another Hellfire missile at its zenith. This time, the North Korean armored unit approaching the ridge had an answer. Three Igla 9K38 portable IR missiles were loosed from a couple of armored vehicles that had them attached. Trailing fine white lines, the anti-air weapons passed the incoming Hellfire and made for the now descending AH-64E.

The sensors on the enemy IR missiles saw the target moving and made adjustments to their flight paths, recalculating intercept points. When the attack helicopter went below the crest, the missiles arced down, slamming into the ridge just below the top, a near miss. The three explosions went mostly unnoticed in the continued artillery fire hitting the position.

"Three-four is up."

The airwaves rang out with "Rifle" calls, informing everyone that an air-to-ground missile was being fired. This game of peek-a-boo continued with the attack choppers only visible for brief moments, thanks to the ability to target the enemy armor from behind cover. Dwight changed up the order several times so that they wouldn't become predictable to the enemy gunners on the other side of the ridge.

Not all the Hellfires found targets. Some were intercepted by the same anti-air missiles being fired at the American attack helicopters appearing from beyond the ridge. But the supply of North Korean MANPADS dwindled as the aerial attacks continued. The valley was marred by dark smoke columns lining the progress of the North Korean attack.

When the company had expended its compliment of missiles, England Dan and John Ford Coley started attacking with what they carried. They would rise, fire, descend, and then move to another location before doing it all over again.

After the sixteenth missile sailed over the top of the ridge, Dwight told the others it was time to head home. A second company, the "Vampires," were waiting for their turn and moved into position when Dwight and the rest of the "Reapers" moved away and began heading south along their pre-planned exfiltration route.

"It's a long, long way home," Coley started crooning a hit from the pop duo as they flew back to refuel and rearm.

"Oh God! Finish me now," Dwight commented. His gunner never disappointed.

\* \* \* \* \* \*

The dull thump of explosions could be mutely heard on the other side of the thick, steel walls of the tank. The massive, almost seventy-ton M1A2 rocked from nearby blasts from North Korean artillery that had been working over the ridge since the early hours of the morning. The brigade was mostly protected in defilades on the back side of the hills while the enemy hammered the top.

Sergeant Brent Carson wondered if there would be anything left of his carefully dug firing positions, or whether it would just be a morass of churned up ground. He was nervous about entering his first foray into battle as a tank commander. Maneuvers and exercises were one thing, a real shooting war? That was something else altogether.

He was confident in his crew, his tank, and the rest of the company. Besides worrying about being hit, his anxiety stemmed from how he would perform in the upcoming confrontation. His dad had been a tanker in Desert Storm and Brent remembered some of the stories he could coax him into telling. He also remembered his dad saying, "You can train and train, think over situations and how you're going to react to them. But," he would say, shaking a finger, "you can truly never tell how you're going to react until you're actually in the shit. Training helps, but it's not everything."

Well, Brent was about to find out how he'd react. Amid the clouds of smoke covering the top of the ridge, he saw several missile streaks head into the explosions. He knew the attack choppers were behind him, firing into the lead enemy units. With their range, they could engage long before the brigade's tanks. But both their presence and weapon launches indicated that it was almost showtime.

The sergeant was looking at drone footage of the enemy on the other side of the hill. The RQ-7 Shadow, which had been tracking the North Korean progress, had dropped back enough so that he could catch some of the artillery rounds exploding on the ridge. He noted that, while the rounds had been centered on where his company and brigade were to come on line, they were now landing almost randomly and seemed to be scattered over a much wider distance.

Brent wondered if this was a planned action by the North Koreans, perhaps trying to catch flanking units, or if something had happened to the enemy's targeting ability. Maybe the drones North Korea was using to spot for the artillery had been taken out? Whatever the case, it would make life much easier for when they were ordered up the hill and into their firing positions.

The thud of exploding rounds abruptly stopped, with

one or two lagging artillery shells hitting several seconds apart. It was almost unnerving going from the ceaseless detonations bombarding his eardrums to near silence. He'd heard rumors of the South Korean 7th Corps being hit by chemical weapons and he hoped to hell the same wasn't being planned here. Even though he was in his full MOPP gear, the very idea of chemical agents being dropped scared the shit out of him.

On the screen monitoring the front line, Brent saw white puffs land both in front of the advancing North Korean armor and at the base of the hill. The pale smoke expanded and drifted on the slight breeze blowing through the area. Soon, the enemy armor vanished behind a screen of almost cloud white.

The sergeant's heart raced as he thought he was seeing chemical weapons being used against his position, but perhaps falling short. When the drone footage altered as the camera was switched to IR, and the thermal images of the vehicles appeared, he realized that it was just an old-school smokescreen being thrown up by the North Koreans. The images weren't as clear as they should have been. Brent then realized that the North Koreans had some chemical disruptor as part of their smoke shells, meant to obscure enemy aiming systems.

"Alpha company, let's get 'em started and move up," the company commander radioed.

The M1 vibrated as the driver started the tank. Tremors continued to run through the Abrams as Brent turned on more of the tank's systems. He had left only a few functioning to conserve the battery while the brigade waited for their orders to move forward.

"Okay, let's go see if we can find our position," Brent ordered.

The driver, in his reclined position under the main gun, placed the tank in gear. Heavy treads gripped the soil as the driver throttled up, the massive, armored vehicle lurching forward. Coming out of its protection, the tank jostled over uneven ground and angled up the backside of the hill.

Buttoned up, the tank started bouncing even more as they entered the ground churned up by the artillery, even as the driver guided it around the deeper craters. As they approached the top, Brent wondered if the North Koreans would resume their artillery fire. He hoped not, as those heavy caliber shells could easily tear through the top armor of the M1. Near misses were one thing, but a direct strike and he wouldn't even know what hit him…or at least he hoped he wouldn't. The last thing he wanted, and one of his greatest fears, was to be trapped in a burning tank. Even though those were troubling thoughts nestled in the back of his mind, the anxiety he had been holding faded as his tank rolled on top of the ridge, accompanied by others of the brigade. The sergeant was now focused on finding one of the three defilades that had been previously bulldozed out.

It was difficult locating much of anything among the chunks of earth scattered throughout the area and in the drifting smoke. Then he was able to make out the outlines of one position, which had one side partially caved in.

"Driver, there's one on the left," Brent stated over the intercom.

"I see it, boss," the driver returned.

The tank swerved left and then right as the driver lined up with the defilade. One side of the tank lifted as it drove over the caved in portion, the weight of the M1 flattening the surface back to its pre-bombardment condition. The somewhat protected, carved-out indentation was angled so that the tank could shoot down into the valley, keeping any enemy under fire for the entire way, even when its gun was depressed to its max of nearly ten degrees. It was also dug deep enough so the Abrams would be hull down, thus limiting the enemy's ability to target the tank.

Rocking to a stop, the view of the valley opened. North Korean armor was spread from one side of it to the other, their treads and the wheels of supporting vehicles kicking up dust clouds as they plowed through the fields. Brent saw other small valleys opening off the main one, leading up into the mountains or connecting with other valleys. He knew from briefings that the flanking valleys had been mined by allied vehicles loaded with the Volcano mine system. Dense, effective minefields could be laid quickly by driving along and basically shooting mines from a moving platform like firing t-shirts into a crowd. The mine system could even be attached to helicopter hardpoints.

The valley was dotted with climbing pillars of smoke, signs of previous airborne and artillery attacks. Brent didn't see how there could be so many armored vehicles, or more correctly, he didn't see how the brigade was going to stop them. There were just too many. For a moment, the fear resurfaced, his breath caught in his throat. The entire brigade was going to get clobbered.

Off to one side, he saw a new column of dark smoke rising from behind some hills, up one of the side valleys. He didn't think friendly units or aircraft were located there, other than the attack choppers stationed behind the ridge, so he thought that the new smoke columns were from additional North Koreans attempting to flank and subsequently running into minefields.

The lead enemy units were about two miles away, with enemy artillery still laying smokescreens. And then, the shells delivering smoke stopped. Enemy vehicles broke into the clear, rolling past the edges of the screen.

"All right, Alpha, let 'em have it," the commander radioed.

Brent went to his screen, which was now depicting the view from his tank, the thermal images of multiple enemy tanks and other armor in the lead showing clearly.

"Target, tank, eleven o'clock, range seventeen hundred yards," Brent called.

"Got it," the gunner responded.

"Sabot loaded," the loader stated.

"Fire."

The tank rocked as the armor-piercing fin-stabilized discarding sabot round shot out from the barrel and sped downward. With the gunner maintaining targeting information on the enemy tank, the tungsten and depleted uranium shell raced toward its rendezvous. Unheard from within the Abrams, a loud *clang* signaled a direct hit. The sabot round struck with a flash, forcing its way past the reactive armor and slamming into the thick steel of the tank's hull.

The force of the collision superheated the round and it basically melted its way through, a hot knife through tiramisu. As the enemy tank was closed tight for combat, the powerful sabot round caused an over-pressurization to occur within the cabin. Overhead hatches blew off and flipped several times before starting their downward arc.

The over-pressurization crushed the people inside, some of their internal organs bursting. Superheated steel from the tank's armor sprayed the interior with molten metal, igniting everything flammable, including the uniforms and flesh of the North Korean crew. The self-sharpening round spalled, ricocheting through the interior, slicing through system lines and severing limbs. Boiling blood sprayed the interior, drying in an instant.

Super-heated gasses ignited everything inside. The ammunition compartment separation proved to be inadequate to contain the pressure. While the entire interior blazed, the crackle of flames engulfing now unidentifiable human beings, the main body of the round punched through the other side of the turret. With the intense pressure inside the tank, the exiting round created a vacuum of sorts. What was left of one crew member was further crushed when their flaming corpse was forced through the exit hole, turning the unfortunate soldier into a hot gooey paste.

This all happened in less than a second. The lucky crew didn't feel the effects as they all died instantly. The North Korean tank's ammunition, heated by the gasses and molten metal, exploded. This added more pressurization which forced the turret off its mount. With flames shooting from the blasted hatches, the tank erupted, the turret sliding off to the side.

"Hit, target destroyed," the gunner called.

"Target, tank, twelve o'clock, range sixteen hundred, eighty yards," Brent said.

"Got 'im. Load sabot," the gunner responded.

"Sabot loaded," the loader replied.

"Fire."

\*   \*   \*   \*   \*   \*

The North Korean Chungjwa, the equivalent of a lieutenant colonel, waited impatiently by the radio. He ordered the soldiers manning the artillery battery's communications to check again on the equipment. His command sent several non-commissioned soldiers scurrying to check connections and to test the cables. It was the fifth such order in the last hour, each test of the entire system confirming that it was operational and able to receive messages.

Looking at his watch while the soldiers went about their tests, the officer wondered what was delaying the orders to resume firing on enemy positions. The leading forces in his sector should have engaged the southern defenses by now — an hour ago — according to the plans. He should have received coordinates and firing missions long ago.

Worried that he had missed a crucial order, he had sent a transmission requesting a status update. So far, even though his technicians assured him that everything was working on their end, he hadn't received a reply. What was more concerning, even though he had heard some radio traffic, therefore verifying that his equipment was indeed functioning, he hadn't heard anything from his brigade headquarters in some time.

He felt flushed from the anxiety and was unsure what to do. If he had missed firing mission orders, the retribution would be swift and his career ended. He could imagine a scenario by which he was demoted and sent to the front lines. At the very least, he'd be shamed. He was on shaky ground with his brigade commander as it was. If he screwed up at the very outset of hostilities, then there was no telling what might happen.

But what was he to do? The plan had called for the resumption of fire once contact was made by the North Korean vanguard. Based on the initial combat results, he was to fire on the leading defense lines or to interdict enemy reserves positioned behind the line. Without any communication, how was he to know which coordinates to send his rounds to?

If he fired on the initial coordinates, where drones had confirmed the southern defense lines to be, and friendly armored units had broken through, he would be firing on his own forces. But if they'd met with stiff resistance and the leading units needed his support, then he would be failing in his mission there as well. Failing his entire nation.

As time went on, the officer's anxiety increased. His battery of towed artillery had taken a beating from southern counter-battery fire. It just took too long to set up and break down the non-mobile platforms, rendering them vulnerable to return fire. He had been left with just over half of his artillery pieces. But without the order to put even those into action, he almost would rather they had all been destroyed.

To make matters worse, he had been ordered to keep communications to a minimum so that the American eavesdroppers wouldn't be able to pinpoint his position or cause interference with their electronic warfare aircraft, and he'd already sent more communication than he should have, but the worry had built to the point where he felt he had no choice. The North Korean officer messaged some of the other batteries of the brigade, receiving replies almost instantly. He had inquired if they had received orders and found the others hadn't heard anything either. They were also equally hesitant. One or two units had stated that they were continuing with their original mission planning and firing on the last known coordinates. The Chungjwa thought that may be the best solution, but the fear that he could be firing on his countrymen successfully achieving a breakthrough, which was the preached outcome, kept him from issuing orders to fire.

Perhaps the Chungjwa and his co-commanders might have suspected the truth: North Korean communications along the entire front had been disrupted from the CHAMP-equipped cruise missile attacks. Without radio and other electronic equipment, brigade and divisional headquarters were effectively put out of action. With North Korea's centralized command structure, this had led to a breakdown in combined-arms efforts, which resulted in a lack of multi-dimensional attacks along the front. The North Korean lower echelon commanders had no idea that their headquarters had essentially been silenced.

This interruption was more consequential than just affecting artillery support for front line units. It led to disruptions in logistical supplies, at least from a brigade and divisional standpoint. Earlier scheduled supplies were still brought forward, but any additional requests weren't fielded. While that wasn't a factor during the initial attacks, it would become a problem when units were pulled off the line to resupply and found the quantities lacking or nonexistent, especially when ammunition expenditures were far exceeding the quotas.

*   *   *   *   *   *

The fear Brent had felt when rolling into the defilade and seeing the vast array of North Korean armored vehicles dissipated as he fell into a focused routine of firing on targets to his front. Amid the crack of tank fire along the ridge, the sergeant also heard several rumbling explosions, muted through the thick steel plating. It appeared that the North Koreans had resumed their artillery fire, although the intensity wasn't nearly the same as it had been when they were hunkered down on the backside of the hill.

*Clang!*

Adrenaline jolted through the sergeant. The tank shook and the interior rang like the inside of a church bell at noon on Sunday. Brent looked up and saw an orange glow on the turret, which quickly faded, leaving behind a darkened spot.

"The fuck was that!" the driver yelled.

"That was death knocking," the gunner replied.

"He can knock the fuck off that shit and go somewhere

else," the driver shot back. "I'm going to need a change of clothes when we're done here."

Brent realized that they had taken a shot which had thankfully hit at an oblique angle and ricocheted off. The enemy tanks had spotted the brigade's line and started shooting back. It was a good thing the brigade had the height and the advantage of being in cover. Looking back toward the battlefield below, he saw flashes coming from the North Korean tanks. Additionally, infantry fighting vehicles and armored personnel carriers were firing, their tracers angling to the sides and lower down the hill as they started engaging the brigade's troopers positioned there.

White trails snaked from the woods and along the ridge as 1st Cavalry soldiers started firing anti-tank missiles. In addition, the attack choppers to the rear were still delivering anti-tank fire from behind. The fight was developing along a multitude of layers.

Off to one side, Brent saw enemy APCs angling toward where the fields and woods formed a boundary. Some of the armored vehicles were already parked at the edge and disgorging North Korean troops.

"Target, APC, two o'clock, range one thousand three hundred yards."

The turret swiveled to the right. "Got 'im. Load HEAT."

"HEAT loaded," the loader answered.

"Fire."

The round sailed across the intervening space and hit a BTR-60. The shell pushed the squat vehicle down as if its tires had suddenly flattened. Time seemed to pause, the armored vehicle seeming to cower in submission before an explosion engulfed the vehicle. Hot metal sliced through the thinly armored skin. Several soldiers who were disembarking on the run stumbled to the ground. Three of the four tried to rise, their legs moving them faster than they could stand. Finally getting their feet under them, they bolted after some of their comrades who had already fled into the woods.

Another crawled forward, perhaps wondering why his

legs weren't working. On fire, two stumbled from inside, their arms waving as if that action was going to extinguish the flames. Other North Korean APCs erupted in fireballs as the tank company on that side of the ridge, and the soldiers positioned along the flanks, started taking them under fire.

Brent redirected his fire back toward the front, engaging North Korean tanks that were now employing their own smokescreens in an attempt to blur the battlefield. Anti-tank missiles shot from the enemy armor that were equipped with those weapons.

The sergeant handed over fire to his gunner when his platoon commander radioed. On the screen, Brent saw a streak flash up the hill, heading somewhere to his left. The lieutenant in charge was issuing an order when a loud noise came over the radio, somewhat similar to the hit Brent's tank had taken. The radio then went silent. The tanker tried to raise his boss to no avail.

Popping the hatch open, the noise of the battlefield entered at full blast. The crack of cannon fire and the duller thuds of arriving artillery was a cacophony of sound that blended into a surreal overload of senses. If he hadn't been in his MOPP gear, Brent knew he'd be smelling gunpowder carried on the gentle breeze.

The one sound he could localize was a roaring crackle of flames, fire coming out of blown hatches from the tank next to him. Because there wasn't anyone on the ground or running to the rear, he knew instantly that his platoon commander and his crew were dead. At irregular intervals, Brent saw other tanks nearby were either smoking or had been gutted by fire. The North Koreans below weren't the only ones taking hits.

"Hey, boss, captain's trying to reach you," Brent heard his gunner say over the intercom.

With a sickened sigh, Brent sank back down and sealed the hatch. Grabbing the mic, he checked that he was going to transmit on the right frequency.

"Alpha one-two here."

"Alpha one-two, Alpha six. Lieutenant Poole's been hit.

You're the new platoon leader," the company commander radioed. "Congratulations."

"Copy that, sir."

He didn't know what else to add. He'd known the lieutenant for a while, showing him the ropes when he had come in as a fresh butterbar out of the academy. The officer had been one of the good ones, eager to learn and not afraid to ask questions, unlike some of the others, who had arrived overly eager to demonstrate their leadership skills. He gave a thought to the entire crew, people he'd known. Back at Fort Hood, they had shared a few drinks together, friends, in a way, by virtue of common goals and purpose. Now they'd just be names in a local paper and carved on a wall somewhere.

Brent shook his head. There was still business to take care of. The blazing tank that was now etched into his memory was a reminder that life could be taken away at any moment.

"Target, tank, eleven o'clock, range one thousand yards."

"Got 'im."

*   *   *   *   *   *

North Korean forces sought to flank the ridge with ground troops. APCs with supporting IFVs delivered soldiers into the tree lines flanking the open fields, hoping to circumvent the solid line and either deliver fire from the rear or force the American tanks to withdraw for fear of being flanked.

A follow-on force was then to drive through the retreating Americans and force a crossing over the southern fork of the Imjin River. Once that beachhead had been established, secondary mechanized brigades were then to keep charging in order to throw the enemy off balance, denying them a chance to form another defensive line.

Intense firefights developed in the woods. Scarred trees were felled by large caliber cannons from the North Koreans firing bursts in support of their infantry movements. The 1st Cav troops responded with anti-tank rounds and supporting vehicles of their own. With the air filled with steel zipping between the trunks, and mortars air-bursting or exploding in the tree tops and at ground level, troop movements became sporadic leaps and bounds, sometimes without regard for the flanks.

It was when the North Korean soldiers ran into prepared minefields that their attack began to unravel. Any movement forward seemed to involve having to look simultaneously to the ground for signs of explosives, and up the ridges to spot the camouflaged outlines of enemy troops. Going to ground when under fire stood the chance of landing on a mine, which sowed confusion and fear among the North Korean soldiers. It eventually made them afraid to move, allowing the defending soldiers of the 1st Cav to maneuver into better firing positions.

The flanking movements became static, even when North Korean officers threatened their troops with insubordination. Some of the frightened North Koreans were executed when they attempted to retreat without orders. This further enhanced the static nature of the flanking attacks. Afraid to move forward or back, the Northern soldiers remained in place and fired into the woods, often at nothing. Positional infantry battles ensued.

The North Koreans achieved some successes farther into the woods, managing to draw even with the ridge line. This was achieved by conducting overwhelming attacks with a greater number of troops. The North Korean units conducting the massed attacks sustained tremendous losses. Coordination between units was lost, and the leading Northern platoons found themselves without their flanks being protected.

Once the line became stabilized, counterattacks by American platoons and companies against the deeper penetrations forced the North Koreans to withdraw or risk being overrun. Casualties within the woods, because of the close-quarter nature of most of the firefights, was great on both sides.

Farther behind the front, North Korean follow-on units attempted to flank up the side valleys. They became enmeshed in dense minefields. The E-8C directing the battles and providing data for the brigade and divisional commanders, showed the enemy movements. Artillery started landing among the lead flanking vehicles, further halting any rapid progress.

F-16s and A-10s, airborne for support operations, were also sent in against the flanking units. Artillery fire against the North Korean attack was halted while the aircraft fired additional Maverick missiles. This was effective in slowing the larger flanking maneuvers by enemy mechanized forces.

A thousand yards from the defensive lines of the 1st Cavalry Division, the North Korean armored vehicles equipped with smoke generators turned them on. Unable to penetrate the defenses thrown up by the division's 1st Brigade Combat Team and supporting units from the field artillery regiments, along with the 1st Air Cavalry Brigade's AH-64Es, the North Korean armored division slated to break through to the southern fork of the Imjin River began to retreat behind smokescreens. American artillery followed the retreating division, damaging the leading forces even more.

The lack of North Korean supporting artillery was telling and allowed for better cohesion between American units holding the defensive line. It also allowed for Southern artillery batteries, originally slated for counter-battery fire, to deliver ordnance into the charging North Koreans.

To the west, the Republic of Korea 7th Corps held firm on the Imjin River, keeping North Korean forces from crossing the barrier. To the east, the 2nd Infantry Division managed to hold against a similar onslaught by the extensive use of their combat aviation brigade. The soldiers of the Stryker brigades often seemed to support the attack helicopters instead of the other way around, delivering volleys of anti-tank missiles against the North Korean armor storming their positions.

After hours of repeated attacks against the defensive lines established on the northern approaches to Seoul, the North Korean units pulled back toward the DMZ, setting up their own defenses while they regrouped and resupplied. The same occurred on the South Korean and American lines as units were rotated to and from the front. The initial intense battles wound down to the occasional artillery rounds landing on both sides and drones being sent and shot down.

# Initial North Korean Attacks

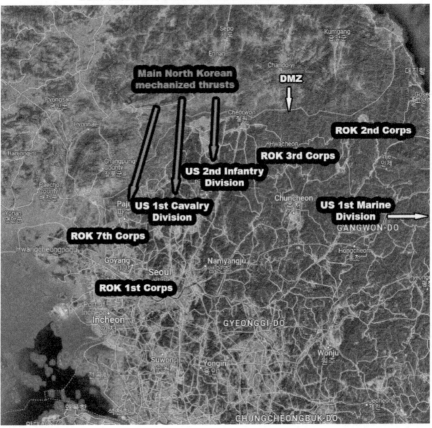

# Chapter Seven

Exhausted from the fight at the ridge, and feeling like he had aged several years over the past few hours, Brent stood on top of his tank. The painted sides were marred with scratches that must have been caused by shrapnel flung from enemy artillery shells landing nearby. One bit of damage particularly caught his eye. He focused on a deep gouge running up the sloped turret, the area around the gleaming metal darkened by heat generated from the impact. Seeing the scar, he realized what a narrow escape it had been. He and his crew could easily have been torched to ash, like his platoon leader.

He eyed the other tanks parked in the rear area. Many exhibited battle damage, their crews, like him, showing their fatigue. Off to one side, recovery vehicles towed several Abrams to forward maintenance areas. Already, personnel were clambering over damaged tanks and other armored vehicles affecting repairs. The bright flare of welders arced as steel plates were welded in place, the sparks flying into the air looking much like when the rounds that caused the damage had hit.

The sights threw Brent off. It seemed to be business as usual when, just a short time ago, he had been in the middle of a hellacious tank battle. People had died and many were injured, as evidenced by medical personnel still carrying wounded from arriving trucks. This wasn't what he had expected since the brigade had been pulled off the line — and yet, maybe it was. He watched as some soldiers were cleaning out one tank where some of the crew had been injured, the rags and water they were using stained deep red.

Brent had sent the rest of his crew to find something to eat. He'd meet up with them when he figured out what was going on. This new position of platoon leader would take some getting used to.

A soldier ran up to his tank. "Are you Sergeant Carson?" the man asked.

Brent turned from his inspection of the damage. "Yeah, that's me," he answered.

"Captain wants to see you."

Brent scanned around the area, looking for signs of a meeting.

Noticing Brent's searching gaze, the man pointed. "They're in that tent."

Sliding off the tank, the sergeant thanked the soldier and crossed the bare dirt field. Pulling open a set of entrance flaps, he hesitated. It took a moment for his eyes to adjust from the sunlit day to the gloom of the tent's interior.

"Sergeant Carson, there you are," an officer greeted him, standing near a piece of plywood resting on two wooden sawhorses. "Come on in."

Brent joined the gathering, recognizing the company's other platoon leaders. Although used to officers, it felt a little strange to be counted as one among them. They nodded at him, one giving him a nod and murmured congrats, the salutation subdued because they knew how the field promotion had come about.

"Okay, I've just returned from Brigade. It appears that the 7th Corps on our left held at the Imjin," the captain stated, pointing to a spot on a map laid out on the plywood. "The same with the 2nd Division on our right. So, even though the original plans called for a withdrawal back toward the river to our rear, we'll be remaining here for the time being. However, I want everyone to be ready to conduct the planned withdrawal at any moment.

"For the time being, we've been pulled back and the 2nd Brigade has been put on the front. According to brigade, we'll be getting reinforcements and replacement tanks sometime today...tonight at the latest. We lost some good people today and we'll be holding a service as soon as the chaplain arrives.

"Until then, see to it that your people get some chow and rest. Given how today went, I anticipate us being back on the line sometime tomorrow, depending on what the North Koreans do. That's it." The officer seemed to remember something. "Right. And before we leave, good job today, all of you. We met the enemy and gave 'em hell. Just remember that communication and coordination is the key. And Seargent Carson, good job spotting the APCs to the east. Keep up the good work.

"That's all I have from higher up." The officers around him seemed to relax, the meeting complete, but the officer drew breath and began again. "Okay. But before we go, let's quickly debrief the day's actions. What did we do right and what do we need to improve on?"

Fatigue was setting in, reflected in these interruptions of his briefing.

Similar actions and debriefs occurred up and down the Southern defense lines. Units hit during the initial engagements were pulled back and fresh units put in their place. Artillery continued to fire over the battle lines, prohibiting enemy force gatherings, disrupting command posts, and interdicting supply depots.

\* \* \* \* \* \*

The last few moments had been filled with one adrenaline rush after another. First there was rolling in on the North Korean formations, the tracers and missile trails streaking from a multitude of sources. It had been difficult to stay focused and zero in on single targets. And he then had to turn around and do it all over again.

Then came the loud *bang* and a myriad of warning lights. That was quickly followed by a loose stick and the ground rushing up. Captain John Faden had been surprised that his heart didn't just give out as he reached for and found the ejection seat handles.

The chill blast of air as the canopy jettisoned added not only to the sudden confusion, but to his overworked adrenal glands. The ride up the rails, although expected, served to ensure that his pulse rate remained north of the one hundred and twenty mark. Then the opening shock made the A-10 pilot question whether he'd ever father another child.

Before he could orient himself, and swinging below a

fully formed chute like a crucible being swung by a priest, John hit the ground. Clicking the releases on the harness, he thought he heard the sound of the billowing chute collapse in on itself. He was alive, but he was keenly aware that his adventures had only begun. He had ejected directly over the enemy forces he had just been attacking.

The sounds of the battle assaulted his ears. The sharp crack of cannon fire, the crackle of flames from burning vehicles, the gunning of powerful engines, the clank of treads, the staccato accompaniment of IFVs and APCs firing in the distance, and the occasional thunderous explosion of an armored vehicle being hit, all combined to create a deafening roar. It was much louder than the relative quiet of the cockpit he had just been thrown out from.

And then there was the smell. He couldn't identify exactly what it could be. He'd been in a foundry once and the odor was similar: burning metal. Also drifting on the gentle breeze was the familiar scent of gunpowder and freshly turned soil.

Without bothering to check for injuries, and having just barely released from the paracords connecting him to the now flattened parachute, the captain rolled quickly to his hands and knees. He was just in time to catch a face full of clanking treads. He dove to one side and rolled as a tank powered past, inches away. The sight of the steel treads pressing deep into the dirt terrified him even more than being hit and ejecting.

The squeal of metal on metal was piercing, and then the tank was past. Dirt kicked up by the rolling treads showered him. John spat clods from his mouth and wiped his eyes clear. He was lying in a field, surrounded by North Korean armor, and had no idea of what to do next. Ejection training certainly hadn't prepared him for this. Should he just lay there and try not to attract any notice? Or should he make a run for it? He was fearful that movement might draw unwanted attention, but he was equally afraid of being seen by those plowing through the fields. And then there was the friendly fire to think about. He knew the artillery had been lifted for his and the other A-10 attacks, but it was only a matter of time before that resumed.

The sight of another tank heading in his direction made him realize that remaining in place wasn't really an option. He quickly disconnected the lanyard to his survival gear. He didn't bother retrieving it as his first encounter with a tank had reduced the container to a flattened piece of junk. The only gear he'd have available was that which was already attached. Looking around, he saw the edge of what he guessed was an irrigation ditch.

What truly spurred him into action was the sound of a machine gun firing nearby. That and the ground erupting a few feet away as bullets tore into the already churned up soil. John sprung like a startled gazelle and streaked for the ditch. The ground lit up behind him and moved toward his rapidly running figure. He willed himself to greater efforts, thinking to outrun the bullets but knowing he was already running faster than he had ever before, could ever have imagined. And the ditch now seemed impossibly far. In his heart, he knew he wasn't going to make it, but he didn't know what else to do except keep sprinting.

A sound like a hammer hitting an anvil rang out, rising above the noisy clamor of the battle surrounding him. The sound of the machine gun and racing engine was drowned out by an explosion that was felt more than heard. A concussive force plowed into him, propelling him forward as a wave of heat rolled past.

In the air and momentarily achieving the kind of flight he only thought his Warthog could do, the pilot flew over the lip of the ditch and landed in murky water with a splash. Spluttering, he half swam, half waded to the bank of the stream and crawled up onto the mud. Hugging the ground just below overhanging edges, John panted, attempting to finally catch a breath that had been a long while coming; one that he desperately needed.

He knew the sounds of the ongoing battle were just as loud, but they seemed muted at the same time. The last five minutes felt like a lifetime as the captain hunkered in cover. It was the first time since ejecting that he'd felt a semblance of control. However, that wouldn't last. He was still amidst the enemy and had to figure out a way to get the hell out of there.

Looking south in the direction of friendly forces, along the length of what he took to be an irrigation canal, he saw a fairly straight path that ended about a hundred yards down. With the sight, any hope he had of using the cover to make his way back to friendly lines vanished. Far up a distant ridge, the captain could see flashes of light emanating from the top. Smoke pillars, similar to the ones he had observed coming from the enemy formations, rose into the clear skies. The North Koreans weren't the only ones taking damage. He knew that was where the ground forces were holding and where he had to make it to. Remembering his escape and evasion training, he knew going back through the lines could often be the most dangerous part.

Pulling out his emergency radio, the captain first turned off the locator beacon and then contacted search and rescue. Due to his position, and with the ongoing battle, he was told that a direct rescue attempt couldn't currently be performed. His best bet was to lay low and make for a nearby community once the fight was over or after nightfall.

The clamor of the battle continued for a long while as John hunkered in the ditch. The North Korean armor seemed to avoid the canal, and he wasn't bothered for the remainder of the battle.

As the sounds of the fight dulled and the clanking of armor faded to the north, John felt that the allied units had defeated the Northern forces. For the time being however, the field and ditch where he found himself was a no-man's land. Search and rescue informed him that the area was still too hot to affect a rescue, but advised he make his way west toward a small community, really just a few abandoned and damaged buildings. Once there, ground forces would try to make their way to him.

For the moment, the pilot that Sergeant Carson had observed going down over the battlefield was alive and mostly well.

\*   \*   \*   \*   \*   \*

Captain John Faden started along the ditch, crouching by the overhanging bank to stay out of sight. That was not only to remain unseen by the North Koreans that had retired from the field, but also to minimize his presence from the friendly forces on the ridge in the distance. He didn't know whether the search and rescue center had notified the front-line forces of his predicament or not, and there was no way any US or South Korean units would inherently know he wasn't a North Korean. They could mistake him for a spotter or some other kind of recon soldier. If they thought him the enemy, they probably wouldn't give it a second thought to bring in artillery or mortars, possibly even direct a tank to fire at him.

The frustrating part was that he was within a mile or so from the friendly lines; a distance he could easily make in nine or ten minutes, perhaps a shade longer over the fields. Pausing in his slow movements, he gazed up to the heights. Columns of dark smoke were still rising all along the ridge. Surely there had to be someone up there, and maybe arranged on the slopes below as well. The prominent position wouldn't just be abandoned.

He was just so damned close. It seemed like it should be an easy thing for somebody to drive out and pick him up, but Voltron, the search and rescue center, had told him it wasn't possible under the current conditions. He paused, his hand gripping a 9mm handgun that was strapped to his vest. The area was nearly silent. Amid the occasional dull thumps of distant artillery fire, he heard the wind whispering over the top of the canal. It was a surreal difference from the sounds of battle he had ejected into.

About to renew his short excursion to the end of the canal, or at least what looked like the end, the captain again sank down into a crouch. The once distant sound of artillery fire seemed to be drawing closer. He saw streaks of white appear from over the top of the ridgeline. Recognizing the sight of missiles being fired, he guessed that anti-tank weapons were being unleashed. They could be from attack choppers or some other vehicle, but the fact that they were launching meant only one thing. There was North Korean armor in the vicinity.

He again hunkered under the overhanging bank, wanting to remain out of sight from pretty much everybody. It seemed like he was once more going to be put in the middle of a battle. Sure enough, it wasn't long before the ground started rumbling from heavy vehicles approaching. Small flashes and streamers of smoke erupted along the heights, the cracks of cannon fire reaching him a second later. Large gouts of smoke roiled upward from enemy rounds striking friendly positions, the noise of the individual cannon shots amplifying to a rolling crescendo of explosions.

The ground tremors also intensified. Small clods of earth dropped and rolled down from the top of the embankment. As he was on one side of the canal, John worried that he might be spotted from armored vehicles or soldiers who might venture close to the opposite edge. One of his greater worries was that North Korean infantry might deploy and use the ditch for cover as they advanced. He shuddered at the thought of enemy soldiers dropping in and seeing the 9mm in his hand. After a split-second's surprise, he would be used as target practice. His time remaining on this earth would be measured in moments following the first clomp of enemy boots hitting the bottom of the canal.

More dirt fell when nearby explosions rocked his position. They didn't quite seem like artillery rounds, but at the same time, they weren't quite like the sharp cracks of tanks firing. He could feel the close ones in his chest, nonetheless. His best guess was that it was enemy armor being hit, but he wasn't about to scramble up and peek his head over the lip in order to validate his speculation. As far as he wanted anyone to know, he was just another lump of dirt resting in the irrigation system.

The battle continued around him. He tensed when he saw an enemy tank turret protrude above the lip of the bank only a few feet away. He didn't know if he could press any farther into the side of the canal without actually becoming buried, but he tried his damnedest each time an armored vehicle came into view.

As before, John stayed hunkered down as an armored battle raged all around him. The air was alive with sounds, the squeal of treads, heavy engines revving, tanks firing and being hit. Hovering just below the nearby reverberations, there were staccato crashes from smaller support vehicles firing. Sometimes, the pilot thought he could pick up the echoes of small arms fire.

The surrounding battle went on for a long while, how long, John couldn't say. In the bottom of the ditch, time lost all meaning. He was exhausted from the continual adrenaline rushes, but he didn't dare lose awareness of his surroundings, so he kept himself on edge for what seemed like hours. And then he became aware that the sounds of the battle were again diminishing.

The sunlight filtering over his position had taken on an orangish-brown hue from the North Korean vehicles burning in the field. With the receding sounds of warfare, John braved a peek from his position under the overhang, only to see that additional smoke pillars were rising from the ridgeline. Still, there was a lull; maybe this time, he could make some headway toward getting rescued.

*　*　*　*　*　*

On the screen, Captain Dwight England saw the North Korean armor begin to pull back. Although many of the tanks and supporting armor started spitting out smoke to cover their retreat, it didn't provide much of a barrier to the thermal images. With his and his company of Ah-64E's ordnance having been expended, all the two could do was watch the enemy withdraw yet again.

Dwight held the "Reapers" in position a touch longer, waiting for the replacement company to draw closer in order to affect the handover. While he didn't see just how close the North Koreans had made it on their last attack, the extent of the tracks in the field gave a pretty good clue. In his opinion, this second armored attack by the North had been halted in nearly the same position. Broken armor, some smoking and others shooting tall pillars of flame into the air, dotted fields torn up by the treads of the forty-ton monsters.

Of course, Dwight understood that it hadn't been a one-sided game as he looked along the ridge that was serving as the 1st Cav's defensive line. The constant stream of medic choppers arriving and departing the flanks where the infantry units were guarding was also a sign that the fight had been a tough one.

The relieving company had called in, and Dwight was about to release his company to head back to prepare to do it all again.

"Hey, didn't we hear somewhere that the artillery wasn't going to be involved in the fight because of a downed Air Force pilot somewhere out there?" Lieutenant Coley asked.

"Yeah, I remember hearing something like that. Why?" Dwight responded.

"Well, take a look down there. About a mile out in that ditch. I swear I keep seeing someone moving," Coley answered.

The screen was on the internal camera. Coley increased the magnification, centering the view on a wide drainage ditch, the bottom filled with muddy water. It was beyond where the vestiges of the North Korean smokescreen were just beginning to dissipate. Near the edge of the embankment, there was a hint of movement. And then there was unmistakably a face peering out. Knowing that the missing pilot was an American, the two tried to determine the uniform, but weren't able to identify whether the one they were seeing was him or not.

"I think it's him," Coley stated.

"How can you be sure? It could be an injured North Korean, a scout, or a spotter. Could be a damned farmer. Hell, it could be a trap to lure us in close. He might have a fucking MANPAD hidden away, just waiting for us to come down," Dwight countered.

"Do you really think so?" Coley asked, his tone questioning.

John shrugged. "No, not really. I think that's probably our guy."

Dwight radioed, telling the relieving company to hold off for a bit longer. He then switched to the JSTAR frequency.

"Ronin two-one, Crazy Horse three-one."

"Crazy Horse three-one, Ronin two-one. Go ahead."

"We think we see the Air Force downed pilot to our front. We're heading out to take a closer look," Dwight stated.

There was a slight pause. "Crazy Horse three-one, negative. It looks like the North Koreans are moving forward again. RTB."

Dwight's thoughts raced a million miles an hour, running through scenario after scenario. Mostly he was deciding if he was going to go against orders and head out into no-man's land in order to positively identify the movement on the screen. He thought about the pilot, how he had survived through two armored battles, and how it must feel to see freedom just a short distance away.

"Well, are we going to go after him or not?" Coley commented from the front seat. "I'm ready for a thrill ride on the wing."

"Okay, fuck it. Be ready with the gun if it is a trap."

Dwight radioed the rest of the company to standby, and let them know briefly what he was about to do. He then switched back to the E-8, deeply sighing before pressing the mic button.

"Ronin two-one, Crazy Horse three-one. We're heading to check on the pilot. Inform brigade to check their fire," Dwight broadcast.

"Crazy Horse three-one, negative. RTB."

"Crazy Horse three-two has command. Three-one heading out."

*In for a penny, in for a pound,* Dwight thought as he increased power.

The AH-64E cleared the top of the ridge and headed across. Below, heads popped up from open hatches and turned to watch the captain as he proceeded out. He passed the lines of

M1A2 battle tanks spread out in their firing pits. Some of the ones he noticed had been burned out with wisps of smoke drifting from their openings. Others were recent, darker smoke roiling from the heated interiors.

Remaining close to the ground, Dwight noted that the entire hillsides had been torn up from enemy fire, either artillery or tank rounds. He didn't know how anyone could live through what must have been hell, but there were troops moving around inside the deep trench lines. A few waved as he powered over their positions, while others stared blankly as though looking somewhere off into a distant view that only they could see.

The two raced across the cratered fields, their wheels seeming to nearly clip fence lines that had been partially uprooted from their post holes. As they neared the location where they had spotted the movement, Dwight slowed. He curved away from the spot, keeping the chin-mounted 30mm chain gun aimed toward that portion of the canal.

"So help me God, if someone pops up with a missile, I'm going to beat you senseless," Dwight stated.

"It's him, I swear it," Coley replied.

"Saying it again doesn't make it so."

Gaining a little altitude, they spotted additional movement and then a face peeked above the lip of the ditch. If the JSTARS hadn't called to inform them that the enemy armor was again on the move, which meant accompanying anti-air weapons of all kinds, then it might have seemed comical. A hand then appeared, causing both pilots to tense. Coley kept his focus on the head, the 30mm trained on the person in the ditch.

Although he kept saying that he was right and that it was the downed pilot, he himself wasn't as confident as he made out. One wrong move, even a suspicious twitch, and he'd obliterate the man to their front. Unfortunately, even this close, it wasn't easy to tell nationalities.

With the downdraft from the attack chopper sending dust and clods of earth outward, the hand raised high above the lip and waved back and forth.

"Told you it was him," Coley said, his eyes still glued to the target.

Dwight only grunted as he slowly brought the chopper closer to the ditch, feeling the wheels caress the ground as he set it down.

"Let's hurry with this. The North Koreans are on the move," Dwight said.

In the distance, he could see dust clouds rising as the enemy armored units were again advancing toward the 1st Cavalry's defensive lines.

Hearing a click as Coley disconnected his communication cord, he saw the gunner give a thumbs up as he began unbuckling from the front seat. The canopy opened and Coley started waving, instructing the man in the ditch to get his butt moving.

The man in the ditch put two hands on the churned soil and vaulted over the edge. Rolling, the pilot, who could now be identified by his muddied flight suit and harness attachments, came to his feet. Sprinting with his head lowered and hands shielding his face from the storm of dirt, he ran toward the waiting helicopter.

Coley stepped on one of the avionics bays that ran along both sides of the Apache Guardian. Crouching, with his flight suit rippling from the downdraft, the gunner guided the downed pilot up and into the front seat. In short order, the A-10 pilot was loaded in and Coley connected himself to the maintenance handholds on the exterior, running a nylon strap through the rung and attaching it to a carabiner.

With the gunner sitting the on the extended avionics bay, practically right next to Dwight, Coley slapped the canopy and gave a thumbs up. Dwight applied power and lifted off. Spinning slowly so as not to throw Coley from his perch, the AH-64E pilot lowered the nose and picked up speed.

"*Warning, missile launch. Warning, missile launch.*"

*Oh shit!*

He was too late and closed his eyes briefly, recognizing that the operator about the E-8C was right about refusing his request to head out.

*"Warning, missile launch. Warning, missile launch."*

*Fuck! Fuck! Fuck!*

He was about to lose the downed pilot, his friend, and his chopper. He tried to let Coley, riding out on his perch, know what was coming. But his gunner's helmet was head down, shielding himself against the battering wind.

Dwight punched out countermeasures, the flares arcing out from the accelerating helicopter. He couldn't maneuver hard lest he dislodge his gunner. As a last second option, while the flares were continually spraying outward, he pounded on the canopy glass. Coley turned his head sideways, looking at Dwight with his face clenched. Dwight motioned radically to the side with his hand, trying to convey that he had to turn hard.

He could identify the "Oh shit!" expression cross Coley's face. The gunner maneuvered quickly, grabbing hold of a handgrip with both hands. Without waiting for a corresponding nod, Dwight banked hard to the right, the opposite side of where Coley was perched. He didn't want to dump the gunner off, but he had to evade those missiles.

Dwight didn't see a missile streak down the left side, but Coley, holding on for dear life and trying not to pass out from the onset of Gs, sure did. He glimpsed something zip quickly past, the anti-air missile trailing white as it sped by.

Neither one saw what happened to the second missile, but those watching from the ridge line and hills watched intently. Cheering the attack chopper on, they saw the first missile pass the banking Apache and speed off over the woods to the side. The second missile went after a series of flares and detonated in their midst. Unheard by any of the three banking across the battlefield, a loud chorus of cheers went out when the attack helicopter successfully evaded the dual threats. The sight of the rescue enlivened many, the lift needed as the duress from the fights was grueling. However, the cheers were short-lived as it was time to get back to business. The next North Korean attack was drawing near.

Tensed and expecting to feel the shock of a hit, Dwight kept the turn going for a moment longer. Then, when the time the missiles should have hit came and went, he reversed his turn, this time not as abruptly. Coley was still next to him, hanging on with white knuckles. Dwight swore that the gunner was praying below the mounts on his helmet.

As he was headed across the battlefield, he radioed the others in his company to begin heading back to base and for the relieving company to move into position. There was one other radio call to make.

"Ronin two-one, Crazy Horse three-one, returning to base with one additional passenger."

"Copy that, Crazy Horse three-one. Nicely done."

And that was that. Although Dwight expected a tongue-lashing for disobeying orders in the middle of combat operations, he was instead welcomed as a hero. The entire company gathered around to help the A-10 pilot from the front seat.

"That was, well, I don't know if I can describe it. And I gotta say, I don't think I'll ever have as much fun again," Coley commented upon landing. "I'm actually a little sad because I think life will be all downhill from here on out. Nothing again will ever match that."

The three, Dwight England, John Coley, and John Faden, would remain friends for the rest of their lives, their families gathering for the holidays, taking an occasional vacation together. As for Faden's concern about fathering more children, he and his wife would add two more in the following years.

* * * * * *

Across the western side of the Korean peninsula, the battles were similar. North Korean mechanized forces attempted to bludgeon their way into the ROK, past South Korean and American defensive lines. In the South Korean 7th Corps, the Imjin River proved too much of an additional barrier for the northern forces to cross. It was also where the PRK commanders seemed to focus their attacks, due to the fact that the area was strategically vital, having the most direct routes toward the Seoul metropolis.

There was considerable pressure put on the 1st Cavalry and 2nd Infantry Divisions as those two units were also blocking two major routes into the capital city. In fact, almost all the roads on the southern peninsula more or less aimed toward the same point. The tank battles of the 1st Cav were slightly different from the fights along the 2nd Infantry lines.

Having fewer tanks, the infantry brigades and regiments relied more heavily on artillery, portable anti-tank weapons, and air support. Because of the shorter nature of the engagements, typical for that type of weaponry, the battles had more close-quarters fights. As a result, North Korean and American infantry units became entangled, the front lines intermixing. North Korean and American soldiers fought each other individually, sometimes not realizing that they were surrounded by enemies to the rear as well as to their front.

* * * * * *

Four soldiers hunkered in the rubble of a partially destroyed building. Concrete blocks, wood, splintered furniture, and an accoutrement of shattered goods lay sprawled across the floor. Part of one wall had fallen in, creating a pile of debris which the four used to shield their presence from the outside.

Moonlight peered in through window and door frames widened by explosive forces, the silver light fashioning an assortment of shapes and shadows which sometimes tricked the mind. It had been a hard day. Attempting to hold the flanks, the partial squad had been cut off from the rest of their unit when dismounted North Korean soldiers had attempted to push past.

The wooded area had been filled with confusion and noise, shouts, gunfire, and grenades. The trees had caused mortar rounds to go off overhead, raining shrapnel down on troops crouched behind trees or firing along prepared trench lines. Darkened figures darted among the woods, sometimes only visible for brief moments as they scurried behind intervening trunks. The MOPP gear prevented the smell of gunpowder from penetrating the senses, but the entire area was carpeted with thin layers of smoke, almost like encroaching fog banks forming in the early morning.

The four soldiers had been cut off when the company was ordered to conduct a counterattack to drive the enemy from the defensive lines. Someone, somewhere, had determined that there was a sufficient gap in the enemy lines to hit one particular enemy attack in the flank. The plan had been to hit the North Korean infantry as they were engaged with another friendly unit, more or less rolling up on the attacking force.

However, as the two units became further enmeshed, the front line became hazy. The four were initially pushed away from the rest of their squad by a mass of retreating enemy soldiers, and the gap they had slid through had closed behind them. The more they tried to go forward, back toward friendly lines, the more it seemed like they were pushed away from their goal. With the sun setting, the four had come upon the small, ruined community and carefully snuck into the demolished structure in order to orient and compose themselves.

During that time, North Korean units filtered through the town, pushing north or south. Several rescue attempts had been made once they had radioed their company of their predicament, but the pushes by units of the 2$^{nd}$ Infantry had been unsuccessful. They had been told to wait it out, that help would soon be on the way. With that, communication intervals had been established and the radio shut down in the intervening times to conserve the battery.

The four had watched the orange of the sunset filter through the openings and the chill of the evening seep into the building. Outside, the sound of motorized vehicles came and went, each time causing anxiety to build. It was tough to remain still, the four desperately wanting to get back to their unit. However, they hadn't known just how far they'd been pushed back until the company commander finally located their probable position. They were much farther behind the lines than they originally thought. The distance increased their fear by leaps and bounds of being captured or outright executed.

As one, their eyes shot up from where they were sitting in the deep shadows caused by the wall's partial collapse. The sound of engines, which had droned on and off for some time, rose above the night and grew louder. Engines revved and fell as if some vehicles were negotiating the wreckage that spewed into the streets. The soldiers pressed deeper into the shadows, their backs trying to become part of the cinderblock wall.

Soon, the clanking of treads penetrated their small hideout. Weak beams of light flashed through the broken windows, competing with the brilliance of the moonlight. Whatever kind of vehicles they were, they halted just outside. The four slowly raised their carbines and readied their remaining grenades. Other clanks of metal-on-metal followed. Voices rose into the night, the language clearly not English. All four thought their position had been compromised somehow, although no one was exactly sure how. But the how wasn't as important as was the fact that North Korean infantry had come upon them.

The squad leader whispered softly into the mic, careful that any reply was also muted. The other three stared out from the darkness, watching for the enemy to make their appearance. Intermittent shadows momentarily blocked out the headlights that sprayed into the interior. Voices grew more distinct, barking laughs heard above conversations. The squad leader reached out and touched each of the other three, shaking his head as they turned in his direction. The signal was clear; don't engage unless they were definitely seen.

The enemy's laughs had tipped the squad leader off that their presence was a coincidence. No soldier was going to laugh and joke like that if they were on the search for an enemy they knew was hiding in the area.

The laughs were cut short by a more commanding voice, the sternness that could only come from an order. Still tightly gripping their carbines, the four shrank back, hoping they could remain hidden and that the enemy would leave soon. They moved slowly or not at all, in order not to dislodge or move any of the broken cinder blocks.

Subdued voices continued and the shadows that had been passing back and forth in front of the headlight beams stopped. The beam was more muted as people stayed in front of whatever vehicles were out there. The American soldiers involuntarily held their breaths as their fear increased. The sounds of bricks being dislodged by footsteps echoed in the ruined interior. It was clear that the soldiers they had heard just on the other side of the damaged walls were approaching.

Flashlight beams wavered, the beams sometimes highlighting part of the interior. The sound of the idling vehicles, the difference in tones telling them there were at least two, fell silent. The headlights dimmed even more, the radiance from the moving flashlight beams taking on more prominence.

Hushed voices came from just outside as the four soldiers pressed into their small alcove and the shadows it afforded. A bright beam of light abruptly filled the structure's interior. Broken memorabilia came into bright focus as the beam panned around. The brilliance flashed over the debris pile behind which crouched the four Americans. The beam hesitated, moving a little back and forth as the holder more carefully investigated the shadows. Each of the four soldiers could see the dimmed faces of their colleagues. If the interlopers took a closer look around the collapsed pile, they'd be easily spotted.

Another light flashed into the interior, highlighting a warped doorway leading into another part of the structure. The American squad leader had thought it a kitchen area, with an upended fridge lying in the middle of the floor. But they hadn't investigated it too much, seeking cover immediately. Silver gleamed off something metallic in the other room when the second light panned through the doorway.

Steps were heard as someone came inside, a concrete block sliding, followed by what had to be a swear. The tone of cursing was pretty much the same worldwide. The beam of light which had been investigating their corner of the room flashed away and a subdued conversation began only a few feet away. If the person who had come inside were to venture just a couple of steps more, the squad's position would be revealed.

The twin beams of light continued to pan throughout the interior, flashing near or past the four soldiers' location several times. Bootsteps could be heard crunching across the gritty floor. It was impossible to say whether it was just the soldier shifting or actually walking, but hands gripped carbines even more tightly.

If it came down to a fight, it would be a short-lived one, as each of the four were pretty sure the vehicles that had parked nearby were APCs and they carried more firepower than the four could muster. Anything near a fifty cal or better would punch right through the concrete walls, disintegrating the remaining structure.

The same commanding voice rang out. Answering responses came from the nearby soldiers. A beam of light again flashed near their position, the radiant light showing four sets of fear-filled eyes. The faces holding the eyes froze, unmoving. The beam held for a long moment, and then flashed away.

Ther interior abruptly darkened, leaving behind only the faint sheen of man-made light filtering in from outside, again fighting with the moon's beams for prominence. Muted voices again began conversing on the other side of the wall. The four let out long-held breaths. The headlights went out and other sounds were heard. Although the four couldn't be sure, it sounded an awful like a camp being readied and their unwanted company setting up for the night.

If it were even possible, the tension among the four increased. They knew from experience that the enemy soldiers would likely position themselves inside one or more of the ruined buildings. It was human nature to seek shelter indoors at night. That meant the odds were high that their lair would be infiltrated. The four listened intently for the first step inside their hideout. All of them knew that the night would end in a firefight. There were few other possibilities.

But an hour passed, and no one came inside. The sounds of stuff being moved continued, but the enemy soldiers had apparently found a different lair. Flickering yellow light transfused inside. Dancing shadows gave sign to the presence of a fire. Subdued conversation followed the wavering firelight as if the two were in concert. It was almost enough to give the presence of comfort, but the fact that they were far behind enemy lines weighed down any ease they might have felt.

A very faint squelch came from the radio. Eyes darted outward, fearful that the sound might alert the enemy nearby. Subdued voices continued without pause, not giving any sign that they had heard. The squad leader hunched over the radio as if his body could shield the noise more than it actually could, his replies barely above a whisper.

"Okay. Good news," he breathed to the others. "Rescue is on the way. When we get the word, we're to dash out the door and head right. Apparently, there's a plaza of some kind a couple of blocks down the road. Don't stop for anything until you get there."

Each of the other three glanced toward the sound of the enemy soldiers.

"Do they know about the armor and soldiers nearby?" one asked.

"I told 'em."

"How are they going to get us? We can't just run out in front of those soldiers. There's too many of them," another stated.

"How in the fuck do I know? They didn't say. When I say go, make a run for it. Got it?"

In the dark, the others nodded, the gestures not seen but known by the leader just the same.

Another soft voice came over the radio, barely heard even though the other three were close.

"Okay, ten minutes," the leader said.

Time seemed to stretch, each one eager to get the fuck out but worried about what that might mean. Were troops inbound? Which would mean a battle taking place basically at their doormat. That didn't sound like it would lead to a happy ending at all.

The squad leader leaned back over the radio, listening to an inbound call.

"Oh shit! Heads down everyone," he said, trying to keep his voice as small as the shape his body was curling into.

The softly muted conversation and the glow from the fire was suddenly interrupted by a whoosh-explosion. The moonlight and yellow glow were replaced by a brilliant flash of light and sound, like thunder and the flash of lightning arriving at the same time. Shrapnel hit the side wall and just outside of the structure. The glow of the campfire was replaced by a more urgent wavering of shadows and the loud crackle of flame. When the blast faded, the four heard the heart-thumping sound of rotors passing over their position.

A second explosion rocked the building, the interior highlighted in stark relief as an intense flash of light traced the outlines of the shattered windows and doorway against the ruined walls and debris-filled floor. The thunder of the blast rolled over the four as they thought the structure was going to collapse in on them. Choking dust filled the interior and chips of concrete rained down on the four.

Outside, a series of smaller explosions blasted through the neighborhood. The dust hanging in the air seemed to stop in mid-fall for a half-second with each detonation, then swirled violently aloft when concussive waves caused pressure differentials. Carbines lay on the floor as the four focused on covering their ears. It felt like their very skulls might come apart.

Each series of blasts was followed by a chopper passing close overhead in the darkness. The squad leader had his attention on the radio, looking rather than listening for a transmission to come in. When it finally did, he frantically patted each of the other three. When they looked in his direction, their faces lit by the outside fire's radiant glow, he shouted, "Go! Go! Go!"

The four leapt up as if they had been sitting on an open

flame. Holding their carbines in one hand, they scrambled out of the shadows.

"Go right! Go right!" the squad leader shouted behind him.

Negotiating their way over and around the debris, the four raced for the door. It was a race they were to lose. A shadow fled past one of the open windows and tore through the wrecked doorway. The encounter surprised both the four Americans and the lone North Korean trooper. Both the squad leader, ahead of the others, and the enemy soldier came to a stop, staring at each other in disbelief.

The squad leader recovered faster, lowering his carbine just as the recognition of danger spread across the North Korean's face. A burst from the M-4 sent the enemy soldier tumbling to the ground, his weapon clattering to the rubble. Coughing once, the man sank to the ground, blood bubbling from his mouth.

Having been surprised, it took a moment to get going. The rearmost squad member rammed into the back of the one ahead, who then hit the one in second place. In turn, the squad leader was plowed into from behind. With the line of soldiers acting like a centipede, the leader took off running again, followed after a brief delay by the second, third, and fourth. They tore through the warped frame of the doorway, and without another glance, turned right and ran into the night.

Guided by the flickering flames of a burning North Korean APC, the leader leapt over rubble strewn across the street. He looked like a running back negotiating an obstacle course of would-be tacklers, each moment expecting to hear gunfire and feel the heaviness of being hit. He was followed by the three others as they ran through the destruction.

Through gaps along the streets, the four fleeing Americans could see tracers descending at angles from the night sky. Flares shot out from unseen helicopters as they made their attack runs. Behind, the crackle of flames faded as they made it a block farther. All at once, the building walls on both sides felt less oppressive. The flames still gave enough light to dimly see their surroundings. A plaza opened before them. With the sounds of a battle in progress, and of rotors seeming to come from every direction, the small squad had made it to their destination.

"We're here," the squad leader shouted into the radio, wanting to be heard above the din.

"We have you in sight," a different voice replied. "Move forward another twenty yards and then don't move. We're coming in."

The four ran forward and crouched. Even though it was dark, they felt very vulnerable being in the open. They might not have their NVGs on, but that didn't mean there weren't a hundred North Koreans who did.

A heavy rhythmic thumping rose above the sounds of battle going on all around. Turning toward the sound, they saw the dark shape of a Blackhawk flying just over the highest rooftops. It came swooping down, the nose pulling up sharply several yards away. When it settled into a low hover, the four jumped up and ran for all they were worth. Each expected to see tracers leap out from the surrounding buildings to sweep in their direction.

When they reached the side of the Blackhawk, a crew member on the ground helped each one up into the open compartment. When all were in, their legs and arms in a tangle, the crew chief jumped in.

"They're in. Let's get the hell out of here," he said over the intercom.

The nose lowered as they gained altitude, the rescue chopper picking up momentum. Flying just feet over a crumbling roof edge, they vanished into the night, the journey back to friendly lines taking only a few minutes. With the successful rescue of the four cut off American soldiers, the attack choppers assigned to the 2nd Infantry Division halted their attacks on the North Korean battalion that had bivouacked in the South Korean village.

"Helluva night, eh, *luogotenente*?" Captain Carl Rowe stated.

"You're not kidding," Lieutenant Cardillo replied from the front seat.

"What, no Italiano?"

"I'm so fucking tired that I don't remember how to speak it."

\* \* \* \* \* \*

While the western sectors facing the 7th Corps, the 1st Cavalry Division, and the 2nd Infantry Division were beset by a constant series of mechanized attacks, the middle sector of the South Korean 3rd Corps was relatively quiet by comparison. Artillery duels took place, but the North Korean armored columns that had been proceeding through the mountainous terrain halted their drive south after crossing the DMZ. Surveillance and electronic monitoring showed the North Korean forces holding up in destroyed allied outposts, even partially reconstructing some into more defensible networks.

General Carswell and the top-level command staff believed the northern armies facing 3rd Corps were digging in. It was assessed that their mission was to pin down South Korean and American units in place to prevent them from reinforcing the main attack from the North Korean troops aimed at Seoul.

That made sense as the central part of the nation was tricky for attacking mechanized units. The narrow passes were ideal for defense, especially as the North didn't possess much in the way of aerial support or attack resources. Their helicopter assets were minimal, and the air force had been decimated since the early hours of the conflict.

Given the nature of the central region, General Carswell contemplated pulling some of the 3rd Corps units back. There was no use subjecting them to artillery fire and having them whittled down for no reason. If he moved them farther south, deeper into the mountains, then they could support any attack North Korea might start there, or be ready to reinforce the west, should North Korea achieve a breakthrough.

As he thought about the strategy, he was concerned that

pulling some units farther to the rear might actually prompt the North to conduct an assault. He didn't want to present any sign of a weakened front which might invite brigade or division level attacks. There was enough to deal with in the west without additional pressure being created along the entire front.

If North Korea wanted to wait this one out in the central region, that was fine with him. Plus, it allowed him to focus his air arsenal on the western sectors. If the North started pushing the center, he'd have to send some of the aircraft in support, weakening the western defenses. It was something he'd keep a watch on and he'd decide on a firmer plan of action within the next few days. As the war was still in its infancy, he wanted to see how things panned out before making changes. For now, the central region was placed on a "watch and wait" basis.

\* \* \* \* \* \*

The eastern seaboard was a microcosm of what was occurring in the central region. The narrow coastal road was easier to defend. And with the lack of interior connecting roads, there wasn't the danger of being flanked and the defense lines circumvented. The drawback was that with the narrowed South Korean defensive lines, the North Korean artillery could concentrate their fire.

The units at the front near the border crossing point found themselves under intense bombardments. For the most part, soldiers spent their time inside prebuilt bunkers. Drone operators kept their birds aloft, searching for signs of forming attacks and infiltrators along the border wall that stretched into the interior.

The forts and outposts along the eastern sections of the DMZ weren't demolished like the others ranging across the southern end of the demilitarized zone. Nor were they abandoned. North and east of the DMZ, drones and other forms of surveillance kept an eye on the river that ran along the DMZ.

Units farther down the coast and behind the lines were slated for rotation to the front, just as before. However, getting there was much trickier than in more peaceful times, as North Korean artillery kept the approaches to the frontier under fire. There was only one way in and out for the members of South Korea's 2nd Corps.

Instead of bunching up behind the lines to quickly respond to North Korean attacks, the units were arrayed up and down the coast. On the eastern shores, the greatest danger lay in coastal infiltrations by North Koreans coming in via fast-attack boats. The United States 1st Marine Division protected part of the coastline south of the 2nd Corps area of responsibility. They were there to provide reinforcements and to guard against North Korean intrusions.

The goal of the 2nd Corps was to prevent the North Koreans from reaching the denser populated shores to the south. There, the coastal plains opened up somewhat and would allow for maneuvering. In addition, several major routes wound through the mountains. If the North Koreans gained access to those highways, then the units guarding the Han River could be hit in the flank. And if the North was able to get even farther south, then roads inland could allow them to completely undermine the Han River planned line of resistance.

Although few roads were in the east, it was vital that the few that did exist were defended. Thus, the greatest fear was of small special forces landings by North Korea. They could wreak havoc with rear area troops and logistics. But a greater danger was that they could take hold of strategic routes and locations, paving the way for mechanized columns to force their way south, into the heart of the peninsula.

The front wasn't one-sided against the 2nd Corps. Their artillery, especially the long-range rockets, which could outdistance their northern counterparts, hammered the narrow defiles of North Korea's eastern seaboard. Like in the central mountain regions, the east came alive with artillery duels, and soldiers hunkered in bunkers.

It was thought by the ROK/US combined forces command that North Korea was threatening the east in order to fix allied units in position. And like with the center, allied support aircraft from the west was minimal. However, the 1<sup>st</sup> Marines had F-35Bs at their disposal, which could provide support for the 2<sup>nd</sup> Corps and for the 3<sup>rd</sup> Corps should it be required.

As remote as the east was, supplies and their delivery was something of a challenge. Should the conflict intensify, the logistics chain would have to come either via air or sea. The few highways through the mountains could be used, but it would take all three to fully supply the units tasked with defending the shorelines. And even that was doubtful, if the ammunition expenditures even remotely approached those of the western armies.

\* \* \* \* \* \*

Aside from the emerging land war on the Korean peninsula, an additional element to the conflict was being fought away from the seaboards. With the lion's share of the United States Pacific naval resources focused on the conflict with China and the upcoming defense of Taiwan, South Korea was mostly on its own with regards to defending its shores.

The South had a greater array of modern warships and submarines, vastly more capable than the coastal patrol ships and subs of North Korea. In the Sea of Japan to the east, with the departure of the guided missile submarine, USS *Ohio* and its LA-class escort, the USS *Topeka*, to rearm, South Korean established a picket line of diesel-electric submarines. Farther out to sea rode the sleek shapes of destroyers and frigates. This line was established to prevent any of the North's coastal submarines and patrol craft from landing small groups of personnel south of the DMZ. It was also to catch any of the enemy's older subs from interfering with the supply routes from Japan to the busy South Korean southern ports. This was the lifeline of the allied land forces.

With the two United States submarines enroute to a submarine tender, the Southern naval forces in the east weren't entirely without American assistance. An E-3C Sentry orbiting over the Sea of Japan provided long range radar coverage for the South Korean vessels guarding the seas. While the airborne command post was primarily there to provide coverage for Japan in case of a North Korean attack, and to control the aerial raids interfering with North Korea's logistics, the data was shared by the allied ships.

Even though it had only been a short time since hostilities began, the trend of the North Korean missile and patrol craft had been to remain close to the eastern shores and harbors. It was thought they were there to protect their coastlines and islands from any Southern intrusion, while also safeguarding the limited number of ships entering their eastern ports. Like their southern neighbors, ensuring the safety of their supply lines was thought to be paramount.

The patrol and missile boats were given an occasional glance by allied surveillance to make sure their assumptions still held. A concern arose when one of the operators aboard the E-3C noticed that several of radar returns began gathering near one of North Korea's southerly ports. As the hours passed, more joined the burgeoning flotilla. In the eyes of the E-3C crew, this heralded something more than protecting shorelines.

The commander in the modified airliner's fuselage looked to the south. There were the South Korean ships that were part of an established picket line.

"Who's in that South Korean task force?" the commander inquired, pointing to the blips representing the patrolling ships.

One of the operators took a moment to pull up a list denoting the allied ships on the screen.

"Sir, there are two South Korean destroyers leading two other frigates; the ROKS *Sejong the Great* and the ROKS *Choe Yeong*."

"Which is the lead ship?"

"*Sejong the Great*."

"Get them on the line."

*   *   *   *   *   *

*Sea of Japan*
*3 August, 2021*

The duty officer in the ROKS *Sejong the Great's* CIC hung up the phone. He glanced toward the situation board showing the vessels in the area. The other destroyer and frigates in the formation were spread across miles of ocean, each patrolling their sectors and listening for any hint of a North Korean submarine attempting to pass through the picket line of surface ships and friendly subs.

Most of the North's submarine fleet were older and only suited to coastal missions. However, at times they had been caught in the deeper waters as they attempted to circumvent South Korea's defensive measures closer ashore. The duty officer knew that friendly submarines were stationed closer to the peninsula to catch any enemy vessels that tried to penetrate the line in the noisier waters. So far, they had been successful in sinking three North Korean subs since hostilities had begun.

However, that wasn't what concerned the combat officer. With the information he had just received from the American *Sentry*, a surface threat could be materializing to the northwest.

"Are we receiving data from the American E-3 east of us?" the duty officer inquired.

"Yes, sir," one of the CIC operators answered. "Adjusting the filters now."

Just as the crewman finished his reply, additional blips appeared near the edges of the map. Seeing returns massing to the northwest, near the North Korean shores north of the DMZ, the duty officer came to the same conclusion that the American operators had arrived at. Without taking his eyes off the board, the duty officer reached for the phone, dialing in the ship's 1MC, their public address system.

"Captain to the CIC. Repeat. Captain to the CIC." After a brief moment he then ordered: "Sound general quarters."

Although the destroyer was already on a war footing, the warship was brought to a heightened alert status. A series of high-pitched sirens rang throughout the vessel, echoing across the nighttime waters. That was followed by another series of gongs.

*"This is not a drill. This is not a drill. General Quarters. General Quarters. All hands man your battle stations."*

"Order the *Choe Yeong, Incheon,* and *Gwangju* to general quarters and have them—"

"Captain in CIC," an order rang through the combat center.

"As you were," Commander Cho Dae-hyun said almost before anyone reacted.

Accepting a cup of coffee, the vessel's captain strode toward the situation board dominating the room.

"What is the situation?" he asked, his eyes roving the placement of the different ships showing.

"Sir, we received a warning from the American Sentry of North Korean surface vessels massing. We and the others in the task force are at general quarters. I was about to send position changes for a more efficient defensive fire. I am working along the assumption that the North is gathering for an attack, possibly a mass firing of anti-ship weapons toward us," the duty officer explained.

"Valid assumption," Dae-hyun nodded, staring at the board. "Very well, issue the orders for positioning the others. See if we can get the *Daegu* and the *Gangwon* pulled from the south. They will need to sail at flank speed if they are to help."

"Aye, sir."

"Oh, and ensure the data is being shared. If the North is planning what you say, we will need careful coordination of our limited resources. See if we can drum up support from the Air Force. I know the American Marines have aircraft near the east coast."

"Aye, sir," the duty officer stated, lifting the receiver to contact the E-3C to the east.

"Sir, the North Koreans are moving," one of the operators commented.

Commander Cho Dae-hyun glanced back to the situation board. The fifty plus number of North Korean ships, massed more or less together, were indeed moving toward the four

South Korean surface ships. Indicators on the enemy vessels showed they were taking intercept courses and increasing their speed.

Several ships were in advance of the enemy flotilla, their rates of speed slower than those behind. Dae-hyun thought those might be the much-older North Korean frigates. Their top speeds were only half of what the North's newer missile boats could make and thus needed to be closer if they were to reach firing distances at the same time as the faster boats.

"Any word on the makeup of the enemy fleet?" the commander inquired.

"No, sir," one of the CIC crew answered.

Commander Dae-hyun imagined that the ones in the rear were fast attack boats. The north had a number of missile craft that carried anti-ship weapons, most of them were dated but still capable. While many had the older Russian-made P-15 Termit missiles, each with a range of around fifty miles, North Korea possessed some newer classes that could carry the KH-35U export version, which had a reported range of one hundred and fifty miles. Some of the missile boats could also carry the C-802 Chinese anti-ship missile with a range of seventy-five miles.

The main board showed the other South Korean vessels moving in relation to the destroyer. The two frigates, the ROKS *Incheon* and the ROKS *Gwangju* were pulling ahead in a staggered line. This was to allow room for each ship to maneuver while maintaining a defensive network and clear lines of fire. The two frigates, mostly geared for anti-submarine warfare, were also spaced to allow for them to continue their ASW missions.

In the commander's mind, if North Korea was going to launch an attack like the one presenting on the screen, then they would surely include some of their aging underwater boats. The demonstration of the North Korean ships could even be a ruse to draw attention away from encroaching submarines. The commander wasn't about to let enemy submarines just freely approach into firing positions.

The other destroyer, the ROKS *Choe Yeong*, was moving

ahead and to the portside, establishing a shoreward side screening position. Fifty plus North Korean ships were closing in on the four South Korean warships at forty knots.

Aside from the vast technological edge the South Korean ships had over their North Korean counterparts, the four warships also possessed a range advantage over most of them. The South Korean SSM-710K Sea Star anti-ship missile had a range of nearly one hundred and fifty miles, matching the best the North Koreans had to offer. The enemy ships racing toward the Commander Cho Dae-hyun and his four ships were well within that range and approaching the firing parameters of their other, lesser missiles.

Commander Dae-hyun ordered the ships under his command to initiate missile actions against the enemy warships.

\* \* \* \* \* \*

The sleek South Korean ships dove into the rolling seas as they increased to flank speeds. Water arced away from the driving bows, hitting the sea with loud hisses. On the moonlit side, water droplets glistened as if they were lit from inside. The bow waves joined the spreading wakes as the warships drove toward the enemy, their silhouettes seeming to hold the tension of the upcoming battle, one in which neither side was likely to glimpse the other.

The fifty plus North Korea missile crafts were approaching the eighty-mile limit of their longest-range anti-ship missiles. As if unable to hold the tension any longer, a gout of flame shot skyward from the lead darkened South Korean ship. The flames towering aloft highlighted the gray superstructure, casting a yellow glow across the adjoining sea.

A cylinder rose from out of the explosion of light and smoke, quickly gaining speed and shooting into the night sky. The SSM-710K anti-ship missile was quickly lost from sight as its turbofan engine engaged, the projectile arcing back toward the sea where it would skim just above the surface as it raced toward its intended target.

Spread over square miles of ocean, additional flares of light suddenly winked into existence as the other South Korean surface ships fired on the encroaching Northern missile boats and frigates. The missiles firing lit up the nighttime like distant flashes of lightning, sparking for seconds and briefly highlighting the warships. In all, forty Sea Star anti-ship missiles left their nests to speed toward the amassed North Korean vessels.

\* \* \* \* \* \*

The North Korean force held off firing their longer range Kumsong-3 anti-ship missiles in order to achieve a single massive firing, hoping to overwhelm the South Korean defenses. Because of the need for South Korean naval escorts near the southern port routes, and due to the few attack aircraft on the eastern shores, the Korean People's Navy on the eastern side had been able to gather their missile boats and frigates without interference.

The North Korean naval commanders knew about the South Korean picket line of warships south of the DMZ. The plan was to overwhelm the surface vessels and then send their coastal submarine fleet south to interdict the southern supply routes from Japan. If they could slow the American supplies flowing into the country, they could push the defensive ground lines back and achieve the breakthrough they needed to unite the Korean peninsula.

With the American naval forces otherwise engaged with China and unable to interfere, the North Korean command thought they had a good chance to achieve their goal. They felt that the logistical routes the Americans had was their weak point. All they had to do was get their diesel-electric boats past the South Korean line of warships and they would be in position to wreak havoc.

The North Korean fast attack craft cut over the Sea of Japan at forty knots, their bows slamming into the rolling crests at that speed. Spread over the surface for miles, the speeding vessels looked like forty-two-foot cigarette racing boats speeding across a moonlit Florida Keys. The jarring collisions with the waves sent jets of water shooting off to the sides, the translucent nature of the sprays catching the moonbeams before disappearing back into the sea.

They were able to speed into firing range before the contingent of South Korean missiles arrived. The first to fire were the longer range Kumsong-3 anti-ship missiles. These were derivatives of the Russian KH-35U weapons, capable of ranges of one hundred and fifty plus miles. However, the fire control systems of the older North Korean vessels hosting these projectiles weren't able to take full advantage of the missile's capabilities. Namely, over the horizon tracking accuracy was minimal at best.

Like fireflies at the edge of darkened woods, flames winked on and off as a series of KN-19 Kumsong-3s were launched from a Nampo-class frigate. This was quickly followed by a North Korean Najin-class frigate letting loose with a salvo of SS-N-25 Switchblades. Two Huanfeng-class vessels each unleashed four C-802 anti-ship missiles.

Last to fire their weapons were missile boats carrying the much older P-15 Termit missiles. The launch platforms were unwieldy at best; the firing of these weapons from the selected craft was considered a hazardous operation. This was doomed from the outset.

One Komar class missile boat virtually vanished in a gigantic white flash. The P-15 had barely left its launch rail when it exploded, tearing into the craft traveling at forty knots. The detonation set off another missile waiting on a second rail, obliterating the missile boat in a vast eruption of water. Another ship was able to fire off their first, but wasn't so fortunate with the second. That one tore the railing apart as it was halfway up. With a loud screech of tortured metal, the Termit missile crashed into the side of its mother ship and detonated.

Several of the antiquated vessels came apart under the dangerous launches, the only evidence that the craft even existed coming from flotsam drifting on darkened waters. Other problems arose from the sixties-era anti-ship missiles. Some of the Termit missiles locked onto nearby friendly vessels, their courses veering from their initial south-easterly trajectories and slamming into North Korean ships.

The crews of two Soju-class missile boats never knew what happened. They had completed their primary missile launches when their time on this world abruptly ended. P-15 Termit missiles fired from ships to the rear slammed into the sides of the speeding craft and exploded inside them. The thin hulls, which were only about the size as ocean-going racing boats, were torn apart. Pieces of hot metal shot outward, skipping across the Sea of Japan.

Nearby ships witnessing the hits thought South Korean missiles had started arriving, even though their screens still showed clear. Many eyes turned nervously toward the twinkling heavens, searching for glimpses of enemy aircraft. Later analysis was unable to reveal whether the friendly fire stemmed primarily from operator error or whether technical issues were to blame.

*　*　*　*　*　*

After firing, the North Korean armada of missile boats and frigates began to maneuver as they went through the tedious reloading process. Not long after North Korea launched the massed volleys toward the South Korean warships, the actual enemy anti-ship missiles began arriving. Some of the larger North Korean vessels had radar systems that could identify and track the incoming threats. However, the older ships weren't fitted with many defensive measures.

Most had automated close-in weapons systems in the form of twin AK-230 30mm turrets. The defensive nature of the missile boats constructed in the sixties and seventies was to turn and run once they had fired their contingent of weapons. This is what many of the amassed craft attempted, turning west to make for the illusion of protection the shores provided. Even racing away at forty knots wasn't much of a defense against an anti-ship missile traveling at near Mach speeds and well within their operational ranges.

Even the larger frigate-sized ships didn't have much in the way of defensive armament. Built chiefly for anti-submarine duties, the North Korean ships carried the same CIWS systems comprised of automated 30mm turrets and manned Igla IR missiles. The infrared surface-to-air weapons weren't connected to the ship's radar systems, so the crew had to manually locate and lock onto incoming threats that were skimming just a few feet above the sea's surface at night.

The first South Korean Sea Star determined that it was inside its terminal phase and turned on its internal seeker. The missile's active radar saw the bright bloom of a Najin-class frigate and made a minute adjustment to its course. The radar altimeter kept the weapon scant feet above the cresting waves as it powered at over eleven hundred miles per hour toward the aging North Korean frigate.

The older radar system saw the threat and initiated fire from the 30mm turrets on the decks. Streamers of fire arced away from the speeding warship, but they were too late. The corrective nature of the system was unable to function well enough and the defensive slugs fell behind the incoming missile.

The SSM-710K slammed into the side of the light frigate, a loud *clang* echoing over the nighttime waters moments before a rumbling explosion drifted over the seas. The ship staggered as it sped over the waters, smoke pouring out of a wide-open gouge in its hull. The vessel immediately slowed from its headlong pursuit and listed toward its injured side. Alarms rang out on the stricken warship as the crew attempted to put out raging internal fires. It took only minutes for the 1970's frigate to roll over. There it drifted on the rolling seas for an hour or more before it gave up and slipped under the waves.

An accompanying newer North Korean warship, a Nampo-class corvette, was hard-maneuvering as its radar identified threats heading toward it. Flares arced into the air as the countermeasure attempted to fool any IR seeker attached to the incoming dangers. This action interfered with the operation of those manning the friendly Igla IR anti-air missiles.

One surface-to-air projectile sped away from the ship, its course seeming to target something beyond the range of vision, when it suddenly altered course and chased after a descending flare. The nearby explosion startled some and made them think that they'd been hit. However, luck was with the manned crew as another sailor found a heat source beyond the flares and fired. The IR missile ignored the countermeasures and sped away into the darkness. Moments later, a distant explosion, barely visible to the deck crew, marked a successful intercept. One of the threats targeting the North's offensive vanished from the radar screen.

A second South Korean Sea Star found the corvette and turned after the speeding warship, closing rapidly as if meaning to avenge the demise of its comrade. Alarms were ringing throughout the North Korean vessel as the captain and crew attempted everything they could to elude the incoming projectile. The chatter of the 30mm turrets were an indication that the ship was only moments away from being hit and potentially sinking like its nearby cousin. Tracers streaked away from the vessel, arcing through the night as they chased after the yet unseen threat.

Columns of water rose where the shells passed the Sea Star missile and slammed into the sea. The computer system providing input to the automated turrets compared the outgoing rounds and the incoming target, making adjustments as it went. Several large rounds hammered into the sea-skimming missile, destroying its internals. The SSM-710K nosed over and slammed into the surface, sending a towering pillar of water to cascade over the Nampo-class frigate. The vessel emerged out from under the deluge as if it had reached the dramatic conclusion of a water park ride.

More sea-skimming missiles began arriving out of the dark. One of the issues now facing the North Korean armada was that very few were built with aerial defenses in mind. Some possessed automated 30mm turrets, but the majority only had manned systems without any computer or radar input. The crews searched through the darkened landscape with their eyes, peering intently for any target. Sadly, finding a flame trail or any other sign of an incoming threat was in vain, as the South Korean anti-ship missiles were driven by turbofan engines rather than liquid or solid propellant rocket motors. The only indication the manual gun crews had of the South Korean projectiles were from the other warships and their arcing streams of tracers reaching out over the seas, pointing the way towards enemy threats like illuminated darts.

Many of the fleeing missile boats sent large caliber rounds in the same direction they saw the automated turrets firing. But the lob-and-run approach led to many instances of friendly fire hitting the fast attack craft speeding over the cresting waves. Even dumb luck strikes once in a while, and a few times, brief flares of fire blossomed in the night when successful intercepts brought down Southern anti-ship missiles. More often though, deep rumbling explosions reverberated across the waters when Sea Star missiles slammed through the thin-skinned warships and detonated.

Columns of fire shot into the sky from the smaller boats as explosions engulfed the forty-foot vessels, blowing pieces of the boats outward. Flames flickered intermittently across miles of ocean as fuel from the stricken ships burned. Seeing the increasing devastation consuming their fellow warships, the basically unarmed missile craft maneuvered violently, seeking to elude enemy missiles that may have them in their sights. More losses occurred when desperately maneuvering ships collided with each other, the darkened silhouettes of other boats suddenly appearing.

The fire control radars aboard many of the missile boats and frigates allowed for collision avoidance, but some of the North Korean fast attack vessels had turned theirs off after launching, fearful that they could be tracked by their electronic emissions. Once the first ships started getting hit, the retreat became "every ship for itself" rather than attempting to coordinate defenses. Again, though, many of the older ships participating in the attack didn't have adequate aerial defenses, instead having to rely on speed to escape retaliatory responses.

One after another, North Korean vessels were hit, destroyed by the enemy, or by their own home team. The smaller missile boats simply disappeared in flashes of light, drifting debris the only sign that they ever existed. Larger corvettes and frigates floundered once they were hit, the seas pouring in through gouges and overwhelming bilge pumps and other emergency efforts to keep the ships afloat.

The American E-3C orbiting miles to the east watched as the radar returns from the North Korean fleet grew fewer with each pass of the radar sweeps. However, there was still an armada of radar blips speedily closing in on the South Korean warships. The nighttime sea battle was far from over.

*   *   *   *   *   *

Commander Dae-hyun looked at the radar plot, his brow furrowed in consternation. He saw the same thing that the operators aboard the American airborne command post were witnessing. The SSM-710K missiles launched from his small task force were wreaking havoc among the North Korean flotilla. He could easily imagine the chaos the nighttime attack must be creating for the enemy commanders as ship after ship was hit. As he stared at the screen however, he knew it was a scene that he would soon be facing himself.

His deeply focused expression wasn't for the elimination of the North Korean ships, nor for the imagined chaotic night, but for the approximately one hundred and fifty enemy missiles now heading toward the four ships under his command.

Dae-hyun knew that many North Korean systems weren't geared for beyond the horizon tracking, so those on the screen would be fired at coordinates. Once the internal INS or GPS electronics determined that the weapon was nearing its programmed location, it would activate its own radar or IR sensors and guide toward any targets it found in the vicinity. They weren't quite the capabilities the newer anti-ship models possessed, but it was the best the North could manage with their older fire control radars. However degraded the anti-ship missile's functions might be, the sheer number of projectiles they'd fielded presented a tremendous threat; it only took one to seriously ruin his night and possibly send his ship to the bottom of the sea.

"Make certain that we are coordinated with the other ships to ensure that the Mark Two decoys are aloft. We do not want to run out in the middle of this," Dae-hyun ordered.

"Aye, sir."

Even though the CIC was slightly over-pressurized, the commander could still hear firing commencing from the vertical launch systems. The medium-range surface-to-air defenses were operating. They were the first lines of defense against an aerial attack toward the ship and the task force.

In a strung out, staggered line, the four South Korean ships were constantly illuminated as they fired SAM after SAM toward the multitude of incoming threats. The two frigates were geared mostly for offensive and anti-submarine warfare operations and thus held a fewer number of RIM-66 surface-to-air weapons. The frigates were given responsibility for deploying electronic and infrared decoys, ensuring that they were kept active. The decoys presented electronic signatures identical to the ships they were designed to protect, while the IR devices were to attract sensors searching along those wavelengths.

One after another, end caps flew open from the *Sejong the Great's* CLS launch chambers. Gouts of flame erupted, catapulting slender projectiles into the night skies. With roars, the missiles sped away from the South Korean warships traveling at flank speeds.

Once the anti-ship missiles had been fired toward the massed North Korean vessels, and the indication appeared that they had been fired upon in return, Commander Dae-hyun had ordered a change in course. Knowing that the enemy weapons would only be searching for targets once they appeared over the horizon, he wanted to be as far away from his previous coordinates as possible. Although the nearly Mach speeds the enemy missiles would be traveling wouldn't allow him to sail very far, he would do everything in his power to evade the huge number of enemy missiles coming at them.

The incoming North Korean anti-ship missiles started running into the defenses launched from the South Korean task force. It wasn't a collective meeting of threat versus protections, but rather a series of individual intercepts.

The first RIM-66 SAM streaked out of the skies, its onboard sensors locating its selected target from among the many North Korean anti-ship missiles streaking over the top of the sea. It arced down, speeding toward the cresting waves. The targeting system analyzed the track and speed of the threat, compared it against its own, and calculated an intercept point. It continually repeated this process, making minute adjustments as the variables changed, matching steps to its partner's dance. Just as it seemed as if the RIM-66 was going to slam into an empty set of waves, a dark, sleek projectile slipped into view. The surface-to-air missile's proximity fuse set off the charge. Fragments from the warhead destroyed the once aerodynamic form of the North Korean weapon, sending the threat plowing into the sea at high speed.

Small flashes dotted the nighttime skies from successful intercepts. Even though their numbers were being reduced, the quantity over quality strategy would pay off as the massive volley of North Korean anti-ship missiles continued closer to the racing South Korean warships. The engagements occurring over the darkened horizon crested the line between heaven and sea. Drawing near to their programmed coordinates, the seekers of the enemy missiles activated.

The variety of North Korean anti-ship weapons saw bright plumes of radar returns. Unable to differentiate targets based on the shape, they opted for the biggest and brightest. Many altered their courses and turned toward the sparkling decoys emitting the same electronic emissions as the ships themselves. A few ignored the decoys, their more advanced systems recognizing that the radar returns weren't moving as quickly, thus classifying them as countermeasures.

When the leading enemy missiles came within six miles of the ROKS *Choe Yeong*, the ship's secondary defenses activated. Being farther out to the shoreward side, it was the first of the South Korean ships to come within range. The RIM-116 Rolling Airframe Missiles, controlled by the ship's point defense computers, began firing. Steel containers hummed as they spun toward the identified threats. Slender projectiles then shot out from their boxes in a continual series. The dual sensors of the RAMs sought after the electronic and IR emissions emitting from the enemy's anti-ship weapons.

Mere miles from the ship, the first of the RIM-116s made contact. Splashes burst into the night as more of the North Korean missiles were downed. Additional streaks of fast-moving flames sped outward from the other ships as their point defense weapons activated.

Commander Dae-hyun watched the screen, willing his defenses to down more of the North Korean threats. The number of missiles tracking his ships had dramatically decreased, but there were still far too many anti-ship missiles homing in on his small flotilla. He knew the danger increased significantly when the point defense weapons engaged. The subsonic, but still speedy threats could close the last six miles in a hurry.

*"Incoming missile. Brace for impact. Incoming missile. Brace for impact."*

The call went through the ship-wide intercom system. Crewmembers grabbed for nearby handles and spread their legs for increased balance, ready for the expected jarring impact of a missile exploding inside the bowels of the ship. Emergency crews grasped their fire hoses and other gear a little tighter, waiting for the hot breath that signaled an impact. Nervous eyes tried to peer through the steel hulls, wondering just where the weapon would enter. Some wondered if they might see the nose of the missile just as it penetrated, the sight heralding their death.

The Goalkeeper CIWS's two computer systems worked

in conjunction with each other. The first identified the targets while the second one tracked and engaged them. The system was set in automatic mode, so anything determined to be hostile, in other words, anything coming toward the ship, was considered unfriendly and fired upon. When the 30mm Gatling gun started spitting out rounds, the crew knew that the possibility of being struck became even more real. The CIWS could fire out to a mile, depending upon which ammunition was being used. With the enemy missiles zipping along at nearly ten miles per minute, it took only seconds for them to cross the mile separation.

The close-in system aboard the ROKS *Choe Yeong* sent burst after burst into the night, the seven-barrels of each platform spinning almost continuously. The computer-controlled defensive fire quickly locked onto incoming missiles and dispatched them into the sea with heavy slugs.

One North Korean missile made it through the thick defensive fire from the rolling airframe missiles and the 30mm Gatling guns. It rolled across the aft flight deck and detonated. The blast pushed the aft end of the ship downward, the bow rising higher over a cresting wave. To those aboard, it felt like a giant fist had reached down and punched the stern. The destroyer staggered under the blow as if it had been grabbed and squeezed hard.

As a large fireball rolled into the night skies, the ship released. Becoming lighter, it almost sprang into the air. The crash of its bow on the backside of a wave sent sheets of water spraying to the side. The bow then plunged deep into the front of the next wave, digging under a wall of water. At its current speed, it seemed as if the ship might just continue diving deep, becoming more submarine than surface vessel.

The luck of *Choe Yeong*, her crew and captain would be remembered always. Although the diving trajectory of the front end of the ship hampered the forward CIWS systems (momentarily rendering them nonoperational against the incoming threats), it also placed the warship below the path of the next incoming enemy missile. A North Korean Kumsong-3 missile sailed right over the partially submerged ship. The onboard sensors became confused, almost as if they were humanized in that short moment. The KN-19 anti-ship missile sped onward and exploded a hundred yards off the starboard side.

With reluctance, the sea released its grip on the warship, the bow rising rapidly. The roller coaster ride slowly smoothed. Those within the CIC, bracing for what they knew with certainty was going to be a second hit, were as confused as the North Korean missile's internal sensors. But they quickly recovered as they were still in the middle of a battle.

The Rolling Airframe Missile and automated 30mm point defense weapons took an immense toll on the North Korean anti-ship missile fusillade. After passing through the South Korean medium-ranged air defenses, the remaining projectiles that didn't chase after the launched decoys, ran into a solid wall of fire. The small RIM-116 surface-to-air missiles presented a continuous series of fiery streaks speeding away from the warships. Tiny flashes of light pock-marked the nighttime horizon as North Korean missiles were intercepted and shot down.

The ROKS *Incheon*, while warding off the North Korean attack as best it could, was also listening for transient noises below the waves. The warship, designed for anti-submarine duties, compartmentalized its responsibilities. Missiles highlighted the superstructures as they rose from within their launch tubes and tracer bursts added staccato streamers of fire.

Inside the Combat Information Center, operators were attempting to keep up with the fast-moving battle. They monitored their own attack efforts and noted that the North Korean fleet was in the process of retreating, their numbers substantially decreased. No new attacks were observed emanating from the gathered warships.

However fast the crew were processing the enormous flow of data, the computerized fire control and search systems were quicker. The tracking system processed all the incoming targets identified as hostile and moved them into differing categories. Those not directly targeting the South Korean task force ships, those falling victim to countermeasures, were placed in a secondary status. The primary targets were given priority for the point defense weaponry aboard all ships.

The computers determined that one North Korean missile had slipped through the defenses and was going to hit the *Incheon*. Alerts were automatically disseminated and the collision alarm was sounded. Crews throughout the ship braced themselves as best they could against the imminent hit.

With alarms sounding and streaks of defensive fire still speeding away from the South Korean frigate, a North Korean Kumsong-3 missile slammed into the side of the fast-moving warship. With a delayed action fuse, the anti-ship weapon detonated inside the ship's combat information center.

The blast decapitated the defensive efforts of the frigate. The flash of the internal explosion darkened the ship, the fire from the defensive weapon systems abruptly shutting down. They were replaced by a glow from deep within the ship, as seen through a huge gash in the ship's superstructure. Smoke roiled out from the damaged side, blending in with the darkness surrounding the frigate.

Those on the bridge recovered from the jarring hit, and immediately began assessing damages. They had moderate control over the steering systems and engines, but recognized that the ship's offensive and defensive measures were offline. Some of the services, to include anti-submarine efforts, were transferred to the bridge. However, the automated fire control systems continued to be inoperative. Recognizing the dangers from being in the forefront of the small task force, the bridge's duty officer, being the current high-ranking member of the ship's crew, ordered the ship to the east, attempting to place them in a less hazardous position.

\* \* \* \* \* \*

A Sang-O-class submarine crept toward the line of ships it had on sonar. The North Korean diesel-electric boat was only capable of doing nine knots while submerged and the captain was afraid that the faster-moving South Korean warships would outpace his coastal vessel.

He was taking a chance moving his aging sub into deeper waters, but his orders were to engage the enemy surface ships at any cost. Only partially aware of the missile attack by other North Korean surface ships, he was taken aback by the sound of explosions coming from the direction of the enemy warships.

Sonar had soundings from four ships sailing at high speeds, with the relative bearings of each one. He had tried several times to close to within the five miles necessary for his Type 53-65KE torpedoes to be within range, but with each attempt, the South Korean ships' speeds had been too great. If he pushed his boat to greater lengths, he'd be heard and likely destroyed before he had a chance to fire. "At any cost" didn't mean the destruction of his submarine and crew without even being able to fire a shot, at least not in his opinion.

"Sir, I have a bearing change for target Alpha Two," the sonarman quietly called. "New bearing is two-zero-zero, moving right to left, range decreasing."

The captain ran his finger over a stained map, mentally tracking the four South Korean ships he was maneuvering on.

"Range?" the captain inquired.

"Sir, ten thousand yards," sonar reported.

The captain saw a chance whereby he might be able to fulfill his orders.

"Increase to nine knots. Ready tubes one through four. Steer heading two-two-zero."

"Yes, sir. Turning to two-two-zero, increasing speed to nine knots. Tubes one through four showing ready."

The North Korean captain was determined to make it within the five-mile range limit of his older Russian-made torpedoes. If he was able to fire on the South Korean ships, with at least a *chance* that his weapons would hit, then he could count his mission orders as being satisfied.

It wasn't that he was being cowardly; the captain was a realist. He knew that his boat was best relegated to coastal interdiction maneuvers or for use with special operations. Directly engaging with the more modern South Korean naval destroyers and frigates was a one-way trip. With his orders, he knew he was placing himself and his crew in peril and was likely dooming them to a grave at the bottom of the sea, with the possibility of having achieved nothing.

When the South Korean warship kept on course and sailed into the waiting arms of the North Korean submarine, the Sang-O-class sub's captain felt a wide range of emotions. He was relieved that he would get the chance to accomplish his mission and not have to face the accusations that would surely follow any failure. He also dreaded issuing the next orders, as he knew that doing so would condemn him and his crew to never seeing their families again. His hope was that he would at least be remembered as a hero of the North.

"Speed and course input into the firing solution?"

"Yes, sir. Data has been input and accepted."

"Fire one," the captain ordered.

\* \* \* \* \* \*

"Sir, underwater transients bearing zero-three-zero, eight thousand yards," one of the *Incheon's* bridge crew reported.

With the combat information center impacted by the missile hit, the offensive measures that the ship was capable of was limited. But the reported underwater sounds could only be from one source, an enemy submarine had maneuvered close to the task force. And the four successive sounds reported would be torpedoes currently homing in on one of the warships. From the perspective of the source's range and bearing, the duty officer quickly assumed that his ship was the target of an enemy submarine's attack. The other ships were out of range from any North Korean torpedoes, at least according to the latest intelligence reports.

"Hard left to heading two-one-zero," the duty officer ordered.

He knew they were already at flank speed, so there was

no use ordering the move any faster. They were sailing at nearly the same top speed that North Korea's arsenal of torpedoes were known to have, so there was a slight hope of outrunning the inbound threats—if they could manage to turn fast enough and keep up their speed.

"Aye, sir. Left to two-one-zero."

"Do we still have control of the torpedoes?" the bridge officer asked.

"Yes, sir."

"Very well. Fire the Blue Sharks down the track's course, and deploy acoustic countermeasures."

Seconds later, three K745 Blue Shark torpedoes were lobbed out from the stricken ship as it leaned heavily into its sharp turn. Countermeasures followed, the underwater devices designed to mimic the ship's acoustics. The hope was that the enemy torps would "hear" the louder signal and start homing in on the decoy.

"Notify the other ships of our situation and change in course," the duty officer commanded.

"Sir, we lost our external comms," a crewman responded.

"Lost our exter…how bad were we hit?"

After the initial reports of the hit, the duty officer had been consumed with evading the current threats against them. The report let him know that the very ship he was attempting to save was in fact already in the process of devouring itself from within.

"Sir, damage control parties are attempting to bring the fires under control. But the blast warped a lot of the surrounding bulkheads, jamming many of the hatch doors shut. They just aren't able to reach the damage quickly and are having to cut access panels," the crewman said, adding that the interior of the ship around the CIC had basically been eviscerated.

"I see. Has anyone heard from the captain?"

The crewman giving the report merely shook his head.

"Tell them…well, tell them to do their best. Get the chopper airborne. They are to give our report to the *Sejong* and ask for assistance when they are able. Alert them to the sub reporting."

"Aye, sir."

Unknown to the duty officer and remaining crew, the North Korean torpedoes were homing in on the turning vessel, their onboard sensors picking up the noise of the frigate's screw sounds. When the acoustic countermeasures from the *Incheon* hit the water and began making noise, two of the North Korean torpedoes altered their course in response. The other two, however, continued chasing after the South Korean warship.

With the turn completed, crews fought against the ship bouncing over the swells at high speed as they sought to release the lone AW159 Wildcat helicopter. As the struggle with the tie downs commenced, the crew quickly went through the startup checklist, communicating the *Incheon's* difficulties to the lead destroyer as soon as the master switch came on.

The two, Type 53 North Korean torpedoes continued the chase, the distance between them and the speeding warship closing. But with the *Incheon* now heading directly away from the threats, the relative speeds became identical, the distance neither closing nor widening. As the torpedo sensors were designed for wake-homing, they weren't able to gain on the ship, as they had to crisscross the frigate's wake in order to track the target.

A minute after the turn, a deep rumble vibrated through the damaged *Incheon*. The ship lurched, its bow diving into a rising swell. The crew on the bridge that weren't strapped in stumbled from the unexpected move, grabbing anything to catch themselves.

"What the hell was that!?" the duty officer yelled after righting himself.

The question was rhetorical in nature as the fire consuming the interior was beginning to make itself known to the parts of the ship seemingly unharmed by the explosion. Engineering systems burned through, affecting the ship's engines. The ramifications were that one of the ship's two turbines went offline, substantially diminishing the ability of the ship to achieve its thirty-knot top speed.

As though a guardian spirit had reached out and touched it, one of the North Korean torpedoes chasing after the *Incheon* ran out of fuel just short of the ship's propeller. The second one, however, caught up to the ship and detonated under the aft end. The blast from the four-hundred-and-fifty-pound warhead lifted the ship's stern clear of the sea. The *Incheon* slammed back into the water, a towering column of water splashing back down where the helicopter had just lifted off. The warship then settled by the stern, its forward momentum slowing to a stop.

The duty officer picked himself off the deck, the blood trickling from his nostrils unnoticed. It was obvious that the ship had been hit again. The darkness of the bridge meant the vessel was in dire trouble. Emergency lighting glowed, the dimness highlighting a bridge crew slowly recovering as they rose from the deck. Stumbling to the wing, the officer saw the ship stern down, the dark waters of the sea washing over the aft railings. Each swell coming over the deck rose higher than the preceding one. The officer knew the ship was sinking by the stern and there wasn't much he could do at this point to halt that fact.

Sticking his head back in the bridge, he ordered: "Abandon ship!"

\* \* \* \* \* \*

The transient sounds emanating from the North Korean Sang-O-class submarine were heard by the other ships in the task force. The ROKS *Choe Yeong* sent two Red Shark anti-submarine rockets from its decks. The rocket motor sent the torpedoes sailing high over the seas, the flame trail fading into the night. In a matter of seconds, the two Red Sharks flew over the enemy torpedoes, the two weapon systems passing each other. Arriving over the calculated location of the underwater sounds, the rockets released their payloads of Blue Shark torpedoes.

Floating under deployed parachutes, the lightweight

South Korean torpedoes drifted down. Hitting the salt water, the parachute harnesses released and the weapons' motors engaged. Onboard sensors immediately began listening with their acoustic guidance systems.

The Sang-O was sailing at its maximum speed. While the electric engines were quiet, the propeller was cavitating ever so slightly. It was enough for the delicate sensors to hear the underwater vessel. As it was designed to drop in its previously programmed kill box, the two lightweight torpedoes immediately began to passively home in on the North Korean submarine.

The first torpedo arrived, the proximity fuse system detonating the warhead a yard from the enemy boat's outer hull. The pressure from the explosion caved in the outer and inner hulls, sending a torrent of water gushing into the sub. A second Blue Shark arrived on the heels of the first, further compressing the small North Korean sub.

Targeting and homing in on the Sang-O-class sub was accomplished entirely by passive means. The North Korean captain and crew never heard the approaching threats. At best, those aboard the coastal sub felt the intense vibration from an explosion before they were overwhelmed by a deluge of water. Escaped air from both the attack and from the sinking sub bubbled upward, momentarily disturbing the surface. The sub, compressed to a fraction of its original size by the two proximate underwater explosions, sank toward the bottom of the Sea of Japan.

The North Korean captain was correct in his assumption that giving the order to attack would end in his demise and that of his crew. However, his attack achieved more than he could have hoped for with the sinking of a modern South Korean frigate. His parting hope, which was no longer a part of this world, was that his comrades in other submarines would be successful in eliminating the South Korean picket line.

The three Blue Shark torpedoes fired by the *Incheon* each heard the breakup sounds coming from the enemy submarine and homed in on them. The subsequent detonations were heard by the remaining South Korean surface ships, attesting that the North Korean boat was most assuredly destroyed. There wasn't much left of their target by the time the three torpedoes arrived, the compressed water finding nothing more to damage on the already crushed sub.

*   *   *   *   *   *

Commander Dae-hyun heard the reports and nodded. Although the fight so far could be counted as a win, he didn't feel that way. He had one severely damaged frigate and another destroyer that had been hit, though still in action. The presence of one North Korean submarine more than likely meant that there were others. A feeling that the North Korean surface attack was a distraction designed to mask underwater attacks against his task force gnawed at his gut.

"Sir, the *Incheon's* helicopter informs us that the frigate is abandoning ship."

The news came as a blow to the commander. He was now faced with a decision for which he didn't have a "right" answer. The three remaining ships of his task force were still in a fight, even with the remnants of the North Korean surface fleet steaming away. There was the possibility that they were just reloading and could turn around for another attack, and his ships had nearly exhausted their anti-ship missiles, along with their anti-air defenses. The two frigates to the south that were racing northward might not reach the battle in time. He needed their missiles if the North Koreans decided to re-engage, along with their defensive firepower.

So, did he keep his three ships in action, leaving the *Incheon* to fend for itself and lose more sailors in the process? Or should he sacrifice part of his firepower, and a key part of his anti-submarine defense, to assist with the evacuation of the *Incheon*? His picket line was key to keeping the North Korean underwater fleet from the Southern supply lines; lines that were crucial to the defense of his homeland.

The commander gazed out over the expanse of darkness

surrounding his ship. Somewhere out there, a sister ship was sinking and South Korean sailors were dying. He knew that the task force and the defense of the supply lines were a priority...no, that was *the* priority. As bad as he felt, it was critical that he keep the picket line intact. Turning to issue orders, an incoming report stayed his lips.

"Sir, multiple tracks suddenly appeared to the west," a crewman reported.

Dae-hyun eyed the situation board where new blips had sprung up, seemingly out of nowhere. His heart skipped a beat, thinking that a fresh attack had commenced on his small fleet of warships. He had heard about the North developing new stealth missile boats. Instead of masking the approach of submarines, was the intent of the North Korean attack actually to mask the approach of these newer craft? If so, he was in a dire situation. There were also rumors that the North had developed the capability to conduct underwater missile attacks, a fear that gripped every South Korean sailor.

The data of the new radar tracks started showing a different pattern. The high-speed returns were definitely missiles, but their courses indicated northerly headings. It dawned on the commander that friendly submarines operating closer to the shores, patrolling along routes the North Korean coastal subs were expected to take, had fired on the massed Northern surface craft. The sudden appearance of the new tracks were submarine-launched Harpoon anti-ship missiles. The realization came at the same time as incoming confirming reports were relayed. Dae-hyun let out an audible, relieved sigh.

"Order the *Choe Yeong* to assist the *Incheon*."

It wasn't long until the destroyer came alongside the sinking frigate, helping to locate survivors and pulling them out of the sea. The area around the sinking ship was lit up as rescue efforts commenced. The entire stern of the *Incheon* was underwater, the deck awash from rolling swells. A flurry of activity started as boats filled with sailors were hauled aboard, individual swimmers guided up ladders, and nets thrown over the side.

A short time later, and with little fanfare, the ROKS *Incheon* vanished from view forever as it started its long journey to the bottom.

\* \* \* \* \* \*

One assumption Commander Dae-hyun had regarding the North Korean submarines was partially correct. While the surface attack by the North wasn't designed to mask other attacks, the smaller coastal submarines of North Korea were there to participate in the attack of the Southern picket line. However, with their limited underwater speeds, they were having difficulties intercepting the Southern ships, which were sailing at thirty knots. Moreso, the reduced range of their torpedoes limited their ability to engage.

When some of the South Korean submarines received orders to fire at the North Korean surface fleet (a command which wasn't relayed to the task force), the scope of operations changed for the North Korean sub captains. Some of the Sang-O-class boats heard the missile launches and determined that they had found easier targets. Rather than struggle to keep changing intercept courses, for what many viewed as futile attempts to get within range of the South's warships, they turned toward the west in the hope of locating enemy submarines.

When the North Korean submarines started their new search efforts, they were unaware that the skies above their heads were filled with ASW helicopters searching the waters for them. The hunters were themselves being hunted.

Commander Dae-hyun had ordered the choppers aboard the remaining ships to be airborne, along with those from the ROKS *Daegu* and the ROKS *Gangwon* steaming up from the south. Although the attack against the *Incheon* had come from farther out to sea, he guessed that any others coming against his task force would come from the landward side. The AW159 chopper from the *Gwangju* would search the waters to the north and northeast. The others, including an SH-60 Seahawk from his own ship, he sent west and to the northwest.

The launching of the Harpoons against the remnants of the North Korean armada had inadvertently kicked off an underwater war. It was a mostly silent one, with the combatants unaware that they were being tracked and fired upon until it was too late.

*   *   *   *   *   *

"I have a passive contact, bearing two-five-zero, signal fading," the sonarman stated.

"Okay. Lift it up and let us drop two hundred yards along course two-five-zero," the South Korean SH-60 pilot said.

The dipping sonar retracted, water streaming off as it rose above the waves. Once clear, the nose of the chopper dropped as it picked up speed. A minute later, the waves lit up as a downward-pointing spotlight illuminated. Froth whipped up from the downwash created a mini maelstrom. Swaying at the end of its cable, a dipping sonar lowered from the hovering SH-60 Seahawk.

As it vanished below the surface, the sensors began listening for the faint sounds of a passing enemy submarine. The operator paused the device at varying depths, listening intently. The chopper was slightly to the southwest of where the contact was heard, but with the sub traveling along an unknown course, it could come from any direction. It could be as easy as hearing it immediately or as hard as having to fly in a wide arc, searching for any faint sound denoting its presence.

The Seahawk hovered over the location for several minutes, everyone onboard hoping for the sonar operator to give encouraging news.

"Anything?" the co-pilot inquired.

"Negative," the sonarman replied.

"Okay, let us try a little farther to the west," the pilot suggested.

All aboard knew the risk of venturing farther away from the task force. If the enemy submarine, which the contact was assumed to be, was after the surface ships, then moving more to the west would place them farther away from the contact's course. This could allow the contact to slip through the outer ring and potentially put them into a firing position.

However, the opposite could be true if they ventured east. It could allow the enemy to fire on the friendly subs the crew knew were positioned to the west. It was a decision that was part intuition and part a roll of the dice. If they came up dry after several more attempts, they would return to their starting position and begin working east, all the while hoping that nothing serious happened. One ship had already been hit by a North Korean submarine. No one wanted to be responsible for the task force losing another vessel.

The sonar was raised and the chopper again hopped a short distance to the west, hoping to get ahead of the contact. Or at least to hear that they had made the right decision in venturing farther away from the task force.

The tension inside the ASW chopper was a physical presence, the air feeling a little more compacted. The sonar slipped beneath the waves, the whipped-up surface mimicking how each of the crew members felt inside. As the dipping sonar descended deeper, the crew heard of other contacts by the supporting ASW helicopters operating over the expanses of sea. The reports slowly coalesced into a pattern, validating Commander Dae-hyun's assertation that the North Korean attack was a multifaceted one. It showed a staggered line of Northern underwater assets arrayed against the task force, forming a ragged arc from the northwest to the west. These reports brought some relief to the Seahawk crew that they were searching in the right direction. But until they actually made contact with whatever had made that one faint sound, they wouldn't rest easy.

The operation in the new location didn't yield any results. The pilot was still reluctant to give up and head back to the east. The contact had faded to the southwest, which indicated that the underwater vessel wasn't heading toward the task force's ships. However, that didn't mean it was continuing on the same course.

"Well, what do you think?" the pilot asked.

The co-pilot shrugged an answer.

"I think we should try a little farther south," the sonarman chimed in.

That was the confirmation bias the pilot was hoping for. When the sonar cleared the water, he nosed the chopper south, zipping to a new location. Bringing the SH-60 into a hover, the pilot waited, the situation seeming to slip out of his hands. With each passing minute without finding the underwater contact, it opened a wider area for the enemy sub to be in. There was a chance that the fleeing sound was the only one they would hear, and that could result in the deaths of many others.

"Contact!" the sonarman stated with equal measures of relief and excitement. "Contact bearing zero-six-zero, signal increasing."

After a half minute, the sonar operator was able to ascertain a general course and speed. It was heading almost directly at them at a speed of eight knots. By raising and lowering the sonar's depth, he was able to get a pretty good indication of the contact's depth. And as the signal grew stronger, he could verify that the contact they were tracking was a North Korean Sang-O-class submarine. For the patient crew of the Seahawk, it was game on.

The data was put into the lightweight torpedo hanging from the SH-60. Seconds turned to minutes as they waited for the closest passage of the enemy boat. Just as the Sang-O-class sub neared, the sonar was raised, to spare it, and to prevent the possibility of the torpedo becoming ensnared in the cable.

"Torpedo One away."

Dropping from a low level, a lightweight weapon splashed into the sea, immediately vanishing. As it was already in its kill box, the torpedo instantly went active. As the engagement was in such close proximity, the pilot increased altitude and moved away so as to not be caught in any resulting explosion that might break the surface.

Below, the North Korean crew heard the first ping

emanate outside the sub. Fear-filled eyes turned toward it, each knowing that the sound spelled their doom. They were already traveling as fast as the vessel would allow, and there was no outrunning a weapon they knew had six times their speed.

"Launch countermeasures," the captain ordered.

Small canisters shot out from the side, the devices meant to create noise and bubbles that could reflect sonar pulses. It was a longshot, and everyone inside knew it.

"Emergency ascent. Blow the tanks."

The captain knew that the odds were against him and wanted to get to the surface before the enemy torpedo hit, or at least as close to it as possible. The North Korean sub didn't make it very far before the explosive compression caused by a nearby detonation crushed the smaller vessel. Bubbles shot upward from a gash that ripped open in the sub's hulls as it was fighting for all it was worth to get to the surface. The submarine, already surrounded by darkness, plunged to even greater depths and was swallowed up by waters so deep they never saw the light of day.

On the surface, the spotlight shining on the water caught the margins of a disturbance. A mound of seawater rose, and then exploded as a shower of water shot upward. Dangling at the end of its tether, the sonar again dipped below, listening for confirmation of a successful action.

"That's a kill," the sonarman stated, hearing the unmistakable groaning sounds of a submarine being compressed even further.

\* \* \* \* \* \*

The battles in the Sea of Japan between North and South Korean surface combatants were over fairly quickly. South Korea lost one of its frigates due to the massed launches of anti-ship missiles which had stretched the nation's ability to counter, and from a North Korean submarine captain taking a perilous chance. North Korea lost the majority of their smaller surface craft due to their lack of anti-air defenses. The daring rush of smaller vessels toward larger ships was a risky proposition, even back in World War II days. With the advent of modernized radar systems, airborne warning platforms which could detect surface vessels for hundreds of miles, and the ability to share live data streams, the reliance on speed to retreat from naval engagements didn't really have a place.

The underwater fight that had started with the South Korean Harpoon launches took much longer to complete. On the North Korean side, submarine captains had to choose whether to continue chasing after the much faster Southern ships or to go after the harder-to-find South Korean submarines. Many turned toward the closer contacts, ones which tended to fade away immediately after firing.

Most of the captains who had tried tracking down the South Korean surface vessels felt frustrated by their inability to get within range of their torpedoes. The limitation of their underwater speeds, coupled with the requirement to get within five miles of the South's ships sailing at nearly thirty knots, made intercepts next to impossible to accomplish. They reasoned that the South Korean subs would be easier targets. This was partly because they already had locations marked from the launch sounds, even though it would take some time getting there. They could ghost along, listening for further indications, figuring they already had an advantage.

The logic employed by the North Korean captains was reasonable, even though many of the Southern boats hurried away from their launch points. Some of the Sang-O-class subs hastened at their top speeds so not to lose the slim advantage they possessed. This proved to be their undoing in many cases, as they were summarily located by the cavitation of their older prop designs.

Hunting helicopters could cover miles of ocean while the North Korean submarines could manage eight-to-nine knots. There was little chance of maneuvering away from patrol zones. In most instances, once they were located, their fate was sealed. Some North Korean captains attempted to use the deeper seas to move about safely, but they again faced the limitations of their vessels. Many couldn't dive deep enough to get under the thermoclines in the area.

Searching dipping sonars of the ASW choppers, along with the passive sonars of the South Korean surface ships, heard numerous underwater explosions. Not all of those were the death knells from North Korean subs. In some instances, the Sang-O-class crews managed to locate and get within range of South Korean submarines. The silent nature of submarine warfare meant that most crews never heard their death approaching, or heard the ping of an active sonar until the last minute. This was true for both sides. Submarine crews died without knowing their end was nigh.

However, the majority of underwater losses came from the Northern side. They were fighting both the limitations of their vessels and the much more modern sensors the South possessed. For a time, an American P-8 out of Japan flew over the area, dropping lines of sonobuoys. They managed to locate two additional North Korean subs and dropped lightweight torpedoes on the unsuspecting enemy. But when their buoys started showing South Korean Sohn Wonyil-class boats maneuvering through their lines, they were called off. The intermixing of undersea hunters, both allied and enemy, made for a high probability of a friendly fire incident to occur.

Over the next hours, South and North Korean submarines hunted each other. The kill boxes for torpedoes were narrowed substantially to prevent misses from circling and finding friendly boats that might be nearby.

The other aspect that allowed the Southern underwater fleet to prevail was the nature of the weapons employed. North Korean torpedoes, with their wake-homing devices, were deadly against surface vessels. That wasn't the case against submarines, who left a much lighter wake pattern and for shorter distances. The acoustic design of South Korea's arsenals allowed for better anti-submarine passive capabilities. The guidance systems could even be programmed to only home in on certain acoustical patterns, decreasing the chances of friendly fire in such a contested zone.

When United States Marine F-35Bs arrived, they were kept on station to the south in case the Northern surface vessels turned around. In the end, they were dispatched back to their bases, many grumbling that the South Korean Navy could have left some of the fun for them.

While the undersea battles were winding down, the ROKS *Daegu* and the ROKS *Gangwon* joined with Commander Dae-hyun's ships and became part of the task force.

By the time the sun rose over the Sea of Japan, the South Korean forces had prevailed. Many of the North Korean submarine fleet had been sent to the bottom, or had fled northward. The Northern plan of interdicting the Southern supply lines had ended for the time being.

Once the submarine-launched Harpoon missiles finished working over the North Korean surface fleet, composed primarily of small missile craft, very few vessels remained. When the remnants of the North Korean surface ships arrived in Wonsan and Rakwon, they were but a shadow of what they had been, leaving the threat of North Korean naval attacks along the eastern shorelines greatly reduced.

\* \* \* \* \* \*

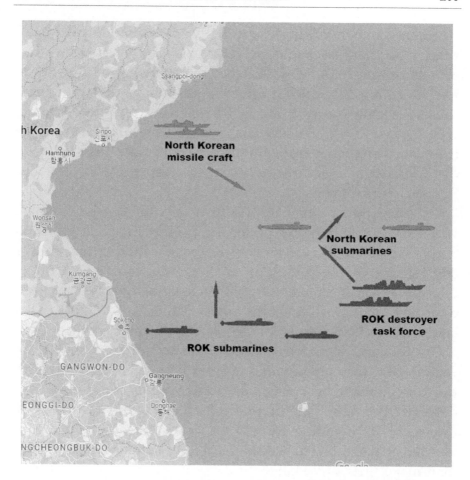

*North of Incheon, South Korea*
*3 August, 2021*

While the South Korean 7th Corps was covering the northern approaches to Seoul, the 1st Corp's area of responsibility was for the city itself. This included the islands of Ganghwa-do, Gyodong-do, and Seokmo-do that lay off the mouth of the Han River. Situated north of Incheon City, and with each island connected by one or two bridges, the first two islands were directly south of North Korea, lying close to the northern limit line. This limit line was an extension of the DMZ and established a boundary between the two countries.

The waterways between the islands and North Korea were silt-ridden passageways with islets of sand emerging between channels during low tides. Too shallow during those times, the channels could only be patrolled by shallow-draft vessels during high tides. Watches were kept on Ganghwa-do and Gyodong-do from tall observation towers and numerous sensors. This was also true for the mainland area near Gimpo, which was just a narrow channel crossing away from an invasion. For that reason, the area was heavily fortified with deep defense lines and ready reserves to respond to any attempt by North Korea to cross.

Since the outbreak of hostilities, any boat, large or small, was immediately brought under fire from both small arms and South Korean artillery. The area resembled little of its pre-war countenance as the rumble of artillery was constant. Artillery duels, both on the mainland and the islands, were carried out day and night from both sides. Craters dominated the landscape, with the lower lands filling with water seepage.

Both sides worried about invasion forces crossing the channel and then circumventing front line defenses. The North Korean command worried that Southern units could cross and descend upon Kaesong, thus cutting off one of the major supply routes for its invading forces. The allied forces of the South worried that the North would be able to come around behind their major line of resistance.

A successful attack by North Korea in this area would undermine the entire network of defenses and force the allied units to fold back to secondary lines. Thus, strong reserves and surveillance systems were in place around Gimpo. With the limitations of the islands themselves, imposed geographically, South Korean forces were encased in underground bunkers dug into the few ridges rising above flat farmlands. The observatories on both northernmost islands were part of an underground network of bunkers, allowing South Korean units to continue monitoring the narrow channels during artillery barrages.

* * * * * *

The crash of incoming artillery rang throughout the northernmost hills of Gyodong-do. On a clear day, the observers stationed there could see the flat landscape of North Korean farmlands, situated just two miles away across tidal mud flats and the silty water channels coming from the Ryesong and Han rivers.

For years, the two opposing countries had observed each other through flocks of arriving and departing migratory fowl that inhabited the mud flats. Similar to how it was throughout the DMZ, small, fortified bases were positioned on the shorelines, each monitoring the other side for any sign of intrusion. Both sides had conducted raids throughout the years of relative peace, seeking to gain intelligence and testing defenses.

Now that the conflict had started anew, the fortified posts had been demolished by the heavy shells of guns hidden away in the folds of the land or tucked into hardened shelters. The sporadic nature of the shellings was due to the gun crews having to emerge from the bunkers, fire, and then return the artillery pieces back before return fire annihilated them. Only mobile platforms survived for long as the tedious nature of setting up stationary weapons left them vulnerable for too long to counter-battery fire. This created a conflict of artillery duels that came and went as the hours of the current conflict passed.

As the leading North Korean units pressed hard to break through the allied defense lines north of the Han River, the posts scattered through the islands of Gyodong-do and Ganghwa-do noted an increase of shells arriving from North Korean batteries situated in the hills around Yonan, Pususan-dong, and along the ridges on both sides of where the Ryseong River emptied. The brigade commanders of the South Korean 1st Corps noted that the area surrounding connecting bridges was being spared, a clear indication that the North Koreans had plans for the islands. They issued warning notices and focused some of the surveillance systems toward the water passageway separating the two countries.

South Korean artillery batteries did their best to suppress

the fire coming from the North, the longer-range rockets sending streamers of fire into the night skies. The horizon on both sides of the line flashed like summer thunderstorms in tornado alley.

\* \* \* \* \* \*

A quick series of flashes sent shockwaves powering outward. Billowing smoke marred the dawn skies, the increasing winds from approaching storm clouds ripping the balls of smoke apart and sending smudges of darker gray to the northeast. The blasts from the explosions battled with the heavy swooshing of stiff breezes as they rolled across the farmland and through the grasses at the island's perimeter. Just as the first blasts started fading, new salvoes began arriving, sending torrents of dirt rocketing upward.

At the mouth of the Ryesong, the waters swollen from a high tide, shells of a different nature started landing on both sides of the river's end. Instead of leaving craters to slowly fill with seeping water, the rounds landed with soft karumphs. Whitish smoke billowed out and spread, the strong breezes trying to tear the smokescreens apart.

In attempts to keep the screening smoke a solid barrier, North Korean artillery crews maintained a continuous salvo. Slowly, the area around the mouth of the Ryesong River and farther upriver became shrouded in a fog-like bank of swirling white. South Korean observers tried to peer through the thickening bank of smoke, desperately attempting to see what the North was up to. The added particles within the smokescreen played havoc with thermal imaging systems, those trying to pierce the veil but not able to see up the river with complete clarity.

Some of the operators aboard the E-8C orbiting south of Seoul were responsible for new movement patterns, filtering out those already established. In this way, they could clear up their screens so they could observe emerging patterns. Some focused on possible supply depots to target for later strikes.

Others monitored for enemy reserves being moved to the front, or frontline replenishments and unit rotations. One monitoring the area north of Incheon, in particular looking for any North Korean attempt to land across the Han, saw new vehicular movements coming from near the mouth of the Ryesong River.

Long columns materialized from the northern side of the waterway, seeming to stem from the hills north and northeast of Pususan-dong. These new tracks went from near the reservoir there to the river and then returned. This was followed by radar returns of moving vehicular traffic coming from the river itself, moving along the channel toward the estuaries between North Korea and the South Korean islands of Gyodong-do and Ganghwa-do. This started a long series of warnings, beginning with the South Korean 1st Corps units in the Gimpo area. Then South Korean naval vessels in the Yellow Sea, along with Southern Air Force units, were alerted to the possibility of a North Korean water invasion.

Drones were launched from the island bunkers and sent into the thickening bank of white smoke that was defying Mother Nature's efforts to break it apart. The drones, with their IR and thermal sensors, scanned the hidden areas. Slowly, warmer shapes began to emerge. All manners of large boats, mostly landing craft for infantry and tanks, started materializing.

A North Korean invasion fleet, hidden in carefully constructed bunkers which had gone unnoticed by the South, had been hastily moved down to the water's edge. Already loaded with soldiers and heavy combat vehicles, the vessels, hovercraft, and older landing craft, raced downriver, making for the island beaches. With North Korean shells landing along the shorelines, South Korean soldiers prepared to man the concrete walls running around the smaller island of Gyodong-do. Armored support vehicles rolled into prepared positions, ready to repel enemy invasion attempts.

Even before the North Koreans appeared from within their smokescreen, South Korean armor began to feel the heat from the enemy's artillery fire. Sheets of flame shot into the early morning skies from direct hits, sending dense pillars of smoke upward only to be shredded by gusting winds.

South Korean artillery fires shifted from counterbattery fire to strike coordinates within the Ryesong River itself. Gouts of water rose above the smokescreen, momentarily clearing small pockets. The grayish-white smoke became ashen in places from direct hits on the North Korean landing craft, the ragged smokescreen appearing as if it had become infected by a disintegrating virus.

Farther inland on the main peninsula, Patriot and THAAD systems came alive as North Korean ballistic missiles again shot into the air. This time, the mobile launchers in the most northern ring, or third ring, became active. Trailing long tongues of fire, and filling the countryside with their deep, rumbling roars, medium- and intermediate-ranged ballistic missiles shot into the morning skies.

The anti-missile systems waited until the enemy threats had reached their zeniths and began falling back through the atmosphere. They then sent their payloads aloft, streaking for the North Korean projectiles falling at high speeds. Successful intercepts were greeted by loud cheers within the control centers. Commanders worried that falling debris might drop into populated areas and eyed incoming communiques with anxiety. It wouldn't be their fault if casualties occurred, but it would certainly affect the status of whether more systems would be allowed in-country at a later point. But even though these thoughts crossed their minds, those were worries for another day. For now, there were additional North Korean missiles to be dealt with.

Most of the Scud missiles launched were downed. However, not all the intercepts had been successful. Streaking out of the dawn skies, warheads began landing and exploding in and around the ridges on the southern parts of both islands. Billowing clouds lifted, the blasts forming deep craters. Cracks radiated outward and rubble fell inside the hardened bunkers of reserve troops. One such shelter collapsed under the weight of a direct hit, burying one entire South Korean company, along with all their gear.

The island of Gyodong-do shook as if it were about to come free from its foundations. Smoke rising along the border walls from ruined equipment carried the stench of burning metal and rubber across the waterway separating the two countries. Nervous eyes watched from their positions, waiting for the first glimpse of enemy craft to emerge from the drifting smokescreen. From the hammering of incoming artillery shells, and the sounds of outgoing rounds, it seemed as if the island might actually sink.

The first darkened hulls of enemy craft became visible, the blunt-nosed landing craft splashing their way toward the island. Up and down the fortified wall, 30mm and 40mm weapons began sending tracers across the silt-laden waterways. Tracers started coming in from mounted weapons aboard the vessels, the seeming slow-moving fire suddenly gaining speed as they raced in among the waiting defenders.

One of the landing craft stalled in the middle of a channel, the loading ramp sparking as rounds from various IFVs and APCs started striking. It then began trailing a line of dark smoke. The emission grew thicker until the craft lost all speed and floundered in the middle of the waterway.

Shells from friendly artillery and mortars sent geysers of water towering upward. It looked like a smaller version of what the Japanese soldiers must have witnessed as American landing craft streamed toward their island shores so many years ago. More explosions followed the craft speeding toward their landing zones.

The mud flats and shallow waters mitigated the explosive impacts of the shells. Some of the artillery rounds became fully immersed in the mud before their warheads detonated and the ensuing blasts barely cleared the surface. Instead, the explosions created eddies surrounding craters that quickly filled with mud and water. However, those created waves circled outward and threatened to swamp some of the unwieldy landing craft.

A gout of fire rose from the middle of another North

Korean landing craft as if fell victim to a direct hit from an artillery round. Debris splashed all around the stricken vessel. Soldiers flew above the rising smoke cloud, tumbling end over end like rag dolls. They fell, their bodies hitting the shallow sea with large splashes. The vessel began sailing in circles, the engine still driving hard with no one left alive to provide steering.

The unrelenting South Korean fire began taking its toll on the North Korean invasion force. Gaps started appearing between the ships, with the damaged vessels floundering. But the distance the landing ships had to travel wasn't far, and the landing craft continued closing on the islands.

*   *   *   *   *   *

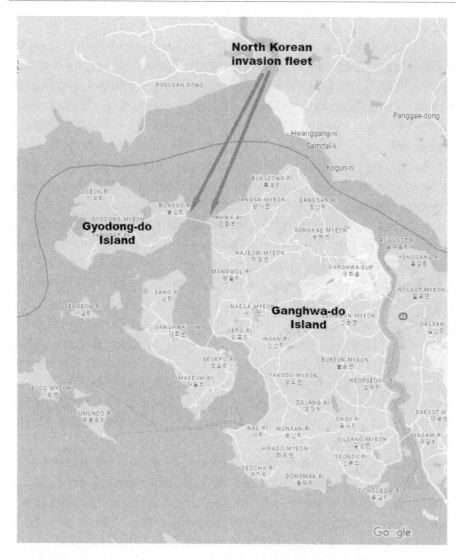

*Yellow Sea*
*4 August, 2021*

In a similar manner to the picket line in the Sea of Japan, the South Korean naval forces maintained a fleet of destroyers and frigates in the Yellow Sea. Many of these modern warships, as South Korea was attempting to establish a blue water navy, protected the entrances to Incheon and Seoul. They not only protected the approaches to these major urban areas, but also watched for North Korean infiltrations of the shorelines and

Han River.

Knowing that the North mostly possessed coastal submarines, they ran a picket line similar to the eastern naval units. Their goal was to protect the southern ports from North Korean interferences. However, the difference lay in the landscape. The waters close to the Han River, with its entrance just south of North Korea's Ryesong River, were shallow. The shallows of the shorelines ran out some distance with submerged mud flats that had several deeper channels running through them.

This left the South Korean destroyers and frigates to patrol farther out to sea while the shore patrols were provided by five Pohang-class corvettes. During times of peace, in addition to patrolling the entrances to the Han River, these corvettes were responsible for actively patrolling the northern limit line north of the Gyodong-do and Ganghwa-do islands. With the outbreak of hostilities and the lack of air defenses (the ships mainly relying on MANPADS for their aerial defenses), they were withdrawn farther south, positioning themselves to the southwest of the island group. Here, they could move quickly and assist with the island defenses in the event North Korea tried to invade.

The ships farther out to sea could provide a measure of protection as well with their anti-ship missiles, preventing North Korean submarines from flanking the corvettes and other small coastal patrol vessels. The capital city of Seoul was in a difficult location to defend from a naval standpoint, and South Korean plans had to adapt accordingly.

When the hundreds of North Korean landing craft were detected coming down the Ryesong River and into the narrow waterway separating North from South, orders were sent to the older South Korean corvettes to move north into firing positions. When a North Korean fleet of older frigates and missile boats was observed heading south around the western heel of North Korea, driving toward the impending battle area, South Korean destroyers were ordered north to intercept. Although some ships remained back to safeguard the corvette flanks, due to the number of enemy ships heading south, only a very few were left behind.

The overnight battle that had developed in the Sea of Japan was beginning to look small in comparison to what was building in the waters to the west of Seoul.

\* \* \* \* \* \*

When the North Korean invasion fleet was discovered, four South Korean corvettes, able to maneuver in the shallower waters, were directed north from their positions south of the islands off the Han River. Their search and fire control radar systems had been upgraded and were able to communicate with the E-8C systems currently tracking the North Korean invasion fleets. The corvettes were directed to move against the landing craft coming down the Ryesong and into the waters near the Northern limit line.

Directly west of Incheon, a Sang-O-class North Korean submarine waited near the bottom of a channel. It had taken the captain and crew a long time to get into their current position. Part of this was due to the slow speed the sub was capable of, part was due to the delicate navigation required to work their way through the shallow waters, and the rest because of the risky maneuvering necessary to circumvent the South Korean patrol boats.

The shallowness of the waters and the movement of the tidal flows created a noisy environment through which the North Korean captain and his crew slowly moved into their position. Now lying near the bottom, they found themselves in a good spot to interdict any South Korean warships that happened to sail within range.

They weren't alone in their endeavors to strike at the South Korean fleet in the Yellow Sea. With patience, and having to endure many close calls, other Northern subs of the same class were also able to work close to the shores and lay low in the underwater channels that fed into the deeper waters of the Yellow Sea.

\* \* \* \* \* \*

The noisy waters flowing around the submarine helped to hide its signature from the numerous South Korean anti-submarine patrols. Although seeming advantageous in general, and though it had helped the captain and his crew get this far, there was a counter-side to the perceived benefit. The tidal waters rushing through the channels also made it difficult to hear enemy ships.

Being enclosed in a steel tub, the sub's sensors were practically the only way for the crew to get information from the world around them. If they couldn't hear the warships they were sent to attack, then they couldn't realistically launch the deadly weapons residing in the four torpedo tubes with any hope for success. They needed to hear the thrashing of propellers to determine bearing and ranges, information required for the fire control systems to operate effectively.

The crew was quiet, hardly daring to move lest they make a sound and give away their position. They knew there were enemy warships out there, most of which carried better sensors than their own aging boat. All attention was focused on the single man with his hands pressed tightly against a headset. The sonarman's attention was a physical representation of the tension and anticipation felt by the entire crew.

Captain Yun Baek's anxiety was no different from the rest of the crew's. While the focus of the others was on the sonar, the captain's was divided. Between glances at the INS system to make sure they weren't drifting with the tidal influences, he was engrossed with the sonarman's facial expressions. Not only would he be the one to find them prey, but he was also the one who would provide the first warning of any enemy actions taken against them.

With the control room filled with building tension, the swirling and swishing sound of propellers coming through the hull was enough to make every heart stop beating for a brief moment. All eyes shot to the top of the room as if they would be able to see the ship that was currently on top of them.

Captain Baek wondered whether the waters were actually so noisy that they had concealed the enemy's approach, or if the ship had always been there, sitting above the small sub. The watery thrashing sound seemed amplified, and he wondered if they were about to be hit. Two or three of the crew involuntarily ducked, anticipating the screeching sound of metal grinding against metal.

The captain walked slowly over to the sonarman. The operator had the headset off and was listening through only one of the earpieces. He was writing on a thin sheet of paper. Yun Baek leaned over the man to see what he was jotting down.

'Pohang class right on top of us. Speed increasing. Bearing three five zero. Same course.'

Captain Yun Baek nodded and patted the man on the shoulder to let him know he understood. The sonarman pressed his headset harder against his ear and concentrated. He then started to write a new message.

'Second Pohang class. Bearing two five zero. Speed twenty knots and increasing. Moving left to right at two thousand yards.'

The North Korean captain could hardly contain his excitement. The laborious hours of working their way through the ASW screens was about to pay off. He had carried doubts that he'd be able to get even a single shot off at a South Korean warship. The limitations of both weapons and sub were hindrances which he thought would be too difficult to overcome. Yet here he was with two targets practically at point blank range.

The noise of the propeller overhead was beginning to fade as the warship pulled away from the sub's position. Yun Baek feared his advantage was starting to slip away. Practically all the South Korean warships had top speeds either equal to or greater than the older torpedoes most of the North Korean underwater boats carried. Any enemy vessel traveling near their top speeds could outrun a North Korean torpedo. And with a range limited to five miles, they wouldn't have to run far or long to outdistance any threat. The second warship was already nearing the top speed of the weapons nestled in the forward tubes. He'd have to move quickly if he was to have a chance at a successful encounter, or any encounter.

"Prepare tubes one and two for the second warship," Yun-Baek quietly ordered.

His thought was to fire at the most distant ship first. It was farther away and therefore the most likely one to escape the trap.

"Tubes three and four for the one overhead," he continued.

The crew moved quickly but silently through the control room. Green lights lit up on an overhead panel, indicating that the four torpedo tubes maintained their watertight integrity and were responsive to commands.

"Tubes one through four ready," the sub's XO responded.

"Fire control data input?" Yun Baek inquired.

"Yes, sir. Both ships' ranges, courses, and speeds are recorded."

Yun Baek nodded. There wasn't a sailor in the control room who thought they'd be able to escape the aftermath. Once the torpedoes were fired, they'd be heard and hunted. With the sub's slowness, there was next to no hope they'd be able to run away. Even knowing the most likely outcome, there wasn't anyone aboard who would hesitate to press the buttons to send the torpedoes on their courses.

\* \* \* \* \* \*

The South Korean corvette, the ROKS *Daechon* received orders to head north. Their mission was to intercept a bevy of North Korean craft that were sailing toward the islands of Gyodong-do and Ganghwa-do. Two similar patrol ships were ahead of them and had already commenced firing operations. Missiles rose from the aging decks, their white trails arcing toward the north and blending with the overcast skies that were coming in from the southwest.

To the west rode its sister ship, the ROKS *Namwon*. From a mile away, it was easy to see the forming bow wave as the vessel accelerated northward. The situation board in the CIC showed additional North Korean ships coming south. In all likelihood, from the speed of the enemy craft, those were fast attack missile boats coming to facilitate the North Korean attack against the islands. At least, that was the initial assumption. The invasion ships coming out from the Ryesong could very well be heading to a landing near Gimpo on the mainland. That would make as much sense as the islands, if not more.

Weapons operations were beginning on the *Daechon*. They were about to send their own SSM-710K anti-ship missiles into the air, hoping to assist with the defense of the islands. With smoke and flame shooting from the deck, the first missile rose with a roar and rocketed into the air. It was the first of the four anti-ship weapons they carried.

The alarm sounded when an operator listening to the towed array sonar heard a series of transient sounds coming from nearby. The first of the sounds was so close that the operator thought it a transient caused by their own firings possibly bouncing off the shallow sea bed. When a second distinct sound occurred, the sonar operator immediately raised the alarm.

Because there were so many North Korean submarines, and the fact that a South Korean ship had been sunk by one in recent years, quick reaction drills were a part of ship life aboard South Korean vessels. These transients were quickly identified as torpedo firings and the data automatically input into the ASW fire control system.

The proximity of the possible submarine contact worried the ASW officer. Although working up to its top speed, the *Daechon* would still be in close proximity to a launched torpedo's kill box. However, if he did nothing, then the result might be the same without being able to get a shot off in return. Knowing the risks, he ordered the triple torpedo tubes to fire.

Along with the continued firing of anti-ship missiles, three K745 Blue Shark torpedoes were launched off to the sides of the speeding warship. They plopped into the waters and circled to the south.

A spout of water rose a mile to the west. The morning sun broke through a break in the clouds and shone directly on the ROKS *Namwon,* as if the ship were an actor on stage being illuminated by a spotlight. The rays gleamed off the rising column of water and showed the stern of the ship above the surface of the sea. It looked like the ship was fleeing a sea monster, lifting itself clear to avoid the swipe of a claw.

A moment later, a second pillar of water rocketed into the air just as the rumbles of the first explosion rolled over the *Daechon.* The *Namwon* fell back into the sea and immediately started sinking by the stern. The trails from the missiles it had fired were still visible as the ship's deck became awash with waves rolling across its surface.

Streaming at twenty-five knots, and knowing that an enemy submarine was active nearby, the *Daechon* strove to clear the area. The topside crew had witnessed two torpedo explosions against another ship and knew that four enemy weapons had been launched. The captain ordered evasive maneuvers as he watched the speed indicator slowly increase. The S-turns were because he knew the North Koreans had wake homing torpedoes and he hoped to avoid being hit by forcing the enemy weapons to conduct their own wider snake turns in order to track along the *Daechon's* wake. Once the ship reached its top speed of thirty knots, he'd head in a straight course to outrun the weapons he knew were homing in on his ship. Until that happened, he held the tension of one who knew they were being hunted.

To the south, three explosive eruptions rose above the surface of the sea. His three weapons, fired in response to the transient sounds, had reached their target. The successive hits demolished the Sang-O-class submarine, a kill verified by other nearby assets. Closer to the stern, towering columns of water rose when the ship's depth charges went off. The South Korean captain had ordered the measure in the hopes that the explosions would either destroy the expected North Korean torpedoes or cause their sensors to become confused by the turmoil in the water. With the enemy weapons designed to navigate between the edges of the wake generated by a ship, it was hoped that the depth charges going off would lead the threats astray.

The measure worked to a degree as the lead enemy torpedo was driven to the side by the turmoil. Coming out the other side, the onboard sensors perceived that the torpedo had ventured too far from the wake and turned back to reacquire it. It didn't find it again and so continued circling until it ran out of fuel.

The second torpedo drove right up the *Daechon's* wake and exploded. Like the other wake-homing torpedoes, the warhead went off right under the ship's stern. A large gouge punctured the hull below the waterline and the ship began taking on water. The captain ordered the ship toward the shore, but the torpedo had damaged the steering and drive systems. Slowing, the ship came under the influence of the tides and winds, turning abeam of the waves.

The fifth corvette, held back to protect the approaches, was ordered to assist both ships. Few of the *Namwon's* crew survived its quick sinking. The *Daechon*, down by the stern, was taken under tow. However, the attempts to save the ship were abandoned after a short while as the pumps couldn't keep up with the inflow of water. It was dispatched by two torpedoes fired from the ROKS *Gongju*.

Driven by tidal currents, Captain Yun Baek and his crew, their bodies compressed in the wreckage of the Sang-O-class submarine, were slowly pushed into deeper waters. The remains of the submarine were never located.

* * * * * *

Six of South Korea's most modern destroyers were sent north to engage the armada of North Korean missile boats and frigates steaming south. Six of the South's Incheon and Daegu class frigates were ordered into the gap between the destroyers farther out to sea and the remaining corvettes racing north closer to the western shores. They were in a position to assist against the North Korean attempts to storm the islands and to help safeguard the destroyers with their anti-air weaponry.

With the enemy submarine attacks against two of the South's corvettes, resulting in their sinkings, airborne ASW assets were diverted. The SH-60 and Super Lynx anti-submarine helicopters from the frigates were given sectors to the north and northeast of the ships assigned to repel the North Korean invasion fleet. South Korean P-3 Orion maritime patrol aircraft were assigned the deeper waters to the west of the destroyers. They were to monitor the permanent lines of sonobuoys positioned as an anti-submarine defensive line, and to actively begin searching by laying sonobuoys of their own.

The Super Lynx choppers from the destroyers lifted off from the rear decks to scout ahead of the racing line of destroyers. With each destroyer able to carry two of the ASW helicopters, the task force sent to face the North Korean missile boats would keep a continual ASW screen ahead and also on the flanks.

\* \* \* \* \* \*

Gray skies rolled in, turning the seas leaden. Brisk winds whipped through the area, blowing sprays of water from the tops of cresting waves. Scattered throughout, dark gray columns descended from thickening clouds, the rain showers merging with waters beginning to frenzy from the approaching storms.

The bow of the ROKS *Munmu the Great* dove deep into a rising swell, sending a torrent of water splashing against the bridge windows. Wipers whisked away the seawater, clearing the view to the front of the Chungmugong Yi Sun-sin class destroyer. The bow rose on the ascending front of the wave as a lid on the vertical launching system flipped open. Smoke shot upward, again blocking the forward view. An SSM-710K anti-ship missile blasted through the shooting stream of smoke, arcing above the ship, which was about to begin another downward plunge into the next wave.

The South Korean warship rode through the dissipating cloud of smoke, emerging as if birthed, the roaring of a rocket motor signaling the event. No sooner had the destroyer cleared the remnant of the missile launch than another burst of smoke and fire rose from the foredeck. This time, smoke and saltwater sprays engulfed the bridge at the same time.

Spread out across the sea, South Korean destroyers and frigates sent a multitude of Sea Star and Harpoon anti-ship missiles after the North Korean northernmost fleet of craft. It was just one of a myriad of tasks the crews inside the combat information centers were performing. Others were tracking the anti-submarine operations being conducted by both their own contingent of ASW helicopters and monitoring the efforts of the P-3 farther to the west.

Before long, the hectic nature inside the CICs became even more frantic as long-range search radars picked up a massive launch by the North Korean missile boats. With the fire control radars working together, essentially forming one large system, the fast-moving targets that were determined to be North Korean anti-ship missiles, were targeted.

The first to engage the new threats were the medium-range RIM-66M surface-to-air missiles. The SAMs streaked from the heaving decks of the South Korean warships, the white trails of the missiles arcing toward the gray heavens before vanishing into the depths of the overhead cloud layers.

One band of showers descending from the clouds looked eerie as streaks of white emerged from within the dark column of rain. It looked as if the rain shower was losing containment, shooting out streamers of fire as it self-destructed.

The distance between the North and South Korean missiles closed rapidly. To the crews inside the South Korean combat centers, it was like watching a video game as blips raced toward each other across their screens. Like matter and anti-matter particles bent on annihilating each other when they came into contact, the blips disappeared when they crossed paths.

Each of the crew, feeling the tension deep within, willed the incoming radar tracks to disappear quicker.

Although the numbers decreased one by one, it didn't seem as if they were being destroyed fast enough. And they were correct. Following the longer-range intercepts, many of the North Korean anti-ship missiles were still coming at near Mach speeds.

At twelve miles, the next surface-to-air missiles roared from the decks of the South Korean destroyers and frigates. The K-SAAM weapons accelerated to Mach 2, arcing through the cloud layers as their dual sensors homed in on the ultra-high frequencies emanating from the North Korean Kumsong-3 missiles.

In addition, the South Korean warships began deploying a variety of countermeasures. Initially, Multi Ammunition Softkill Systems were launched. These devices broadcast emissions across the electromagnetic spectrum. They gave off ultraviolet, infrared, radar, electro-optical, and laser emissions that mimicked the ships they were designed to protect. Additional decoy systems were fired, their emissions meant to draw the threats away from the warships.

The K-SAAM anti-air missiles began arriving among the numerous North Korean projectiles skimming just a few feet over the tops of the cresting waves. As the incoming threats were making incremental adjustments in the blustery wind conditions, the South Korean weapons dove into them. Locating the enemy threats with IR homing sensors, the K-SAAM's proximity fuses detonated their warheads adjacent to or slightly ahead of the North's Kumsong-3 missiles. Blast fragmentations punched through the outer casings and destroyed systems in most instances. In others, the force of the blasts drove the missiles into the heavy seas. The small geysers created by the North Korean missiles diving into the water were mostly lost in the wind-whipped seas.

Although the number of incoming missiles was again decreased, many more made it through the second layer of defenses. By now, the North Korean missiles were no longer having to track via INS coordinates as they were now over the horizon, where they could themselves identify individual targets. Their radar systems saw a number of targets being presented across a wide area.

A majority of them altered course as their dual sensors located brighter radar and IR returns. Inside the ships' combat centers, the automated systems, although still classifying all of the missiles as threats, lowered the threat levels of those no longer on intercept courses with the ships themselves. The remaining defenses were directed toward those that presented specific threats to each individual ship. From here on, the combined efforts of the combat systems dissolved. Each ship would protect itself with its own point defenses.

Rolling airframe missiles shot out from the Southern ships. The computerized systems took into account the rolling decks as rocket after rocket left the sides of the warships. Even though those on the bridges, in many cases, couldn't see through the rain showers that engulfed some of the ships, the fire control radars could. The point defense weapons shot into a void of rain, the IR sensors picking up the fast-approaching heat signatures.

The situation boards within the CICs were surrounded by a multitude of radar tracks, all aimed toward the center. Every gut was clenched. It was a race to see whether the defensive missiles could destroy the enemy tracks before they closed in. When the CIWS systems, whether Goalkeeper or Phalanx weapons, engaged, the crews knew the battle had neared dangerous quarters.

Gongs rang out over ship-wide intercoms, with warnings to brace for collisions. Aboard the *Munmu the Great*, the Goalkeeper close-in weapon system sent a string of 30mm slugs outward. They collided with a North Korean Kumsong-3 missile, shredding the projectile. With a bang that shook the destroyer, the detonation ringing throughout the ship, the enemy threat exploded just a few yards short of its intended destination. Shrapnel from the explosion pinged against the ship's side. The last threat against the Chungmugong Yi Sun-sin-class destroyer had been eliminated. A cheer ran through the CIC, although it resonated more like a sigh, a release of held tension.

As the South Korean point defense weapons were engaged with the sea-launched anti-ship missiles, North Korea launched an additional wave of Kumsong-3s. These missiles were fired from land-based mobile tracked platforms which had emerged from hardened bunkers ranged near the southern shorelines of North Korea. This additional launch was meant to completely overwhelm any remaining defenses the South Korean warships had.

The destroyers and frigates had few medium-range anti-air defenses left. A few desultory missiles left the decks of the South Korean warships, but the outgoing tracks were a dismal showing compared to the incoming projectiles. Hands aboard the ships hastily replenished Rolling Airframe Missiles in their weapon systems, knowing that they were racing against time they may not have.

No sooner had the outer doors closed on the platforms, and the systems brought back online, than the newly reloaded rockets raced from their individual tubes. The loaders watched as the slender missiles raced out over the leaden seas, each streaking toward an incoming threat.

Countermeasures were again foisted aloft, hoping to lure the enemy anti-ship missiles from the ships. Many were drawn away from the warships plowing into rising waves, the RIM-116's infra-red seekers going after true threats. These were soon joined by the rotating barrels of the CIWS, the turrets swiveling toward new targets after successful intercepts.

The new wave of North Korean subsonic missiles was again slowly reduced in number, but there were so many involved in this second round that they proved to be too much for the defenses to handle. The first South Korean warship to be hit was the ROKS *Wang Geon*. A Kumsong-3 blew past the inner defenses and slammed straight into the bridge. The blast took out the entire bridge crew, showering the deck with shards from broken windows. Smoke roiled from the hole gouged into the top of the superstructure. The explosion also blew away the radar and communications systems, while severely damaging the scanned array radars on the side of the forward structure.

With the loss of the radars, the CIWS systems went offline, leaving the ship defenseless. And, with the bridge crew decimated, there wasn't anyone directly steering the ship for the time being. A second North Korean missile plowed into the side of the struggling ship, exploding deep inside. Key systems were disrupted from a series of ensuing blasts. Emergency crews responded but were powerless to contain the fires, especially with the ship heeling over as it turned abeam to the waves.

The *Wang Gong* wasn't the only ship hit by the second wave. Two other destroyers were hit by missiles that penetrated their defenses, along with two frigates. The South Korean task force had seemingly been lured into a trap from which they had difficulty escaping. In the battle, two corvettes, two frigates, and two destroyers were sunk or put out of action.

When the South Korean frigates assigned to defend against the enemy landing craft turned to the northeast, an additional ship ran into the sights of another North Korean Sang-O-class submarine. Although transient sounds were recorded and acoustic countermeasures put into the waters, the wake homing torpedoes again found their mark.

The ROKS *Chungbuk* fell victim to two of the North Korean 53-65KE weapons. Taking on water through massive holes, the vessel initially settled by the stern. It then rolled over and sank within minutes of being hit, taking a chunk of the crew with it. The waters to the west of Incheon were smudged by oily smoke plumes driven by increasing winds. Seven ships of the South Korean western naval forces had been damaged or sunk.

The battle wasn't one sided. The North Korean submarines that had lain in wait were in turn hunted down and decimated by ASW helicopters seeking to avenge their motherships. In addition, the P-3s operating farther to the west heard a number of the North's underwater boats as they attempted to transit permanent and temporary buoy lines. The hunting grounds were proving successful, so much so that the South Korean sub hunters had to be reinforced so they could return to rearm.

As for the missile boats and frigates sent south by North Korea, like those that were sunk in the east, they turned back toward the north as soon as they'd fired their contingent of anti-ship missiles, but their attempts to speed back out of range also proved fruitless. Arriving South Korean SSM-710K and Harpoon anti-ship missiles struck with near impunity. The only defenses the Northern vessels were able to muster were an assortment of automated 30mm guns.

Frigates foundered and the smaller craft simply vanished as warheads detonated. Only a handful of those sent out returned to their ports. As the storms strengthened, they drove flotsam from the destroyed ships, both Northern and Southern, onto shores. North Korea had dealt the South Korean Navy a hard blow, but it had come at great cost.

# Yellow Sea Naval Battles

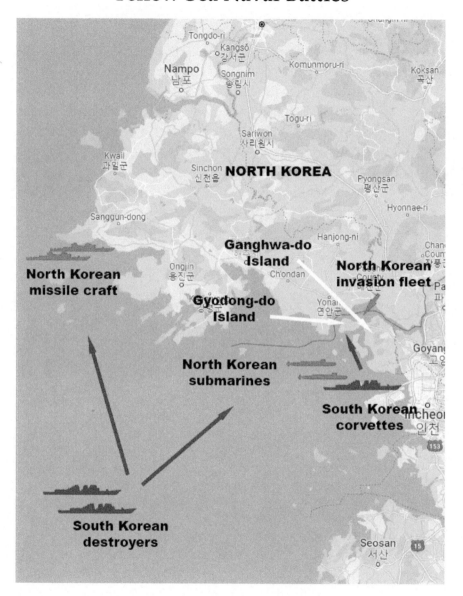

# Chapter Eight

Water crashed from the blunt bows of the North Korean landing craft, the increasing wind driving the spray back into the faces of the soldiers enduring the crossing. The bay separating the two countries was littered with debris and floundering vessels. Thick, black smoke poured from boats that had been hit, which was then whisked away by strong gusts. Still, the numerous attacking fleet came on toward the island shores, with more appearing from behind the ragged edges of the North Korean smokescreen.

Rain showers moved through the area, at times blocking the attacking swarms of landing craft from view. At other times, they slowly revealed the remaining vessels that drove through relentless fire. The South Korean targeting systems didn't notice the rain squalls much, as their sensors were able to pierce the scattered sheets of water falling from gray clouds.

On the South Korean shorelines, wind-driven smoke rolled away from stricken vehicles positioned along the defensive walls. Northern artillery fire hammered the shores, the fire intense until the North Korean guns had to reposition. Counterbattery fire from units of the South Korean 1st Corps engaged in distant battles with their North Korean counterparts. Over time, counterbattery from the Southern artillery managed to reduce the amount of incoming Northern suppression fire.

Tracers from 25mm, 30mm, and 40mm fire zipped across the intervening waters. Sparks flew from enemy landing craft as rounds found their mark. Return fire from the boats hammered into the seawall, ricochets streaking into the leaden skies. Replacement armor and soldiers crossed the still intact bridges connecting the two northernmost islands with the mainland. South Korean attack helicopters swooped in to unleash barrages of rockets and missiles, darting away trailing flares and chaff. The fight for the islands was in full swing.

The anti-ship missiles fired from South Korean frigates and corvettes sent to intervene began arriving. Streaking low over the islands and alongside them, the projectiles weaved as they conducted evasive maneuvers. When their onboard sensors located enemy ships, they entered their terminal phases. Accelerating, they plowed into the culled armada of vessels.

Meant for larger warships, the anti-ship weapons obliterated the older and much smaller landing craft. The warheads detonated over or inside the open-topped vessels, completely surrounding the LSTs in fire. With smoke pouring out from inside, some of the North Korean vessels that were hit came out the other side as if they'd been scalped. Bent and twisted, the top gunwales lost any form of cohesion with many looking like sculptures of modern art. Losing most of their compliment of soldiers, the stricken ships slowed and became adrift in the rising waves.

Other LST craft simply vanished under the booming explosions. The force of the blasts pushed the shallow draft vessels under the waves at depths from which they weren't able to recover. Soldiers splashed about in the wind-tossed waves, many succumbing due to the weight of their equipment. Their bodies added to the flotsam gathering in the stormy bay.

South Korean reinforcements were instantly placed along the seawall, filling the gaps from destroyed and damaged equipment. White trails from missile fire sped away from the edges of the islands. Weapons meant to eradicate tanks were used against thinner-skinned naval craft with effect.

From within the smokescreen, which was becoming more ragged as the storm winds increased, a line of Kongbang-class hovercraft materialized. Racing over the choppy waters at nearly fifty miles per hour, the craft transited the war-torn waters in the blink of an eye. Towering columns of water fell across the speeding vessels as they raced for the South Korean shores.

Nearing the halfway point, one of South Korea's 30mm IFV cannons began impacting one of the Northern air-cushioned vehicles. Sparks flew from the forward housing, followed by pieces flying behind the hovercraft. As the rounds found their way into the raised fans, the ACV slowed. Sparks showered from the tail end when one of the twin fans started coming apart, and dark smoke began to trail the vessel.

Additional weapons joined in and the Kangbang-class craft turned sideways to the waves. More sparks flew from the newly exposed side. The heavy caliber rounds penetrated the sides and smoke poured from the holes. With a final choking cough, the vessel sank lower to the water. When the inflatable sides lost their air, the ACV settled into the pounding waves and developed a severe list, partially sinking.

The other North Korean ACVs turned toward the narrow strip of water separating Gyodong-do and Ganghwa-do. Speeding ahead of arcing tracers which attempted to follow, the hovercraft again divided. Half of the surviving vessels ran up on the Ganghwa-do shores near the Gyodong Bridge.

Driving right over compromised seawalls, the ACVs settled into plowed fields on the other side of the defensive works. North Korean special forces soldiers leapt from within. With fifty men emerging from each craft, the specialized troops quickly established a perimeter. Others raced for the Gyodong Bridge.

South Korean reinforcements currently crossing the span came immediately under fire from the newly landed enemy troops. Anti-tank Guided Missiles raced toward the slow-moving vehicles. Explosions rang out as multiple vehicles were eliminated in a short span. Small arms fire crackled around the bridge's entrances.

In the confusion, North Korean soldiers advanced with only sporadic return fire coming from the startled South Korean convoy. Additional missiles made short work of South Korean armored vehicles and troop transports.

It was over in minutes. Sheets of flame and dark smoke rose from destroyed South Korean vehicles. Bodies littered the roadside, the injured crawling away from the carnage. Small pockets of South Korean resistance remained near the bridge, but those few were quickly eliminated by the fast-moving North Korean special forces. Inside the space of five minutes, North Korea had established a small foothold on the island of Ganghwa-do.

On the opposite side of the bridge, North Korean ACVs drove up onto the shores of Gyodong-do. In a similar sequence of maneuvers, the other side of the bridge was secured. With the bridge under the control of North Korean forces, the perimeter was expanded to include a small community on the northwestern point of Ganghwa-do. North Korea had pushed inside the seawall defenses and had secured the only bridge connecting the two islands. For the time being, South Korean units on Gyodong-do wouldn't be receiving reinforcements or supplies.

Some South Korean observers noted the landings, but their forces were already engaged with North Korean boats still attempting to push across the waterway. Artillery units on the islands were continuing to conduct their counterbattery or direct support missions. Coordinating with South Korean command units on the islands, the E-8C monitoring the ongoing battle sent a request for long-range artillery units to open fire. Providing the coordinates, the staff aboard the airborne command post coordinated a volley of fire from HIMARS-equipped 1st Corps artillery assets.

Turning aside from their missions against the enemy landing craft, South Korean Apache Guardians were sent after the new landings. Rockets flew from their chambers, erupting in scattered explosions. In return, streaks of white rose from North Korean positions. Even with countermeasures accompanying the South Korean aerial attacks, two attack choppers were brought down within a short span of time. With few airborne assets remaining, the remnants of the attack choppers were pulled away. They continued launching indirect fire from a distance.

As the North Korean long-range artillery was prepping the targets, additional hovercraft sped out from the mouth of the Rysesong River. Following on the heels of the leading vessels, these new arrivals also made their way between the islands. After sustaining several casualties among the ACVs as South Korea began to prioritize the speeding craft, additional soldiers arrived, along with lightly-armored vehicles.

The support vehicles moved to take up positions along the road, ready to defend the bridgehead against anticipated counterattacks. Anti-tank weapons bristled from attachment points and the special forces units began deploying small minefields along the perimeter.

On the Gyodong-do side, anti-tank equipped vehicles expanded outward. The heavily equipped scout vehicles started probing to the north. The goal was to come upon the South Korean defenders from behind and systematically eliminate them, thus opening up a section of beaches for the invading forces to land. Those ordered to protect the bridgeheads began to dig in, setting up small mortar pits and overlapping fields of fire. Anti-armor strongpoints with ATGMs were arranged on the higher points.

Having lost contact with a reinforcing unit and with several other scout units, the South Korean command on the islands soon realized that their defenses had been breached. Drones were dispatched, many of which were shot down before they were able to establish a clear picture of the North Korean landings. However, some video came through that showed enemy soldiers erecting defenses. With most of the units on Gyodong-do committed to holding off the invasion forces, and with the resupply route temporarily out of commission, there was little the outer island command could do.

A small number of reserves were hastily put together. Comprised of lightly injured and supply personnel, they were sent to establish a line of defense. They weren't to attack the infiltrators, but to resist any further expansion. It was decided that any force capable of pushing the North Koreans off the islands would have to come from the Ganghwa-do and mainland side. This was worrisome. Every minute the enemy was allowed to remain on the islands was another minute they could dig further in.

The North Korean lightly armored vehicles turned north before any Southern units could effectively block them. Missiles streaked across fields and slammed into South Korean armor established along the defensive seawall. The South Koreans weren't entirely surprised as some of them had been able to observe the fights at the bridge. Return fire came in the form of 30mm rounds and ATGMs. Vehicles on both sides were hit in the ensuing battle. Additional pillars of smoke rose above the tree lines, only to be carried off by the brisk winds.

The attack from the rear, even though not a total surprise, caused enough chaos that the South Korean units manning the northeastern peninsula withdrew. Had they known that they had destroyed or damaged most of the North Korean vehicles sent against them, they might have acted differently. As it stood, the northeastern section of Gyodong-do wasn't under anyone's direct control.

The arriving rockets from 1st Corp's artillery units on the mainland was devastating. A concentrated barrage landed among the North Korean special forces' soldiers setting up defensive lines. Small buildings exploded from the tremendous blasts. The roof of one toppled end over end as it arced through the humid skies. Smoke completely engulfed the northwestern peninsula of Ganghwa-do. When it cleared, North Korean soldiers lay among the ruins of a community, some crawling for cover, seeking to move away from the pain.

A third wave of ACVs emerged, racing for the juncture of the islands. Fire from Ganghwa-do sped across the intervening waters, causing a couple of the North Korean ACVs to lose steam. Others managed to make it, landing reinforcements on both sides of the bridge and on the unattended northeastern section of Gyodong-do. The small North Korean bridgehead was slowly expanding.

The smoky trail of a flare curved over the choppy waters of the waterway, exploding into a burst of green. Blown away by the wind, the residues of the flare's path could still be faintly traced to the northeastern corner of Gyodong-do Island. Seconds later, a second flare arced from Ganghwa-do's northwestern edge.

The two green bursts caused a change in the North's landing craft. As if steered by a single hand, the vessels altered their courses, making for the island sections from which the flares originated. Behind the remaining North Korean landing craft were the wrecks of the vast armada. Smoke rose from drifting hulks, debris rubbing against the sides as waves rolled past. Driven by winds and tides, floating bodies were slowly pushed toward the North Korean shores.

The sounds of grinding metal marked the first of the Northern landing craft to hit the shores. Motoring over flooded tidelands, they pushed against rocky beaches. With metallic clanks, the front doors of the landing vessels came crashing down. Met by a few of the remaining special forces teams, North Korean infantry leapt from the open-topped craft. Thrilled to be out of the death traps, more than a few of them were seasick. However, all of them were relieved to have made it through the carnage of the approach. The North Korean soldiers began to fan out. More importantly, the sound of engines being revved announced the arrival of armored infantry fighting vehicles. A couple of vessels that had started crowding the shores carried the more heavily armored main battle tanks. Amid suffering immense casualties, North Korea had managed to gain a tremulous foothold on the islands west of Incheon.

With the landings, North Korean artillery concentrated their fire on the western parts of Gyodong-do and the eastern sections of Ganghwa-do. For their part, the remnants of Gyodong-do's defensive units pulled back from the seawall and began forming a defensive line meant to hem in the North Korean intrusion. But the South Korean efforts to amend and fortify their defenses were hampered by the North's artillery fire. Large and small caliber shells fell among the defenders, the fire adjusted by drones loitering over the seas and North Korean shores.

Without bothering to organize units, the North Korean special forces command, in overall charge for the initial phases of the operation, put together an ad-hoc force based on whatever, and whoever, arrived on the shores first. With troops positioned atop IFVs and three main battle tanks, the first North Korean forces pushed quickly outward.

In the shadow of a tall ridge jutting up to their left, the

Northern force sped along the main road heading inland from the Gyodong Bridge. Their goal was to reach the open fields past the ridge and establish a defensive line. During exercises rehearsing the invasion, it became obvious that extending the perimeter to the open fields early on was imperative. If the Northern forces were unable to reach this critical juncture, then they could easily become trapped on the northeastern peninsula. They had to beat any South Korean units to the western edges of Daeryong. If they could manage that, then any South Korean attacks would have to come across long, open fields.

That reasoning and strategy was also known to South Korean units stationed on the island. The commanders knew that they had the chance to contain any enemy invasion, and that setting up along the higher terrain would create a distinct advantage. Whoever held the higher crest could observe the rest of the island and direct operations.

North Korean special forces were already enroute up the eastern slope. A second armored force was put together when additional armor and troops landed. This column was sent along the southern coastal route to come upon Daeryong from the south and blow past another containment point that could effectively lock North Korea into the northeastern sector. The two sides were racing each other to reach the important intersection of Daeryong.

Artillery fire from both combatants was directed toward these obvious routes and the observed gathering points. North Korean landing boats still had to face artillery falling amongst them, even though they had reached the perceived safety of the shores. Reinforcements were arriving, but the exploding shells created havoc among the North Koreans as they attempted to move armor, soldiers, and supplies off the shore.

On the South Korean side, artillery fell among the units attempting to coalesce and move east. Moving barrages followed dust trails, which rose from places where the rain showers hadn't yet touched. And all the while, counterbattery measures fired by both forces tried to stop devastation from happening. With South Korea unable to receive reinforcements on the island, the destruction of armor and casualties severely reduced their available firepower. Not only that, but artillery rounds on the island itself began to run low.

As the South Korean 1st Corps wasn't engaged with the main North Korean mechanized units south of the DMZ, they had reserves they could rush toward the islands. The units in prepared defenses had to remain in place, but the artillery, which was presently assisting with 7th Corps fire missions, were forced to readjust their fire. This reduced the amount of support the 7th Corps could call upon to hold their lines.

Smoke belched from the end of a long barrel, a tank rocking back on its treads. The crack of the cannon fire rolled across the shores of the lake. Those who had listened to the distant rumbles of the battles along the northern shores turned their eyes skyward, wondering if the gray they saw portended more than rain showers. A second later, a vehicle parked across a causeway erupted in a shower of sparks and fire. Flame shot out from blown hatches. South Korean soldiers tumbled from the tops as the crew clambered desperately to escape from within.

A white streak of smoke sailed from within the tree line, powering across the lake in the opposite direction. The anti-tank missile clanged into an armored behemoth and an explosive ball of fire enveloped a North Korean T-72 main battle tank. Tracers from infantry fighting vehicles and light armor crisscrossed the southern end of the lake. The battle was short-lived as the South Korean forces were very few. They had attempted to forestall any North Korean advance but were simply overwhelmed by the firepower the North was able to bring to bear.

In short order, the two remaining Northern tanks rolled past the fiercely burning South Korean APC. Unmoving bodies lay along the shoulders of the road, barely noticed by the North's IFVs as they continued rolling toward Daeryong.

Driving through a small roadway passage that ran between two hills, the lead North Korean T-72 tank emerged into the northern outskirts of the village. It and the other trailing armor separated. The armored vehicles took refuge in several large sheds that dotted the landscape. Soldiers dispersed into tree lines and set up along dikes that ran alongside the main roadway. They had won the race to the strategic village.

\* \* \* \* \* \*

A platoon of North Korean special forces began the climb along an elongated ridge that sloped down from a sharp-crested top. Trees dominated the north-facing side with the south portion of the ridge line pockmarked with moderate-sized copses. The team moved fast, continually scouting the terrain ahead using small drones. A squad to the left and right of the platoon provided flank protection and could also maneuver against any enemy they encountered.

When a drone located trenches near the top, the light, fast-moving special forces soldiers held up. Movement along the trenches revealed South Korean soldiers manning positions along the line. A quick count showed there to be an equivalent number of South Koreans facing them. But being entrenched and uphill, the defenders held the advantage. The eyes of the North Koreans searched the gray skies through the canopy, looking for any sign of a South Korean drone or that the enemy was aware of the special force's presence.

The drone operators also swiveled their cameras to see if they could detect any small aerial vehicles. With none to be seen, they again focused on the trench line and the soldiers there. The South Koreans seemed alert with some of the soldiers manning the bunkers and machine guns. The rest had their carbines at the ready and were focused downhill.

The jagged line of the trench, with branches off the main trunk ending in bunkers and other covered positions, gave the terrain a scarred, almost angry look. As the drone continued zooming in on the defenses, the North Korean operator and unit commander saw a thin metal aerial that was most likely a communications antenna. The men marked a nearby bunker as possibly being a small command post.

Trying not to draw attention to the drone, the camera zoomed in and panned along the trench line. It appeared that most of the South Koreans manning the defensive network were concentrated on the route the North Korean special forces platoon was taking. The northern and southern edges didn't seem to be covered. If they were, then the soldiers along those axes were hidden in bunkers. For all intents and purposes, it appeared that the South Koreans were meant to tie in with additional responding units. If so, then those supporting units hadn't yet made it into position. And if all went well with the North Korean armor moving west, then they wouldn't have that chance. From the initial look, it seemed that the northern and southern flanks of the trench were undefended for the time being, or at least marginally so.

To the south, the land was more open, which allowed for better observation of the enemy positions. The northern side was more or less hidden by the forest, with only partial views through the canopy. The North Korean officer was confronted with a choice. He discarded a frontal assault on the defensive line. They'd be chewed up before reaching the bulwarks. The northern route would offer cover nearly up to the edge of the trenches, but he wasn't able to identify all of the defenses there. If he attacked in that direction, it could be that he would be faced by a hidden force, sending his men to death. He could see that the southern side wasn't well-defended, but that route also meant that he would be attacking over open country.

With little time to take over the commanding view of the countryside, which was allowing the South Koreans to pinpoint artillery fire on the columns heading west, the North Korean officer opted to hit the line from the south. Any route had its risks, but he felt that this was the one that offered the best chance of success without being drawn into a lengthy firefight.

He ordered the squad south of him forward. If they took fire or if the South Koreans in front of him spotted their movement and reoriented, then he and his platoon would attack. He held back the northernmost squad. They were to be a reserve to either draw fire or to reinforce one of the units.

Viewing the tiny screen, he saw the southern squad starting to move forward. One team would cover the trench line above them while another moved from cover to cover. They would then leapfrog each other, each team taking over the previous one's role. The officer's gut was tied in a knot, waiting for the first gunshot or burst of fire to ring out.

When the first soldier rolled across the raised berm and slipped inside the trench, the North Korean officer felt his held breath escape. Other soldiers followed the first one in. They covered both sides of the trench line. Using the drone as guidance, one team of the squad began moving east, toward the South Korean troops facing him and his platoon.

Near one corner of the zig-zag trench lines, the officer held up the team. The video from the drone showed a group of enemy soldiers manning the berm.

"Hold position. Four enemy troops around the next bend, all looking east," the officer radioed.

He then ordered his platoon up. They would engage the enemy from cover, the sound of their battle hopefully covering any gunfire or explosions the flanking team might make. His troops were in a good position and he didn't want to squander the advantage. If he had the squad just open fire as they went along, the opposing forces would reorient and the trench battles could easily then become a bloody affair. He couldn't afford the manpower or time that kind of battle might take.

The platoon opened fire on the South Korean trench line from a distance. The sound of small-arms fire erupted, penetrating the forest. Flocks of birds took wing with the sudden cacophony. Return fire peppered the platoon. Splinters of bark and torn leaves rained down on the North Korean special forces.

"You still have four around the next bend, firing in our direction. Move now," the North Korean officer ordered the southern team, involuntarily ducking as something exploded nearby.

Without pause, the lead soldier on the southern team rolled around the sharp corner. With his carbine in front, he immediately saw an enemy soldier firing over a slightly raised berm. Firing a quick burst, he watched the man jerk and crumple to the ground. The falling of the South Korean fully revealed the next soldier in line. The man's attention was also focused downhill, but the North Korean could tell that the enemy soldier had seen something amiss to his side. Before the South Korean became fully aware of his danger, he too was slumping over his carbine. Moving quickly forward, the man took down the next two defenders.

"Lane clear," the officer said over the radio.

The team moved along the trench to where a branching trench line exited.

"Bunker five yards up the trail," the officer said, following the action via the drone and giving instructions.

Pulling a grenade from his pouch, the North Korean soldier peeked quickly around the corner and back. He then mentally visualized more fully what the quick look had revealed. The trench went to a darkened hole in the hillside with a makeshift cloth doorway. The winds gusting through the area caused the doorway to twist and bend, showing only darkness beyond. Arming the grenade, the soldier again quickly peeked and tossed the explosive device through the doorway. A few seconds later, a muted *karump* was heard and the ground above the bunker rose slightly. The soldier then moved quickly past the branch and farther up the main trench line.

When he came to the next corner, his carbine held ready in front in case an enemy suddenly materialized, the North Korean paused.

"Four enemy. The two nearest are ten yards down and are waiting for you. Two are farther away and firing downhill," the radio stated.

Two of the team readied additional grenades. The lead soldier tossed his to where he thought the trench and enemy soldiers were. The device detonated, sending a shower of dirt spraying across the trench lines.

"You were too long by two yards," the North Korean officer stated.

The soldier relayed the info and his companion tossed his. The resultant blast was more subdued and on target.

"Two down, two staggered."

The soldier went around the corner firing. He saw two figures covered in dirt lying on the floor of the trench. He put a burst into each before firing at two others who were stumbling down the trench line. They went down and he shot the rest of his mag into the still bodies, ensuring they weren't merely injured and could still cause harm.

"Line cleared, no bunkers."

The southern squad moved up to the next corner. The lead North Korean ducked as an explosion went off, sending clods of earth to rain down upon him. A grenade had been tossed, thankfully missing the trench, like his previous one had.

With the sounds of the battle intensifying, explosions mixed with dozens of carbines and heavier machine guns, the lead soldier and those behind lifted their weapons over the top of the trench and blind fired toward the enemy. They had to be careful in order to avoid sending rounds toward their main force, which was ahead and off to their right.

Slamming a fresh magazine in, the radio again came alive in his earpiece.

"Lead soldiers reloading."

The North Korean rounded the corner without pausing and fired into kneeling enemy soldiers. He could see surprise and fear registering on their faces, the two emotions blending into one. His rounds slammed into their chests, their fatigue tops blossoming dark, liquid stains. The first South Korean soldier was sent flying backward. The other slumped forward as if folding around the damage inflicted on his body. He then fell forward and off to the side. Two more bursts were sent toward two other camo-clad figures, knocking them against the trench walls.

At the same time, the lead North Korean felt something hard slam into his side. For a moment, he wondered if he'd missed an enemy soldier that had nailed him with a bat of some sort. Without knowing how, he found himself on the trench floor, staring at clumps of dirt. The sound of the battle became muted and he found it difficult to breathe. Without knowing how or why, or truly caring at that point, darkness closed in, forever enveloping him in its embrace.

The next in line finished off the two who had fired. Reaching down to the bloodied body of his comrade, he saw open eyes staring at nothing. Removing the radio, he placed the earpiece in and moved down the trench toward the next corner.

The North Korean officer saw the lead soldier go down and the next in line pick up the radio. They'd cleared some of the trench line without sustaining too many casualties. The rest looked to be more difficult as the South Koreans were now aware that they had company within their fortifications. He then ordered the northern team up to engage the trenches from the other side.

\* \* \* \* \* \*

As the northern and southern North Korean squads worked their way along the trench lines, using drones as overwatches and to direct the best times and ways to strike, the North Korean officer in charge began pulling back the platoon. The accidental firing on their own troops was becoming a higher probability. He then sent the platoon around the southern flank, behind where the squad had initially entered the South Korean trench line. The platoon went up and over the defensive network, angling farther up the hill.

Maintaining control over the fight from his secured position, the officer had the platoon send a small team toward the trenches. The team came upon the South Koreans and began firing on them from above. Now surrounded, the South Koreans put up a valiant, but short-lived fight. The remaining southern unit holding the hill surrendered. The North Koreans had broken through another of the defensive lines South Korea had established to hold the invaders from extending beyond their beachhead and reaching the interior.

Keeping just below the crest in order not to silhouette

themselves against the skyline, the platoon kept moving along the ridge. One team stayed behind to guard the South Korean prisoners while the other squads moved along the trenches. The drones flew slightly ahead of the moving units, searching the woodlands and clearings for any sign of the enemy. The squad was responsible for clearing the rest of the trenches while the platoon moved forward as quickly as possible, with the goal of reaching the western edge so they could establish an observation post over the island.

Normally used to going along slowly to avoid detection, the lead platoon was moving quickly. They wanted to press their advantage, especially with the almost certainty that the South Koreans were now aware of their presence. The radio tower near the initial trench lines was likely used to inform other enemy units of the attack, and with the lack of responses, it would be pretty easy for the South Korean leadership to deduce that the position had been overrun.

For that reason, eyes not only searched among the tree trunks, but took in the gray skies. Drones would provide easy recon of the slopes, just as had those of the North Koreans. Artillery landing on the ridge behind the advancing North Korean soldiers verified that the South Koreans were indeed aware of the penetration of their lines. However, the Southern artillery units found themselves overwhelmed with fire missions. The North Korean landings had swamped the local batteries, with the long-range guns needed everywhere.

Moving as quickly as they did, the North Korean special forces platoon was able to keep any South Korean response off balance. They intercepted and ambushed Southern reinforcements coming up from a Buddhist temple located halfway up the slopes. With the North Koreans using connected trench lines and having the higher ground, the firefight was intense but was shortly finished. The South Koreans had to drag their dead and wounded down the hillside under fire.

Once they were assured that the South wasn't going to send additional troops into the attack, the Northerners moved on. It was a wise decision, as artillery was soon falling on their previously held positions.

As word disseminated of a North Korean breakout on the ridge, South Korean artillery began focusing on the hilltop. That left fewer shells hitting the landing zone on the shorelines of Gyodong-do. Although the boats running the gauntlet of the open water were still under fire from Ganghwa-do, the easing of artillery fire from the beaches allowed units, equipment, and supplies to land and move inland a little easier.

Reaching the western edges of the ridge, the North Korean special forces platoon set up a perimeter. Their positions were hidden under the swaying canopy, with a small opening that allowed the observation post to overlook the island to the west.

\* \* \* \* \* \*

Artillery rounds peppered the fields to the north of Daeryong. The South Korean artillery was ranging in on the lead North Koreans who had taken positions there. Whitish-gray smoke, attempting to mimic the color of the skies, blossomed across the farmlands. Craters pockmarked the surface, turning the once peaceful and scenic terrain into an alien landscape.

Lines of dust rose upward from South Korean APCs and IFVs charging hard across the fields. Smoke shot from barrels and trailed behind the racing vehicles as they engaged presumed enemy positions. In return, shells began landing adjacent to the Southern attacking forces as North Korean artillery across the water tried intercepting the South's assault.

North of the community, a gout of smoke shot out from an open shed, a cloud of dust rising into the air below the long barrel of a North Korean T-72. The crack of the cannon fire threatened to bring the aluminum building down around the main battle tank. The round screamed across the brown fields.

The South Korean drone hovering over the battlefield showed the abrupt flare of a hit against one of the armored vehicles conducting the counterattack. A ball of fire roiled and dissipated, the APC lurching to a halt. Smoke billowed from a blown hatch with South Korean soldiers pouring from within and running away from the smoldering vehicle. A few fell shortly after exiting and were helped by others as they sought safety.

The video had also identified the North Korean tank. A streak left another armored vehicle, racing back toward the focus of the attack. An explosion rocked a storage shed and smoke started billowing out from the structure. Flame followed, which quickly built to a raging inferno. An intense explosion destroyed the building and brought it down on the destroyed North Korean tank.

More of the South Korean armored vehicles were hit by anti-tank guided missiles that were fired from the edges of the farmland. Heavy caliber tracers crisscrossed the open lands and still the South Korean force was able to race closer toward the small contingent of North Korean armor.

Another Northern tank shell found its mark, annihilating a South Korean infantry fighting vehicle that was supporting the attack meant to throw the North Koreans back from their positions. If South Korea could manage to defeat the small force that had made it through the gap and seal it, then they could possibly contain the invasion. Once isolated, the invasion force could then be systematically reduced and the island defenses restored.

The attackers outnumbered the defenders and sought to use their firepower and speed to overwhelm and roll through the North Korean unit. With IFVs and a small number of tanks to fix the North Koreans in place and to keep their heads down, the APCs would close in quickly to disembark soldiers near the North Korean lines. The troops would then begin the process of eliminating the positions.

The North Korean platoon sitting on the ridge watched the battle's progress. Although the South Koreans were taking losses, with smoking vehicles strewn across fields, they were quickly drawing near to the North Korean lines. The battle, although bloody, looked to be lost. North Korean armor had also absorbed punishment and added black columns of smoke that were quickly blown away. The North Korean officer, having caught up with the lead platoon, grabbed a radio mic and began giving a report.

\*   \*   \*   \*   \*   \*

Several streaks angled skyward from the south, seeming to attack the clouds scudding past. Smudges of smoke marked where heat-seeking MANPADS had knocked South Korean drones from the air.

As it drove toward the North Korean lines, a South Korean APC exploded in a fountain of flame. The intense pillar of fire rose high above the farmland. A second APC slewed to a sudden stop and started belching smoke. Soldiers climbed out, struggling to get clear of the smoldering vehicle. Tracers from the North Korean line converged on the stumbling soldiers, knocking many to the ground.

Eyes turned toward the hamlet of Daeryong. The crack of a tank cannon rolled across fields already filled with the sound and smell of battle. A South Korean tank blew up, the barrel slumping to the ground as if running out of energy. More of the attacking armor fell victim to a North Korean armored force flanking from the south.

Coming around via the coastal roads, the second North Korean armored unit had picked up its careful advance when the special forces officer, observing from the heights, had radioed concerning the other force's predicament. They had come upon the fight just in time as the South Koreans had almost advanced into the Northern lines.

More South Korean armor erupted in flames before they could even think about doing something regarding the second Northern armored force that was now engaged in the fight. The flanking attack seemed to take the wind out of the South Korean attack. IFVs and APCs started withdrawing, racing backward as they delivered fire into the newcomers. Smoke generators aboard the vehicles started, but their efforts were whisked away without doing much to hide them.

More South Korean losses were taken as they retreated and the North pressed their attack. Tanks and IFVs followed the South Koreans, reducing their numbers slowly but surely. A few additional North Korean armored vehicles moved through the gap and turned north, toward the shoreline. While South Korean artillery arrived near the northern part of Daeryong and North Korean guns hammered the eastern part of Gyodong-do, this third force secured additional beaches for the North's landing craft.

Although significantly reduced by South Korean attacks, North Korea possessed hundreds of the open-topped invasion vessels. With new landing zones opening, they could now cross the waters away from Ganghwa-do's defenses.

Harried as they withdrew, South Korea's defenses on the island of Gyodong-do began unraveling. The remaining armor pulled back to the northwest, taking refuge in a bunker built into a series of ridge lines there. There were also remnants of South Korean defenders hunkered in hardened shelters within ridges to the southwest. After quick breakthroughs through thin, hastily erected defenses, the North Korean invasion forces secured much of Gyodong-do.

They were harassed by long-range artillery coming from Ganghwa-do and the mainland, but without the ability to resupply, the remaining South Koreans on Gyodong-do weren't able to do much about the North resupplying and reinforcing the island.

\* \* \* \* \* \*

With the rapid advances by the North on Gyodong-do, the fight over the islands, from a South Korean perspective, switched to becoming one of containment rather than defending against or overcoming the North Korean threat. Being so close to Incheon and Seoul, the South couldn't afford to have both islands taken. This could lead the circumvention of the planned main line of resistance at the Han River. It would also allow

North Korean artillery to move closer, which could place them within range of several important bases. It became imperative to close off the damage and contain it, in much the way one might treat a serious wound. Minimize the harm and take measures to not lose an entire appendage, even if that meant losing part of it.

North Korean armor and infantry that had managed to land on the shore of Ganghwa-do secured the immediate area, including the Gyodong Bridge approaches, then moved east to establish positions near a defile that cut through two ridge lines to the north and south. South Korean armor from 1$^{st}$ Corps moved to seal off the eastern routes from the enemy bridgehead.

*   *   *   *   *   *

Craters pockmarked the few farms adjoining the main road that led to the Gyodong Bridge. More shells fell around the highway as South Korean artillery attempted to weaken the North Korean forces involved in the invasion. A continuous rumble of explosions reverberated off the hills rising above the lowlands. Smoke and dirt filled the small valley.

The blasts suddenly stopped, the echoes still ringing in the ears of the North Koreans manning their outer perimeters. Cautiously, South Korean armored vehicles started forward, moving to engage enemy troops still recovering from the artillery barrages.

Coming through the narrow passage, cannons from infantry fighting vehicles sent rounds toward any likely enemy positions. Large caliber tracers tore off into tree lines and the smoldering remains of buildings that lined the highway. A gas station and convenience store blazed mercilessly. Towering flames licked the gray skies, propelling a thick, dark column of smoke upward. Falling embers threatened to ignite the dry hillsides, further inflaming the countryside.

Missiles shot out from concealed positions, converging on the narrow line of South Korean armor. The lead vehicles erupted in flame as the ATGMs struck home. The smaller pillars of smoke from the damaged South Korean IFVs were added to the destruction happening all around the vital bridge.

Tanks accompanying the assault force tried to overpower the North Korean units defending the small beachhead. Cannon fire blasted at the North Korean cover. The response was additional anti-tank missiles flying up the highway. One of the South Korean K1 tanks was hit, losing a tread and slewing to the side. Stalled in deeply furrowed ground, additional North Korean ATGMs slammed into it, obliterating the tank. With the loss of three armored vehicles in as many seconds, the other armor withdrew. The initial assault on the North Korean bridgehead on Ganghwa-do had failed. It was decided that additional resources were critical.

*   *   *   *   *   *

Looking like something out of an older war, a string of bombs fell away from the South Korean F-15K Slam Eagle. The Korean GPS Glide Bombs, looking like they were aliens clutching eggs, dropped out of the sky. Wings from the attached bodies sprouted, carrying the Mark 82 bombs with them. High above the rapidly descending glide bombs, the South Korean aircraft turned back toward their bases.

Dropped from fifty miles away, the five-hundred-pound bombs angled toward the North Korean positions located near the Gyodong Bridge. The GPS sensors adjusted their glide paths and the many groups of weapons fell through the varying cloud layers. Not being far from their bases, the Slam Eagles were lining up for their instrument approaches by the time the weapons began arriving at their targets.

The narrow valley with the pockmarked fields erupted as if the Earth's fury had been unleashed. Five hundred pounds of explosive power tossed dirt, rocks, trees, and humans alike. Each blast came so close to others as to seem like they were one. Twelve of the Korean GPS Glide Bombs from each of the strike fighters detonated in long lines, tearing into the hasty defenses put up by the North Korean infantry, armor, and special forces troops.

Offshore to the south, the remnants of the South Korean naval forces also received new orders. Although the Yellow Sea fleet was still smarting from the loss of warships during their sea battles, and had retreated to a standoff position to the southwest of Incheon, the remaining ships still carried a tremendous amount of firepower.

From the decks of the destroyers and guided-missile frigates, Hyunmoo-3 and SSM-750K land attack cruise missiles lifted off. Again, the spread-out fleet of South Korean warships became enshrouded in smoke as volleys of weapons soared aloft from within their vertical launch chambers. Streaking low on the waters of the Yellow Sea, these cruise missiles sped toward targets that were currently being swarmed with glide bombs dropped from miles above.

With planned timing, the hills were still ringing from the last of the glide bombs detonating when additional explosions ripped through the turmoil of dirt and smoke. The narrow valley leading from the Gyodong Bridge became a smoky mess, smelling of freshly turned earth, gunpowder, burning metal and rubber, and bodies ripped apart.

Behind the front line, additional missiles began arriving at the beachhead itself. Soldiers hurriedly unloading landing craft and disembarking armor were caught in a sudden barrage of fire. The entire landing zone was momentarily lost from view. When it again reappeared, contorted bodies lay among smoking armor. North Korean landing craft drifted with the tide as they were pushed off the tidal flats by the series of concussive hammers that hit them. Stacked ammo supplies burned fiercely, with missiles and rockets firing randomly in all directions.

Immediately following the intense bombardment, South Korean armor and infantry again came through the narrow defile. As before, guns blazed away through the smoke-filled valley. Overhead drones searched through fallen trees and shattered buildings for signs of enemy movement, redirecting fire from the armor when any was found.

With fire support from IFVs and tanks, APCS rushed forward to suspected enemy lines. Very little return fire from the North Koreans was encountered as South Korean soldiers poured from personnel carriers. Firing immediately toward suspected enemy positions, the infantry stormed tree lines and came upon partially ruined buildings. Slowly, they moved through the initial North Korean defenses. Some wounded were taken prisoner. The initial phase of removing the North Koreans from the shores of Ganghwa-do was completed without much more than a few scattered firefights. North Korean positions that put up any kind of resistance were overcome with the help of drone operators.

Back at the Ganghwa-do beachhead, the North Koreans were attempting to recover from the intense barrage. Vehicles that could still move were quickly sent across the bridge toward the Gyodong-do side, along with whatever remaining soldiers that could hitch rides. The command posts had lost contact with the advance units placed to the east. Drones sent aloft showed a picture that wasn't heartening; South Korean forces were advancing down the highway.

The hold on Ganghwa-do had been tenuous at best, and it was decided, in order to prevent the loss of the smaller island as well, they would abandon the larger one and transfer any remaining equipment and personnel over to Gyodong-do. When the last of the functional forces were across, the North Korean special forces blew the bridge they had rigged upon arrival. Two spans of the Gyodong Bridge collapsed into the shallow waters. Now a narrow waterway separated the two forces.

The North Koreans continued to land equipment, supplies, and reinforcements along the northern and western shores of Gyodong-do, bypassing the South Korean bunkers still holding out. South Korean artillery attempted to interdict these landings, but the North kept changing the zones, making any substantial interference problematic.

For all intents and purposes, North Korea now held Gyodong-do Island, though considering they were continually harassed by airstrikes and artillery, they couldn't do much with it for the time being. The South Korean 1$^{st}$ Corps did their level best not to allow a North Korean buildup on the island. Both Gyodong-do and the western shores of Ganghwa-do became gray zones, with South Korea building defenses to prevent North Korea from crossing the narrow channel between the two islands.

# Initial battle for Gyodong-do

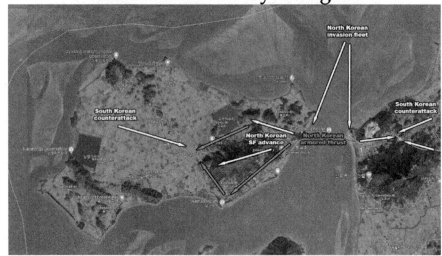

# Subsequent Battle for Gyodong-do

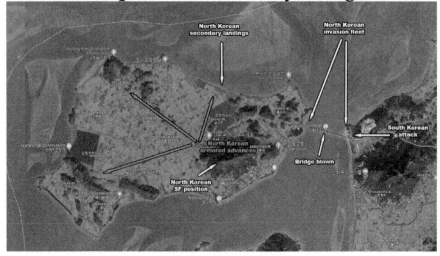

# Chapter Nine

Moonlight gleamed off the light gray wings as two turbofan engines propelled the E-7A Peace Eye aircraft through the night skies. Billowing clouds to the southwest, their tops shining white, indicated that a change in weather was approaching. It was the last month of the monsoon season and rains were expected, which could alter the battlefield to some degree. Even though the Southern attack fighters were capable of operating in all types of weather, the heavy rains would alter the frequency of their use. For one, takeoff and landing separations would be increased, especially as instrument landings would have to be flown.

The South Korean airborne early warning and control aircraft circled over the central part of the peninsula, having taken over duties from an American E-8C JSTARS. Together, the airborne command posts of the United States and South Korea shared shifts surveilling the lands to the north and strategically directing the battles being waged just south of the DMZ. The aircraft type was also able to share responsibilities with the American E-3C Sentry crews directing and coordinating the aerial missions conducted by both the United States and South Korea.

Part of the AEW&C mission was to track moving targets north of the DMZ. This gave the command staff an inside look at possible North Korean plans by analyzing vehicular movements. The capability was also able to identify supply depots by the type of actions; the arrival and departure of vehicles from certain locations identified logistical supply dumps and provided coordinates for long-range artillery strikes.

There was another threat that the airborne command posts were responsible for, and one that General Carswell had considered to be a priority. That was to track down North Korea's mobile missile launchers, in particular, those that carried short-, intermediate-, medium-, and long-range ballistic missiles. In his opinion, the North's large inventory of ballistic weapons, coupled with their demonstration that they were willing to use chemical agents, were a big threat to the Southern defenses. And as always, the bigger worry was that they would detonate nuclear weapons, should their offensive become stalled, which in the early hours of the land battles, it seemed to be.

Therefore, operators within the fuselage noted individual vehicular movements. The process was made easier with the initial ballistic launches. They had a starting point from which to monitor the movements of the identified individual launchers. However, the rough terrain sometimes prevented full monitoring, as trees and ridges blocked views at times. Even though the war was technically only hours old, the process seemed agonizingly slow.

However, as the hours passed, the data being returned from the primary and secondary belts of ballistic launchers was able to track most the vehicles that fired short and intermediate-range Scud missiles. Using current tracks and the historical data of the mobile TELs, the operators aboard the previous E-8C and current E-7A aircraft were able to pinpoint several locations where the now empty transport erectors had moved to.

Using methods similar to those used to locate supply depots, intelligence officers were able to find what they presumed were missile storage sites nestled in the North's mountainous center. The movement tracks of several launchers joined at particular locations. Further surveillance from drones found that the coordinates were likely hardened bunkers, which seemed prevalent throughout the northern country. The allied forces of South Korea and the United States had found what they believed was the place where North Korea was storing a large inventory of ballistic weapons.

* * * * * *

The general's eyes shot open. The transition from deep REM sleep to abrupt wakefulness was momentarily confusing. In the dim light, Carswell was able to recognize his operations officer. Being wakened like this could only mean something important was up. A small burst of adrenaline filled him as he envisioned that something had gone horribly wrong on the frontline.

"General," Jim said another time, gently shaking his shoulder.

"Yeah, Jim. I'm up," Carswell answered, swinging his legs over his temporary bed. Reaching for the light at his side, he continued. "What's going on?"

"One of the Peace Eyes found something...or several somethings...that I thought you should be aware of. The information is time sensitive, but take a few minutes to wake up, sir," the operations officer said.

"Okay, give me two to get ready and I'll meet you in the ops room," Carswell responded.

"Coffee, sir?"

"As strong and dark as you can make it and still be considered a liquid."

Jim chuckled. "It'll be waiting for you, sir."

As he dressed, the general wondered what could be important enough to wake him, yet not sufficiently vital that he could take his time getting ready. Many scenarios ran through his head. It couldn't be a North Korean breakthrough or his ops officer would have been more harried. Maybe the North had pulled back and are saying, "Sorry, it was all a mistake. Our bad."

Like he'd have that kind of luck. Buttoning up his fatigue blouse, he really couldn't come up with any plausible explanation. Walking out of his small bedroom off to the side of the command bunker and still straightening himself, he met the operations officer and took a proffered steaming cup of something that looked like used oil.

Taking a small sip that nearly scalded his tongue, Carswell said, "That'll do nicely. Okay Jim, what do you have?"

The operations officer briefed on what the intel shop had come up with regarding North Korea's possible missile storage sites.

"Okay, why am I standing here in the middle of the night? Why aren't there birds already in the air? You don't need me to authorize an attack," Carswell stated once the operations officer had finished. "But now that I'm awake, let's get tasking orders arranged and planes into the air."

The ops officer hesitated. "Well, sir. We would have, but there are a few additional factors to consider. Intel thinks there is a strong possibility that the North Koreans are staging their chemical weapons in the same location as their missiles."

General Carswell growled. For one, he wasn't particularly fond of being told there was something he couldn't do. It was a trait that came from being bombarded by a range of diverse information and sometimes not having enough time to carefully weigh each and every decision, yet being expected to make one. It was something he knew about himself and was trying to correct, or at least modify. Although his attempts to change weren't truly done wholeheartedly.

Taking another sip, Carswell nodded. "Okay. You're right, Jim, as usual. Let's get the weather shop in here. In the meantime, show me these locations."

Sipping the cooling coffee out of a deeply stained cup, the general pored over a map. He brought himself up to speed with any updates on the battle lines forty plus miles to the north. His finger kept wandering over to the location where he had identified an enemy brigade vanishing.

"Jim, any update on where that brigade went?" Carswell asked, pointing to the site.

"Nothing as yet, sir. Intel believes it may be a reserve unit or perhaps a follow-on one waiting in a hardened bunker."

"Hmmm...any movement to or from there?" Carswell inquired, taking another sip.

The operations officer went to a console and typed out a few commands, looking at historical data in the area. He then shook his head, "No, sir...nothing that has showed up."

The general's gut told him something was up with that place, but he couldn't figure out what it could be. Perhaps his intel shop was right and reserve forces had been placed underground. It made sense. Or, it could be…

"Sir, weather is here," Jim stated, interrupting the general's thoughts.

"Good, get 'em over here."

A young officer nervously made his way over to the general and the situation map. Highlighted were the locations observed by the surveillance aircraft.

"Yes, sir," the weather officer said.

"I want to know what the winds are in these locations," General Carswell inquired, pointing to each of the potential bunkers.

"Uh, yes, sir. What altitudes would you like?"

The general thought about it for a moment. "Jim? How high do you think a plume would go?"

"Well, sir. Given that we'd have to use some type of bunker buster, it's going to shoot up there quite a bit. Two, three thousand feet? Maybe more."

"How about ground to say, five thousand feet?" Carswell said, addressing the Air Force officer.

The junior officer gulped, unused to talking to a four-star general. "Uh, one moment, sir."

The officer fumbled for a moment, trying to pull up the information. Carswell laid a hand on the officer's shoulder.

"Take your time, lieutenant…and relax. I'm not nearly as rabid as they say."

The operations officer coughed from behind, his hand covering his mouth. The general chuckled. "Apparently, some may disagree with that conclusion."

The lieutenant looked up and smiled, unsure of how to respond. He thought there was no way he could agree or disagree without being wrong.

"Okay, sir, here we are. Surface winds are out of the southwest at two-two-zero, moving toward two-zero-zero at five thousand. They'll swirl a little in those mountains due to the terrain, but they'll generally move in the same direction. There's a weather system coming from the southwest that will push winds in the same direction," the Air Force lieutenant briefed.

The general looked toward his operations officer. "See, Jim. If anything is released, it'll be pushed back towards their own homeland. Serves them right if they're storing the stuff there."

"But what about the general populace? If word gets out that we knew about what was there and a catastrophe happens, Washington will have your ass, and whatever's left the UN will chew up. You know, sir, if there's to be any condemnation and they need a scapegoat, you understand that you'll be at the bottom of said hill."

"I'm okay with that, Jim," Carswell answered. "Let's look at the alternative. Let's say that we don't do anything because of the risk and those bloody bastards launch an attack that annihilates our command or defenses or supply ports. Whose head do you think will roll if we lose this bloody thing, especially if we could have prevented that?"

The general, now perturbed, looked toward the lieutenant, who had been typing all during the conversation.

"What is that bloody clacking all about?" Carswell asked, turning on the Air Force lieutenant.

The junior officer jumped back as if he was facing a snarling dog. "I...I, uh, sir, considering the winds, I have, uh, fallout projections for the sites you mentioned."

The officer slid back, revealing the screen he had been working at. There, at the sites identified by intel as being missile storage sites, were elongated ovals outlining what the lieutenant said were fallout projections.

The general and operations officer stared at the screen. None of the shaded ovals encompassed communities or populated areas. General Carswell grasped the lieutenant's shoulder.

"Well done, son...err, lieutenant. Well done. Jim, see that the lieutenant here is in line for an early promotion."

"Will do, sir," the ops officer replied, taking down the officer's information.

"So, can we get the birds in the air now?" Carswell

grumbled.

The operations officer nodded, hurrying off to put things in motion.

*   *   *   *   *   *

With a bump of the throttles, the South Korean F-15K edged forward, easing out of its hardened shelter. Even with adverse weather in the forecast, the canopy was left open. The cool evening air settling in the cockpit felt good to Captain Kwon Dae-jung. The pilot looked along the parking area, seeing three other Slam Eagles nose out of their shelters. Turning out of the parking area, the captain rolled onto the first taxiway.

Blue taxiway lights trundled past on each side, exhaust from the jet's twin exhaust pipes blurring the markers for those taxiing behind. Dae-jung glanced up to see the brighter stars twinkling across a velvet sky. The moisture in the atmosphere cast a halo around the orbiting moon. It was a night made for flying, the cooler air enhancing the F-15Ks performance, the clear air providing stellar views of the heavens.

Dae-jung loved to fly the South Korean version of the American Strike Eagle. Strapped in the cockpit of the powerful jet, he couldn't believe he was actually allowed to pilot the attack fighter. It was a feeling he had every time he taxied out, every time he ran the throttles up on the runway and felt the aircraft leap forward in response, every time he felt the wheels leave the ground. It was a joy that could only be understood by another fighter pilot. He felt he had formed a bond with the jet, perhaps a closer one than most any other he had made in life.

Although his family didn't have a lot of money, Dae-jung never really noticed the lack during his childhood. He'd always felt rich, or at least loved and cared for. His parents had come from the North, escaping in their early years. They almost never talked about the event, mentioning it only a few rare times that the captain could remember. When it surfaced, he could feel the chill that came over his mother and father, along with a distant look that would come into their eyes. He could tell from the scant stories and expressions that it had been a harrowing experience, but the young pilot never knew if that was from what they escaped or from the border crossing itself.

His father had passed two years ago, his mother doing her best to make ends meet. Dae-jung made sure that a large portion of his paycheck went to support his mother and sisters. Every time he tried to bring up life in the North, his mother would respond, "Kwon Dae-Jung, you don't worry yourself about such things." He supposed he would never know about his parents' past lives.

Growing up, he had watched the jets fly overhead, pausing in whatever he was doing to stare at the passing aircraft until they faded from view. Although he'd wanted to be a pilot ever since he saw his first jet, he never in his wildest dreams thought he'd ever fly one, or even could. In his mind, that was for, well, he never could pinpoint who he thought flew them, but knew it wasn't him. Perhaps it was that thought that spurred him on. Whatever it might have been, he felt he was living a fortunate life.

He didn't really think much about the war in terms that he was fighting his relatives, or perhaps even family. His family had escaped the Northern regime and as far as he was concerned, he and they were South Korean. Someday, he hoped that difference would be changed, and the people could just once again call themselves Korean, instead of having that volatile North-South divide. But there was someone invading his country now and it didn't matter what they called themselves. He would protect his homeland, with his life if need be.

Dae-jung ran the canopy down as he taxied into the runup area near the runway. In unison behind, the others of his flight closed their cockpits. Flights did everything at the same time, a mental exercise so that they became one entity comprised of four different parts. When the last jet rolled into position, the blue taxiway lights winked off. It was part of the established blackout procedures. Even though technology had practically erased the notion that a target had to be seen to be hit, the measures were more out of habit and to not give any spotters or potential saboteurs free intelligence.

The roars echoed across the seemingly desolate airfield as the four jets ran their engines up, checking that all was in order prior to racing into the night skies. After verifying that the instruments showed that his aircraft systems were working, Dae-jung glanced out to the wings. Air defense missiles nosed out from under the leading edges, looking menacing under the moon's rays.

However, the main purpose of the mission almost seemed out of place attached to the sleek outlines of the Slam Fighter. The flattened top of the Taurus KEPD 350 cruise missile looked alien, kind of like it was more of a maintenance platform rather than a weapon meant to penetrate hardened sites.

When the rest of his flight signaled that they were good to go, the captain contacted the tower. The clearance was immediate, the runway lights illuminating on their low setting. Dae-jung loved how the F-15K responded when he applied just an ounce of power. Rolling onto the active runway, he throttled up. Twin streams of flame shot out from the burner cans in the rear, the attack fighter lunging forward.

The acceleration kept increasing, forcing the pilot and weapon system operator back into their seats. It was a thrill that the captain would never cease enjoying. Still increasing speed, the nose wheel lifted free of the paved surface, the main gear departing the runway a second later. With a jerk on the gear lever, the wheels retracted and folded into their compartments with a *thunk*. The flaps were raised and the cleaned-up F-15K shot into the darkened skies.

Dae-jung started a circling climb while the other three attack fighters joined up on his wing. Still gaining altitude, he sent them off into a tactical formation. Given the range of the air-launched cruise missiles and the proximity of not only the border, but the targets themselves, the flight would be a quick one. It could easily be recorded as one of the shortest combat missions in the history of flight.

Flying to a desolate area in case any of the weapons

malfunctioned, Dae-jung went over the pre-release checklist with his WSO. Given the short duration of the flight and the busy nature of firing on such a shortened itinerary, he didn't get to enjoy the night as he normally might. The brief time he was given during the ascent was spent on watching the glow of cumulus clouds building to the southwest. The moonbeams brightly reflected from the billowing masses, the towering columns could be seen rising rapidly even from a distance. Monsoon-like rains were on their way, although the season for them would soon be at an end.

The F-15K lifted as over three thousand pounds of missile fell away. Dropping through the night, the KEPD 350 cruise missile deployed its mid wings while the turbofan engine fired up. Slowly, the darkened shape pulled away from the Slam Eagle, its altitude decreasing as it sped north at just under Mach 1.

Seconds later, another weapon fell from its pylon. Shaken from over six thousand pounds, the aircraft almost seemed to shiver as if it had shed a weighted backpack from its shoulders. Not far away from base, Captain Dae-jung brought the throttles back and pointed the nose earthward. Descending back toward darkened runways, the F-15Ks dropped out of the night skies, leaving the cruise missiles to head north on their own, like fledglings leaving the nest for the first time.

*　*　*　*　*　*

The KEPD 350 missiles kept on their descending path, dropping out of the stars as they headed north toward the DMZ and beyond. The South Korean variants had specialized GPS receivers onboard that had an anti-spoofing module designed to minimize enemy jamming attempts. The GPS signals remained spotty because Chinese and North Korean electronic warfare equipment were attempting to jam the communications between receivers and the satellites. It was a game of jamming and taking measures to work around it. North Korea and China expanded their efforts based on what the South and the United

States tried. Some of the anti-jamming systems worked flawlessly while other older modules had a more difficult time maintaining a connection with the satellites. The Selective Availability Anti-Spoofing Module was one of the systems that was able to circumvent North Korea's jammers.

Even without the GPS, the guidance systems in place allowed for precise flight path navigation. Flying a hundred feet over the mountainous terrain, the missiles used a thermographic camera for high-resolution images to verify the correct flight route. The images were compared to planned 3D models stored in the computer system. Spread across the peninsula, the weapons frequently altered their courses to evade any countermeasures and to disguise their true targets.

One of the first air-launched cruise missiles rose over a ridge. The onboard sensors showed it was on course and nearing its programmed target. Computers calculated the optimum popup point, analyzing the various atmospheric conditions. At the right moment, the missile conducted a bunt maneuver, whereby it climbed sharply. After calculating the optimal angle to both acquire the target and penetrate it, the ALCM nosed over and started a steep descent.

The KEP 350 was designed to go after hardened targets buried deep underground. The double warhead system was named Mephisto, or Multi-Effect Penetrator Highly Sophisticated and Target Optimized. The first charge went off, clearing the soil and penetrating the hardened underground bunker. The explosion strobed the surrounding area with a brief flash of light. Crashing deep underground, this pre-charge created a bulge in the earth's surface, the dome growing larger by the millisecond. In slow motion, it looked like a caldera rising and rupturing.

The bulge grew larger and then fractured. The explosion burst free, sending tons of soil and stone rocketing into the night. The ground rumbled from the seismic activity, nearby trees toppling as the earth shifted from the deep underground blast. The route to the North Korean underground missile storage site was cleared.

Once deep inside the facility, the delayed fuse detonated the thousand-pound main warhead. A second explosion rose through the crater created by the initial penetrating charge. More debris was upthrust through the hole, the ground cracking all around the crater's rim due to the tremendous pressures applied far underground.

The secondary explosion that followed was one for the ages. North Korea, in order to save time between reloading their mobile transporters, had kept many of their short and intermediate range Scud missiles loaded with liquid fuel. Those weapons detonated with a force many times that of the initial South Korean warhead. A series of blasts shot through the opening, chasing after the path of least resistance.

Flames shot hundreds of feet into the air, blowing a wide gap in the earth. Winds adjacent to the crater rapidly approached gale forces as oxygen was drawn in from the eruption, feeding the fires pouring from deep inside the earth. Thinking that the subterranean storage site would be next to impossible to find, let alone bomb, the North Korean leadership had placed the liquid fuel storage for the rockets in close proximity.

A blinding white flash rose high into the night, casting the surrounding woods in stark reliefs of light and shadow. Trees nearby were tossed over as if swatted by a giant hand, several splintering into toothpicks. The roiling ball of white and yellow flame spewing into the night quickly faded as the fuel was almost instantly consumed, the dark shape of a mushrooming cloud blotting out the stars and dimming the moonlight.

Seismic readings alerted many of the world's monitoring facilities, geolocating the size and location of the eruption. NORAD and the Indo-Pacific command were immediately alerted. The initial indications were that something large had detonated inside of North Korea. At first, it was thought that a nuclear device had gone off, the evidence of an accidental or deliberate explosion unclear.

The national resources of many countries were initially

brought to higher levels of readiness. Some of those monitoring the situation and with active seismic listening devices, thought that American retaliation for North Korea's chemical attacks had arrived, and the profound hope was that the retaliation hadn't been nuclear, though many agreed on that possibility.

When other facilities blew up from the attacks on identified North Korean missile storage sites, the world presumed that the tactical nuclear retaliation had taken on a more widespread basis. Many held their breath, waiting for the ugliness of a nuclear war to break out on the Korean peninsula, or to spread across the Pacific as North Korea escalated attacks to Japan, Guam, or Okinawa. With a world waiting with bated breath, the expectation was for nuclear weapons to start exploding up and down the Korean peninsula.

It wasn't long until American monitoring facilities identified that the sources of the explosions weren't the result of nuclear devices. Word went out globally that nukes hadn't been involved. The held breath of many was slowly let out, although some still feared the worst.

South Korean and American sites across the Pacific were put on alert, expecting that North Korea might still think the worst *had* happened and retaliate. Ballistic missile defense systems were all on alert, waiting for the slightest sign of North Korean launches. As time passed, tensions eased as the North remained relatively quiet.

The disruption of the North's communication systems had an effect none could have imagined. It wasn't until much later that command knew that many of their missile storage sites had been destroyed. Had the communications been uncompromised, it was highly conceivable that the Northern leadership would have misinterpreted the events and done everything in their power to get nuclear warheads in the air.

The violence and heat from the secondary detonations also destroyed most of the stored chemical agents meant to be mated to the ballistic weapons. Some of the agents were able to escape from the giant sinkholes and dispersed into the local area, the chemicals becoming inert after several days. When the detonations subsided, several prominent ridges had vanished, the rock and debris scattered around giant craters. Those who manned the facilities simply evaporated, a very few suffocating as the explosions instantly burned up all the available oxygen.

# Chapter Ten

*White House, Washington DC*
*3 August, 2021*

The past few days had been hectic ones, not to mention that last few hours. If he regretted running for a second term, then the information coming out of Korea certainly reinforced that notion. As feared, the conflict with China had expanded, war spreading to the Korean peninsula. From the daily briefings, Frank understood that the military resources in the Indo-Pacific region were spread thinly.

The South Korean and American defensive lines were holding against the North Korean aggression, although the president wondered for how long. The North seemed to have an unlimited array of soldiers and equipment, while those in the South were considerably limited. South Korea had a large reserve of soldiers, but the process of recalling them was still in its infancy. It took time to properly train them so they could be integrated into the active combat forces. Many hadn't served in some time. Tactics and equipment evolved, along with the rusty training that had to be shaken loose. Until then, the scant forces holding the front lines had to make do, and according to his advisors, they had to do it for at least two months.

The pressures of being in office were oftentimes overwhelming. He hardly recognized himself while shaving in the morning. The person staring back was a stranger; the tired eyes, the rapidly graying hair, and cheeks that seemed to sag under the weight of the office, continually at war, or so it seemed.

The news coming from the Korean theater didn't help matters. The chemical attack on the front lines and civilian infrastructure, while somewhat expected, came as a shock anyway. Then there were the subsequent attacks, which intelligence had shown the North Korean missiles had been carrying chemical agents. Many of his military commanders had wanted to retaliate, urging him to authorize the release of tactical nuclear weapons. While the reasoning that it would likely bring an end to the war with North Korea was solid, it wasn't something he had been ready to approve. If the use of those types of weapons continued, he would revisit the subject. But until then, he would try his damnedest to keep things from escalating too far.

That was especially true with the latest scare coming from Korea. The initial reports of the large blasts had been scary to say the least. The fact that the entire global leadership had been terrified that the United States had unleashed nuclear weapons demonstrated that the scenario was within the realm of possibility. And that was a worrisome place. Each hour that passed without a North Korean retaliatory missile launch was another ounce of tension that could be released.

No, it wasn't much fun being on the leading edge of information. He'd much rather be one of the citizens going about their days and nights without truly knowing what was occurring in the world. He doubted there was even a small percentage that were aware of the decisions he faced on a regular basis, especially with the conflicts raging in the western Pacific.

Frank glanced at the time. It wouldn't be too long before the United Nations would meet in response to North Korea's use of WMDs. The president thought it would be interesting to see exactly how China reacted to the fact that North Korea had used weapons of mass destruction. Considering how they used the Northern country for their own ends, and had probably goaded them into this act of aggression against South Korea, would China now distance themselves from their neighbor? Would they condemn the North, support them more stridently, or go on as if it didn't happen?

China was in a peculiar situation. Considering their role in the global marketplace, and their desire to become the number one market economy, they couldn't really risk the prospect of a global condemnation. Were they currently attempting to curtail North Korea's use of chemical weapons? Or did they go as far as to actually propose or condone their use in the hopes that the North would break through allied lines?

The United Nations would certainly be in an uproar over the use of chemical weapons, but what power did the organization really have? They could issue condemnations, but that was about as far as they could go. Direct action could only be taken if the security council were to actually all agree, and that wasn't likely. China or Russia would surely block anything the United States proposed, just the same as the NATO nations blocked anything China or Russia wanted.

Sanctions could be issued, but would that influence North Korea? After all, the sanctions already in place hadn't budged the Northern nation, although it did keep them from upgrading their military equipment. That was something, given the current state of the peninsula.

The United States would use the issue of WMDs to set conditions on the world stage, even if that was demonstrating its constraint in the face of chemical attacks. It would seek to improve its world standing, potentially alienating China even more. Already, fractures were forming among China's allies, with more of the nations friendly to them starting to back off.

There was once a time when the whole of Indonesia and countries bordering the South China Sea were under China's sway. But that was changing with China's aggression in the area. The Philippines was a good example, although the "change" in leadership was the predominant reason. Someday, Frank would like to sit down with his CIA Director over a beer and find out what had really happened on the other side of the Pacific.

\* \* \* \* \* \*

*United Nations, New York*
*3 August, 2021*

Elizabeth Hague stepped out from the council chambers. The hall was empty at the moment, the silence almost a relief from the tempers that had flared inside the security council meeting on the other side of the doors. She leaned against the wall, the back of her head resting on the cool surface. The job she held was a demanding one and downright infuriating at times. She both loved and hated the politics and gaming that went on inside the United Nations.

As with the others who negotiated the corridors, she sometimes lost sight of the fact that the games played here had real repercussions for the men and women on the battlefields. There was the mistaken notion that the true battles were fought inside the many UN chambers and she had to sometimes pull out of her reality to realize that Americans were dying in foreign lands. The actions taken by the UN were meant to halt casualties, but the games played within the walls of the building often did the opposite. There were some, maybe even venturing toward many, that fought to still hostilities. But those voices mostly went unheard. Agendas were being played out, often to the detriment of actual human soldiers.

The greater council of member nations had voted to condemn North Korea's use of chemical weapons by a vast majority. There were those who were in China's corner, who either voted against the resolution or abstained. It was the Chinese ambassador to the UN who was the most vocal, not accepting the evidence put forth by the United States and South Korea. All the while, he sought to soften China's position, citing that China was against the use of such weapon types.

"China does not condone the use of weapons of mass destruction. China does not undertake the use or threaten to use weapons of mass destruction, especially against non-nuclear states or nuclear-weapon-free zones at any time or under any circumstance. We have always upheld our policy of 'no first use rule' while maintaining a sufficient deterrent retaliatory measure for the defense of our country," the ambassador had spouted.

He went on to reiterate that China doubted the veracity of the data presented by the United States and their South Korean puppets. China was playing the sides, not coming across as supporting the use of WMDs while also saying they were against condemning their use by one of their allies, who were fighting against the same foe as they were. Everyone saw it for what it was, but there was nothing that could really be done about it. The resolution sent a strong message that the world was against any use of chemical, biological, and nuclear weapons. But that was about the extent of what the United Nations could do; send a strongly-worded letter. The security council resolution to freeze the Korean conflict and send in UN troops to impose a buffer zone was vetoed by China, citing the usual cliché-ridden message they had spouted to the general assembly.

Elizabeth felt like she needed to bathe after the rhetoric put forth by the Chinese ambassador, but she also hadn't expected anything different. It was all part of the game. China's concern, especially with their economy starting to tank, was that some of the nations, especially those in Africa whom they were attempting to win over, might view a continued relationship with China as risky. That was what this was all about, the swaying of parties to one side or the other. China would only listen if it hit their pocketbooks. But it had to be done. To do anything differently would be effectively handing China an open invitation to escalate matters as they saw fit, and not just in their corner of the globe. At least this resolution was a way of drawing a line, and showing them where it was.

She couldn't really blame the ambassadors. They were fearful, as they rightfully should be with two nuclear superpowers fighting each other. It could easily tip into an all-out war, whether purposeful or through some misunderstanding of events, which could end then the human race. Yeah, they had a right to be worried.

The voices that had risen inside the chambers varied. She knew that some of the nations were opposed to anything the United States did. Secretly, they wished that North Korea had actually used nukes. There were those who weren't so secret, and Elizabeth speculated that the Chinese ambassador had arranged for those scenes to transpire. They appeared to be drawing their own lines in the sand.

Others, without stating so in public, had told Elizabeth

that the United States should end the North Korean menace once and for all. The implication being that the U.S. should bomb the troublesome country out of existence. Most though, worried about the conflicts escalating, as it seemed events were inching the doomsday clock ever closer to humanity's end.

Those nations called for peace at any cost. But who was to compromise their position remained nebulous. They gave statements without answers. Most of the nations didn't want China controlling the South China Sea, yet some of those same countries weren't sure they wanted the United States acting as the world's police. Mostly, people didn't want China and the United States to edge closer to a nuclear exchange, and there was the feeling that North Korea's actions brought that possibility nearer to becoming a reality.

The call for increased sanctions against North Korea didn't pass, just as Elizabeth had expected. You really couldn't sanction a country more than the Northern country already was without being accused of genocide. The United States and a few allies were on the verge of issuing additional sanctions against companies and individuals still doing business with the Northern regime. But with many already in place, there were few ways to increase the measures.

With a sigh, Elizabeth pushed away from the wall. The doors to the council chambers swung open and members started exiting. A few nodded in her direction, but for the most part, she was just like the paintings adorning the walls, noticed but not really seen. As she strode down the wide hallways, she lifted her cell phone and dialed. It was time to notify the president what had transpired. There wasn't much to brief.

* * * * * *

Frank listened to the words coming from the United Nations. It was a victory of sorts, at least as much as could be expected. A vast majority of nations had voted to condemn North Korea for the use of chemical weapons. Perhaps that should be enough to prevent their continued use. But the

Northern regime had proved time and time again that they didn't care one bit about what the world thought of them.

The reaction from China wasn't a surprise. Hell, he could have written that script beforehand. As a matter of fact, he could easily see himself responding in the same manner had the circumstances been reversed. Or any other nation, for that matter. He supposed the game must be played.

The biggest worry for Frank was that North Korea would try to use WMDs again. The Pentagon had stated that they had destroyed large stockpiles that the North had, but that didn't mean they were depleted. And if the North didn't have chemical agents to use, would they then resort to launching nuclear-tipped missiles? Either possibility worried the president to the point that he was sure he was getting an ulcer from thinking about it.

Now that the UN resolution was in place and everything in the open, if North Korea again used WMDs, then his hand would be forced to respond in kind. There were still calls for him to authorize the use of tactical nukes; to obliterate the country from bottom to top. He was used to the ultra-nationalists voicing their opinions, but now some were coming from within government offices and those had a way of picking up steam. He had to handle the situation carefully if he was to avoid the trap those voices presented. Push them down too far and they only seemed to grow louder and multiply. Do nothing, and the same could happen. He just hoped that the message to North Korea, and more importantly to China, was heard. He hoped that the power in China would deliver the message to halt any further use of chemical, or nuclear weapons.

The problem was that there were those in the world who were applauding North Korea's actions. They were calling on them to annihilate the forces of the Devil, by any means. They were also calling for the true believers to begin a Jihad against Americans wherever they might be. The world was truly a volatile place, much more so than it had been in years. And with Russia gathering on Ukraine's borders and Iran starting to again rattle sabers, it was going to be difficult keeping things under control and not letting matters escalate past a point of no return.

And in the middle of the extreme ends, there were those who called for the United States to cease all hostilities. If it were only that easy. The United States was already in too deeply to arbitrarily pull back. The message that would send to the rest of the world, both ally and unfriendly nation alike, would be deadly. That would only give opponents the message that America wasn't up to the task. If anything, violence throughout the world would only get worse, bringing the doomsday clock ever closer to midnight. Frank felt that the rope he was having to walk was a thin one indeed.

*   *   *   *   *   *

*Hwacheon County, South Korea*
*4 August, 2021*

The motorized cart drove past tank after tank idly sitting in long rows. The officers riding in the vehicle silently observed the long lines of Chonma main battle tanks. The tanks were interspersed with infantry fighting vehicles and armored personnel carriers. It was an awe-inspiring sight to witness so much armored firepower arranged by the regiments in which they belonged. Behind the armored might were mobile artillery vehicles and their towed howitzer accompaniments. And farther to the rear of the miles long convoy of armor were the supply vehicles which would accompany the regiments.

Sangwi Kang Yun, a North Korean company officer with one of the regiments, felt the might emanating from the firepower the armored vehicles represented. What amazed him every time he made the journey toward the front of the columns was that they were technically miles south of the DMZ and the battles currently being waged.

The North Korean captain peered up at the roughly hewn stone, wondering just how many tons were held up. Being deep underground, he envisioned the mass above him just collapsing and burying the thousands of troops that were contained in the miles-long tunnel.

More amazing was the fact that they hadn't been located by the Southern forces. He'd heard about the other tunnels that were meant to convey soldiers past the DMZ defenses and strike into the heartland. Those had been only several feet wide but were rumored to be able to carry some thirty thousand troops per hour through their narrow passages. Four had been dug deep under the DMZ. All of those had been discovered using ground penetrating radar and deep holes drilled all along the border. Kang Yun found it incredulous that a tunnel as large as the one he was transiting hadn't been found. But then again, this one ran deeper than the others and great care had been taken to avoid detection. The captain wondered just how long the Northern leadership had been constructing it. He thought it possible that it had been started the moment the cease-fire had taken place. It was really the only way to explain how vast and long it truly was.

Sangwi Kang Yun wasn't exactly sure how many regiments waited for their orders, but he guessed that it had to be at least four. It was possible that it was many more, but his commanders were very tight-lipped about the size of the gathered force, just as they were about their eventual mission and goals. The captain didn't even know where the tunnel would exit, but given the amount of time it took to get near the front of the columns, where his company resided, it was many, many miles. The tunnel curved numerous times, supposedly to minimize the weight of the stone straining from above (at least that's what someone had said a while back).

Branching tunnels along the way led to quarters housing the numerous soldiers which would participate in the surprise attack. Strung lights followed the vehicle as it rolled past the armor, casting shadows among the tanks and other vehicles. It made the resting vehicles take on a more ominous appearance. Ductwork running along the ceiling exchanged the air, meant to expel the exhaust from vehicles and bring in fresh oxygen. Smaller ducts carried the electrical and communication lines.

The vehicle stopped at times to drop off other officers,

delivering them to their assigned units. Kang Yun stepped off the cart when his turn arrived. Being assigned to the lead company, he was the last to depart. Stepping onto the dust-laden rocky surface, he could tell that the land was sloping upward. Ahead of his company of main battle tanks, heavy machinery waited.

Although he wasn't privy to the details, he assumed they would clear the way once the tunnel end was blown. He would then lead the rest of North Korea's armored fist out to strike the South Korean and American forces. That much he'd surmised from his company's position at the front and the large machinery ahead. From his summons to meet with regimental command, he also guessed that the time when they would emerge from the tunnel would be soon. He had another meeting scheduled in three hours. Perhaps he would learn more then.

*   *   *   *   *   *

The captain sat in the upper hatch, the Chonma-216 main battle tank idling. The smell of diesel exhaust permeated the tunnel and he inhaled the fumes with each breath. The overhead ducts absorbed much of the exhaust, but not enough and it left him feeling a little light-headed. As far as he was concerned, the sooner things started moving, the better.

He had finally received the orders he and others had been patiently waiting for. They would incredulously emerge from the underground only a few miles north of Chuncheon, which sat in the middle of the central highlands. The captain had known the tunnel was lengthy, but he had no idea it penetrated the South as far as it did.

His orders were to attack south with the rest of the regiment, aiming for Chuncheon itself. Moving quickly, they would destroy any reserve and rear area units the South Koreans had and set up a blocking force along South Korea's National Route 46 to the west. Another unit would accompany them and block the highway to the east. Accordingly, a third force would proceed straight south and take National Route 60, the main highway heading from Seoul to the east coast.

Once established there, the attack would proceed west, taking Seoul from south of the Han River. According to his regimental commander, that move would roll up the enemy defense lines and force them to retreat south. It would also trap thousands of enemy soldiers and armor, bringing the Southern forces to their knees. In one fell swoop, they would occupy a large section of South Korea's northern provinces and eliminate a large part of the enemy forces.

Units emerging from the tunnel would also head east and west, setting up additional blockades. One last regiment was slated to attack north, hitting the troops of the South Koreans manning the front lines. With staged North Korean units then attacking south from the DMZ, they would trap a majority of South Korea's central corps between them. In Kang Yun's mind, it was a risky attack, but one that could win the war.

A deep rumble rolled down the tunnel. It was followed by a slight gust of wind. It didn't feel refreshing, like he had envisioned, but it was obvious to him that the time had come. The heavy machinery had moved out some time ago and now the soldiers, acting as guides in front of his company, motioned them forward. The North Korean main battle tank lurched as the driver engaged the transmission and began driving.

# # #

# About the Author

John O'Brien is a former Air Force fighter instructor pilot who transitioned to Special Operations for the latter part of his career gathering his campaign ribbon for Desert Storm. Immediately following his military service, John became a firefighter/EMT with a local department. Along with becoming a firefighter, he fell into the Information Technology industry in corporate management. Currently, John is writing full-time.

As a former marathon runner, John lives in the beautiful Pacific Northwest and can now be found kayaking out in the waters of Puget Sound, mountain biking in the Capital Forest, hiking in the Olympic Peninsula, or pedaling his road bike along the many scenic roads.

# Connect with me online

Facebook:
**https://Facebook.com/AuthorJohnWOBrien**

Twitter:
**https://Twitter.com/A_NewWorld**

Web Site:
**https://John-OBrien.com**

Email:
**John@John-OBrien.com**

Printed in Great Britain
by Amazon

27224637R00175